Ihsan Abdel Kouddous is one of the most prolific and popular writers of Arabic fiction of the twentieth century. Born in Cairo, Egypt, Abdel Kouddous graduated from law school in 1942 but left his law practice to pursue a long and successful career in journalism. He was an editor at the daily *Al-Akhbar* and the weekly *Rose El Youssef*, and was editor-in-chief of *Al-Ahram*. The author of dozens of books, his controversial writings and political views landed him in jail more than once. *A Nose and Three Eyes* is his second book to be translated into English, and his first was *I Do Not Sleep*.

Jonathan Smolin is the Jane and Raphael Bernstein Professor in Asian Studies at Dartmouth College in the US. He is the translator of several works of Arabic fiction, including *Whitefly* by Abdelilah Hamdouchi, *A Rare Blue Bird Flies with Me* by Youssef Fadel, and *I Do Not Sleep* by Ihsan Abdel Kouddous. He lives in Hanover, NH.

Hanan al-Shaykh was born and raised in Beirut. She is the author of *The Story of Zahra*, *Women of Sand and Myrrh*, *Beirut Blues*, and *Only in London*, which was shortlisted for the Independent Foreign Fiction Prize. She lives in London.

Praise for *I Do Not Sleep*

"[One] of the best new works from around the world."
—*The Irish Times*

"This 1950s Egyptian epistolary novel is told by a young woman looking back on the misery, patriarchy and middle-class life that surrounded her upon her return from boarding school."
—*New York Times Book Review*

"Fresh, unpretentious, and irresistibly cinematic."
—*ArabLit*

"A must-read book set in Cairo."
—*Electric Literature*

"A classic of Egyptian Literature. It's great that books like this are being published and that Ihsan Abdel Kouddous's work is available to the English reader in such a good translation."
—Raphael Cormack, author of *Midnight in Cairo*

A Nose and Three Eyes

Ihsan Abdel Kouddous

Translated by
Jonathan Smolin

hoopoe
AN IMPRINT OF AUC PRESS

First published in 2024 by
Hoopoe
113 Sharia Kasr el Aini, Cairo, Egypt
420 Lexington Avenue, Suite 1644, New York, NY 10170
www.hoopoefiction.com

Hoopoe is an imprint of The American University in Cairo Press
www.aucpress.com

ISBN 978 1 649 03359 8

Library of Congress Cataloging-in-Publication Data

Names: 'Abd al-Qaddūs, Iḥsān, author. | Smolin, Jonathan, translator.
Title: A nose and three eyes / Ihsan Abdel Kouddous ; translated by
  Jonathan Smolin.
Other titles: Anf wa-thalāth 'uyūn. English
Identifiers: LCCN 2023033172 | ISBN 9781649033604 (hardcover) | ISBN
  9781649033598 (trade paperback) | ISBN 9781649033611 (epub) | ISBN
  9781649033628 (adobe pdf)
Subjects: LCGFT: Novels.
Classification: LCC PJ7804.Q3 A8313 2024 | DDC 892.7/36--dc23/
eng/20240202

1 2 3 4 5   28 27 26 25 24

Designed by Adam el-Sehemy

We see people as we want to see them . . .

Ihsan

Foreword

Hanan al-Shaykh

WHEN I LEARNED THAT JONATHAN Smolin had taken on translating some novels by Ihsan Abdel Kouddous into English and was writing a book about his fiction, I remembered a letter that Ihsan sent me in the summer of 1980. "I read in the press that your novel *The Story of Zahra* has been translated into French. Congratulations. I wish, my dear, that you could suggest to your French publisher to translate what they like of my work since I long to see one of my books translated into a foreign language."

I still remember how I rushed to call him from London, where I lived, and how he told me at the end of the call "Hanan, you have to help your teacher. Don't you remember, my dear, when I was the one who was an important writer?"

I met Ihsan for the first time in Cairo in early 1963, when I enrolled at a local secondary school to get my degree in literature. At that time, I was able to convince my father that this was the only way to qualify me to go to university to specialize in journalism. The truth of the matter was that I wanted to free myself and travel and live in Cairo, the city of writers and novelists. My eyes had been opened to the love of reading and writing. I was writing reflections and publishing them in the student page in the daily newspaper *Annahar* in Beirut. In my writing, I focused on the personal freedom that I dreamed of achieving by any means, even if it meant resorting to tricks. I started conducting interviews with Lebanese politicians about their first loves and publishing them in Lebanese newspapers.

In Cairo, I took everything that I'd written and published, and I went to *Rose El Youssef*, where the doorman accompanied me to Ihsan's secretary who brought me into his chic office. After initial pleasantries, we agreed that I'd write what I wanted on the condition that I wouldn't be paid for anything that was published.

As soon as I left his office, I felt that I had fallen in love with him.

I tried as hard as I could to write something to entice him to publish it. And what happened was that the evening after I visited him, the supervisor of the girls' dorm where I lived told me that I had a phone call from *Rose El Youssef*. It was Ihsan asking me if we could meet the following day on the Nile corniche, opposite Shepheard Hotel at six in the evening.

Ihsan was married and had two sons.

We fell in love without thinking about the age difference. I was eighteen and he was forty-four, even though when I asked him how old he was, he was quick to say he was forty. He took me all over Cairo as we talked, having a good time, laughing. He took me to beautiful and relaxing places. We kept meeting and he showed me Alexandria, making me fall in love with it, as well as Fayoum with its lake full of birds and rose-colored pelicans.

But the corniche along the Nile was our favorite place for an outing. We'd drive around as we looked at the al-Saghir Mosque glitter on the Nile at night.

That summer, Ihsan met me in Lebanon, and we traveled together from Beirut to Rome, London, and Paris. I told my father that I'd won a literary prize and that I had to go get it in London.

I came back to Beirut three weeks later to face a storm in the local newspapers and magazines, which were talking about Ihsan Abdel Kouddous marrying a Lebanese girl named Hanan al-Shaykh and that the newlyweds spent their honeymoon in Europe. The hotel workers where Ihsan stayed in Beirut for a week before we left confirmed that we were married after they saw me with him inside the hotel almost nonstop, in addition to the fact that he gave the hotel our passports to get visas for us for the three European countries.

When I arrived at the Beirut airport, I was full of longing for Ihsan who had said goodbye to me at the airport in Rome. I was going to Beirut, and he was heading to Cairo, after we had spent the happiest and loveliest couple of weeks in Europe.

I got out of the taxi, took my bag, and carried it up the stairs of our house. I heard the clamor of the neighbors calling out, "Hanan's back! Hanan's back!" As soon as I got in the house, everything went crazy. The exhausted voice of my brother, as if he was hitting me with a whip, yelled out, "We know everything. We know that you traveled with Ihsan Abdel Kouddous. Tell us what happened!" And my father, acting like he only just heard the news, said, "What? My clever daughter

Hanan was tricking us like that?" Then my brother said, "Let's go and see how clever she is when we take her to the gynecologist for a virginity test."

My anger, craziness, and longing to be with Ihsan made me run to the door and open it, yelling, "Okay, prison guards, take me to a thousand doctors!"

It seemed that my acting and confidence filled my father and brother with doubt and confusion. My desire to protect Ihsan had become unbearable. I quickly found myself asking to reveal a secret to them, a secret that had to stay between us or I'd wind up in jail. I told them that I did, in fact, travel to Europe to meet Ihsan and bring him thousands of pounds that I was smuggling for him from Cairo. This was because the Egyptian authorities would only let Egyptians take out a limited amount from the country. My brother then whispered in fear, "You really are crazy. How did you do that? Where did you hide thousands of pounds?"

I responded by pointing to my hair: "Here." And then, standing firm, I continued, "And in my bra, inside my pants, in my belt, around my waist, in the sleeves of my jacket, in the hem of my skirt."

I took a deep cleansing breath, congratulating myself for my quick thinking, but things didn't exactly go smoothly from there. My father cried out the Arabic saying, "Close the door that brings wind into your house and relax." He continued, "We're not letting you go back to Cairo!"

I yelled and screamed that they were blocking the path of my future, stopping me from going to university in Cairo now that I had my Egyptian secondary school degree.

My brother defended the decision by explaining that if I went back to Cairo, I'd be confirming the rumors that the newspapers had printed about my marriage to Ihsan, showing that it was all true and not simply rumors, and that people would start talking about it again.

None of my yelling, pleading, crying, or threats of suicide were successful before my family's insistence on preventing me from going back—in other words, preventing me from inhaling the breath of life.

I found myself determined to flee and go back to Cairo, especially since I had the return ticket that Ihsan had bought for me when we were in Europe in case of an emergency, but the strict supervision of my family stopped me. I found myself threatening to end my life. I stopped eating and drinking water, and I refused to speak. It got to the point that I ran to get on top of the kitchen chair pretending that I was going to throw myself out of the window. My tricks eventually worked, especially when I didn't leave the bathroom for two days straight pretending to be vomiting and hallucinating. I finally heard my father utter the famous Arabic expression, "Seek knowledge, even if it is found as far as China"—in other words, agreeing to let me travel for school—while my brother started begging me to open the door, swearing on his honor that I could go to Cairo whenever I wanted.

I remember when I was with Ihsan in London and we had some Egyptian friends with us, including a former Arab queen. Ihsan sat next to her talking to her the whole evening. Afterwards, I chided him and told him that he was being self-centered by ignoring me. That surprised him and he said, "I'm a writer and a novelist. I take stories from life and people and their experiences. You want me not to feel curiosity about a former queen and ask her about her life?"

When we read the novels of Ihsan Abdel Kouddous, we experience what's happening in the psychologies of the characters emotionally, socially, and politically. He exposed and corroborated the intimate relations between the individuals of society, particularly between men and women. He was among those who called for the freedom of the individual, something that he considered a life-jacket in the turbulent sea of life.

I once heard Ihsan say "If I give up my freedom, I've lost my soul."

It's true that the dramatic situations in his novels extended to the two of us when I saw Ihsan drive by me quickly with a young woman next to him, the two of them deep in laughter as if they were in total harmony. I was nailed to my spot, feeling crushed that he was with another woman. I became a chimney letting out dark smoke.

Should I, I wondered, do what I was hearing from the supervisor of the girls' dormitory and stop seeing Ihsan? My Egyptian friend Sharifa was also telling me that Ihsan changed lovers like he changed neckties. She advised me to wake up to the fact that every meeting with him was hurting my reputation.

When Ihsan next took me to the Mena House Hotel opposite the pyramids, I felt sad, depressed, and lost. I was silent and distracted. He put his head between his hands leaning on the table and then looked up and told me that he had read my letter about what happened, which was twenty-four pages long. He didn't agree that he wasn't responsible for what he did. He said that I was wrong about the way I saw the reasons for his betrayal, and for using my personal philosophy of love, that our feelings contradict our desires, to try to absolve him. Nor did he appreciate my telling him that he ought to be completely honest with himself as to why he was excited to meet with another woman.

In a sudden movement, he took my hand, kissed it, and said, "Three women and a man. I wonder how each of them sees him? Hanan, this is the novel that I'm going to start writing tomorrow. I'll call it *A Nose and Three Eyes*. The third eye is Lebanese, but the nose is the man!"

When Ihsan started writing the novel, things began to change. Ihsan was feeling isolated and disillusioned at the time, anxiety overcoming him about things in his life and work. He suffered in silence. Our relationship also began to change. He no longer called me daily as he used to. He started asking me to meet him in his apartment while he was writing the novel, whereas in the past, he would insist that we go out almost every day together to restaurants and hotels where we'd dance the tango and watch the most famous Egyptian belly dancers.

I still remember how, in June 1964 as he was writing the third eye, Ihsan started writing something and then kept tearing it up until he finally finished. I asked him what he was writing, and he said that it was a letter to the writer Tawfiq al-Hakim. I thought that maybe Ihsan was asking him to intervene with the authorities on his behalf, to return him to his position as chair of the board of *Rose El Youssef* after he had been informed that a former director of a dried fish factory had been appointed in his place. Ihsan's sadness turned into pure anger that spewed lava like a volcano. As a result, he decided to resign from the position of editor-in-chief of *Rose El Youssef*, which he also held, contenting himself with just taking part in the editing.

When I heard from Jonathan Smolin that the novel *A Nose and Three Eyes* had created a crisis in official circles and even with President Gamal Abdel Nasser personally, I was surprised. Feelings of grief and confusion overcame me because Ihsan never said anything to me about all these developments. Was it because I didn't read the newspapers and magazines and had contented myself with living in the cocoon that I enjoyed in Cairo? I blamed myself because I didn't pay attention to something that was being inflicted on Ihsan!

And now I'm wondering after more than half a century, did Ihsan want to protect me and prefer not to have me share in the weight of his worries and put his troubles on my young shoulders at that time?

Is that, I wonder, why he hid from me the turmoil that was happening around *A Nose and Three Eyes*?

I said goodbye to Cairo at the beginning of summer 1966 and went back for good to Beirut. Some months after my return, I accepted a request from a Lebanese journalist to talk with him about the novel *A Nose and Three Eyes*, since I was the third eye. The interview was published with photos of me as I was holding a Kleenex with a kohl pen and some money, talking about boredom and freedom exactly like the third eye in the novel.

I admit that I represent the third eye. But Ihsan denied it and said that he took inspiration for the characters of his novels from the world of the imagination, even though he frequently took them from situations and experiences that he lived for real. The third eye of *A Nose and Three Eyes* was the embodiment of a generation that believed in existentialism and modern society with progressive values.

I remember when we were sitting together in his apartment as he was writing the third eye and how I'd read in disbelief his incredible talent and cleverness. Even things that I said to him made their way into the dialogue and the plot.

Rereading the novel now reminded me of how the name Rihab was the name of my Lebanese friend whom I knew when I was living in the girls' dorm in Cairo. Like the character in the novel, I also lived in Cairo with a Lebanese family after I was kicked out of the dormitory. This family had immigrated to Egypt from Lebanon at the beginning of the nineteenth century and, like in the novel, suffered from the nationalization of their factories.

I remember how I was the one who made up the story of smuggling money from Egypt to Europe and I was a young woman who was holding a kohl pen, money, and Kleenex in my hand, not in a handbag.

But, unlike the heroine of the third eye, I had passionately fallen in love with Ihsan.

Nonetheless, I agree when Ihsan said that Hanan al-Shaykh isn't the third eye. When I became a writer, I discovered that when I wrote about people I knew, they inevitably became different once they were cast as characters in a novel. If I decided to write the biography of these people, I'd be turned from a novelist into a historian or an employee at a health insurance company!

As a writer, I find myself getting on a train and traveling with a character on an open journey whose destination is unknown to me, nor do I know who we'll meet or what will happen when the train stops at the coming stations. That's how we learn on the journey of writing, and we discover the truths of life that we didn't understand before.

If Hanan al-Shaykh is not the third eye, who, then, is Hashim in the novel? Is he Ihsan himself when he wanted to be transported from one relationship to another? Or did he mean to profoundly understand the depths of women?

My dear Ihsan, here are some of your writings translated into English, which means that they still stir up controversy and debate, in addition to shining light on the past, on the history of a particular story from which we can learn about the present and future.

And here I see Ihsan Abdel Kouddous and his famous smile covering his entire face and that of whoever he spoke to, holding his translated novel and reading his name and the title in English, declaring, "Yes, this is great."

Introduction

Jonathan Smolin

BY FALL 1963, WHEN HE started writing and serializing *A Nose and Three Eyes*, Ihsan Abdel Kouddous was already a legend on the Arab literary, cultural, and media scenes. Widely known in Egypt and the Arab world by just his first name, Ihsan rose to fame as a precocious journalist, magazine editor, and short story writer in the 1940s. He befriended Gamal Abdel Nasser and the other Free Officers in the early 1950s, using his platform as editor-in-chief of *Rose El Youssef*, perhaps the most important political–cultural weekly in the Arab world at the time, to uncover scandals among the Egyptian ruling elite and to call for revolution. Ihsan was so close with Nasser that when the coup was launched on July 23, 1952, Nasser called Ihsan down to the barracks, making Ihsan the only civilian to participate with the Free Officers on that fateful day. For the next four months, Ihsan was perhaps the most prominent and forceful supporter of the Free Officers, calling on the public both in the press and on the radio to support their reforms. All Ihsan's support was based on the assumption that Nasser and the Free Officers were working to install democracy in Egypt and that they would withdraw from rule once the country was ready for free and fair elections. As became clear by late 1952, he was tragically mistaken.

By January 1953, Ihsan had gone from one of Nasser's most ardent supporters to a thorn in his side, pressing him both privately and publicly in his *Rose El Youssef* editorials to leave the military, form a political party based on his platform, and participate in democratic elections like any other politician. Now entrenched in power, Nasser was having none of it. By spring 1954, Nasser became so annoyed with Ihsan's persistent dissent that he decided that it was time to teach his former co-revolutionary a lesson. He jailed Ihsan for three months, a deeply traumatic experience that demonstrated once and for all that Ihsan's dreams of a democratic Egypt were nothing more than fantasies.

Like any prominent editor-in-chief at the time, Ihsan continued to write editorials in *Rose El Youssef* after his release, but, unlike before his jailing, these were almost entirely devoid of political dissent. Instead, he now turned to fiction to use the tools of metaphor and allegory to retell his deeply fraught history with the revolution and dissent against Nasser. He used fiction as a cover to explore his deep sense of regret, guilt, and despair at his own role in inadvertently helping to turn Egypt into a military dictatorship. Unlike Naguib Mahfouz, who carefully completed his novels before serializing them, Ihsan typically wrote each chapter of a novel or short story only hours before it went to press. This establishes a powerful lens through which to read Ihsan's fiction, offering unique opportunities to tie events in the politics of Egypt to each installment of his fiction exactly as he was writing it.

Starting in fall 1954, immediately after his release from jail, Ihsan wrote and published an installment of a novel or a short story—sometimes both—in seemingly every issue of *Rose El Youssef*. Until fall 1963, when he began writing and publishing *A Nose and Three Eyes*, Ihsan wrote nearly all of the classics that made him so famous, including *al-Wisada al-khalia* (The Empty Pillow), *La anam* (I Do Not Sleep), *Fi baytuna ragul* (There's a Man in Our House), *al-Banat wa-l-sayf* (Girls and the Summer), and *La tutfi' al-shams* (The Sun Never Sets), among others. Each of these works not only boosted the circulation of *Rose El Youssef* and became bestsellers when printed as books, but they were also adapted into some of the most popular works of Egyptian cinema in the twentieth century. Ihsan's highly fraught relationship with Nasser continued behind the scenes during these years, with Nasser intervening in a variety of ways to both punish and reward Ihsan for what he wrote in the press. On multiple occasions, Nasser, who was a devoted reader of Ihsan, relayed his anger at his fiction, demanding immediate changes as Ihsan was writing and serializing a novel. By spring 1960, Nasser had not only jailed Ihsan and intervened to shut down dissent in his editorials and shape elements of his fiction, but he also nationalized the press, confiscating Ihsan's magazines and turning them into the property of the state.

Between spring 1960 and fall 1963, there seemed to have been a détente in Nasser's relationship with Ihsan. During this period, Ihsan avoided metaphorical criticism of Nasser in his fiction. He also published a number of editorials in the press that were particularly enthusiastic in praising Nasser and his achievements. On 16 December 1962, Nasser appeared to reward Ihsan for his recent loyalty, giving Ihsan the Order of First Merit for his service as chairman of *Rose El Youssef*. Despite the ceaseless turbulence of their relationship during the 1950s, it appeared by mid-1963 that Ihsan had finally moved on from his regret and sense of betrayal at what became of the Egyptian revolution.

Something happened in fall 1963 to change that. We know that Ihsan was in a romantic relationship with the young Hanan al-Shaykh at the time. Unlike other married famous writers who hid their affairs behind the doors of their bachelor apartments, Ihsan refused to participate in the charade of social hypocrisy. As Hanan told me: "Ihsan was a free spirit. He did not comply with any rules. He was like a teenager, falling in love again and again. He was so courageous in defying society. He was a great rebel." When Ihsan took Hanan to Europe on vacation in summer 1963, an episode that she describes for the first time in her foreword to this translation, word spread of the famous writer dating a young Lebanese woman, sparking scandal in its wake. When Ihsan returned to Cairo, he discovered that the secret services had not only been monitoring him, but that they even confiscated a love letter that Hanan had written to him from Beirut. Anwar Sadat, the future president of Egypt, then took Ihsan for a stroll along the Nile to warn him to stop seeing his young Lebanese girlfriend. Nasser had already punished Ihsan multiple times for his fiction and editorials, even confiscating his magazines as part of the nationalization of the press.

Ihsan no doubt felt that Nasser was now intervening in his love life as a new form of punishment.

Whether it was the concerted effort to end his relationship with his young Lebanese girlfriend or, perhaps, something else that we have no record of, Ihsan suddenly became intensely defiant just as he began writing and publishing the installments of *A Nose and Three Eyes* in fall 1963. While the novel can certainly be read outside of any political framing as a brilliant narrative of the passions and pains of romantic love, Ihsan's relationship with Nasser—and Nasser's romance with Egypt—provides a crucial lens through which to understand the work. The novel is divided into three sections, or "eyes," each narrated by a different lover of Dr. Hashim, a thinly veiled double of Nasser himself. Each section appears to be a metaphorical retelling of the three distinct phases of Nasser's relationship with the nation, with accompanying condemnation. In the first section, which takes place during the early to mid-1950s, Amina, a double for both Egypt and Ihsan himself, divorces her husband, a marker of the corrupt previous era, on the delusion that the manly, strong, and enticing Hashim will marry her. It is a bet on the future that will lead Amina, like Ihsan, to regret, despair, and, ultimately, a haunting sense of degradation. In the second part, the sick Nagwa is healed by Hashim, who now appears as a messianic figure, mirroring and, perhaps, mocking the widespread public depictions of Nasser during the mid- to late 1950s as the sublime savior of the nation. Finally, in the third part, which spans the late 1950s until the early 1960s, Hashim is a shell of his former self as he chases after a young, rebellious Lebanese woman, an obvious parallel for Nasser's delusional infatuation with Syria in his failed romance with the United Arabic Republic.

During the 1950s, Ihsan repeatedly criticized Nasser and dissented at the trajectory of the revolution in his novels. Nonetheless, this subtext of his fiction was mostly opaque to readers who knew little about Ihsan's personal relationship and history with Nasser and the coup. In *A Nose and Three Eyes*, Ihsan had finally gone too far. While the exact details of what happened behind the scenes are unclear, we know that a crisis erupted surrounding the novel by the time he was midway through serializing the second eye. In the installment when Uncle 'Abdu follows Nagwa into her bedroom after "purchasing" sexual rights over her from her mother, Ihsan included a note that read: "I feel the stupidity of the writer when he's forced to say that the characters of his stories aren't particular people or that any resemblance between them and any real person is pure coincidence. But I'm forced to be stupid and repeat these words to try to end all the talk since I began this novel. The heroine of the "first" or "second" or "third eye" or Dr. Hashim are in no way real people . . . I apologize for saying this, but I'm forced to since I'm tired of all the rumors." By the time he was finishing serializing the second eye, the crisis had reached the point that a member of parliament took the unprecedented step of charging Ihsan with "harming public morality" with the novel, demanding that serialization cease immediately and that it never be adapted into any other format, including cinema, radio, or television.

The scandal took a massive personal toll on Ihsan.

With Hanan al-Shaykh at his side, Ihsan wrote a letter to legendary playwright Tawfiq al-Hakim the day before the case was discussed in parliament, saying "I'm suffering a psychological crisis and a horrible feeling of loneliness. I'm alone, alone to a terrifying degree." Ihsan rushed to complete *A Nose and Three Eyes* to put an end to the scandal and to leave Egypt, at least for the summer. This helps explain why the third eye is so much shorter than the other two and ends so abruptly. Before he left Egypt, however, he was interrogated by the police about the novel. The case was then turned over to the public prosecutor, who also interrogated Ihsan. When it was transferred to the morals police, Ihsan had had enough. As he wrote in a letter to the "Dean of Arabic Literature," Taha Hussein, in 1966, "I couldn't bear that a novelist in our age could be held to account before the morals prosecutor like a prostitute or a pimp." Ihsan asked his close friend, former army officer, and fellow writer Youssef El Sebai to intervene on his behalf with Nasser. The case was subsequently dropped but the damage had been done.

In the wake of the scandal, Ihsan was removed as president of the board of *Rose El Youssef*, the magazine that his mother had founded and that he had worked at since the 1930s. It was an unbearable public and professional humiliation. For the next two years, Ihsan was forced into social and literary exile, publishing almost no editorials, fiction, or cultural pieces, by far the longest period of silence in his career up to that point. It was what he would later call a "literary execution." As Ihsan wrote in the same 1966 letter to Taha Hussein: "I found myself fighting a terrible psychological crisis that distanced me from everyone, all centers of movement, everyone I love . . . For the past two years, this suffering became more than I could bear." As Ihsan became more and more isolated, irritable, and distracted, he began to see Hanan al-Shaykh less and less. Their romantic relationship came to an end, an outcome that must have pleased Nasser as perhaps a final punishment even worse than imprisonment.

This tragic toll of the novel, however, is not the end of the story. After two years in exile, Nasser eventually brought Ihsan back to the public sphere by naming him editor-in-chief of the leading weekly *Akhbar Elyom*, a high-prolife position that Ihsan embraced with relish. He managed to expand the weekly's circulation to over a million copies, a striking milestone for a periodical in the Arab world. Ihsan would eventually return to publishing novels after Nasser's death and, under Anwar Sadat, he would be named as chairman of *al-Ahram*, the daily newspaper of record in Egypt. Even though their romantic relationship ended, Ihsan would remain lifelong friends with Hanan al-Shaykh and it was no doubt a point of tremendous pride for him to see her become one of the most important writers of Arabic fiction in the twentieth century thanks to classics like *The Story of Zahra* and *Women of Sand and Myrrh*. And despite the crisis surrounding *A Nose and Three Eyes* at the time of serialization and attempts to ban the novel, it would indeed go on not only to be published as a best-selling book but also adapted into a classic film with an all-star cast that included Mahmud Yassin and Nagla' Fathi, a sultry radio play featuring Omar Sharif himself as Dr. Hashim, and a shocking television series starring a young Youssra. And now, some sixty years after the scandal that rocked Ihsan and the Arab literary world, this brilliant classic is finally appearing in English for readers outside of the Middle East to enjoy. Ihsan would no doubt have been proud to see his most controversial and explosive novel reaching the widest audiences despite unprecedented efforts to repress it.

The First Eye

1

THERE'S NO SUCH THING AS love.

I scoff at the foolish girls who go crazy at the sighs of 'Abd al-Wahhab and the wails of 'Abd al-Halim Hafiz. They pour their youth out into the lines of romance novels and movies and then hitch their fantasies to the first guy they meet, tearing up their hearts with their fingernails proclaiming, "We've fallen in love!"

No, girls.

No, deluded girls.

There's no such thing as love.

Believe me.

I know. I'm an expert. I have long, bitter experience.

What we call love is only, how to put it, habit. Yes, just habit. You get used to a man and habit takes root deep inside you until you think it's love. Or what they call love. Exactly as we say that a man loves whiskey. Does it make any sense that a man falls in love with whiskey? We use the word "love" for whiskey, as we use it for romantic relationships, because the basic element that brings together a man and whiskey is what brings together a man and a woman. It's habit. Getting used to something. When we say that someone loves whiskey, we mean that they've gotten used to it. When we say that someone loves someone, we mean that they've gotten used to them.

So, if this is true, why does a woman love one man in particular and not another? Or, more specifically, why does a woman get used to one man in particular and not another?

It's a matter of taste.

While one man is used to whiskey and another to cognac, a third might prefer wine, and so on. It's the same with girls. One girl likes brown-haired guys while another likes blonds. One girl likes heavy-set guys while another likes thin guys, and so on.

Despite that, there's not a girl out there who started her romantic life with just one guy. Girls always begin by casting their gaze onto more than one guy, just like they flip through the pages of fashion magazines. And she likes more than one dress. More like ten dresses or twenty. She also likes more than one guy, or ten guys or twenty. She checks out each of them and she hopes to touch each one, hear each voice on the phone, see each set of lips, and sample each taste herself. She tries different men, or at least some of them, and she stops at the one that most fits her circumstances.

There's no difference between a kiss from any of the ten or twenty guys she likes. It's the same taste, the same trembling of the lips, the same feeling savored in silence. The difference is between a kiss that she's gotten used to and one that is new. If she got used to the kiss of any of the guys that she longed for, I'd call this love, just as I'd call my habit for Hashim love.

What was between me and Hashim couldn't be more than that.

Simply habit.

I didn't love him. It couldn't have been love. I don't want it to be said that I loved him. It drives me crazy whenever I hear someone say that I loved him. I only got used to him.

Habit has harsh rules. It controls you, makes you submit, degrades you, and erases your personality. A man who got used to whiskey might lose it if he's denied whiskey. He might destroy everything around him and then destroy himself. All that happened to me because I got used to Hashim.

How did I let this happen when he was so bitter, so repulsive from day one?

I don't know.

Whiskey also has a bitter and repulsive taste.

And I got used to both.

I got used to Hashim.

Then I got used to whiskey.

And . . .

I laugh. I laugh at myself, at my defeat, at my suffering.

I'm trying to make out like I'm some philosopher here, but these words aren't mine. They're some of my boyfriend's. He told me all this once to dry my tears. Then he kissed me to get me used to him so that I might get rid of my habit for Hashim's lips. I remember that night. I let him take more than that. I let him take all of me to help me get rid of my habit for Hashim. I believed what he was saying that day.

But I'm not a philosopher.

I was a girl like all the rest. I was crazy about the sighs of 'Abd al-Wahhab and the wails of 'Abd al-Halim Hafez. I poured my youth out into the lines of romance stories and movies.

I was beautiful. My hair was the color of hazelnuts. It was long, down past my shoulders. My eyes were wide and amber. My mouth was small, my lips tight and cheerful. My lower lip was fuller than the upper one. I had an infectious smile. My skin was white, the color of milk. I was five foot six, tall but not too tall, and I had shapely legs.

My breasts were like two sunflowers. My waist was thin, not more than 22 inches. I had a beauty mark the color of chocolate on my shoulder. And another one, I won't say where.

I was infatuated with my body. I'd lock my bedroom door and stand naked in front of the mirror. I'd inspect every part of me, every line, every fold. I wanted to put a little weight on my arms since they were so thin. I wanted my breasts to come up a bit so that my collar bones were a little less prominent. I'd dance in front of the mirror. I'd smile at my waist as I bent forward, at my chest as it shook, at my thighs as they swung softly and calmly, as if I was swimming in air. I loved dancing, but only my mirror saw me dance. Even my mother had not seen me.

I never thought about a man as I stood in front of the mirror staring at my body. Never. I never thought about who I'd be giving this body to. Never. All that was far from me. I'd notice the eyes of men pursuing me. I felt pleased by it, but I'd brush them off like I was swatting away flies, not letting a single one land

on or cling to me. There was never one man in particular, never one man I yearned for. My head was full of
movie stars. Rock Hudson, Gregory Peck, Dean Mar-
tin. Just fantasy, just dreams that didn't excite anything
real in me. My body was mine alone. I felt that I was
the only one who had the right to enjoy it, to examine
it and discover its secrets. I preserved my treasure, only
opening it in front of the mirror.

Have I gone on too long about it?

Sorry.

But that's how my story begins. It begins the day
I started feeling that I was beautiful, the day I became
infatuated with myself.

I was the most beautiful girl on Salah al-Din Street
in Heliopolis. Suitors started coming to my father when
I was fifteen.

And then I got engaged.

At the time, I was sixteen. I was living with my
mother, her husband, and my three half-siblings. My
mother was a goodhearted woman. She prayed and
fasted. Every month she made an offering to one of the
awliya—an offering to *Sayyidna* al-Hussein for her son's
success, an offering to Sidi Abu al-'Abbas when my sister
recovered from measles, and so on and on. She went to
fortune tellers for them to read their coffee grounds and
tarot cards. Despite her preoccupation with all this, she
was a happy woman. A day didn't go by without her getting together with some of her many friends, who made
up half the women of Cairo.

My mother used to spoil me and worry about me
more than my siblings. Maybe because I was living with

her and I didn't have a close relationship with my father. She used to cover up my mistakes so her husband didn't find out about them, while she'd complain to him about my siblings. She'd complain to him about every little mistake and then he would hit them.

Her husband was the kind of man who makes out like he's harsh and firm, but he's an imbecile you could make fun of and dupe easily.

One afternoon, my mother and I were leaving the salon when a man saw me. He walked behind me. He drove after our car all the way home. He asked the doorman about us. And the next day, he came to propose to me.

I don't know how he convinced my mother to agree to our engagement. 'Abd al-Salam was thirty-six. Twenty years older than me. Guys younger than him had come before to propose. Guys from well-known families had come before. Even a guy with a doctorate had come. 'Abd al-Salam wasn't cultured or educated or from a well-known family. But he was rich. He worked as a trader in Suez. Even though someone richer had come before, my mother accepted 'Abd al-Salam. He was the kind of guy who could mesmerize older women.

My stepfather agreed quickly. Maybe to get rid of me so he could be free from my mother's endless indulging me.

My father opposed it, but his opposition wasn't worth much. My father didn't have any weight, and no one took him seriously. He was irresponsible, living only for himself. At the time, he was married to his fourth wife. My mother used to say that he had a bachelor pad where he'd meet another woman who would one day become his fifth wife.

I gave in to my mother. I was happy with the engagement ring. It had slender diamonds and a lattice. It had a solitaire of fifteen karats. I loved the new dress and the party and all the attention from my five aunts. I was happy because I was engaged before my cousins Riri and Farida. My happiness those days was overwhelming. It made me forget everything, even my fiancé himself. I'd see him as I saw other men, just in passing. I didn't try to scrutinize his features. At the time, I didn't see the pores across his nose that you could only see if you looked closely. I didn't see the gold tooth on the side of his right jaw that looked out at you whenever he laughed. I didn't see that all his pants were too big from the back, as if the tailor had almost made a loose robe and then changed his mind at the last moment.

My fiancé left for Suez the day after the engagement was announced. He started coming to Cairo every week to spend Friday, Saturday, and Sunday there. Each of my aunts made a big lunch for us. My father invited us once for dinner. That day, I felt he was carrying out an unwanted responsibility and he almost kicked my fiancé and me out immediately after dinner. But I wasn't angry at my father. I knew how my father was and I loved him.

My fiancé and I were never left alone. My mother was always with us. When she had to disappear for a few moments, she insisted on leaving her husband or my younger brother with us. My fiancé didn't ever try to get me alone. He didn't even try to whisper something my mother wouldn't hear. He didn't try to squeeze my hand or give me any of the glances that I read about in stories. All he would insist on was performing the five prayers at the right time. His whole aspiration was that I'd pray like him. My mother reassured him that after the marriage, I would definitely pray.

My happiness with the engagement began to fade. Everyone in my family and all my girlfriends had already seen the two rings that he gave me. The new dress became old. All the chitchat became boring. And then, when I stood in front of my mirror to dance naked as usual, I felt for the first time that my body was no longer mine alone. I now had a partner. I saw in the mirror the face of my partner—my fiancé—and, for the first time, I became aware of his features, which I had taken in without realizing it, without paying attention. I saw the pores on his nose. I saw his gold tooth. I saw his pants sagging down. My image of Rock Hudson and Gregory Peck disappeared. There was no longer anything in front of me but this reality of my fiancé. A tremor ran through my body. And, that day, I couldn't dance. I couldn't even stand there. I ran and hid as if I was hiding from the wide eyes of my fiancé.

From that day, my body began making me anxious.

I began to feel the treasure that I kept hidden my whole life was on the verge of being discovered. I began to feel the picks that were digging down on top of it to get to it, that something was getting close to my lips, my neck, my chest, my waist, my legs.

I was certain then that my treasure would be discovered. I had no way out. I couldn't hide it forever. Someone was going to reach it. But I didn't want that person to be my fiancé. I didn't want him. I was fleeing from him. He disgusted me. His hands were like pieces of lumpy dough. His eyes on me were like drops of oil. His words fell from his lips like pieces of clay. There was no tenderness, nothing in him that dazzled me. There was no skill of the explorer, the treasure hunter.

Could I break off the engagement?

Maybe if I'd tried then, I would've been able to. But I didn't. I was weak. I was too weak to stand up to my mother and tell her how I really felt about my fiancé. But I didn't know then what I wanted. I couldn't understand what I really felt. I understood that I didn't want him, but I believed that my fate was just that of any other girl. Sometimes I felt oppressed by my situation, and sometimes I felt I shouldn't even be thinking about breaking off the engagement, that I should fear God and not be ungrateful. Other times, I felt a rage fill my chest that could tear me to pieces. I'd put out the fire by burying my head in the pillow and telling myself, "Girl, be reasonable!"

This hesitation brought me to submission. But this submission pushed me to a kind of defiance, defiance of my weakness, my hesitation, my mother, my lot in life. It was a kind of repressed defiance. I didn't admit it to myself. But it pushed me, pushed my thinking, my reactions, my behavior.

This defiance pushed me to look for another explorer for my body, someone other than my fiancé 'Abd al-Salam who would be the first person to touch my lips.

My eyes began scouring the terrain around me.

I no longer chased away the flies arrogantly, as I usually did. I started looking for flies. I was happy whenever a fly landed on me. I learned how to look from the corner of my eye, how to see every guy without him noticing that I was looking at him, without my mother or 'Abd al-Salam noticing that I was looking at anyone. I began collecting information about every guy in Heliopolis. I was looking at every guy and comparing him to my fiancé, imagining him as an explorer for my body.

One night, I was sitting at the Heliopolis Club with some girlfriends. My mother was sitting with her girl-friends at another table. Muhammad sat at the edge of the swimming pool and stared at my face with delight. I was bored. My friends were talking about something trivial, so I smiled at Muhammad. And Muhammad clung to my smile. He ran after it. He started chasing me. He would circle his car around my house. It was a white Chevrolet. And he was always behind me at the club, at the movies. Even when I was with my fiancé, he didn't stop chasing me. He fed my conceit and filled my emp-tiness, even if he didn't match the image of the explorer that I was dreaming about. He was twenty. He was a university student, a great swimmer, nicely put together, known in Heliopolis as a catch. He was my girlfriends' dream guy. But he was missing something. I didn't know what. He was like the taste of something cooked on a high flame. If it were cooked on low, it would be richer and more delicious.

The phone began ringing in my house. My mother would pick up, but no one would respond. It would ring again, and my stepfather would pick up, but then no one would respond. The ringing continued. And no one responded. This went on for days. And the comments started. My mother started directing her questioning eyes at me. I became afraid. I was afraid of her and my stepfather. Once, the phone rang and I picked up. My mother was next to me. I heard my aunt's voice and I started repeating: Hello? . . . Hello? I pressed the receiver against my ear to hide my aunt's voice as she was shouting on the other end: Hello? . . . Hello? I then hung up and turned to my mother.

"No one responded," I said innocently, just to put an end to her doubts.

I stayed next to the phone until my aunt called back.

"Is your phone broken?" she demanded.

"Not at all, Auntie," I responded. "How are you? How's Riri?"

A few days later, the phone rang again. I was next to it and my mother was far away. I heard Muhammad's voice. It was the first time I'd heard his voice, but I knew immediately who he was. I don't know how, but I knew it was him.

"This is Muhammad," he said conceitedly.

"You're the one who's been calling and not saying anything?" I asked in a sharp whisper, turning to the next room to keep an eye on my mother.

"Yes," he said as if he was proud of himself.

"Don't call again," I said. "Understand? You're causing problems for me."

"If you don't want me to call you, call me."

"Fine," I said, taking down his number. "I'll call you. Bye for now."

I hung up, smiling, feeling like a princess ruling over men.

I started talking with Muhammad on the phone.

After about three weeks, I went out to meet him for the first time. It was my first meeting with a man. My mother let me go visit my friend Huda by myself. I called Muhammad and I asked him to wait for me in his car on Baron Street. I got in next to him.

I didn't hesitate. I wasn't nervous. I sat next to him as if we were at the movies. I turned to him, waiting for the show to begin. I had the engagement ring on my finger.

Muhammad was more anxious than me. He didn't know how to begin the show I was waiting for. He stammered and struggled to get his words out, talking quickly and seeming to be out of breath.

"Was that your fiancé with you and your mother the day before yesterday?" he asked.

"Yes," I said looking out of the window.

"But he's old."

I turned to him with a sharp look.

"He's got nothing to do with you," I snapped.

I was ready to slap Muhammad in the face if he'd kept going. For some reason, I was defending my fiancé. I don't know why. Muhammad wasn't wrong. 'Abd al-Salam was indeed "old." And more than that, there were black pores on his nose, a gold tooth in his mouth, and his pants sagged down like a clown. But I wouldn't accept hearing this from someone else. Maybe I wasn't defending 'Abd al-Salam. I was defending myself, my fate, my weak personality, my submission.

"I'm sorry," Muhammad said.

He then reached out, took my hand, and squeezed it. I let him keep my hand in his for a moment. I then pulled it away quickly. I remembered 'Abd al-Salam and I was afraid to compare his hand with Muhammad's. 'Abd al-Salam's sweaty hand was lumpy and doughy. Muhammad's hand was hot and gripped mine, squeezing hard, almost crushing my fingers.

My meeting with Muhammad didn't last more than fifteen minutes. Afterwards, I went to visit my friend. I then went back home as if I was coming back from the movies. I stood taking my clothes off before the mirror and I examined my body. At that moment, I didn't think about Muhammad. I thought about 'Abd al-Salam, his face looming over me from the mirror. I scowled in disgust despite myself. I then squeezed the image of Muhammad into my mind. I began imagining him as the owner of this body, its explorer. But no, Muhammad was missing something. I didn't know what. I didn't think he knew the way to my body. But he had to know more than 'Abd al-Salam.

I slept terribly that night. I wasn't regretful, I was just empty.

Did I feel guilty because I went to meet a guy when I was engaged to someone else? Not at all.

I didn't meet Muhammad again for another month. My mother's supervision didn't give me much of a chance, but I wasn't so motivated to figure out a way to trick my mother again to go meet him.

Our second rendezvous was quick too. He tried to kiss me, but I only gave him my cheek. Then I opened the car door and ran off.

Four days later, the date to sign my marriage contract to 'Abd al-Salam was set. I became busy preparing the dress and the big party that would be put on for me at the Semiramis Hotel. I was totally preoccupied. My emptiness was filled for the time being. I no longer thought about Muhammad or my fiancé. I even forgot about my body and my mirror. I was busy from the moment I opened my eyes until I went to sleep. I was completely exhausted, a delicious kind of exhaustion.

Maybe the whole point of the craziness preparing for the big day is to occupy the bride, so she doesn't think or feel or search her heart. It's a kind of negation of the will.

I was on the wedding dais when my eyes began to focus again on what was around me. I began to wake up from the preparations that had taken hold of me, wake up from the dress that I wore and the white veil on my head. The belly dancer Thurayya Salim led my procession and Nagat al-Saghira sang. The ring was on my right hand. Words of congratulations were repeated endlessly. My five aunts threw themselves down on chairs to rest. My mother was broken by exhaustion.

My mind was filled with the image of my fiancé, without me even looking at him. I saw the pores on his nose, his pants sagging down. I scowled. I was bitter that this man was the one who would discover me, who would reveal my body. My eyes roamed around the faces of the other guys there. And I wondered . . . which of them is more deserving? I wondered this as I sat on the dais with roses all around me and the guests eating and drinking in front of me.

I went back home.

I wasn't happy.

I was tired.

This was still only the party for the marriage contract, the actual wedding was still a long way off. 'Abd al-Salam was building a villa in Suez and it wasn't finished yet. We couldn't even buy the furnishings before it was finished.

So 'Abd al-Salam was not yet my husband officially, and the only thing that happened after signing the contract was that my mother started leaving me alone with him. But he didn't try anything. He kissed me on the cheek when we met and when we parted. He'd kiss my hand sometimes. Once, he gave me a quick kiss on my lips. It passed like a touch of cold air. He got nervous afterwards. His face blushed. I feigned bashfulness and shyness. And then he tried to kiss me again.

"What'd we agree to?" I snapped, moving away. "There's none of that before we move into our house."

The good man submitted.

I remained a virgin bride.

The reality was that 'Abd al-Salam preferred sitting with my mother and my mother's husband instead of being alone with me. He was comfortable with them. And lost with me.

Emptiness enveloped me.

I went back to filling my emptiness by talking on the phone with Muhammad. I became freer than before. My mother let me do whatever I wanted as if she was finished with me. Despite that, I didn't think about meeting Muhammad again. He was pressuring me. But I refused. I felt that I'd become bigger than him. In my eyes, he became a child. I was now an adult, an engaged woman. I wanted something more.

When 'Abd al-Salam was in Cairo, I insisted on him taking me out for dinner every night. I'd pick the place, which I'd usually read about without seeing. The Hilton, the Mena House, the rooftop at the Semiramis.

It was at the Semiramis that I saw Hashim for the first time.

Dr. Hashim, known to one and all.

I looked at him for a long time. His shoulders were broad. His eyes were puffy as if he'd just woken up. His glances seemed to hang in the air. You didn't know if he was looking at you or hadn't noticed you at all. His lips were thick and always slightly parted. You couldn't tell if he was smiling or grimacing. His nose was curved and prominent. He looked like the American actor Robert Mitchum, even if he was a little taller and a little broader. He was the kind of person you found yourself looking at for a long time because there's something about them that sets them apart from everyone else.

I didn't know if he was looking at me with his puffy eyes or if he was glancing at me unintentionally. But looking at him brought strange feelings to my body, to my body and not my mind. With an involuntary movement, I found myself pulling my dress over my knees and lifting my palm and covering my arm with it, as if I was protecting myself from him.

I spent that night looking at him, stealing glances that my fiancé sitting next to me didn't notice. I don't know why I stole those glances. There was nothing between us. But I kept stealing looks at him. After every glance, I decided it would be the last. But then I looked again. I was furious, furious at myself and at him. I became enraged. His glances at me were stirring me up. He made me think about getting up and slapping him across the face and pulling his big nose. He seemed conceited and arrogant as if he owned the entire world.

My fiancé saw him.

"That's Dr. Hashim!" he whispered breathlessly as if he'd seen something incredible, as if he'd actually seen Robert Mitchum.

It was the first time I heard his name. I heard it from my fiancé.

At that moment, I was furious at 'Abd al-Salam too. I was angrier at him than at Dr. Hashim. Why was he so dazzled? He was small, trifling. I felt scorn for him, disgust.

"He's an exceptional doctor," he continued still breathless, his eyes glued to Hashim. "Imagine, my cousin went to all the doctors in Cairo. No one knew how to treat him but Dr. Hashim."

I didn't respond. I shook my shoulders and turned my lips as if I wasn't paying attention.

My fiancé sat up straighter as if he was proud to be sitting in the same place as Dr. Hashim.

"I'm going to go say hello to him," he then said, still dazzled. "He must remember me from when he was treating my cousin."

"No!" I whispered sharply. "If he remembers you, he'll come say hello on his own."

He shot me a surprised look and then didn't say anything.

Hashim didn't remember my fiancé and he didn't come over to greet him. I didn't see anything in his vacant glances telling me that I had caught his eye. I went home feeling a failure.

My fiancé kissed me in the car in front of the house. He kissed me on the cheek. He then went back to the hotel he usually stayed at whenever he came to Cairo. I sat with my mother, telling her about the evening.

"We saw Dr. Hashim," I said indifferently.

My mother was dazzled like 'Abd al-Salam.

"Really?" she said. "Who was he with?"

"A few men and women," I said surprised at her reaction.

"You know," my mother said full of delight, "he's the one who treated Susu, Madame Hosniya's daughter. He brought her back to health. They say he's a miracle worker."

I felt miserable.

"I don't know why this man doesn't get married," my mother continued, biting her lip. "The only thing he's lacking is a wife!"

I got up without responding to her.

I stood in front of my mirror. I took off my clothes and examined my body. I inspected it closer than ever before. I examined every line, every fold. A sudden question jumped to my mind like a flash of lightning cutting through the dark emptiness.

Could Hashim be my husband instead of 'Abd al-Salam?

2

FROM THAT DAY, I COULDN'T get the image of Hashim out of my head. The question kept coming back to me: why don't I marry Hashim instead of 'Abd al-Salam? It was a fantasy, a kind of distant waking dream, as if I was dreaming of marrying Rock Hudson or Robert Mitchum. But why should marrying Hashim be just a dream? Why was I thinking about him like Rock Hudson or Robert Mitchum? He was a normal man, simply a successful doctor. Any girl who married him wouldn't have anything more than me. But I had bad luck. My lot in men was 'Abd al-Salam, who my mother stupidly engaged me to. She didn't appreciate the value of my beauty. She didn't appreciate the value of the body that the man who was going to marry me would discover.

Hashim had stirred up doubt in myself. He made me anxious. And he didn't even know me. Maybe he hadn't ever seen me. He was a fantasy, a reflection of my own ambition. I hated to describe myself as ambitious, as ambitious girls lacked something, so they say, but I didn't lack anything. And who was Hashim to stir all this up? He was a man like all the rest. With a snap of my fingers, he'd fall at my feet. All I needed was to calm my imagination, thank God for my lot, and keep quiet.

I saw Hashim again when I went with my fiancé to have dinner at the Hilton. And a third time when we went to the Mena House. Every place I went to, I saw him, as if fate pulled us to one another. My aunt's husband recommended that we go have dinner at Le Grillon, a restaurant I'd never been to or even heard of. As soon as we arrived, I saw Hashim leaning on the edge of the bar, drinking a glass of whiskey. I almost cried from anger. I didn't want to see him. He was stirring me up, making me anxious, but I couldn't stop stealing glances at him. In return, his gaze hung in midair, and I didn't know whether he'd seen me or not. His lips were parted, and I couldn't tell if he was smiling or grimacing. My fiancé next to me looked at him dazzled, a smile on his lips, ever hopeful that Hashim would one day recognize him and come over to say hello.

I went back home feeling like a failure, feeling that I couldn't turn his head, even in passing.

The next day, I got up exhausted, crushed under the weight of my anger. I had no energy to change out of my nightclothes or brush my hair or look at my face in the mirror.

At one thirty, I picked up the phone and dialed Hashim's clinic.

"Please get the doctor right away," I barked at the nurse who answered.

"Who is this?" he asked politely.

"We have an urgent situation," I said. "We need the doctor immediately."

"One moment, please."

I heard Hashim's voice for the first time. It was thick, deep, and slow, as if he was yawning.

"Could you tell me where you'll be spending the evening?" I snapped.

"Can I know why?" he asked, unfazed.

"So I don't spend the evening wherever you do."

"Okay," he said simply. "Don't go to the Semiramis tonight."

Then he hung up.

That scoundrel. He hung up on me. It was my mistake. I should've hung up on him before I heard him respond.

The feeling of failure seized me again, harsher and more bitter. Rage boiled up inside me.

When my fiancé came by to have lunch, I insisted that it wasn't necessary and that we have an early dinner that night at the Mena House. I told him in a loud voice as if I wanted Hashim to hear me.

That night, when I stood in front of the mirror to get ready to go out, I found myself changing my hairdo. I let my hair hang down over my eyes. It was more enticing that way. I put on the padded bra that I'd bought two weeks ago. I pressed my lipstick on my finger and rubbed it on my cheeks to make sure they weren't pale. I put more kohl around my eyes to make them look wider, and more prominent. I put on my white dress. It was tight, alluring. I turned around in front of the mirror. Did my back look smooth? Yes, but still I changed into a dress that was more revealing.

I rode beside my fiancé in his car. We headed to the Mena House as we'd agreed in the morning. I was quiet.

I was trying to convince myself that I really wanted to go to the Mena House, that I wouldn't change my mind. But, before we got the Qasr al-Nil bridge, I turned to 'Abd al-Salam.

"What do you think about going to the Semiramis?" I asked, smiling. "It's closer."

He smiled broadly, revealing his gold tooth.

"As you wish. We can go wherever you'd like."

"Thanks."

Why'd he listen to me? Why didn't he protect me from myself?

He didn't know. He didn't know that I was chasing a fantasy and that there was a husband other than him in my imagination.

We got to the Semiramis. Hashim came late. He sat at a table packed with men and women. He turned his head to scan the rest of the tables as soon as he sat down. I imagined he was searching for me, but his eyes didn't stop on me.

From that day, I gave in to myself and to this fantasy: I hoped Hashim would be my husband instead of 'Abd al-Salam. I admitted this. I didn't know how to achieve it and I didn't know how to end it. I would go out with my fiancé when he was in Cairo to look for Hashim. I'd always find him. It was strange, but that was what was happening.

Once, we went to the Hilton and I stayed until eleven o'clock, but Hashim didn't show.

"I don't like this place," I said. "Let's go to the Mena House."

We went to the Mena House and I saw Hashim there.

I'd insist 'Abd al-Salam extend his stay in Cairo. The poor slob was happy. He thought I was becoming more attached to him.

In the evening, I'd sit with my mother and extract details from her about Hashim. I'd get everyone to talk about Hashim, including my girlfriends and my aunts. I wanted to know everything about him. I learned that he lived with his sister in a villa in Maadi and that he'd announced his engagement five years ago but then broke it off two months later. No one knew the exact reason, but it had been to a woman lots of people knew named Nahid. She'd loved him for two years, then they split up. No one knew why. Maybe because she was older than him.

My imagination was taking shape before me. I almost felt Hashim sleeping in my bed, his breath on my pillow. I tossed and turned in my sleep, pulling the sheet with me and dreaming that I'd pulled it from on top of him as he slept next to me. I'd wake up smiling.

Everything seemed easy. I could get to him. I could marry him. Maybe my mistake, and my mother's mistake, was that we hadn't chosen 'Abd al-Salam, but 'Abd al-Salam was the one who chose me. If I'd waited until I met a man I wanted and decided to marry him, maybe I would've married Hashim. I'd have had the most wonderful, important name: Mrs. Dr. Hashim.

All the girls did that. They picked the man and then set a plan to marry him.

But I didn't have a plan.

Believe me.

I acted rashly, without thinking.

I called his clinic in the morning and made an appointment for an examination. The nurse gave me an appointment at one o'clock in the afternoon. Standing in front of the mirror, I tried to pay particular attention to my appearance, but I couldn't. I was nervous. Actually, no. I was preoccupied. There was no problem with me going out alone. I was all but married and my mother no longer had any rights over me. I left without a single word of what I'd say to Hashim in my head. I was lost in thought. All I did as I went into the building where his clinic was located was take off my ring and put it in my purse. I felt embarrassed by it on my finger as I went to the man I wanted.

I sat in the women's waiting room. It was packed. It seemed to me that all the women there were healthy, that like me they'd come to meet Hashim, only to get to know him. I hated them all. There was a girl there about my age. What was she doing there? She didn't seem sick. Her cheeks were the color of tomatoes. She had a bold look in her eyes. Her body was full of vigor. She could raze a mountain. I looked daggers at her. She must be one of the spoiled, vacuous girls who visited doctor clinics to pass the time. I smiled. I was one of those spoiled, vacuous girls too.

I turned my gaze from the girl, the smile still on my lips. My eyes fell on my finger from which I'd taken off the ring. I was suddenly seized by the feeling that I was naked. I covered my finger with my palm quickly.

I tried to be calm. I tried to collect my scattered thoughts to think about what to do. I needed to drive all these fantasies from my head and go back to my house and my fiancé, the good-hearted man.

But I couldn't stay calm. The nurse came and took two pounds from me as payment for the exam. He gave me a receipt. Was this the first time that a girl has paid to meet with a man? Two pounds to see my man. It was a humiliating feeling, a feeling that degraded me. I tried to convince myself that it was as if I'd paid for a movie ticket, as if I was on my way to see a Robert Mitchum movie. He too filled my imagination. It's only that the ticket for Dr. Hashim was a little more expensive than for Robert Mitchum. And, no, I didn't experience that shuddering, trembling feeling when I went to the movies. The humiliation came back to me, the feeling that I was paying to meet a man, buying him with money.

I tried to get rid of this feeling, to think calmly again, but I couldn't.

The old woman sitting next to me leaned over me with her entire body.

"What's wrong, sweetie?" she asked.

I hesitated for a moment. I hadn't decided on the kind of illness I would have.

"I feel dizzy," I said, hesitating. "I have a constant headache."

"You have appendicitis," the old lady said smiling, confident that she knew everything. "My niece had it."

The polite nurse saved me from her. It was my turn.

"Please, miss," he said.

I felt nailed to my seat for a moment. I didn't want to go to him. I wanted to go back home. I got control over myself and managed to get up. I walked behind the nurse feeling the eyes of the other women boring into my back. They saw my trembling and knew why. They envied me because I got to go to paradise before them.

I found myself with him.

With Hashim.

For the first time.

It was in a subdued office, dimly lit. Humid air came out of the air conditioner. There were two phones on the desk, one of them white. He was standing up, tall and broad, his nose strong, wearing a suit with no white coat on top, as I'd imagined. He looked as if he was standing to greet a guest at home.

His eyes sparkled and had what seemed to be a look of surprise in them. He then lowered his eyes from me and I noticed a slight smile that passed quickly. He pointed to a wide chair next to the desk.

"Please," he said in a low voice.

He walked around the desk and sat down.

I sat on the edge of the chair, still trembling and confused. Should I look at him? Should I look in front of me? At my shoes? I didn't know what the color of my face was at that moment. Was I blushing or was I pale? I didn't know whether to say something or keep quiet. Then suddenly, I found myself talking, trying to shake off my nervousness.

"I feel dizzy, doctor," I said. "I always have a headache. I don't feel like eating. When I wake up, I feel dizzy. And when . . ."

"What's your name, please?" he said, cutting me off, taking out a piece of stationery from his desk drawer as if he hadn't heard a single word that I said.

"Mitou," I said, accidentally using my nickname.

He raised his eyes to me in surprise, a big smile on his lips.

"Amina. Amina Salim," I said, correcting myself.

"Mrs.?" he asked, writing down what I said.

"Miss," I said, after a pause.

I didn't lie. I really was a miss since we hadn't had the formal wedding yet.

"Age?" he continued, his face serious now.

"Nineteen."

He raised his eyes quickly as if sensing my lie. No, he couldn't have known. I'm tall and everyone who sees me thinks I'm older than seventeen.

"Have you had any surgeries before?"

"Appendix. Tonsils." I said, taking the opportunity of him looking down to write to fill my eyes with him.

"Did you get your vaccines when you were little?" he asked. "What have you been sick with?"

I began to feel annoyed. He was questioning me like I was a little girl. He seemed to think I was here because I was actually sick.

"I had measles," I said. "I don't remember more than that."

He sat up and gave me a serious look.

"So, tell me. What's wrong?"

I couldn't bear his scrutiny. I lowered my eyes and began to reel off every symptom I could think of: headache, dizziness, stomach cramps, loss of appetite, constipation, diarrhea, heartburn.

He looked at me confused.

"Let's take a look," he said.

He rang a bell next to him and leaned over to write something on the paper in front of him.

A door inside the room opened and a heavyset female nurse who looked about forty and seemed to be foreign, Greek perhaps, appeared.

"Please, come this way," she said in broken Arabic.

I was afraid.

I stayed in my chair. I looked at Hashim as if asking him for help, but he was still writing. He raised his head and seemed surprised that I was still in my chair.

"Please, go ahead," he said, gesturing to the door that had opened.

I got up, my knees trembling. I went into the examination room and the nurse closed the door behind us. She then pointed at the screen at the side of the room.

"Please, get undressed," she said in her strange accent.

"Is that necessary?"

"Yes, Miss."

"Isn't it possible for the doctor to examine me on top of my dress?" I asked, my eyes filling with tears.

"No," she said. "It's not possible, Miss."

I stood in front of her astonished, my feet nailed to the ground.

"Please go ahead," she said again, impatiently.

"What do I take off?"

"Everything."

I lowered my head. I stepped behind the screen, sheltering behind it, protecting myself from the nurse and the doctor, and from myself. I stood for a moment motionless. Why was I subjecting myself to all this humiliation?

I didn't think this would happen, but I couldn't go back now. My lie had grown too big.

I started taking off my dress slowly, shyness burning in my chest like fire. More than shyness, it was a feeling of scandal. Tears collected in my eyes. They were tears of humiliation. In the middle of all this deluge of feelings, I remembered I was wearing a run-of-the-mill undershirt made of jersey fabric. I had a white lingerie undershirt embroidered with lace on its sides and back. Oh, why hadn't I worn that?

The tears I was holding back were burning my eyes.

I looked out from behind the screen to make sure that Hashim hadn't come in the room yet. I then walked toward the nurse and stood in front of her, silent and embarrassed.

"Sorry, Miss," the nurse said as she lifted her eyes to me. "The bra and the garter too. Leave only your slip on."

"No," I said sharply. "This is enough."

"That's not possible, my dear," she said, smiling, as if I wasn't the first girl to resist. "How can the doctor examine you?"

She then reached out quickly behind my back and unsnapped my bra. She leaned over, trying to unsnap my garter, but I got to it before her.

She took me by the hand and guided me onto the examination table. She covered me with a white sheet.

I pulled the sheet to my neck and gripped it with my fingers, a terrified look in my eyes.

The nurse went and opened the door for Hashim.

He didn't look at me.

He didn't look at any part of me.

He sat on a chair at the side of the table. The nurse handed him his stethoscope and he put it in his ears. He then tried to pull down the side of the sheet from on top of my chest, but I clung to it. I looked at him with scared eyes. I begged him, I pleaded with him.

He gave me a sharp look.

"Please," he said in a firm tone.

I looked at him for a while, tears almost spilling from my eyes. I then turned my head from him and raised my arm and covered my eyes with it.

I didn't want to see him. I didn't want to see myself. Every part of my body was on edge and ready to defend itself.

I felt his fingers get close to my chest. Were they his fingers or the stethoscope? I didn't know. But I felt violent pounding on the door of my body, that I'd been discovered. For the first time, I'd been discovered. I was so afraid.

"Take a deep breath," I heard him order me.

I inhaled as if I was pulling my breath from a deep well. My chest was trembling. It felt every movement of his fingers and maybe imagined some that didn't happen. My arm was still raised, covering my eyes.

"Please sit up," I heard him say.

He then reached his hand out and took my arm to help me up. I sat on the table, the sheet wrapped around my chest, still trembling.

He put the stethoscope on my back. All I could feel was his warm breath brushing my back and his cold fingers colliding with my flesh.

"Breath, please," he said.

Please have mercy. There's no longer anything in me to breathe. I was bathed in sweat. Couldn't he see that?

I breathed . . . because he wanted me to.

He laid me down again. I glanced at him quickly. His face was severe and serious as if he hadn't discovered anything, as if there was no treasure in his hands, as if I were just some bag of cotton whose warmth, trembling, and energy his fingers hadn't detected.

He reached his hand under the sheet and pressed down on my stomach.

"Does this hurt?" he asked.

Now every part of me hurt. His fingers lit my nerves on fire. I felt them in my head, under my skin.

I closed my eyes again and put my arm across them.

"No," I whispered.

He moved his fingers and pressed them all over my stomach as if he was a child amusing himself with a half-inflated ball. He then took my pulse and my blood pressure.

"Thank you," he said suddenly, getting up from beside me.

He disappeared into the room next door.

The nurse helped me get up from the table. I was exhausted, crushed by my embarrassment and resisting the feelings that Hashim's fingers had stirred up.

I put on my clothes feeling a dizziness that almost made me collapse.

The nurse opened the door for me. I went out to him.

He was standing far from his desk. He greeted me, with a slight smile.

"There's nothing wrong with you," he said. "I'm going to give you some medication for anxiety. Take one pill before bed."

He handed the prescription to me.

I took it from him with a shaking hand.

I stood there staring at his face with wide eyes. I didn't move. I couldn't. We couldn't be finished already. Something else must happen. I didn't know what. Maybe at that moment, I wanted him to ask me for my address so he could come and propose to me. And why not? He'd knocked on the doors of my treasure. 'Abd al-Salam saw me on the street and followed me to find out where I lived and came to propose the next day. Why couldn't Hashim do the same?

I wanted even less than that. Just one word, any word. But he was silent. He looked into my eyes without saying anything. Only his smile widened.

"I've seen you before many times, Doctor," I found myself saying to him in an unsteady voice.

"I've seen you a lot too."

He then fell silent.

I smiled. Thank God. He'd seen me just as I'd seen him. I thought I hadn't caught his eye.

I didn't want to move.

That couldn't be it.

I stood before him like a cold statue, my eyes fixed on his, my lips trembling, filled with words that I couldn't define or articulate.

His smile widened.

He pulled the prescription from my hand. He then leaned over his desk, wrote a number on it, and gave it back to me.

"If you feel sick again," he said smiling, "call me at this number."

I looked at him in confusion.

I then pulled my eyes away.

And I left.

I was lost in thought.

His fingerprints were all over my body.

3

THE CONFIDENCE THAT WE FELT at that time was strange. A huge, incredible confidence, a confidence of optimism, of being alive. We moved in life like the waters of a small stream, bubbling happily past rocks that were in its way, not even noticing they were there. At the end of the road, the big ocean would swallow it.

We didn't see the big ocean or hear it. We rushed forward joyfully, scoffing, confident in ourselves until it swallowed us, that big ocean.

I left Hashim's clinic with a stormy feeling of self-confidence, of strength. I'd never felt as strong as I did that day. It's true that a tremble still ran under my skin, but it was a delicious tremble. It was the tremble that follows a successful adventure, as if I'd jumped over a high wall and landed safely. I laughed. I let out a loud laugh that filled my whole chest. I was victorious, victorious over Dr. Hashim. I duped him. I got to him.

I went back home.

I stopped suddenly in front of the door before ringing the bell.

I almost forgot.

I opened my bag, took out my wedding ring, and put it back on my finger. I didn't feel naked like I had when I took it off. Instead, I felt like I had put something heavy on.

I went in to my mother and sat down next to her. Of course, I didn't tell her I'd been at Hashim's clinic. I told her I was out window shopping. I discovered at that moment that I could be good at lying, that I was good at avoiding going into detail so my lie wasn't revealed.

I left my mother and went to my mirror. I stood in front of it looking at myself eagerly as if I was going to see something that had happened to me, that had happened to my body. Maybe I was looking to see if my stomach had gotten bigger, or my chest had filled out. I smiled at these fantasies going around in my head. I then started taking off my clothes. I was looking at the mirror, searching my body for something, for the traces of his fingers. No. He didn't leave any traces. But I felt them. I felt them on my stomach, my chest, my back. His image filled my head, his puffy eyes, his big strong nose, his lips half open.

He must be thinking about me too. Maybe I was distracting him from his patients. No. I excuse him from thinking about me so he can devote his attention to his patients. Then I imagined the girl I'd seen in the waiting room entering the examination room. I saw her taking off her clothes as I did, lying on the long table, his fingers tapping on her chest, her heart beating fast. He couldn't have smiled at her the same way he smiled at me. He couldn't have written his phone number down for her the way he did for me. I ran to my bag, opened it, took out the prescription, and read the number. It wasn't the number in the phonebook. Maybe it was the number for the other phone, the white phone.

I wanted to run and dial the number.

No. I played it cool.

I danced around the house with delight in my eyes and joy in my heart. I was swept away with love. I loved my mother, my siblings, my stepfather. I loved the chairs, the curtains, the walls. Happiness almost lifted me away. A hint of bashfulness almost cut through my happiness whenever I remembered myself naked with him in his examination room. I then laughed at myself, happy with what I had done.

Did I think of my fiancé?

Not at all.

I forgot him as if he was a nobody, as if he wasn't an obstacle on the road of my dreams.

When he came back from Suez that evening, I didn't wake up from my fantasy. It was as if he had nothing to do with me. I met him with a bigger smile than he was used to from me. But I didn't ask him to go out for dinner. I didn't want Hashim to see me with him anymore. He didn't know that I was engaged.

That night, we went to the movies. We then went out and bought a sandwich, which we had in the car. Hashim was with us, in my imagination, at the movies, in the car. The way I thought about him was changing quickly. I began to think about the problem that I'd have when he asked me to marry him. I'd be forced to break off my engagement. When that happened, I was sure my mother would help me break it off. She wouldn't hesitate to help me, especially if I was going to marry a man like Dr. Hashim.

I didn't sleep that night.

But I wasn't tired in the morning.

I resisted the phone until noon.

Then I couldn't resist anymore.

I dialed the number.

No one answered.

Maybe he was in the examination room.

I dialed the number again fifteen minutes later.

I heard his voice.

I felt the tremble running under my skin.

"Good morning, Doctor."

"Good morning," he replied in a hurried tone. "Who's this?"

"You don't remember me?"

He paused for a moment.

"Oh, how are you?" he then asked.

"I'm calling to thank you. I really am feeling better and . . ."

"Excuse me," he said, cutting me off.

"Are you busy?"

"Very," he said in a more delicate tone. "The clinic is full, and I've only seen two people so far."

"Okay, I'll call you later," I said quickly, trying to hide my embarrassment.

"Not before three o'clock."

"God willing," I said. "Goodbye."

I hung up before he did.

I felt annoyed, like he'd insulted me. Maybe I was expecting him to leave his patients and just sit and talk with me.

I didn't call at three o'clock.

But as the hours passed, I started feeling better. I started coming up with excuses for him, that his patients have more right to him than me. If he was a doctor who ignored his patients, he wouldn't have become so famous. I told myself a lot of things until I forgave him, as if I'd been fighting with him.

The next day, I called at three o'clock.

No one answered.

He must have finished with his patients and left.

I called in the evening, during clinic hours.

He was busy.

He spoke quickly as if he wanted to get rid of me.

Ten days passed without me being able to have a conversation with him that lasted more than a minute. Despair was creeping into me. All I thought about now was seeing him again. He was more difficult than I imagined.

I picked up the phone and dialed the number.

"I'm very sick, Doctor," I said as soon as I heard his voice.

I imagined him smiling.

"I can see you," I heard him say firmly but in his usual rush.

"Where?" I said quickly, afraid he'd get away from me again.

"You know Hassan Sabri Street in Zamalek? Number thirty-two, apartment fourteen."

"But . . ." I hesitated.

"Is four o'clock good?" he asked, cutting me off.

I was quiet for a moment, thinking carefully about what I was doing.

"Yes."

I put the phone down without saying goodbye.

I ran to my room and threw myself on the bed on my stomach. I began hitting the pillow with my hands. I was furious. I felt like he'd conquered me. I wouldn't go. No. Who'd this man think I was? Just like all the other girls?

Then my rage abated. Why was I furious? I couldn't wait for Hashim to follow me home and then come to propose, like 'Abd al-Salam did. This kind of man doesn't get married like that. Someone like him needs a big love story.

He wanted me to meet him at his bachelor pad.

What was wrong with that?

My friend Huda met her lover at his bachelor pad. And Samira. Muhammad had one that he and some of his friends rented. He tried to invite me there once when I was talking with him on the phone. In Heliopolis, there's a building with a bachelor pad that some of the guys at the club rent. A lot of my girlfriends knew about it. I'd pass in front of it and look up at it cautiously, half expecting to see a naked man or woman on a balcony.

It was natural for Hashim to have a bachelor pad. And it was natural for him to meet me there. He was a man with a reputation who couldn't be seen with me in his car since I was engaged. And it wasn't good for me to be seen with a man who wasn't my fiancé.

But why go to him?

I had to resist.

I wouldn't go.

His fingerprints were still burned onto me.

I couldn't make up my mind.

I left my room and went to sit next to my mother, seeking protection in her company. I thought a hundred times that I'd tell her everything. Why wasn't I honest with her? Maybe if I'd been honest with her back then, even if I'd hidden some of the details, she would've helped me help myself, pulled me out of my crisis.

But I didn't tell her anything.

At three thirty, I went out.

I walked quickly and anxiously, looking for a taxi. I felt like I was on the run. When I was in the taxi, I took out my little mirror and stared at myself. I was pale. The line of kohl under my eyes was shaky. My lipstick was rough, thick on one side and thin the another. I began to fix my makeup and pinched my cheeks until they were flushed.

I remembered to take off my ring and put it in my bag.

I got out of the taxi in front of the building. The driver didn't have trouble finding the address, as if every taxi knows where the girls go.

I looked at my watch. It was quarter to five. I was very late.

Good, I thought.

I went into the elevator with a spring in my step. Everything in me was silent, my mind, my heart, my nerves, my body. The silence of a terrified woman waiting for the big event.

I didn't have to look for the apartment. It was as if I already knew it.

My hand wasn't trembling as I pressed the bell.

He opened the door for me wearing a shirt and pants, no jacket. His shirt collar was open, showing the edge of his undershirt. His tie was hanging down on his chest.

"You're very late," he said.

I smiled and didn't respond.

"You know I have to be at the clinic at five thirty. I wanted to have more time with you than this."

I didn't respond.

He was standing at the door as if he wasn't going to let me in.

I stood in front of him silently, my eyes locked on his.

Finally, he came to and moved away from the door.

"Please, come in," he said as if regretting inviting me.

I went inside.

I first saw the outer salon. It had soft lighting like his office. The wooden shutters were closed. All the furniture was dark. It wasn't at all what I'd imagined. It was the furniture of a family house, not that of a bachelor's apartment.

I sat on a wide chair. I purposely sat on the chair, not the couch.

"Would you like me to make you a coffee?" he asked, sitting beside me on the edge of the couch, resting one arm along its back and, with the other, running his palm over his black wavy hair.

"No, thank you," I said.

His smile widened.

"You know why I have this apartment?" he asked. "To make coffee for myself here. I'm the best at making coffee. I'm just as good at making coffee as I am at being a doctor."

"Why don't you make coffee at your other house?" I asked, gripping my dress on top of my thighs.

"My sister doesn't let me," he said laughing. "It's incredible that she lets me into the kitchen at all."

"You have this house just to make coffee?" I asked, looking away.

"To relax here," he said. "Most days, I can't get out to Maadi after the clinic, so I come here to relax."

"So, you're not in love with anyone?" I asked, hesitating, looking at his fingers.

"I'm in love. But not with anyone."

I looked at him, not understanding.

"I love my work."

His eyes relaxed and his smile widened. He pulled his eyes off my arms. I saw him as he was in his clinic.

"You don't know how much I love my work," he said enthusiastically. "I love it like the love you read about in novels. I'm both tortured and delighted by it. Sometimes I feel misery, sometimes nothing but hope. When I examine a patient, you can't imagine what I feel. I feel that everything inside them is inside me. When they say this part hurts, I feel the same part hurt me too. I sit analyzing the pain that I feel and try to diagnose it."

His voice was dreamy, with love in his eyes. He was no longer looking at me.

"That's why you're so successful and well known."

"Love always elevates you."

My feelings softened, the fear melted away.

"I didn't think you were so sensitive," I said, my eyes settling on his face calmly as if they were two butterflies that had set down on a flower.

"Don't be fooled," he said, letting out a laugh. "I'm not always so sensitive."

He looked into my eyes. His gaze searched my face as if he was seeing me for the first time, as if he was discovering something new in me. His eyes lingered. He was no longer laughing. His smile faded. There was something serious in his look, something I didn't understand. I was looking at him too, waiting for something, waiting to be reassured or to submit.

He reached out and put his hand on mine. I felt its weight, its warmth. His fingers weren't silent or cold like the fingers that pressed down on my stomach when I was at his clinic. There was new life in them. These fingers were alive, sending messages to every part of me, to my heart, mind, chest, waist.

He looked at his watch.

"I'm late for the clinic," he said. "It's five ten."

I woke up.

"Do you want to leave first?" he asked, getting up, fixing his collar, and pulling his tie up. "Or should I?"

He was decisive now.

I stood up feeling I'd been insulted.

"No," I said. "I'll go first."

He walked ahead of me and put his hand on the doorknob.

I went over to him. I raised my eyes to him, standing silently, still waiting for something.

His eyes met mine.

He raised his hand from the doorknob.

He walked the short space separating me from him and then, without saying anything, he enveloped me in his arms, delicately, tenderly. He pressed his cheek against mine. My mind was alert, aware of every movement. I wanted to stay like that. I wanted to know what would happen next. He pulled his cheek from mine to put his lips in its place. It was a silent kiss. I closed my eyes. I don't know why. But I couldn't stand to keep them open. His lips touched mine. I was silent, frozen. I hoped that moment wouldn't end. My eyes were still closed.

He lifted his lips from mine.

"Sorry," I heard him say.

I opened my eyes to find him looking at me with a curious look.

"I shouldn't have kissed you. It's the first time we're meeting . . . Not like that."

I lowered my eyes. I didn't respond. Nothing of the sort had occurred to me.

He put his hand on the doorknob again.

"When will I see you?" he asked.

"Whenever you want," I said, unable to swallow, my voice unsteady.

"Tomorrow at four?" he asked.

I nodded.

"But don't be late," he said.

"Okay," I said, smiling.

He opened the door.

And I left.

I walked in the street distracted. I didn't try to look for a taxi. I wanted to walk. His kiss was still on my lips, burning them, running through my veins. I felt it on my chest, on my feet.

After a bit, I noticed him in his car. It was a '51 Buick, last year's model. He didn't see me. He was in a rush, rushing to his big love, his clinic.

I found myself on Fouad Avenue. Still dazed, I hailed a taxi to take me back to Heliopolis. A strange happiness flooded me, a happiness that I couldn't quite grasp. I felt that it wasn't stable, it wasn't real.

I went into my house still preoccupied. I don't know what I said to my mother.

"Where's your ring, Mitou?" I heard her ask.

I woke up.

I thought quickly. I was good at thinking on my feet.

"I was looking at stockings," I said. "I was afraid I'd rip them, so I took off the ring."

I quickly opened my bag, took out the wedding ring, and put it on my finger.

I drifted off again.

I lay down on the bed replaying every moment that happened, every movement and every glance.

I closed my eyes to hear his voice and see every piece of furniture that was around us.

But . . .

Something strange.

I was feeling my body.

It was as if I hadn't felt it before. I felt it bloomed, it was thirsty, wanting to drink.

I raised up my hands and squeezed my chest, my waist, my thighs, imagining Hashim.

I want Hashim.

I got out of bed and snuck over to the phone. I dialed his number. I heard his voice. I didn't respond.

I smiled. His voice was enough for me. I went back to my room.

I was in love.

Those days, I believed in love.

I thought that was love.

I lived enraptured in love.

I went to him the next day. I was half an hour late. He was angry. I loved him more when he was angry. He stayed angry for a few moments as I hid a big smile in my chest. He then turned to me.

"If you're late again, you know what I'll do to you?" he asked. "I'm going to hit you."

"You couldn't," I said, looking at him, my smile on his eyes.

"I could," he said. "You still don't know me."

He then pulled me by the hand and brought me into the kitchen to show me how he makes coffee for himself. The kitchen was organized, neat. I'd never seen a kitchen so organized and neat.

"You're an excellent housewife," I said, looking all over the kitchen.

"Not me," he said, turning on the stove. "It's Mahmud, the doorman."

He then started making coffee as if he was performing a mathematical operation. Everything by calculation. His eyebrows were knitted as if he was concentrating all his thought on the coffee.

He took a sip.

We laughed. There was nothing but laughter around us. Every part of us was laughing. He wasn't Dr. Hashim. Only Hashim. Happy, simple. His eyes were wider, sometimes sparkling to the point that I was afraid of them, and then so serene I could drown in them.

My inexperienced lips got their second lesson. His fingers were pressing down on my arms, squeezing me. Every inch of my body was blooming, drinking but still not quenching its thirst.

I plunged in more.

I went under to the deepest depths of love.

Or what I thought was love.

I went to our third meeting, late again. This time by twenty minutes. Was I late on purpose? He let me in and then closed the door behind me. He stood in front of me silently, his eyes raging, his face scowling, his lips pursed. I tried to smile, but I couldn't. I was afraid of him. Not exactly fear, but a kind of worried anticipation of the unknown, a feeling that I was on the precipice of a new adventure.

Suddenly, he raised his hand and slapped me hard. Everything shook in front of my eyes. And there was a ring in my ears. Shocked, I put my hand on my cheek.

"I told you if you were late again, I'd hit you."

And he slapped me again on my other cheek. He then pulled me by my hair and dropped me to the ground. I found him on top of me. I no longer knew what was happening. It was faster than I could take in. His lips were on mine and then on my neck. I felt his fingers opening the buttons of my blouse. A piece of my flesh was uncovered and then another piece. He was crazy, ravenous. I was resisting, but my body was thirsty.

From that day, I got used to inflaming him.

And he got used to hitting me.

We only met like that, both of us crazy, one of us almost tearing up the other. And then we'd calm down. I'd go back to how I was. My carefree attitude, smiling like a naive girl. And Hashim would go back to Dr. Hashim, serious and dignified. He'd go off to his great love, his clinic.

I lived in this madness. I let Hashim discover more of me until he'd completed his exploration, revealing all of me. No, he did leave a little for my fiancé.

Was I thinking about my fiancé? Was my conscience haunting me? Was I confused? Did I feel sin? Did I hate it?

Not at all.

Nothing like that.

My fiancé had nothing to do with it. What I was doing did not concern him. It was enough that I took off his ring whenever I went to Hashim out of respect for him.

I sometimes thought about the fate of my relationship with Hashim, about the future. I'd go back to thinking about my plans to get married. What was important, though, was meeting Hashim, not marrying him. I started living to meet him, not to marry him. I was hiding my feelings about the future behind my intoxication in the present. I was driven forward, eyes closed, mind closed.

Until one day, three months later, I was with Hashim. He was lying in bed bare-chested, his brown muscles soft in relaxation, while I sat in front of the mirror in my undershirt, combing my hair.

"How much do you love me, Hashim?" I asked smiling at his image in the mirror.

I didn't mean anything by it. I just wanted to hear some sweet words.

"And you? How much do you love me?" he asked with a tight smile.

"You still don't know?"

"Not yet."

"All this time and you don't know?"

"Sometimes I don't think you love me."

I turned to him.

"So, what's all this?" I asked surprised.

"Maybe you want to marry me."

I became furious, my breath catching in my chest.

"Everyone I get to know wants to marry me," he continued. "I think women don't know love, only marriage. They can't live on love, only on marriage."

I turned away.

I grabbed my bag, took out my ring, and tossed it in his face. I went back to looking in the mirror and combing my hair.

He took the ring.

I watched him in the mirror.

He sat up, staring at me.

"What's this?" he asked.

"My engagement ring," I said, dragging the comb through my hair.

"You're engaged?"

"Wedding contract signed," I said coldly.

He jumped out of bed and came over to me.

"Since when?" he asked breathlessly.

"A long time ago. Since before I met you."

"Why didn't you tell me?"

"Because . . ." I said, shrugging my shoulders.

He fell on his knees and embraced me. He pressed his face against my neck.

"It felt right. I really thought . . . I thought I loved you," I said, turning my face from him.

"My dear," he whispered.

I hated him at that moment, but I still wanted him. I thirsted for him.

I went back to him, just as I'd gotten used to.

I was in deeper and deeper with him. I began to be jealous of him, his patients, his social circle. It was a repressed jealousy. I was always wondering where he went at night, even if he'd told me. He had dinner at the Semiramis and then went home. Or he was invited to a party . . . or . . . or . . .

But my mind was not at ease. A man like him couldn't spend every night alone.

A mad idea erupted into my mind.

I could meet him one night.

My mother gave me a key to our apartment for when I was going out with my fiancé so I could spend the evening out without me bothering anyone when I came back. I agreed with Hashim that he'd wait for me on Salah al-Din Street at half past midnight. Hashim tried to refuse. He tried to end this madness. But I insisted and accused him of having a woman that he met at night, so he gave in.

I went out with my fiancé. We went to the movies. I then claimed that I had a headache and the poor slob believed me. He brought me home and kissed me on the cheek. All he'd gotten from me was still just a kiss on the cheek.

"Take an aspirin and have a glass of tea," he told me with idiotic tenderness as I was getting out of the car. "And shut your bedroom window."

I waited a bit until I was sure he'd driven off. I then went back down to the street and ran to where Hashim was waiting for me. I threw myself in his car. He took off looking at me, surprised at my audacity, my recklessness. We went to the Zamalek apartment.

The girls who say that anything that happens at night could happen during the day are fooling themselves. More happens at night. Maybe because people's eyes are closed or because the sky is black. I took more at night than I was used to taking during the daytime. And I gave more too.

I went home at three o'clock in the morning, The entire house was asleep. No one noticed me.

It continued. I wanted an adventure every day. I wanted to inflame Hashim and for him to hit me. I wanted to quench my thirst.

Then, suddenly . . .

Seven months after I met Hashim, my fiancé came back from Suez insisting on moving the marriage forward. He didn't want to wait until the villa was finished and fitted out. He felt that we were growing apart from each other. He wanted us to get married the following week. He insisted stubbornly, and he convinced my mother, my stepfather, and my five aunts. Everyone was on my case, pressing, insisting.

No one wanted to listen to me. I was told that the guy had waited a long time. All he was asking for was his right.

I ran to Hashim.

"I'm finished. I'm going to get married."

"No way. When?"

"Next Thursday."

His face darkened. He turned his back to me as if he was upset. But I felt at that moment that he was putting on a show.

"I was waiting for this day," he said sighing. "The day you'll come tell me you're getting married and going to live in Suez."

I was quiet for a moment, staring at him.

"Hashim," I said, my voice trembling. "You can't marry me?"

He raised his eyes to me quickly and then lowered them.

"No," he said, turning his head.

"Why?"

"Because I've decided not to get married," he said in a severe voice, looking away from me.

I cried.

My tears poured out, tears of rage, humiliation, submission to my own weakness.

He came over to me. He said a lot of things that I didn't hear. He kissed me. He kissed me some more.

Then, he abandoned me.

All of them abandoned me.

They left me to marry 'Abd al-Salam.

And my story began.

4

I GOT MARRIED WITHOUT A wedding.

I traveled the same night to Suez to live in my husband's house, with his mother, until the new villa that he was building for me was finished.

Should I reveal all the details?

I'm not the first girl who married a man she didn't love, this is a well-known story.

I wonder, though, if Hashim hadn't entered my life, could I have gotten used to my husband? Could I have let myself get used to him? Could I have enjoyed life with him and lived happily ever after with lots of kids?

Maybe.

In those days, I didn't believe that life was about habit. I thought life was love. And I'd already started getting used to Hashim, his touches, his breath, those quick hours that he stole from his patients to give to me, that violent recklessness that we were living in.

The day I got married, I could've forgotten Hashim, liberated myself from my habit of him. Our relationship had only lasted for seven months. But I didn't try. I never tried. Not for a single moment did I try to forget him. Not for a single moment did I try to be a faithful wife. It never even crossed my mind. I wasn't thinking about my husband at all.

As I rode in the car next to 'Abd al-Salam on our way to Suez, I thought about Hashim. I was thinking how I could meet him and when. When I lay down on my husband's bed that night, my mind was full of Hashim, not feeling the other man next to me, not feeling what he wanted. I wasn't afraid or expecting anything. My body was dejected and tight. All I sensed was the stench of the bottarga coming from my husband's mouth. I turned my head to get away from him. The poor slob was doing everything he could, thinking that I was still just a teenager. He decided that I couldn't yet be a wife.

And he fell asleep.

He left me to myself to think. I was furious with Hashim, because he let me get married. I felt that he had tossed me aside and wounded my dignity. Despite that, I was driven toward him with my entire being. I made excuses for him. He hadn't deceived me. He didn't promise me something and then abandon me. But still I wanted to take revenge against him, to humiliate him just as he humiliated me. And then I'd be full of hope. Maybe I could still marry him.

The next day, the morning after we got married, my husband left for his office, which was near the house. I stayed in my bed. I didn't want to get up. There was nothing to get up for. I didn't wash my face or change my shirt or comb my hair. And for perhaps the first time, I didn't yearn for my mirror. Every part of me was thrown into neglect, as if I could do without it all. I felt nothing but dejection.

My mother-in-law came in with her big, fake smile.

"Good morning to our bride!" she said, a phony ring of joy in her voice. "You've brought light to all of Suez!"

Her smile made me feel worse. I felt like she was a school principal coming to remind me I had assignments to do.

"Aren't you going to get up and tidy yourself up, my dear?" she continued with the big smile still fixed on her lips. "Someone might come around. All the ladies of Suez want to see you."

"I really can't," I said, yawning. "I'm tired. I don't know what's wrong with me. I don't think I can meet anyone now. Leave it to the afternoon."

She looked at me, her gaze scrutinizing me.

"Why not, my dear?" she asked, oozing cheerfulness once again. "Rest up. I'll call and tell them to visit in the afternoon. Do you want me to bring you breakfast in bed?"

"Please," I said pretending to be tired. "And please could the butler bring me the phone so I can call my mother?"

She shot me a quick look.

"Of course, my dear," she said again. "He who doesn't have goodness in his family, doesn't have goodness anywhere."

I hated her.

I felt an intense longing for my mother. I felt that I'd become an orphan. I wanted my mother beside me to protect me from my mother-in-law.

The butler came with the breakfast tray, but he didn't bring the phone. I kept quiet. I had two bites of my breakfast, but my stomach was in knots. I then pressed on the bell to call the butler.

"Next time, don't bring me marmalade," I barked. "I don't like it. Take the tray and go bring me the phone."

"But the mistress of the house is talking on it," he said politely.

"Fine. After she's finished, bring the phone."

The butler left. My nerves were frayed. Rage was collecting in my chest. The long day extended before me like a snake opening its jaws to swallow me. Emptiness was eating me up. Time passed, but I don't know how much. I then rang the bell again.

"Go tell your mistress to bring me the phone!" I demanded.

After a moment, my mother-in-law came in herself with the phone.

"I'm sorry, my dear," she said, trying to seem gentle and polite. "I was inviting the ladies who'll be visiting us this afternoon."

"Thank you," I grumbled.

My mother-in-law gave me a look and then left.

I called my mother.

As soon as I heard her voice, I cried. All my tears poured out. I felt like I'd found her after years of searching.

"What's wrong, Mitou?" my mother asked anxiously.

"Nothing, mommy," I said, swallowing. "It's just that I miss you. I miss you a lot."

"Still, Mitou?" she said, her voice filling my chest with tenderness. "Don't act like that. You're a grown-up now."

"Come, mother," I said, trying to quiet my tears. "Come here. You can't leave me alone like this."

"I'll come next Friday, God willing," my mother said, trying to be firm. "What's going on?"

I insisted that she come to see me. She was being patient and gave me advice, lots of advice that went in one ear and out the other. She advised me about 'Abd al-Salam and then asked to talk to my mother-in-law, but I refused. I told her she was busy. My mother insisted so I asked the butler to call her. My mother and mother-in-law started to exchange false niceties with each other while I sat in bed with a faint smile on my lips and the traces of tears in my eyes.

The conversation ended.

My mother-in-law loomed over the bed, looking at the phone.

"Can I speak with my father too?" I asked, pretending to be shy.

"Of course, my dear," she said immediately. "This is your home."

She went out of the room, leaving the phone for me.

I didn't feel that I was at home but in a hotel, a guest at my mother-in-law's. I don't know why I hated my mother-in-law so much. She wasn't really so awful. On the contrary, she was trying not to annoy me so much that it was annoying me.

I wonder now if I'd lived with my husband in our own house from the day we got married, would I have been happy? Would I have loved my mother-in-law?

I don't know.

I was still in bed.

The phone was in my room.

I looked at the open door.

I hesitated for a long time.

I couldn't resist.

I picked up the phone, dialed the number to place a long-distance call, and gave Hashim's phone number, all in a rush.

Half an hour passed. All of me was ready, alert. I looked at the open door. I then looked inside myself and sometimes I felt afraid of my compulsion. Sometimes I felt I was too infatuated with Hashim, that it was making me lose my self-respect. Sometimes it filled me with the pleasure of the adventure. I smiled imagining the look of surprise on Hashim's face when he heard my voice.

I heard his voice.

My heart beat fast between my ribs.

"How are you, my bride?" he asked in the brisk tone that he usually had on the phone. "Where are you calling from?"

"Suez," I said, my hand shaking as it gripped the receiver, my smile trembling.

"I know you're calling from Suez," he said. "Where in Suez?"

"From my house," I said, surprised at his question.

"You're really crazy," he said, with a little laugh.

"Did you miss me?"

"So much. When will I see you?"

It was as if I hadn't gotten married, as if marriage couldn't stop us from meeting. Or as if he'd gotten used to meeting married women.

"Did you forget that I got married?" I challenged him.

"I didn't forget. I can't forget that I miss you."

"You like it like this?" I asked, trying to be wicked.

"Like what?"

"You like that I got married and I can't see you?"

"There was no other choice. In any case, I'm not important. You're what's important. What's important is that you're happy."

"I wish, Hashim."

I heard the sound of footsteps coming toward my room.

"I'll call you back later," I said quickly. "Bye for now."

I hung up.

I put my head on the pillow. I had taken a sip of life, at least temporarily. My entire imagination was full of Hashim, and this flowed through my body as I remembered his touch. I was thirsty for him.

My husband came back. He found me as he left me in the morning, in my nightshirt with my hair disheveled, the traces of sleep, mixed with tears, filling my eyes. He smiled at me as if I was the most beautiful girl in the world. He sat on the edge of the bed and leaned over to kiss me.

I pushed him away from me.

"Leave until I get dressed," I told him in feigned delicateness.

I got out of bed. It was after one o'clock. I put on a silk robe embroidered with lace. I stood in front of the mirror looking at myself through Hashim's eyes. Hashim never saw me in this robe. He never saw me as a bride on the morning after getting married.

I put on my makeup like I was putting it on for Hashim.

I went downstairs to have lunch with my husband and mother-in-law.

The entire conversation was about the families of Suez and who I was going to meet that evening.

We went back to our room after lunch.

I didn't want to go.

"Don't you want to rest a little, Mitou?" my husband said, pulling me by the hand.

I gave in to him and walked behind him feeling a heavy embarrassment in my chest as my mother-in-law watched her son with happiness and pride, like he was some virile hero.

"Take me out and show me Suez a little," I told him, giving him the most beautiful smile that I could, trying to throw him off.

"How I'll show you around!" he said, getting near me, wrapping his arms around me, his gold tooth shining in his mouth, the black pores visible on his nose. "I'll lay all of Suez at your feet. But let's stay here now."

"Do it for me," I pleaded.

"Do it for me too," he said, putting his mouth on my lips. "Are you afraid, my sweet?"

I gave up hope of sparing myself from him. So I submitted.

The poor slob tried.

Disgusting attempts.

But he couldn't.

He couldn't discover me.

I was like a sheet of ice.

He was frustrated with me.

He left me panting, sweat dripping from his forehead, scorn in his eyes.

"Don't be so childish," he said.

He then started to get dressed.

"I'm going back to the office."

He slammed the door behind him.

I didn't care.

I didn't even feel pity for him.

I sat thinking about my lot, about the mess I was in. I didn't think for a single moment about how to please this husband, about how to become a wife. I only ached with desire for Hashim.

I woke up to the voice of my mother-in-law asking me to get ready to receive our guests.

I started to get ready.

I imagined offending all the ladies of Suez. I felt that I was superior to them, like someone coming from Paris to the countryside.

I put on my most beautiful dress. I paid great attention to my appearance. I left them waiting for more than half an hour. Maybe they saw me as beautiful, but I was sure they all thought I was uptight and snobbish. I liked that.

And that night . . .

There was my pathetic husband.

The following day, I talked to Hashim on the phone. I started talking with him every day. Sometimes I'd talk with him twice a day. He told me I had to be careful since the phone bill would give my husband a record of the numbers that I asked for, including his. My husband might ask me about this number and discover something.

"Don't worry," I responded to him indifferently.

I was sure my husband wouldn't find out anything. A husband only finds out something if he is looking for it. He wouldn't unless he became suspicious. And my husband wasn't suspicious of me.

Long, heavy days passed.

The distance between me and my husband grew by the day. He got irritated every night. He started blaming me. Then, not even six days after getting married, I asked him to go back to Cairo to visit my mother.

He agreed quickly.

I was delighted.

I traveled as if I was going to meet Hashim.

'Abd al-Salam sat talking with my mother after we arrived. He was alone with her for a long time as I ran to my room and lay down on my bed, recovering from the torture of the last week.

'Abd al-Salam left the house, and my mother came to sit with me. She began to tell me all kinds of unexpected things. She was instructing me how to please my husband. How to help him, as she said. How to excite him. I was shocked that this was my responsibility. My mother went on for a while. We were in sync, talking like two friends, saying things that were making me laugh. I asked her for details and then covered my eyes with my hand as she responded to me. I was shrieking with laughter and disbelief. And my mother kept going, giving me more details.

My mother didn't know that she was coaching me onto a long road that would destroy me. She didn't know that by teaching me how to belong to a man that I didn't want, even if he was my husband, she was placing my feet on the edge of the abyss. A woman who gets used to a man she doesn't want, regardless of who he is, will find she can be with dozens of men she doesn't want.

The same day, I called Hashim. I asked him to meet me the following day at eleven in the morning.

"I can't, Mitou. You know the schedule of the clinic."

"But my husband is with me," I said. "I can't meet you except at that time. Can't you be a little late for the clinic?"

"It's not possible," he said firmly.

It was as if I didn't amount to anything more for him, not even half an hour of his patients' time.

"So, when can I see you?" I was shocked by how much I longed for him.

"You know. Either four or nine o'clock."

I could've set a time with him right away, but I was too proud and wanted to play games with him.

"Fine," I said. "We'll see. If I can, I'll call you again."

I knew I couldn't resist for long. I knew I was weaker than him, too weak to resist.

I called him the next day. We agreed to meet at four o'clock.

I told my husband and my mother that I was going to the hairdresser. My husband actually took me in his car to the hairdresser and I told him to come back and get me at six.

I went into the hairdresser's and made an appointment for five thirty. I then left quickly and got in a taxi.

I went to Hashim.

I was furious on the way over. I felt butterflies in my stomach from this adventure, but my feeling of rage was greater. I don't know why I had all this anger. I was going to him as I used to go to him every time. Maybe at that moment, I felt that I was chasing him instead of letting him chase me. I was sacrificing everything while he was sacrificing nothing, not even half an hour of his patients' time.

I got there fifteen minutes late, but he wasn't angry. I didn't see the usual cloud on his face.

He pulled me by the hand and closed the door behind me. He then embraced me to his chest.

"I missed you," he whispered in my ear, squeezing me in his arms. "I missed you so much."

I didn't relax into his chest. I was anxious, unable to rest. I couldn't be happy or angry. I couldn't submit or resist.

He moved me away from him and then pulled me by the hand and sat me down next to him on the couch.

"Tell me," he said with a bigger smile than I was used to from him. "What's going on?"

I started telling him everything. I told him I was exhausted by my life, that I couldn't stand my husband, my mother-in-law, all of Suez. He told me to be patient, to put up with it. Words were coming out of his mouth, ready-made phrases, but he wasn't listening to what I was actually saying. His hand reached out to my hair, gently pushing back the locks from my forehead and then plunging into the folds. He got near me, wrapping his arms around me, looking in my eyes.

"You're oppressed, Amina," he said in a gentle tone that I wasn't used to. "We've wronged you, both your husband and me."

He then pulled me to him.

His hand rubbed my back.

I knew what he wanted.

But I wanted to cry.

I resisted my tears with all my will.

He kissed me. I didn't want that, but I wasn't annoyed. I didn't feel the annoyance that I felt with my husband, or the coldness. This was a familiar road, one I'd gotten used to, even if I didn't want to go on it right then.

He gave himself more freedom.

He was anxious, in a rush to get back to the clinic on time.

Then, I cried.

At first, I cried silently. It started as a quiet sob.

He pulled me gently to his chest and began to console me. He was talking, trying to be gentle. There was no use saying anything. No words could solve my problem. He was rushing. I knew that. He wanted to get back to the clinic.

"You're late, Hashim," I said moving away from him. "I'll go now."

He got up silently.

I turned to leave.

"When will I see you?" he called after me.

"I don't know. I'll call you."

And I left.

Humiliation was eating me up, as were anger and confusion.

I went back to the hairdresser. I sat there thinking about how to free myself from Hashim. Could my husband free me from him?

I decided to follow my mother's lessons to try to please my husband.

Maybe I'd get used to him. Maybe he could free me of Hashim.

The pathetic slob came at six o'clock. I gave him the biggest smile I could, as if I was promising him something big, something new. I then left him waiting for me for a whole hour until I finished with the hairdresser.

That night, we went back to Suez after we had dinner at my mother's house.

And there . . . in our room . . .

I was exhausted. I couldn't begin to implement the lessons that my mother gave me. Besides, it was too much for me to belong to two men in a single night. I felt cheap and vulgar. My body was trembling. My skin shriveled up whenever it touched my husband.

But I tried the following night. Oh Lord, how I tried!

It was torture, humiliation. My stomach was in knots, but I kept trying to give him everything my mother said . . . and more . . .

I felt I was deceiving Hashim, cheating on him with my husband.

'Abd al-Salam was delighted.

I didn't call Hashim that day or the following day. Three days passed without me calling him, days that stretched out long and empty before me.

The efforts that I made for my husband nauseated me and only drove me further from him. I felt disgust, a snake opening its poisonous jaws wide to swallow me up.

Then I called Hashim.

I went to meet him when we went to Cairo the following week.

A state of indifference engulfed me.

Indifference at everything.

Indifference at my makeup, my clothes, my mother-in-law, the families of Suez and what they were saying about me, even my mother.

I was reckless about going to see Hashim. My indifference was pushing me to be bolder about calling Hashim from Suez. I was talking to him sometimes three times a day. I'd meet him every day I was in Cairo. I'd invent excuses to go meet him after nine in the evening, after the venerated clinic appointments ended. I'd stay with him until ten or eleven o'clock. I even got my husband used to leaving me alone in Cairo for a day or two so I could go to Hashim more freely.

Gradually, my body resigned itself and no longer felt the same nausea when I lay next to my husband. Sometimes boredom took hold of me. I'd wander around my room like a caged animal, wanting something to do, something to divert me from myself.

I called my husband at the office.

"'Abd al-Salam, come," I told him flirtatiously.

"I can't, Mitou. I have work."

"I'm all yours. I want to see you."

The pathetic slob gave in. I took off my clothes, all of them, and lay in bed covered only with a light sheet, a wicked look in my eyes. I'd entertain myself at the sight of his bulging eyes as he pulled the sheet from me, drool almost running from his chin as he touched my body, his movements hilarious. I was having fun, pure fun, just to pass the time.

I didn't care.

This feeling of indifference was a thin curtain over the grief, loss, confusion, and dissolution that I was feeling inside. This curtain would get pulled back sometimes. A memory or a thought would blow it off and I'd see my torture underneath it. I'd cry. I'd cry a lot in my room. My room was the only place that I had in this house. The rest belonged to my mother-in-law. My personality was so weak that I couldn't stand up to her or ask for anything. All I could do was escape so she'd leave me alone, alone to my feelings of disgust and the long empty days.

I played with my body, my only toy.

With time, though, I got tired of this toy and the curtain of indifference began to get ripped. I found myself forced to confront my problem with all its weight, all its disgustingness.

I knew how to solve my problem.

The only solution was to marry Hashim. He was the only man who could make me a complete wife, the only one who could fill my emptiness, the only one who I could wait for without disgust.

Then . . .

I got pregnant.

5

It was a surprise when I found out I was pregnant.

I was stunned.

I knew the day would come when I got pregnant, but I imagined it would be far off, very far off, after two or three or four years. Once I got married, people were always wishing for me to have a child. May the bride be so fortunate! We want to celebrate a baby! Give us a baby beautiful like her mother! But I wasn't thinking of any of that. Or the sting of my mother's disappointment when she'd ask me how I was feeling whenever we met. Or the look of my mother-in-law every time I got my period. None of that made me feel like I'd get pregnant anytime soon.

Maybe because I was living in my crisis.

I was living my life hour by hour, day by day. My mind, my feelings, my body, everything in me was stretched between my husband and Hashim. I wasn't concerned about anything but balancing the two of them.

I wasn't expecting to get pregnant by either of them, and certainly not that quickly.

I got worn out by taking all the precautions and I got lazy.

Especially with Hashim.

I was so infatuated with him that I'd forget everything except the moment we were in.

I think this happens to us all.

We're weak.

At that time, I wasn't only feeling weak, I was indifferent.

The first thing I wondered was . . . who put this in me?

I hoped Hashim was the father. He'd be a father I could be proud of. My child would inherit from him the strength of his personality, his intelligence, and his big nose. I laughed imagining my child with a nose like Hashim's.

Then, I stopped laughing and I became afraid. I was so afraid that my heart was almost ripped out. How could it be Hashim's when I was 'Abd al-Salam's wife?

At that moment, I didn't see the problem fully. I found myself drowning in a thick black fog, the word "shame" hanging in front of me. I was afraid of the shame I would bring on my child, afraid of God, of people, of the future. I was afraid for my child, not me.

Then, through this thick fog, I started to feel that the baby I was carrying was my husband's.

I began to think about all the nights that I was with my husband during the five months that passed since we got married.

I remembered all the details, all my feelings, everything. It was incredible that I remembered all these details so precisely, and one night in particular when I was sure I got pregnant.

Thank God. My child is legitimate. I wouldn't have to fear God or society or the future.

Then, when I was sure, I began to feel a kind of regret, a kind of anger. I was furious because I was pregnant by 'Abd al-Salam, as if he didn't deserve to get me pregnant. I didn't feel that gentleness and openness for the new life that every young woman feels as she yearns for motherhood. I felt there was a chain setting out from my stomach to tie me to a man I didn't want.

I went back to hoping that it was Hashim's. I closed my eyes and felt better about it. I smiled. Maybe if Hashim was sure it was his, he'd make me divorce my husband and marry me. He wouldn't want his child to be raised by another man.

The word "illegitimate" bothered me. I shook my head and changed my mind again. Please, Lord, don't let him be Hashim's. Don't let him be illegitimate. Make him legitimate. Make him 'Abd al-Salam's.

How could Hashim be sure that it was his? He wouldn't be certain unless I gave birth and the baby looked like him and not my husband. But it could be a girl that looks like me. And I'd live my whole life not knowing, which would torture me.

In the midst of all these dark thoughts, I told my husband I was pregnant.

The slob was delighted. He was so happy he was walking on air. He stood in front of me like an idiot. He didn't know what to say or do for me.

My mother-in-law was delighted. She was happy, like she'd gotten her return on the dowry and the marriage gift.

My mother was delighted. She came to Suez and stayed with me for four days. She then took me with her to Cairo to take me to a doctor to be sure since she didn't trust the doctors in Suez.

The only one who wasn't delighted was me.

I didn't say a thing to Hashim.

I went to him the same day I went to Cairo with my mother. I went to him with a new feeling, a strange feeling. I wasn't going to him alone, there was another person with me, another creature, a stranger living inside me. This creature was observing me and holding me accountable, afraid for me. Hashim wouldn't be taking me alone this time. He'd be taking me with this other creature which had no will other than mine. What did he do wrong? He didn't love Hashim like I did. He didn't want Hashim like I did.

This feeling made me anxious.

"What's wrong?" Hashim asked as soon as I sat down next to him.

"Nothing," I said exhaling deeply.

"You're not your usual self. I've never seen you so sulky."

"I'm upset," I said, covering my eyes with my hands.

"About what? Did something else happen?"

"Does something have to happen for me to be upset? Isn't what I'm in enough?"

He leaned back on the couch and took a breath, annoyed that I'd ruined the mood. He didn't respond.

I was silent for a bit. I then raised my head to him and stared him in the eye.

"Hashim," I said, pleading with him for help. "I have to get divorced. I'll go crazy. I can't stand my husband. I can't stand him. He disgusts me. I'm disgusted at myself, disgusted at my life. If I don't get divorced, I'll kill myself."

"Don't be crazy," he said tenderly, running his hand through my hair. "If every woman who's upset at her husband divorced him, if every man who's upset at his wife divorced her, there wouldn't be anyone married left today. Divorce isn't easy. It's something big. Divorce means a home is destroyed. You only just got married. You haven't given it a chance yet. Maybe if you tried more, you'd be able to live with him."

He was talking to me like I was some stranger, as if he wasn't the root of my misery and the mess I was in. He was talking to me like an advice columnist.

"I'm not just annoyed at him," I snapped. "I love someone else. Did you forget?"

He pulled his hand away from my hair and turned toward me.

"So, leave him," he said firmly. "It's easier than divorce."

My eyes widened, full of surprise and pain.

"You could leave me, Hashim?"

"I can't leave you," he said coldly. "Because there's no reason for me to. But you could leave me because you have a reason. If you had to choose between your home and me, you'd have to choose your home because you have no future with me."

Just like that. He said it so simply.

I raised my head as if trying to maintain my dignity.

"At any rate," I said trying to give him a disdainful look. "If I get divorced, I won't be getting divorced for you. I'll be getting divorced because I can't stand the man I'm married to. I can't stand being with you while I'm married. I'm not afraid of the future. I'm still young and beautiful. A thousand men still want to marry me. Anyone is better than the one I'm married to."

He didn't respond.

He got up and walked over to a bookcase and began flipping through one of his medical journals.

I was quiet. My chest was tightening with my breath. But I didn't cry.

Hashim didn't notice there was another person inside me. My stomach wasn't big enough yet that anyone could notice.

He turned to me after a while.

"What are we fighting about?" he asked, closing the journal and tossing it back on the shelf.

"I don't know," I said miserably.

"Fine. Why are you mad at me?"

"I'm not mad."

He came and sat next to me.

"You're crazy," he said plunging his fingers into my hair, giving me a big smile.

He then brought his lips close to mine.

I turned my face away quickly.

I didn't want him to kiss me.

He looked at me in surprise.

"Leave me alone, Hashim, please."

I then got up from next to him and stood up in the middle of the room.

He joined me and looked at me as if he was trying to figure out what I was really thinking. He then wrapped me in his arms and pulled me hard to his chest.

"Don't be crazy," he said. "You've never been mad at me."

He then dropped his lips to mine, giving me this forceful kiss that I knew meant that he wanted to finish with me quickly so he could get back to the clinic.

I yanked my lips from his, letting his kisses fall on my neck.

"I can't, Hashim," I said nervously, trying to get out of his arms. "Leave me alone. I can't."

I really couldn't.

Maybe for the first time, I felt I couldn't stand Hashim's kiss.

He raised his sleepy head from my neck and looked at me with surprise. He then let me go and stood in front of me with a feeble smile.

I fixed my hair and I straightened my dress.

"I have to go now," I said, looking away.

He didn't respond.

He kept standing there with the same smile.

I walked toward the door.

He was still standing in his spot.

I put my hand on the doorknob.

I hesitated a little and then I went over to him and gave him a quick kiss on the cheek.

"Don't be mad at me," I said, going back toward the door. "I'll call you."

"Goodbye," I heard him say.

And I left.

There was a small smile on my lips. I was happy because I resisted him. For the first time, I didn't give him what he wanted. I was looking at the person inside me as if I was proud at the strength of my will.

I took a taxi thinking about divorce.

Yes, divorce.

I was thinking about divorce, feeling like I was defying Hashim. I didn't want to get divorced only because I couldn't stand my husband or because I was cheating on him, but to defy Hashim, to convince him that I'd get divorced even if he hadn't promised me to get married.

I felt a tremor as the thought of divorce hit me. I felt the seriousness of what I was thinking, but it was still driving me forward. I couldn't look back.

I got home and my mother's husband met me, jubilant. He hugged me and kissed me on my forehead.

"God is Great, Mitou. You're going to have a child!"

He started being nice to me as soon as I got married because he was no longer responsible for me.

My mother met me, worried.

"Why are you so late, Mitou? You shouldn't be out and about like this. You have to rest in bed from now on."

A lot of things were said to me, but I didn't hear a thing. All I was thinking about was divorce.

I couldn't stop thinking about it and whenever my thinking hit an obstacle, I found a way around it.

How could I ask for divorce when I'm pregnant? It was better than giving birth to a child to live with a cheating mother or a duped father, I'd tell myself. I would ask for divorce for my child.

Maybe it was better to wait until the child was born? No, now was better, so the child didn't tie me down as I sought a divorce.

I wasn't only thinking about being pregnant. I was really thinking about Hashim.

Comparing him and my husband focused my thoughts on the big differences between them in stature, appearance, character, manliness, everything. If I could have a man like Hashim, why would I marry someone like 'Abd al-Salam? If I had married him, why would I submit to my fate? I was young and beautiful. I still had time for adventure.

I was deluded of course.

My love for Hashim was filling me with delusion and resolve. I couldn't appreciate the danger of what I was embarking on.

The question was, how to force my husband who loved me to divorce me without cause? And how to convince my family?

I didn't know.

But there had to be a way.

My husband called me from Suez two days later and asked me to come back. I refused. I told him I was tired. I wouldn't be able to bear traveling on the bumpy road back to Suez. The pathetic slob actually believed me. And so did my mother.

I didn't go to him.

I went to Hashim.

And that time, I couldn't resist him. I needed him. I needed something violent to distract me. I needed something more forceful than my thoughts, than this creature living inside me. Hashim could always be violent. But when he was about to hit me this time, as he usually did, I started pleading with him.

"No! Don't hit me! Please!"

I wanted to keep a shred of dignity left in me for the creature in my belly, I wanted to maintain some kind of self-respect.

But Hashim hit me anyway.

I forgot everything.

I was immersed in this insanity.

Then I woke up.

All my thoughts woke up at once. I turned my head away from him.

He turned to me and took me in his arms again, gently, calmly.

"I love you so much, Mitou," he said in a pure tender tone.

I looked up at him quickly. It was the first time he said the words "I love you." He said them honestly, deeply. I believed him. At that moment, a path strewn with roses opened up before me, a path emitting light on both sides.

I plunged my face against his neck and pressed him to my chest, to my heart, with all my tenderness, with all my emotional energy.

"Me too, Hashim," I whispered through this cascade of emotions. "I love you so much . . . so much."

We stayed like that in each other's arms, with peaceful smiles like two butterflies asleep on the leaves of the roses.

"Hashim, I'm pregnant," I found myself saying involuntarily as if I could no longer bear hiding anything from him.

His lifted his head suddenly.

"What?" he asked, his voice troubled and his tenderness gone.

I turned to him.

"I'm pregnant."

"Are you serious?"

I nodded my head.

"Since when?" he asked, becoming more agitated.

"I'm in my second month."

"You really are crazy."

He looked me in the eye as if waiting for me to say something. He seemed to be getting ready to defend himself.

He didn't say anything. I noticed a cloud of confusion pass over his face.

"Why are you in such a rush?" he murmured in a low voice.

"What do you want me to do?" I asked, looking at him, happy at his confusion.

"You should've taken precautions. You haven't even been married for five months. You haven't settled into your marriage yet. You should've waited until you settled in, until you organized your life, so you could build a good life for your child. You were telling me two days ago that you want to get divorced and now you're telling me you're pregnant."

Each of us looked the other in the eyes. There was a hint of doubt that we didn't want to acknowledge. He looked confused. I was happy at his confusion. I knew why he was confused. He wanted to ask me who got me pregnant, but he couldn't. And I wasn't telling him. I wasn't going to put him at ease.

"Why am I the one who should be taking precautions?" I asked, pretending to be furious.

"Because you're the one who gets pregnant."

He jumped up and started getting dressed.

I looked at him reproachfully. I was still lying in bed half naked.

He turned to me as he stood in front of the mirror tying his tie, his shirt hanging down on his bare thighs, his eyebrows knitted. I knew what was on the tip of his tongue.

But he didn't say anything.

Neither did I.

I don't know why we couldn't face the subject head on. Maybe because each of us respected the life that was forming inside me. Each of us were afraid for it, afraid of the word "shame."

He finished getting dressed. I was still lying in bed. He walked toward me, trying to gather his thoughts, his fears and confusion.

He sat next to me on the edge of the bed.

"I have to leave before you," he said placing his hand on my bare shoulders. "I'm late."

I knew he had enough time to wait for me to get dressed and leave before him. But I knew what he was going through. I felt his confusion, anxiety, and need to be alone to think. I too needed to be alone to think. I nodded my head and agreed.

"Who's the doctor that saw you?" he asked with shaken tenderness that didn't seem genuine.

"Dr. Sadiq Fuda," I told him.

"Great. He's very good."

He then leaned over and gave me a quick kiss on my cheek. He raised his head and stood there for a moment looking at me with pity in his eyes. He came back to me and gave me a long gentle kiss on my lips.

"Take care of yourself. Call me tonight, after the clinic."

And he left.

He left me thinking. My thoughts opened up many doors of hope, bringing me to the height of happiness. He loved me. I was sure of it that day more than any time before. I knew I could risk my entire life and divorce my husband for that love.

Maybe my problem with Hashim was that he got to know me when I was engaged, I told myself. If he'd gotten to know me beforehand and loved me like this, then . . . who knows? Maybe he would've married me. I just needed to know him while I was free.

I'd make him bear full responsibility for me.

I'd fill his entire life with mine.

Then, he'd marry me.

But he didn't want to get married. He'd decided not to. That's what all men say, though. It's the conceit of the man who's dining out on a girl's infatuation for free, without marriage. A man's decency comes into play and he weakens before his love. He gets tired of being a vagabond and he gets married. I'll be waiting for just that moment.

I'd have to work for that moment, to set a plan to get there.

I was smart. I could rely on my intelligence and beauty, and his love.

But first . . .

How could I get rid of this husband? That pathetic slob.

I didn't know.

I only knew that I had to try, to do everything I could.

I got out of bed and as I walked around the apartment in my undershirt and bare feet, I felt a strange strength filling me with confidence, liberating me from my weak personality. I became capable of anything. I wouldn't ever be weak again after that day.

I smiled at the walls and the furniture as if bidding them goodbye. I wouldn't live in this apartment after marrying Hashim. It was small and inappropriate for Dr. Hashim and his wife. And who knows how many women had come to this apartment before me? Maybe there were still women coming while I was rotting in Suez. I was stung with jealousy at this thought. I took a deep breath, threatening all the ladies chasing after Hashim. My imagination set off looking for a big apartment overlooking the Nile. Maybe in the Lebon building, where the actress Fatin Hamama lived, next to the aquarium, with Aubusson tapestries, a *capitonné* bed, rose-colored walls.

I began to get dressed, my imagination running wild.

I went back home.

In love . . .

At nine o'clock, I called him.

"Don't distract me so much again," I could hear him smiling. "I didn't know how to do anything today. Patients that usually take me half an hour took a whole hour."

That's how much he loves me.

My problem became his problem.

"How am I distracting, Hashim?" I asked flirtatiously.

"You don't know? When we meet next, I'll tell you."

We spoke for a long time.

For the first time, he wasn't in a hurry to head out with his friends, as he usually did after the clinic.

It was something new.

All this love, all this attention. Maybe he thought the baby was his.

I smiled in happiness and wickedness.

Our conversation ended with us agreeing to meet the next day.

I heard my mother praying the evening prayer.

I raised my head in supplication along with her.

Oh, Lord, please grant me a divorce.

6

I ALWAYS DID WHAT I wanted. No one could stop me on the path I set out on. I sacrificed everyone who tried to block me or change my mind. And everyone who I sacrificed were people who loved me. They gave me their hearts, but I stabbed them with the knife of my desires. I rushed past their wounds until I reached the end of the road, where I found the most terrifying obstacle of all: time itself. Hashim stood above it like a ghost. I couldn't grab him. I couldn't get to him. I couldn't even leave him behind.

I didn't mean to cast everyone aside. I didn't want to. I only did it to cut my path. The only one I wanted to rid myself of was Hashim. I wanted to tear up his flesh into small bits and toss them to the dogs, but I couldn't.

He is still standing there, like a ghost. I still see him with his eyes open. I see him with his eyes closed as I reach out to choke him, hearing his mocking laugh.

Why am I saying this now? We are still at the beginning of my story, but I see it from the end. However much it was filled with tears, there was sweetness to those times, the sweetness of my youth, the sweetness of hope, the sweetness of self-confidence, of only see-ing half of the truth. And then we grow up, and we see more of the truth until we see it all. The half-truth is more beautiful and more terrifying. Like the moon, half of it is exciting and beautiful while the other half is dark and terrifying.

I live now in the dark, terrifying half.

I was still in the illuminated half as I thought about divorcing my husband. The light around me was the light of pride in myself, of my infatuation with my beauty and youth. I couldn't see how disgusting my thinking was. Even my feelings toward what was growing inside me, of becoming a mother, evaded me.

There was no reason to get divorced except that I wanted to. My husband didn't prevent me from meeting Hashim. Hashim didn't promise me to get married. I was pregnant and my husband loved me.

But I wanted to divorce.

I had to invent a reason.

Not to convince myself.

I had to convince my mother.

I spent a month in my mother's house. Every day, my husband called and pressed me to go back to Suez. I refused on the pretext of being unwell and scared for the baby. He was coming to Cairo every week and as soon as he arrived, he'd find me in bed, claiming to be sick. He'd sit next to me looking at me longingly. I'd tell him what I'd heard about pregnancy cravings, but I wasn't having cravings. Nor did the smell of smoke bother me. Not at all. It was as if I wasn't pregnant. I feigned it all when-ever my husband came to Cairo so I could block him from sleeping next to me or kissing me, all on the pretext that I couldn't bear his scent or because I had cravings. And that slob gave in to my orders.

"He's obviously becoming demanding . . . like his mother!" he said, smiling.

"Like his father," I said.

He was full of conceit. His chest was puffed out like a rooster, as if he'd seen his son and saw that he looked like him. I made him sleep at a hotel. We didn't have a bed for him except mine, and he wasn't going to sleep there.

My mother noticed how I was treating my husband. She noticed how harsh I was with him. She noticed I went out almost every day when my husband was in Suez and I stayed home whenever he came to Cairo. She began to doubt the reasons I gave to stay at her house.

She didn't say anything, but I could see it in her eyes, the piercing way she looked at me as if trying to reveal my secret. I became afraid of her eyes, so I transitioned to the second act of the play that I was putting on. I began to feign sorrow and distraction. I'd always stay in my room, alone. Whenever my mother came in, she'd find me miserable, on the verge of tears.

She'd look at me and become quiet, searching my face, trying to figure out what was going on.

One day, I came back from meeting Hashim, and I put on the mask of sorrow before going in. I hurried to my room, took off my clothes, and sat on my bed with my head in my hands as if I was in pain.

My mother left me alone for a while and then came in and sat next to me.

"What's wrong, Mitou?"

"Nothing, Mommy," I said looking away.

She was quiet for a bit.

"Could you tell me where you keep going?"

"Nowhere," I said. "I go walking. I like wandering around."

I looked up at her.

"Because I'm fed up," I continued. "You don't know what I'm dealing with. You never ask yourself what your daughter feels. You never ask yourself if I'm happy or miserable. That's it. You married me off and tossed me away. You don't care. Like I am . . . or I was . . . some curse that you exorcized."

My mother suddenly became anxious.

"What happened, Mitou?"

"What happened?" I repeated, starting to feel my eyes burning from how much I was squeezing them to make myself cry. "It happened a long time ago, since the day you married me off. You can't imagine how much I've been tortured, Mommy. That's it, I can't bear it anymore. I can't live with him. I can't stand him. I can't stand him for another day!"

My mother gasped.

"Who says something like this!" she said, striking her chest with her hand.

I finally managed to make my tears pour out. I threw myself on her chest.

"Save me, Mommy," I sobbed. "Please, you have to save me. Just as you tossed me away, you have to save me!"

My mother pushed me off her chest.

"I don't understand anything at all," she said, staring at me. "Talk to me. Help me understand."

"You should've understood a long time ago," I said, looking for my kerchief to dry my tears. "You married me to someone more than twenty years older than me. He's ugly, a country bumpkin, uptight. His breath smells like fish eggs . . . and . . ."

"Did I marry you to him without you seeing him?" she asked, cutting me off. "Why didn't you tell me that from the beginning?"

"I was young," I snapped. "I listened to you, like I was supposed to."

"The man isn't bad looking and we didn't smell his breath."

"It's not only how he looks," I screamed. "He's disgusting! He makes me sick. He only showers once a month. We don't know how to say two words to each other. And his mother! You never asked what my mother-in-law is doing to me. Imagine, she's locked up everything in the house. If I want a piece of cheese from the fridge, I have to ask for permission. If I ask for something from the butler, he goes to tell her. She treats me like I'm a dog, feeding and dressing me for her son to play with."

"The villa will be finished soon," my mother cut me off again. "You'll live there by yourself. You'll be free of your mother-in-law soon enough."

"And how do I know she won't come live with me?" I screamed again, hitting the pillows with my fist.

"She can't," my mother said resolutely. "If she tries, I'll talk to her."

"Even if I live alone," I said, my tears pouring out again, "I can't. You can't imagine, Mommy, how it is in

Suez. I'm living jailed in one room. I can't even go out to the salon. All of Suez hates me and I hate them. From the moment I went there, I've been thinking about nothing but divorce."

My mother's eyes widened with terror.

"Don't say that!" she said, her voice nervous. "And don't forget you're pregnant. Instead of thinking about divorce, think about the child you're bringing into this world. Put up with it for the child."

I stared at her.

"Why didn't you put up with it for me? Why did you divorce Daddy?"

My mother couldn't face me. She lowered her eyes.

"I put up with a lot for you, my dear," she said in a sad, quavering voice. "I put up with it for three years. I could've put up with more."

"So, you want me to bear it too for three years and then get divorced? Since not getting divorced now is better, even though I still have time to find a decent husband?"

"Your father wasn't like 'Abd al-Salam," she said in a low voice.

"At least my father was a human being! At least he was good looking and understanding. You married me off to an animal!"

My mother jumped as if she'd been stung.

"You're upset, Mitou," she said as she exited the room. "We'll talk later."

She left.

I had declared war.

I had to continue down this path.

I felt the heaviness of the coming war on my chest, the road of violent defiance and blind insistence extending out in front of me. My head was like a beehive, filled with buzzing. Jumbled words and images tumbled through my mind, as I tried to grab on to them and imagine the scenes to come between me and my husband and between my mother and me.

I was tired. My nerves were frayed. I got up to talk to Hashim on the phone. Maybe he could calm me down. Maybe he could quiet the buzzing in my head. He's the only one I could take refuge in, the only one by my side in this crisis. I was doing all this for him because I loved him. Hashim was busy with his patients, as usual, then he was heading out with his friends after the clinic. He tossed me two quick words, as if he was throwing a bone to his spoiled dog and hung up, promising to meet me the next day.

I went to bed cowering, defeated. Hashim didn't feel the storms blowing in my head. He didn't feel the path of thorns that I was walking on barefoot for him. He didn't feel me except when he was taking me. When I was with him, I felt all of him was mine. I felt he occupied every part of me, every breath. But afterwards, he was lost to me, lost among his patients and friends, abandoning me as if he was finished with me forever.

I spent the night trying to convince myself to backtrack on the divorce. Or at least to resign myself to fate and not do anything, to leave myself in God's hands. For a fleeting moment I'd think I'd settled things, but it wasn't long before I went back to thinking about divorce, planning the path I would take.

*

I headed out to Hashim the next day, but my mother stopped me before I left.

"Where are you going?"

"Out," I said coldly and defiantly.

"I want to know where." She lowered her voice so her husband didn't hear.

"I don't know," I said, opening the door. "I'm going to walk around town. Maybe I'll go see my friend Nihad."

Then I went out and left her standing at the door in disbelief.

I got to Hashim's apartment at exactly four o'clock. I rang the doorbell, but no one opened the door. He hadn't arrived yet. This wasn't the first time that I'd got there before him. I remembered the days that he'd get here before me and I'd purposely make him wait to enrage him.

I stood next to the locked door, pathetic and abject. Whenever I heard the sound of the elevator or one of the neighbor doors open, I turned to the wall so no one would see me or my shame.

Hashim came at four fifteen.

"I'm sorry, Amina," he said sincerely, leaning on my cheek and kissing it, taking out a key chain from his pant pocket, opening the door. "I've been at the clinic until now. I still haven't had lunch. I left as soon as I finished with the last patient."

I didn't respond.

I didn't want to take him to task. I didn't want to talk to him about my problems. All I wanted was for him to distract me.

Hashim was very tired. He threw himself on the couch and closed his eyes. He seemed on the verge of falling asleep.

I tried to get him talking, but his responses were curt.

I got up to wander around the room. I moved the chairs around. I flipped through the medical journals and then tossed them aside. I turned on the radio and then turned it off. I picked up the ashtray and then slammed it down. He'd open his eyes and watch me, and then close them again.

"Keep it down, Amina," he said in an exhausted voice. "I'm tired. Leave me alone a little so I can relax."

I didn't respond.

I kept bothering him.

"I'm telling you I'm tired," he yelled. "Be quiet."

I picked up the cushion on one of the chairs and threw it at him.

"What have I done wrong?" I said, angry but with the sweetest smile on my lips. "You're tired every time I see you."

He took the cushion and put it down next to him.

"Amina," he said, looking at me angrily. "Please, just fifteen minutes."

But I didn't have any mercy.

I picked up the other cushion and threw it at his face.

"Not one minute," I said. "Treat me like one of your patients. Sit and talk with me."

His eyes opened wide. He looked ready to kill me. He took the cushion and threw it at me with all his strength. My hair fell over my eyes.

"You don't stop for a minute," I heard him say angrily.

I picked up the ashtray as if I was going to throw it at him. He jumped up, rushed over to me, and snatched it from my hand. He pulled me by my hair and tried to throw me down on the ground.

"Hashim!" I yelled. "Watch my stomach!"

He stopped for a moment as if deciding what he should do with me, his fingers still gripping my hair. He then pulled me to the other room.

He poured all his frustration onto my body.

"You know," he said, lying next to me in bed, looking at the ceiling, his breathing rhythmic, his hand tenderly on my inflated stomach. "Sometimes I think it's mine."

I turned to him in surprise.

It was the first time he'd broached this subject directly. A month or more had passed since I'd told him I was pregnant and both of us avoided talking about it. Neither of us wanted to know the truth.

"Don't talk like that, Hashim."

"Imagine if it's mine," he said as if he hadn't heard me, still looking at the ceiling dreamily. "I'd go crazy. I'd die."

"Why?" I asked, delighted to hear about his dreams.

"Why?" he said, giving me a look of surprise, and then looked back up at the ceiling. "Imagine I know it's mine and then I see him living with another man."

"He won't live with another man," I said with a small smile.

He turned to me.

"How's that?"

"Because I'll get divorced," I said calmly.

He turned fully to me. His face was very close to mine. His big nose was pressing against mine. His lips were breathing onto mine.

"Listen, Amina," he said in a serious voice. "You have to give up what's in your stomach. You have to have an abortion . . ."

"Don't say that," I cut him off sharply, recoiling from him. "You have no right over what's in my stomach."

"Listen, Mitou," he said. "Don't be selfish . . ."

"You're a doctor," I cut him off again. "And you talk like that? If a woman came to you and asked you to abort her, would you?"

"I know I'm a doctor," he said, sighing as if summoning all his patience. "I know religion, medicine, and the law forbid it. But giving birth not knowing who the father is, when you know you'll get divorced, what will happen to the child? Medicine permits abortion when the mother is sick and can't bear the pregnancy. Your circumstances are making you sick and unable to bear being pregnant. Even in law, there's no judge who'd say that you should give birth."

"Please, be quiet. You're afraid of responsibility."

"I am not. But I'm talking to you with my conscience. You're being selfish. If you thought about the child for just one moment, you'd hear what I'm saying."

"Of course I'm thinking about myself," I said, getting up from beside him, starting to get dressed nervously. "What if I die while having the abortion?"

"You won't," he said calmly. "You're healthy. If something was going to happen to you, I'd be the first to be concerned."

"You're not concerned about me. You're only concerned about yourself. Relax. This isn't your child or my husband's. It's mine. And I'm free to do what I want."

"You're crazy." He looked at me in disgust. "Cuckoo, stupid, selfish. There's no use trying to make you understand. Yes, it's my fault that I am concerned about you."

He started getting dressed too.

Before I left, he held out his arms to me and I hugged him with all my heart.

"Don't tell me I'm stupid, Hashim."

"I'm stupid too," he said, pressing me to him. "Each of us has a smart and a stupid side. You know what's the smartest thing about you?"

"What?"

"Your kiss," he said, smiling. "Your lips."

He then leaned over and I gave him one of my smart kisses.

I left happy, happier than I'd been since I got pregnant. I wanted to have the baby so Hashim would be confused about the child, so he'd spend his whole life wondering if it was his or not. I wanted the baby as a weapon with which I could challenge Hashim, stir him up and be stronger than him.

When I got back home, I sat with my mother, the veil of gloom over my face.

"I'm going to get an abortion, Mommy," I said with determination.

My mother hit her chest in shock.

"Who gave you that rotten advice?"

"No one. But I have to abort it."

"Why? What's changed?"

"Nothing. But as long as I'm going to get divorced, I have to get an abortion."

"You're not getting divorced!" my mother screamed, forgetting about her husband. "You're not getting an abortion! Understand? I spoke with 'Abd al-Salam and he's on his way."

We held a conference. My mother, 'Abd al-Salam, and me. My mother told him my complaints about his mother and Suez. 'Abd al-Salam took it with genuine worry. He started defending his mother, but then he promised he'd fix everything.

"You shouldn't upset yourself, Mitou," he said with a sincere look. "Don't forget you're pregnant. You have to think of the child."

"I don't want it!" I screamed. "I'm getting an abortion! This child and its father can go to hell!"

'Abd al-Salam's eyes bulged like he was being choked.

"Don't listen to her, 'Abd al-Salam," my mother implored him. "She's anxious. The pregnancy has exhausted her."

'Abd al-Salam calmed down, but I kept threatening him with getting an abortion. Whenever I had to sit with him or my mother, I insisted. And whenever I was with Hashim, I insisted on keeping it.

My husband stayed in Cairo for three days. They didn't leave me alone: my mother, 'Abd al-Salam, my five aunts, my stepfather. Finally, I was forced to go back to Suez to put an end to all the talking.

As soon as I got to Suez, I lit the house on fire. I didn't know I could be so horrible, so shameless, practically criminal. I didn't know I had all that destructive energy in me.

I drove 'Abd al-Salam crazy. I drove his mother crazy. I didn't give them a moment of peace. I revolted at every little thing.

"Divorce me! I don't want you! I can't stand you!" I screamed in his face.

I forbade him from my bed, even from my room. I insulted his mother in front of him. I made him take me to Cairo when he was trying to work. I left him when we got there to go to meet Hashim. I then went back with him under pressure from my mother. The slob thought I was acting like this because of the pregnancy. My mother convinced him of that.

One day, I stood on top of the dresser and threw myself off in front of him to try to abort the fetus myself. That day, the poor slob screamed and cried. It didn't scare me or stir up a single ounce of sympathy for him. It only made me more disgusted.

The fetus clung to me, clung to life.

My husband and his mother put up with me as calmly as they could for the sake of the child. They looked at me with pity like I was crazy.

Three months passed.

I was in the sixth month.

My stomach was big.

My husband was late one day at his office. Suddenly, without thinking, I got up and got dressed.

"Where are you going?" his mother asked in a voice trembling with fear.

"Out," I said without turning to her.

And I left.

I got in a taxi and told the driver to take me to Cairo. I had an intense feeling that this was my last attempt to get divorced.

I got to Cairo at eight o'clock that night. I got out of the taxi in Opera Square. I began walking in the streets. I was trying to kill time until Hashim finished with his clinic at nine, but my heavy stomach wore me out before it was eight thirty. I called him.

"When did you get here?" he asked, his voice rushed.

"Now. I have to see you right now."

"I can't. I still have a lot of patients."

"But I'm in the street. I'm tired. I don't have anywhere I can go. I have to see you."

"Fine. Go to the apartment and tell Mahmud to let you in."

"Okay," I replied submissively.

I took a taxi to Zamalek. I stood in front of Mahmud the doorman humiliated, feeling like a beggar as I asked him to open Hashim's apartment for me.

Mahmud looked at my inflated stomach in disgust. He got up lazily without saying a word and opened the apartment door and let me in. He gave me a horrible look and locked the door behind me.

I went into the bedroom and tossed myself on the bed. I was tired, broken. I tried to sleep, but I couldn't. I kept listening to the sound of the elevator, expecting Hashim to arrive at any second.

But he was very late.

He still hadn't arrived at ten.

I got up and made myself a cup of coffee just for something to do.

I sat in the salon with the cup of coffee in front of me.

Hashim arrived at ten thirty.

He hurried over, worried, and sat next to me.

"What happened, Mitou?" He put his arm around my shoulder.

My tears suddenly poured out, tears of exhaustion and loss. I found myself sinking off the couch until I was at Hashim's feet, my belly protruding before me so that the baby inside knelt at his feet too.

"I have to get divorced," I pleaded. "I have to. That's it. I can't do it anymore. Don't make me go back to Suez again. Don't let them take me back again."

"Don't cry," he said tenderly, embracing my face with his palms. "Anything's possible, but . . ."

"There's no but," I said, cutting him off, sobbing. "Don't try. I won't listen."

"That's it, then. Get divorced. I didn't agree with you before. But if it's this bad, do it."

He lifted me off the ground and sat me next to him. He kissed the tears on my cheeks.

"But how will you get divorced? Maybe he won't agree to it."

"He has to."

He shook his head and fell silent.

"Have you thought about what you'll do after you get divorced?"

I looked at him as if I was asking him the same question. I then lowered my head.

"No. I'll get divorced first and then I'll figure it out."

He shook his head silently.

He didn't say anything.

He didn't promise me anything, as if he wasn't the reason for this entire disaster, as if I wasn't getting divorced for him, as if he had nothing to do with my story.

I started telling him everything that happened in Suez. He was listening silently.

"It's midnight," he said. "Are you going to get going?"

"No, not yet."

"But you're very late."

"Don't worry. I won't ask you to let me stay here."

"I'm afraid for you," he said, with pity.

"Don't be," I replied, my tears coming back. "I know what I'm doing."

He took me in his arms calmly.

We stayed there until three in the morning. Then we left.

For the first time, I took the elevator down with him. For the first time, I rode in his car next to him. I wasn't anxious as he drove through the streets of Cairo. On the contrary, I looked out the window hoping everyone would see me, proud to be next to Dr. Hashim.

I asked him to take me to my Aunt Sa'diya, who lived near us in Heliopolis. She was a widow and lived with her two daughters.

"You're not going to your mother's?" Hashim asked in surprise.

"No. Aunt Sa'diya is better."

"What are you planning to do?"

"You'll find out later."

I got to my aunt's house, the details of my plan forming in my head.

I rang the bell with my ice-cold hand, everything inside me shaking. It felt like a year passed before the lights came on inside the house.

"Who is it?" I heard my aunt ask nervously.

"Amina," I whispered. "Mitou."

She opened the peep hole. As soon as she saw me, she threw open the door and hugged me.

"Mitou, my dear," she said. "Everyone's looking for you! Where were you?"

I didn't respond at first.

I threw myself on the first chair and put my head in my hands, crying.

"Let me tell your mother you're here," she said, hurrying over to the phone. "She's so upset. We thought you did something to yourself!"

She dialed the number.

"Mitou's here . . . Relax. She's fine, thank God . . . You want to come now? No. Don't. It's the middle of the night. Don't do that to yourself. She's here with me. The morning is better . . . Mitou, take the phone and talk with her to make her feel better."

My aunt then gestured to me to come over.

"Calm her down," she whispered. "Don't upset her."

I took the phone.

"That was some thing you did!" she screamed as soon as she heard my voice. "You are causing a scandal for us! Where have you been?"

"Nowhere," I said, sobbing.

"Tell me where!"

"No," I said, sobbing louder. "Unless you get me a divorce."

I then hung up on my mother.

7

I SLEPT THAT NIGHT AT Aunt Sa'diya's.

I slept next to her. She told me that 'Abd al-Salam called my mother from Suez at nine o'clock and told her I had disappeared. My mother waited until eleven and when I didn't show up, she began to go crazy. Both 'Abd al-Salam and my mother were calling police stations and hospitals. My poor mother cried and cried, while my five aunts tried to console her. Nothing helped.

Aunt Sa'diya told me she came back from my mother's at midnight. If her daughter hadn't been sick, she wouldn't have left. But the poor girl's condition was terrible.

I wasn't moved by my mother's suffering. On the contrary, I felt that the first part of my plan had succeeded.

"So, tell me," Aunt Sa'diya said like she was my friend. "Where were you?"

"I won't say until they divorce me," I said, turning my back to her.

"Forget the divorce for now," she said, patting my shoulder. "Tell me where you were. I'm your youngest aunt, the one who understands you the most."

"No."

"Tell me and I won't tell anyone, not even your mother."

"I'll only say when I'm divorced. And if I don't get my divorce, I'll go back to where I was."

My aunt kept insisting.

"Please leave me alone," I said, my eyelids heavy. "I'm tired. I'm dying of exhaustion."

As soon as I closed my eyes, I fell asleep.

I had a strange dream. I dreamt, I was running on a dark terrifying road, bearing my heavy stomach, with a horrifying specter running after me. I couldn't make out the face of the specter entirely. Sometimes it had the features of my husband. Sometimes, the features of my mother's husband. As I ran, I was trying to scream, calling out to Hashim. But I'd lost my voice. I couldn't speak. I opened my mouth, but my voice didn't come out. I kept running and running with heavy steps. I was filled with terror. Then I noticed a lot of lights coming from the end of the road, like there was a wedding. I saw Hashim sitting on a big chair wearing a tux with roses around him. I looked at the chair next to him which was reserved for the bride. And I didn't see anyone on it. There was no bride next to Hashim. I kept running to sit on the bride's chair. But the specter caught me and grabbed the side of my dress. It began to pull me back roughly as I screamed out to Hashim. But he didn't hear me. He looked around, waiting for his bride. He didn't see me. I was afraid that another bride would beat me to him.

When I opened my eyes, I saw my mother's face staring down at me. She was scowling. She had on a black dress as if she was in mourning.

She was shaking me by the shoulder.

"Mitou! Get up. Wake up!"

I looked up at her and then closed my eyes again.

"Leave me alone, Mommy," I said. "I want to sleep."

"Did you let anyone sleep last night?" she barked. "Get up. You can sleep later."

I opened my eyes, casting away the rest of my dream. I sat up exhausted.

"I had a very bad dream," I said rubbing my eyes.

"I don't want to hear about your dreams," my mother snapped. "I want to hear what happened last night."

"I'm not awake yet."

My mother sat on the edge of the bed.

"We're waiting."

"What time is it?" I asked, trying to regain my cool.

"Nine thirty," my aunt responded from the door of the room.

"Ugh . . . I've only slept two hours."

"That's not important." My mother was about to explode. "Speak!"

"Just wait, Fawziya," my aunt said. "The girl is worn out and she hasn't slept. Go, Mitou, wash your face with a little water."

She turned to my mother.

"Fawziya, come, we'll have coffee in the salon."

My mother fixed her wide angry eyes on me. I ignored her and got up slowly to go to the bathroom.

I took my time. I was gone for more than half an hour. My aunt knocked on the door twice to hurry me up, but I kept tarrying. I then went out to my mother, ready to play the ice queen.

I sat on the chair opposite her. Her face was flushed, her eyes even angrier.

My aunt ordered her daughters to go to their rooms. She then sat with us.

"Listen, Fawziya," she said. "I don't want you to upset yourself or Mitou. Everything has a solution."

"Please, speak, Miss Mitou," my mother said.

"What do you want me to say?" I asked coldly.

"I want you to tell me what happened," my mother said, raising her eyes to the ceiling, appealing to God for help with me.

"Nothing," I said calmly, shrugging my shoulders, both hands on my stomach. "I want to get divorced."

"We know that," she snapped. "What I want to know is, where were you until three in the morning?"

"I won't tell you until I get divorced."

"No, you'll tell me!" my mother screamed. "You'll tell me whether you like it or not!"

"Take it easy, Fawziya," my aunt interjected.

My mother fell silent, her breath tortured.

"You're not ashamed of yourself staying out all night with your belly sticking out like that? If not for the child in your stomach, I'd give you a good beating. What am I going to do with you?"

"Divorce me," I said coldly.

My mother blew up again. My aunt calmed her down. The conversation was endless. We went around like that for an hour or two, saying the same things we'd been saying for months. I wouldn't say where I was the night before.

Finally, my mother got up and pulled me by the hand.

"Come with me," she said.

She then turned to her sister.

"Leave us alone for a little, Sa'diya," she said.

My mother then brought me into the bedroom and closed the door behind us.

"Sit down."

I sat on the bed, and she sat right next to me.

At that moment, I wanted to put my head on her shoulder and let go of my stubbornness. I wanted to kiss her, so I did and then I cried.

"Listen, Mitou," she said, patting me on my thigh tenderly. "I'm ready to have you divorced. But before I do, I have to be sure. And I'll only be sure if I know everything. Tell me. Are you with someone else?"

"What do you mean?" I asked, raising my eyebrows, feigning innocence.

"I mean," she said, looking at me with a bitter smile, "are you in love with someone?"

"No," I said, turning away from her.

"Tell me. It's not a crime. All girls fall in love. I made a mistake when I married you off before you had opened your eyes and seen the world. If someone else has come along, you have that right."

I looked at her, trying to believe her. I felt my heart pound in my ribs. I lowered my head silently. The tears flowing down my cheeks revealed the truth.

"Can I know his name?" she asked, a bitter smile on her lips.

"No. That's impossible."

My mother wrapped her arms around me and pulled me to her.

"I'm your mother, Mitou," she said. "If you can't tell me, who can you tell? You've never hidden anything from me."

I leaned my head on her shoulder. I wanted to relax. My head was aching from the lack of sleep and all the talking.

"I won't, Mommy. I won't tell you."

"Can't I just know who this heartthrob is?"

"You'll know soon enough," I said.

She was quiet for a moment.

"Did he promise to marry you?" she asked, hugging me, my head still on her shoulder.

"How could he promise to marry me if I'm already married?"

"So, you haven't agreed that you'll get divorced and then get married?"

"Just like that? Like some business transaction?"

"Then why do you want to get divorced?"

"Because I love him. Because I'm sure that if I wasn't married, he'd marry me."

"You don't think it's possible for a young man of today to destroy your home and then disappear afterwards?"

"He's not a young man," I said, raising my head in protest. "He's thirty-five."

My mother looked at me as if she was trying to read my mind.

"Is that who you were with until three in the morning?"

I got up and moved away from her.

"Oh my God," I said, feigning anger. "How could you say that? He hasn't laid a finger on me."

My mother looked at me as if she didn't believe me.

"So, who were you with?"

"No one," I said sharply. "I won't tell you."

"You still won't tell me who you were with. Why?"

"Because if you don't get me divorced, I'm going back to where I was with no one knowing where I am. There will be a scandal."

"And who will let you do that? Do you think you're free to do whatever you want?"

"No one can stop me," I snapped.

"I know you were with this man," she said, sighing.

"If you knew, you'd know that he wasn't that type. He wouldn't stay with a married woman until three o'clock in the morning."

"Fine. Introduce me to him."

I didn't say a word. My mind was spinning.

"Tell me. May our Lord guide you."

"I can't. I won't. If he knows I told you, he'll stop talking to me."

"My dear, I'm afraid for you more than you're afraid for yourself," she pleaded, looking me in the eye. "I swear. May the Lord destroy you and all my children if I say a word. Tell me. Don't forget that I'll help you. I'm the only one who can."

I hesitated.

"That's it," she said, sighing deeply, her patience wearing thin. "I'm done. Go find someone else to divorce you."

She started getting up, but I grabbed her.

"His name is Hashim," I blurted out.

"Hashim who?"

"Dr. Hashim," I said, lowering my head.

She hit her chest in shock.

"Dr. Hashim 'Abd al-Latif?"

I nodded my head, looking away shyly.

"But half the girls of this city are running after him!"

My mother was staring at me.

"I'm better than half the girls of this city," I said sharply.

"They say he won't get married."

"I know that he loves me. I'm sure of it."

"Since when?"

"About a year."

"How did you meet him?"

I invented a big lie on the spot. I told her I met him at the club. One of my girlfriends introduced me to him and he called me afterwards. I went out with him a number of times in his car, and he kept calling me. I didn't tell her anything of what had really happened.

My mother looked at me, her eyes full of pride.

"You're incredible. I didn't know any of that."

She was then quiet for a bit.

"Does he know you're getting divorced?"

"Yes."

"Didn't he tell you what he'll do after the divorce?"

"Of course not, Mommy," I said, scolding her. "He's a good man. It's impossible for him to push a girl to divorce so he can marry her. He understands that I'll get divorced because I don't love my husband and because my husband isn't a good man. I'm sure that if I get divorced, he'll marry me."

"How so?" she was interrogating me.

"Hashim always tells me that if he met me before I was engaged, he'd have married me. He always tells me he can't ever do without me. I know he can't lie. There's nothing making him lie. Like you said, half the girls of the city are running after him. He doesn't need to tell me all that unless he loves me for real."

I could see my mother beginning to imagine herself as the mother-in-law of Dr. Hashim, boasting about me with all her friends, imagining herself in the big palace she could build from her naive ambitions and cheap desires.

"I really can't believe it. Dr. Hashim is quite an item!"

"Do you want me to call him in front of you?" I asked, smiling at her naivete, feeling superior to her.

"Call him," she said, biting her lip. "Prove it."

I jumped up enthusiastically, ready for my big performance. I went to the salon and came back with the phone.

"What did you two agree on?" Aunt Sa'diya called after me.

"We're still talking," I called back.

I then closed the door and sat next to my mother. I dialed the number as she watched closely, full of curiosity. It was eleven thirty. Hashim was at his clinic.

"What's up, Mitou?" he asked as soon as he heard my voice. "What's going on?"

My mother listened next to my ear on the receiver.

"The whole family is against me, but don't worry. Everything will go as we want."

Hashim was quiet for a bit, not sure what I meant.

"Be reasonable. Don't go crazy."

"I'm calm. I know what I'm doing. Don't worry. Just focus on your patients and leave everything to me."

Hashim was quiet again, trying to understand what was going on.

"Keep me posted," he said in a hesitant voice.

"Yes," I said gently.

I put the phone down and turned to my mother. Her eyes were wide, breathless. There was a big smile on her lips like she was applauding me for my brilliance.

"What's important now is that we get rid of that 'Abd al-Salam," she said, having made the decision to get to work immediately. "The truth is, my dear, you're right about him. He's unbearable."

When we went back downstairs, she told her sister, "It's no use, Sa'diya. The girl has to get divorced."

That's how my mother yielded to me. She gave up her principles and submitted to her cheap aspirations and base greed. She didn't know then the filthy, torturous road I'd drag her down.

My mother joined forces with my aunt and they came up with an action plan. They agreed to contact 'Abd al-Salam in Suez and tell him I was at my aunt's all night and that my aunt didn't know because she was at my mother's house. They'd then ask him to come to Cairo.

The poor slob believed everything.

I went back home with my mother.

"Won't you tell me where you were last night?" she asked again when we were on the way back.

"No," I said smiling. "Only when I'm divorced."

My mother was quiet.

The truth was that I couldn't think of a believable lie. And I couldn't tell my mother the truth.

We got home.

I fell asleep as soon as I went into my room. I fell into a calm sleep, feeling I had arrived at a port of safety after a long journey. My mother sat with her husband, and she started trying to convince him to agree to my divorce, using the reasons that I made up. Her husband grew weak, but he still hesitated. He kept looking for some way to save the marriage.

When I woke up, 'Abd al-Salam was at the house. I refused to see him or even to look at him from a distance. My mother convinced him that he shouldn't insist on seeing me, for the sake of the baby it was better I wasn't agitated. She began to persuade him of the divorce. Her husband began to support her in the conversation. My mother would come to my room and sit with me to relay what was being said. We'd then talk a little about Hashim and we'd laugh. She'd then put a serious look back on her face and go out to 'Abd al-Salam and relay to him words from me, half of which I didn't say.

'Abd al-Salam stayed in Cairo for three days. He came to the house in the morning and then left to have lunch. He came back in the evening, staying until the middle of the night and then he slept at a hotel. My aunts stayed with us. The house was in non-stop commotion. It was almost festive, not like a divorce.

On the third day, I was surprised to see 'Abd al-Salam open the door of my room without asking permission. His face was angry, full of violent anger. I was surprised when I saw him. He'd lost weight. He looked younger and like his personality was stronger. He even looked more handsome.

I looked at him with surprise, as if seeing a stranger. This wasn't my husband, 'Abd al-Salam. I thought at that moment that even his pants seemed not to sag down from behind.

I woke up from my surprise quickly. He got near me, his eyes raging. My mother rushed in behind him. He turned to her.

"Leave us alone, please, Mrs. Fawziya," he said in a firm voice that I hadn't heard from him before.

My mother hesitated. She looked at him and then at me.

"Don't get upset," she said to me. "You still have to talk to each other."

She then winked at me from behind his back and left.

'Abd al-Salam was raging. I looked at him, shocked at this strength of character which I'd never seen from him before. I even felt afraid of him.

"What do you want?"

"You know," I said, recoiling in the corner of the bed. "I don't love you."

"So why did you marry me?"

"I thought I'd be able to love you."

"We still haven't had enough time for you to know whether you can love me or not."

"It's no use. I won't be able to love you."

"And the child in your stomach?"

"I don't want it. I never wanted it. Take it when it's born."

"I didn't get married to get divorced seven months later. You have to stay to raise my child."

"God willing, it'll be born dead!" I screamed at the top of my voice. "I can't stand you! I can't stand you! Listen, 'Abd al-Salam, if you don't divorce me, I'll cheat on you. Understand what that means? I'll go and sleep with another man!"

Before I knew it, 'Abd al-Salam raised his hand and slapped me so hard that it lit a fire across my face.

"Mommy!" I screamed out. "Mommy!"

"I'll divorce you," 'Abd al-Salam said, standing up stiffly in front of me. "Not because you want to get divorced, but because you're no good as a wife. You're no good as a mother. You weren't raised right. You have no principles. You're deviant. I'm divorcing you because I was wrong to marry you."

My mother rushed in.

"He hit me, Mommy!" I screamed out. "He hit me!"

"You hit her, 'Abd al-Salam?" she asked, hitting herself on the chest. "No one has ever laid a finger on her before!"

"Get out of here!" 'Abd al-Salam screamed without turning to my mother. "Amina, you're divorced . . . divorced . . . divorced!"

He had divorced me.

He stormed out of the room.

"Wait, 'Abd al-Salam," my mother yelled after him.

But he left.

I heard the sound of the front door slamming behind him.

I threw myself on my stomach, crying.

I cried with everything inside me. I hadn't cried in my life as much as I cried that day.

My swollen stomach shook before me as if the baby was crying with me.

A volcano of emotions erupted in my chest, contradictory, dark, and painful. 'Abd al-Salam's slap still burned my face. Unlike Hashim's many slaps, it tore up my dignity. It was a slap of anger, not desire. It revealed a truth that I had not seen before: he was a man, a strong man. I felt a violent wave of regret. Oh, Lord! Why hadn't he slapped me before? Maybe I would've woken up from this madness. Why did he spoil me so much? Why was he so permissive? Why did he leave me to Hashim?

I thought about Hashim. I turned to my mother as she was standing next to me, trying to quiet my crying.

"Bring me the phone!" I screamed at her.

"Who do you want to talk to now?"

"None of your business!" I screamed. "Bring me the phone."

She left and came back with the phone.

I dialed Hashim's number.

"Are you happy now?" I screamed at him through my tears. "I've just gotten divorced. Come and marry me."

He was quiet for what felt like an eternity.

"We'll talk later."

I couldn't bear it.

I threw the receiver onto the bed. My mother took it and put it back in the cradle calmly.

"What did he say to you?"

"Nothing," I said sobbing. "Leave me alone, Mommy. Please, leave me alone!"

And my mother left.

I cried alone in my room.

The house was somber. My aunt's presence now made it feel like this was a funeral, my funeral.

And I slept.

No, I didn't sleep. I passed out.

The next day, I woke up thinking about meeting Hashim. I felt that I'd become weaker before him. I'd lost my confidence.

I called Hashim.

"Can I see you today?" I asked, my voice sad and weak.

"Really, I can't, Amina," he said like nothing had happened. "I have consults at four o'clock. I can't miss them. Call me tomorrow."

Was he beginning to flee from me?

I didn't want to know. I didn't want to think about that.

"Okay," I said in misery and resignation.

The day moved sadly and sluggishly. My mother couldn't console me. She was sad too, regretful.

The next day, Hashim refused to meet me again.

"Really," he said sincerely. "I'm busy. I swear. I can't. Call me tomorrow."

I believed him. I had to.

And then he met me.

I told my mother I was going to meet him.

"Be careful, Mitou," my mother said, anxiously. "You're now in *'idda*, the period of waiting after a divorce.

Until it's over, 'Abd al-Salam can do with you what he wants like he's still married to you."

I smiled. I liked the phrase "the period of waiting after a divorce."

I was happy about it as if I'd bought a new dress that I'd been dreaming about. I kept chewing on the phrase, cracking it in my mouth like a piece of gum.

Hashim was waiting for me.

He sat next to me listening to the details of what happened. Then his face became serious.

"Listen, Amina," he said looking at his hands. "I want to talk to you seriously . . ."

"I know what you're going to say," I cut him off, turning my face from him. "I don't want to hear it."

"What am I going to say?" he asked, turning to me with a dead smile on his lips.

"You're going to tell me that if I get divorced, it doesn't mean that you'll marry me. I told you a hundred times that I didn't get divorced for you to marry me."

"I don't want to deceive you," he said.

"I know. Please be quiet."

But did I lose hope that I'd marry him? Not at all. It was this hope that would propel me to the end of the road, and then toss me on the side into the mud. Those days, I was too weak to express my hope honestly and to defend it. I realized that I was afraid of Hashim. I believed that I respected him because he was honest. But, in truth, I was afraid of him, afraid that he was so impudent that he'd have no need to lie.

Fifteen days later, 'Abd al-Salam sent me the divorce papers.

He divorced me without conditions.

The right to the balance of the dower was five hundred pounds. He paid it as soon as my mother mentioned it to him, as if he was selling me at any price.

I was divorced.

I was nineteen and pregnant in my seventh month.

Fear and terror filled my heart.

I had become free, chained only by the heavy weight I carried in my stomach.

I was confused in the initial weeks about what to do with my freedom. I met Hashim every two or three days for an hour or two. I had endless conversations with my mother about the divorce and my marriage to Hashim and the big hope that I was building my lie on. My stomach grew and I went out to walk around Baron Street, getting ready for the birth.

The days passed, slow and boring. I put the boredom down to being pregnant and the waiting period after the divorce that meant I couldn't do much out of fear that 'Abd al-Salam was keeping tabs on me. I knew he wasn't, though, and that he hadn't come to Cairo since he divorced me.

But . . .

It wasn't boredom.

It was something else.

It was fear.

It was a fear that I was trying to ignore. As the birth got nearer, so too my fear increased, into terror. Not at the pains of childbirth, but at fate. At bearing the responsibility for the child alone, without a husband beside me. I felt I was giving birth to an orphan. I saw a long life stretching out before this child, a life that it was going to live alone, fatherless.

My certainty that I was pregnant by 'Abd al-Salam began to shake, shake violently. I wasn't so confident anymore. I had a wicked hope that it was Hashim's. Hashim, at least, would be beside me. He could bear with me the responsibility for this child even if he wasn't my husband.

The torture of my conscience pressed down on me. I even entertained reconciling with 'Abd al-Salam. I even called him. I tried to be gentle with him. I talked to him about the approaching birth, trying to stir up his sympathy. He was cold with me and I gave up that hope.

I submitted to fear, torture, and loss.

I took refuge in Hashim. He was as he was, nothing weighing on him. He'd lead me sometimes to his bed, even though he knew that in only a few days, I was going to be lying on the birthing bed.

When I went into the hospital, it felt that the baby was carrying a knife, cutting a path for itself to life. I screamed, pushing with all my strength to expel this creature from my body. I suffered. Oh, Lord, have mercy on me. I thought this kind of pain wasn't natural. God had to be punishing me. He was pouring His vengeance on me.

The pain didn't numb my mind. Even in the worst moments, I was dying to meet my baby, to find out who the father was.

The nurse brought the baby to me, the thing that was torturing me.

It was a girl. I looked at her face eagerly. And from the first glance, I knew.

She was 'Abd al-Salam's.

I was enraged.

I looked again at her face. All of her was 'Abd al-Salam. Her coloring, her nose, her lips. I thought that if she opened her mouth, I'd find a gold tooth in it.

I looked at her fingers, at her feet.

Nothing from Hashim.

Or me.

I praised God without any joy.

'Abd al-Salam came to visit.

"You're now a mother, Mitou," he said holding his child in his arms, his tone serious and threatening. "The girl needs to be raised correctly. She can't be raised right if her mother isn't good."

He tried to be nice. He brought me a bunch of roses. He paid for the hospital expenses.

My mother and my five aunts surrounded my bed.

I was exhausted.

I woke up the next day and the feeling that I had no man beside me was even worse.

I called Hashim.

"Girl or boy?" he asked, without a care in the world.

"Girl," I said miserably.

"Beautiful like her mother?"

"You're not going to come to visit?" I asked.

Hashim hesitated, but I convinced him to come at ten that evening. I promised him no one would be with me. He accepted, embarrassed.

I pretended to go to sleep at eight o'clock and everyone left, even my mother.

Hashim came at ten.

His arrival stirred up the whispers of the nurses. They came out to see him. His manner was serious as it would be with a patient. After the nurse left, he loosened up. He looked at my daughter in the crib at the side of the room. He gave her a single glance, out of courtesy. She didn't interest him at all.

"She's beautiful. What did you name her?"

"I haven't decided yet. What do you think?"

"Name her after your mother."

"No. What did the poor girl do wrong? I'm not giving her such an old-fashioned name."

"Name her . . . Huda . . . after my niece," he said.

"Yes," I responded. "That's it. Huda."

Hashim looked at Huda again for longer this time, searching her for something. He then looked at me with a smile.

"I have to give you a gift," he said sitting on the chair next to my bed, leaning over me until his lips touched mine. "I don't have time to go looking through the stores. From now on, you have to get yourself used to buying gifts from me."

He then took fifty pounds out of his pocket and put it in my hand.

I tried to refuse.

But my refusal was just not convincing. I was too weak to say no.

"That's way too much, Hashim," I said feebly.

Fifty pounds was the most money I'd ever had in my hands at one time, at least at that point. My husband never gave me more than ten pounds for personal expenses.

"Nothing is too much for you," Hashim said. "Everything I have is yours."

"But what do I tell my mother?"

"Hide it until you buy something with it."

8

I WAS LIBERATED AFTER I gave birth to my daughter. My regret over my divorce turned to misery. And this misery soothed me.

My daughter didn't concern me. I left her to my mother. I had no use for her except when I wanted to show myself off as a new mother in front of guests or when I put her in the stroller and went with her to the Heliopolis Club. I pushed her in front of me proudly, as if I had on a new dress or had got a new haircut. I didn't feel the worry or fear, nor the sense of pride or self-respect, of a new mother. All I felt was selfishness. I felt that Huda was my daughter, my possession. I left her to my mother, who bore all the responsibility for her, but from time to time needed to make my mother feel that Huda was really mine. I'd invent little fights with her about things connected to Huda. I'd insist on her doing things how I wanted so she didn't forget that Huda was mine.

Maybe I was too young to take on the responsibility of a mother. My daughter was simply a doll that I was having fun with. I was too preoccupied with my own future to think about Huda's.

I was totally free. I was like a girl who hadn't gotten married yet. I went back to behaving younger than my age. I dressed like a young girl. I wore pants and I rode a bike in the streets of Heliopolis. All my friends were single girls. We went to matinee movies and ate sandwiches at Bamboo on Sulayman Pasha Street. I didn't hear my mother when she reminded me that I was a divorcée and that divorcées have a special place in society. Nonsense. A divorcée might be different from a married woman, but she wasn't different from a single girl. Neither has a husband. Whatever a divorcée can do, an unmarried girl can do too.

The only thing limiting my freedom was my love for Hashim.

Hashim was my only man, my sole preoccupation.

I talked to him on the phone more than once in the morning and more than once in the evening. I asked his permission before I went out. I'd tell him good night before I went to sleep. I listened to him. I lived to meet him, every two or three days, for an hour or two.

Hashim didn't change.

I was more embedded in his life, but he didn't give me anything new. The only thing he did was give me the phone number of his sister who he lived with so I could talk to him there after midnight when he got back from his night out with his friends. I was happy to have his sister's number. I was happy when I heard her voice when she answered. I even purposely called knowing Hashim wouldn't be home, just to hear her voice. Or, more precisely, to insert myself into her household. I'd tell her my name openly and I'd speak with her delicately and shyly.

Despite the distaste with which she'd respond to me, a distaste masked by politeness and respect but clear nonetheless, I considered her a friend. When talk of Hashim would come up among my mother's friends, I'd claim falsely that I was his sister's friend.

Soon, what I was taking from Hashim was no longer enough. I wanted to meet him every day. He was always busy, and I realized he met me on specific days—Saturdays, Mondays, and Thursdays. Outside of those days, if I called him at the clinic, he'd be in a rush. If I called him at home, he was also in a rush, saying that he needed to sleep or go out.

The only person I could talk with about him was my mother. And what I told her was three-quarters lies. I couldn't tell her where we met or what we did or what we talked about. I made up a naive innocent love story, with a smiling happy future.

Then, I could no longer keep my secret just between me and my mother. I had to reveal it to someone else.

I whispered it to my closest girlfriend. Then to another. And a third . . . and a fourth. None of them believed me, as if Hashim was something bigger than me that I couldn't reach, so I'd talk to him on the phone in front of them to convince them.

I didn't know that when I revealed my secret, I'd discover an entirely new side of Hashim's life. I discovered that I wasn't the only one.

Each of my girlfriends brought me a story about him, about some adventure of his. One swore he had a relationship with a married woman. Another swore he had a relationship with a university student. A third was sure he loved a girl from the Gezira Club, and on and on.

I didn't believe it.

A man like Hashim had to be surrounded by rumors. If he said hello to a girl and smiled at her, people would make up a story about it.

The ease with which I started seeing him proved that he was a man of many adventures.

I began to get jealous. I started feeling like dozens of cockroaches were crawling inside my heart and a hive of bees was buzzing in my head.

I told Hashim what I was hearing about him.

"Don't believe it," he said, letting out a laugh. "You think someone like me can remain unmarried and people aren't going to talk? If what people say was true, I'd have gone out with half the women of Cairo by now."

"Why don't you get married, then, so people stop talking?"

He stopped laughing and gave me a serious look.

"If I wanted to get married, I would have."

"Why don't you want to?"

He didn't respond. He got up from beside me, picked up one of his medical journals, and began reading it as he usually did when he was angry at me.

I decided to keep silent, but jealousy gnawed at my heart and filled my head.

One day, before leaving Hashim's apartment, I put the ashtray in a particular spot so that if I came back and found it moved, I'd know he was in the apartment. As long as he was in the apartment, he had to have been with a woman.

And when I came back, I found the ashtray in a different spot.

"Were you here yesterday, Hashim?" I asked, suppressing my emotions so I didn't explode.

"No."

"You didn't come here at all since we were together?"

"Not at all," he said calmly.

"Liar!" I snapped.

He raised his eyebrows in surprise, almost impressed by my boldness.

"I know you were here!" I screamed again.

"How so?" he asked coldly.

"I won't tell you, but I'm sure."

"As long as you won't say how you know, don't ask me."

"I put the ashtray here myself," I said challenging him. "Care to tell me how it moved? Did it jump there on its own?"

"You're being ridiculous," he said, smiling. He got close to me and took me in his arms.

"Why?"

"You forgot that Mahmud comes up to clean the apartment every day," he said, laughing. "He must've put the ashtray in a different spot."

I wasn't satisfied.

I started going to the apartment like a hunting dog. I'd smell the pillows looking for the scent of another woman. I'd check the cigarette butts. Maybe I'd find one with lipstick. I'd search the kitchen. Maybe I'd find something. I started opening drawers that I hadn't been interested in before. I'd search and search. Hashim would let me search without objecting.

Until I finally found something.

I found a woman's picture. She was about my age, holding a girl about the age of my daughter. I stared at it and my heart jumped to my throat.

"Who's this, Hashim?" I asked in a trembling voice.

He came and stood behind me.

"This is someone I knew before you," he said indifferently.

I began to stare at the photo.

I was more beautiful than her, a thousand times more. And my daughter was more beautiful than hers, a thousand times more.

"Why didn't you tell me about her?"

"You know I don't like talking about anyone from the past," he said, moving away.

I kept starting at the photo.

I calmly took a kohl pencil from my bag, and I began to draw a mustache and beard on the woman's face. I then smeared the girl's face with the kohl and tossed it back in the drawer.

Jealousy for Hashim had taken control of me. The stories that girls were telling me about him didn't stop. I'd go crazy when I called and didn't find him at the clinic or at home. He had to be with another woman.

One day, I was shopping on Sulayman Pasha Street and I passed in front of the clinic. Suddenly, I had this feeling that Hashim had to be with a woman. It may not have been just jealousy that I felt at that moment, but also that I was entitled to impose myself on him, that I had more rights over him than any other woman. I craved him, even just a single glance of him.

Without thinking, I went up to the clinic and the polite nurse met me. He pointed me to the women's waiting room.

"I'm not sick," I told him resolutely. "I'm a relative of the doctor. I want to see him for a minute. It's an important matter. Tell him it's Amina."

"Please wait until I pass the message to him," the nurse said politely, looking at me as if he didn't believe me.

"No," I said resolutely. "Tell him now. He knows me."

The nurse looked at me again as if he still didn't believe me. He then went into Hashim's office and came back a few moments later.

"The doctor asks you to wait your turn," he told me without losing his politeness.

I felt the blood rise up into my cheeks, scorching my face.

"Don't worry about it," I said, swallowing the insult. "I'll call him later."

I left feeling drops of sweat wet my dress. I wondered, if I was his wife, would he have refused to meet me? At that moment, my position with Hashim became crystal clear: I had to sneak to him in the darkness, out of sight. I'd always have to come in through the back door.

I rebelled. I wanted to save myself and to take revenge against Hashim, who was happy to have me in this position.

I called again.

"How could you show up at the clinic like that?" he screamed. "Have you gone crazy?"

"How could you refuse to see me?" I asked, trying to match his tone.

"You know I can't see you at the clinic unless you're sick." He was still yelling. "And when you're sick, you have to wait your turn."

"I wanted you just for a minute," I said, backtracking.

"Even half a minute! If my mother rose up from her grave, I couldn't see her at the clinic. Understand? The clinic is only for sick people."

He then hung up on me.

I couldn't bear his anger. I tried. I managed for an entire day not to call him. But I couldn't manage for another day. I couldn't bear to stay angry at him. I craved him.

I called the next day.

He was evasive. A week passed and he was still evasive.

I cried to him on the phone.

He finally met me.

Jealousy pressed on me and took over. I abandoned the role of the girl that I had been playing immediately after Huda was born and became a jealous woman, with all the violence and insanity that entailed.

I discovered that the only way to have relief was to fill Hashim's time, not to leave him a single minute that another woman could enjoy.

I invented endless reasons to leave the house to go to meet Hashim.

I began to clash with my mother's husband. He took me to task. He constantly reminded me that I was a divorcée and forbade me from going out. Sometimes he'd come in as I was talking on the phone and bark at me in his military tone.

"That's enough! I want the phone."

My mother would help me sometimes but, most of the time, I felt she was inflicting him on me to limit my freedom.

I started spending more time with my father to get free of my mother's husband.

He couldn't block me from visiting my father.

At that time, my father had divorced his fourth wife and married the fifth. She was a woman about twenty years younger than him. She was dark-skinned and poor. She worked as a teacher in one of the public schools. My mother claimed that he hadn't actually married her, but that she'd been living with him in his second place, in his bachelor pad, for two years. Then, after he divorced his fourth wife, she came to live with him at his house, without getting married.

I didn't care what my mother was saying. I didn't discuss it with my father. My father's life was no longer a subject for discussion. He lived for pleasure. He drank a bottle of cognac every day and filled his belly with fatty food. He talked about sex openly and used foul language all the time. All his jokes—even in front of me—were crass and sexual. Every year, he sold one hundred acres of his land, so he didn't have to work.

Despite that, he was a good man. He was just weak. He loved me. I was his only daughter. He kept a room for me at his house, even though I didn't live with him.

His life was totally different from the life that my mother lived with her husband. It was a life free from traditions and principles. No one could change him. He was fifty and he was a hopeless case. It was pointless to try to preserve the rest of his land, his inherited wealth, that he was intent on selling off.

I didn't want to live like my father. I loved him and I even pitied him.

Hashim pushed me to that life, maybe without meaning to.

I began to go by my father's a lot to get rid of my stepfather's supervision. I'd stay with him for an hour or have lunch with him and then leave to meet Hashim. Of course, my father didn't ask where I was going and my mother never checked on me at my father's since her husband forbade her to talk with him except on official occasions like when I got married . . . and divorced.

I started spending the night at my father's on the pretext that he wanted to spend time with my daughter. I'd take Huda and spend a night or two with him, during which I'd try to win the friendship of the woman living with him, whether she was his wife or not. I didn't care what kind of woman she was. All I cared about was that I get her on my side so she could help me cover up my goings out. I then started going to my father alone, leaving my daughter at my mother's. I'd go to spend the night at his house, but I wouldn't sleep there. I'd sleep at Hashim's.

Hashim would take all this casually. We'd spend crazy nights together.

Then, in the morning, he'd go back as he was—Dr. Hashim, who only troubled himself with his patients. There was no room in his mind except for his patients.

At least I felt that I was keeping him from other women.

I felt that I was taking over his life. But, at the same time, I was tearing up my own life. I was careening down a dangerous road. I'd try to turn back, but my resistance was always short-lived.

I had gotten used to him, used to Hashim, to this insanity.

I was sure he wouldn't find another girl like me, at my age and with my beauty, from a decent family and divorced, giving him everything.

My mother hadn't given up hope that I'd marry Hashim. She'd ask me every day. She kept pressing it.

"Mommy, there are circumstances preventing him from moving forward now."

"Why do we have to pay for these circumstances?" my mother would ask. "People are starting to talk. We have to find a solution."

I made up a story for her. I told her Hashim's father engaged him before he died to the daughter of a close family friend, and he therefore couldn't get married now. He was trying to end this engagement. We had to wait.

My mother had gotten tired of waiting. She began to look for a husband for me. My five aunts set out to look with her.

I didn't say anything.

Part of me understood my future was perilous, but still I hoped my love would be victorious.

Then, one day, I was on my way to visit my father and, as I was passing through Zamalek, it occurred to me to go by Hashim's apartment. I don't know why, but

I had a funny feeling. It was four o'clock. The time that I usually met Hashim, but I didn't have an appointment with him that day.

I saw his car in front of the building door.

I stopped the taxi. A fire burned through me. I was possessed.

I leaped out of the taxi as if it too was on fire.

I ran up the stairs. I rang the bell with my trembling hand, the blood draining from me.

Hashim opened the door after a while. A long while.

He was wearing a shirt and pants.

"Why are you here?" he asked, blocking the door.

"Can I come in?" My voice trembled.

"It's unbelievable, Amina, that you're doing this . . ." he said, still blocking the door.

"Let me in," I cut him off.

Hashim saw the cloud of pale insanity on my face. He glanced toward the neighboring apartments and, afraid of a scandal, he moved away from the door and let me in.

I charged through the salon and into the bedroom.

There she was.

I later learned that her name was Mervat.

She was standing in the corner of the room, fully dressed. She was young, but not as young as me. She was beautiful, but not more beautiful than me. She was shaking in fear.

"What are you doing here?" I screamed with Hashim standing behind me.

She didn't respond. She was still shaking.

"Don't get upset," Hashim said calmly. "Talk to me."

"Don't you know he loves me?" I kept screaming, fixing my eyes on her face.

Hashim pulled me by the arm to get me away from her.

"I said, don't get upset!" he said.

Mervat took the opportunity to flee. She ran to the door and left.

"You're a criminal . . . a scoundrel!" I screamed, turning to Hashim. "What more do you want?"

A red cloud filled my vision.

I was pacing around the room like a lunatic, still screaming at him.

"You're a criminal. You're a scoundrel!"

I then picked up a vase and smashed it onto the ground.

Hashim raised his palm and slapped me hard. It dropped me to the ground next to the broken vase.

I clung to his legs as he stood straight, my body at his feet.

"Don't do that again, Hashim!" I said crying with all my tears. "Swear that you won't do that again. I don't want you to be with anyone but me ever . . . ever!"

He fell next to me on the ground and took me in his arms.

"You're crazy," he said.

He always said that to me.

I searched his lips as if I wanted to make sure they were still mine. I threw myself at him with all my passion, all my fire.

We disappeared into this insanity.

*

"Why did you do that, Hashim?" I asked, slumped next to him in bed, my nerves shredded.

"You're the reason," he said, smoking his cigarette.

"Me?"

"It's unbelievable. You get married and then you want me to sit around alone. What do you want me to do? Sit and cry? Commit suicide?"

I believed him. I smiled calmly.

"Who was that?"

"A girl."

"I have to know who she is."

"Just a girl," he said, turning his face to the wall. "There's nothing between us."

"If there's nothing between you, what's she doing here?"

"It's over. Forget it."

"So, you won't be with anyone else ever again?"

"Never."

"Me neither," I said smiling.

That day, when I got home, I cried. I cried all night. I felt that I was weak, weaker than ever before.

I kept my promise. I refused all the suitors my mother and aunts brought. At first, I concocted excuses. Then I began to confront them. I didn't want to get married.

My insistence revealed how much I loved Hashim. All the women in the family found out about him. They were all on my back, warning me, saying Hashim won't marry me, presenting me a new suitor practically every day, reminding me about my daughter and her future, and what people were saying about her mother.

I was crazy.

Life was oppressing me. Everyone was against me. They were choking me, choking my freedom. I started to hate everything except the moments I spent with Hashim.

I even hated my daughter. I couldn't stand her crying anymore. I couldn't stand having to deal with her.

Then, a crazy idea occurred to me.

I ran to Hashim.

"Listen," I told him, trying to think calmly. "I'll say that we're engaged."

"Who are you going to say this to?"

"My family. You don't know what they're doing to me. They're talking about you all the time. They're trying to marry me off. If I tell them we're engaged, at least they'll stop bringing me potential grooms."

"But we're not engaged," he said coldly.

"I know. But that's what I'll say."

"That won't solve anything. We can't say we're engaged and meet each other in secret. Your family doesn't know me, and I don't know them."

"I'll tell them we were engaged in secret," I insisted.

"And people will believe it?"

"I don't care what people believe. All I care about is that they leave me alone."

"But I don't agree. And if someone asks, I'll tell them we're not engaged. I won't even admit that we know each other."

"Say what you want," I said. "And I'll say what I want."

"Be reasonable, Amina. You can't live in a lie."

But I insisted. I insisted on living a big lie.

9

I THOUGHT I'D SOLVED MY problem when I started telling my girlfriends that I was engaged to Hashim in secret. He was just waiting to break off his engagement to the daughter of their family friends to announce our engagement. This lie spread. It got bigger until I started living it. I began to face people fearlessly, shamelessly. I talked about my relationship with Hashim openly. I backed up the lie with a silver engagement ring that I bought and put on my finger. I let people think it was platinum. I let the women working in the stores on Sulayman Pasha and Qasr El Nil Streets see it.

"Congratulations," they'd say. "You've gotten engaged?"

"Soon," I'd respond with a bashful look.

"Dr. Hashim, right?"

"Who'd you hear it from?" I'd ask, feigning surprise.

"The entire town knows."

I'd smile, silently. I was so happy it was like I really was engaged.

I had built a house of cards, and it didn't take long before it came crashing down. I don't know what led me to run so far with this lie. Maybe because I was so insecure about being with a man who wouldn't marry me. The way people looked at me, those who knew my story with Hashim, wounded me and I wanted to fill their eyes with dirt. And I was fed up with my family's attempts to marry me off. Their endless chatter got on my nerves: Aren't we looking forward to seeing you married, Mitou! Why don't you pull yourself together, Mitou, and bring us a groom? May it be the same for you, Mitou! And on and on, words that would drive me crazy and make me feel how inadequate I was. I wanted to shut them all up with this lie.

Only a slight echo of this huge lie reached Hashim. Hashim didn't move in the same social circles as me. He didn't go to the club. He didn't shop at the stores of Sulayman Pasha and Qasr al-Nil streets. He didn't spend his summers at Miami Beach on the North Coast. He spent most of his time at the clinic, only raising his ear from one patient to lower it on another. His patients respected him so much that none of them would dare ask about his personal life. His friends didn't ask because they knew he wasn't going to get married, not to me and not to anyone else. The few times the rumor actually reached him, he just shrugged his shoulders and repeated what he always said: She's crazy. She won't be the first or the last.

But the rumor reached his sister.

Then he was angry.

"Listen, Amina," he snapped. "You have to stop this story that we're engaged. It's enough."

"I'm not saying a thing," I said, challenging him. "People gossip. How can I stop people talking?"

"I know you're the one who started this rumor," he said, looking at me in disgust. "Even if you're not spreading it, you're not denying it."

"You want me to lie and say what?" I screamed. "Say that I'm only going out with you? At least when people say we're engaged, it's better than saying I'm your mistress."

"I don't care about people, Amina," he said, backtracking. "You're what I care about. This talk hurts you more than me. But I want you to face the truth so you know where you're headed . . . where you're going."

"If I can't bear the situation I'm in, what will you do? Will you marry me?"

"No," he said, getting up from beside me. "If you can't bear it, you have to leave me."

"If I could've left you, I would have a long time ago," I said giving him a pathetic smile.

My tears ended the conversation.

My mother soon heard what people were saying. She shook her head in grief, not knowing how to respond. Sometimes she'd participate in the lie.

"But it's still not official," she'd say.

"His whole family is blocking him," she'd say.

Sometimes, she'd get angry at people.

"No," she'd say. "That hasn't happened. You want to put an end to the girl's market or what?"

She'd cry and beg me, using my daughter and my youngest half-sisters whose futures might be affected by people talking about me. She'd beg me to accept one of the suitors that she and my five aunts were bringing and leave Hashim.

Her pleading would wake me up from the big lie I was living. I'd feel the veil rise up from my eyes to see a bleak dismal road before me. At that moment, I'd decide to forget Hashim. But then I'd go back to wondering . . . Why don't I get married, but stay in my relationship with Hashim? I'd then feel the veil cover my eyes and defy my mother all over again.

Then, 'Abd al-Salam intervened.

He'd come to visit about once a week to see his daughter. He usually wouldn't find me at home. He'd come in the morning, and I'd still be out. He'd come in the evening, and I'd be gone. Sometimes he was told that I spent the night at my father's. I wasn't avoiding 'Abd al-Salam. It was just how I was living. I couldn't bear to stay at home, not even for my daughter. 'Abd al-Salam began to object. He wanted an ideal mother for his daughter, a respectable mother, a mother who'd raise his girl and stay home with her. When he said this to me, I'd argue with him.

"You think you're still my husband? You have no rights over me. Only my mother and father have that."

But 'Abd al-Salam didn't let it drop.

He bribed my daughter's nanny to keep tabs on me. He heard the rumors. He heard the story about Dr. Hashim. He tried to talk to me about it, but I exploded.

"What is there between us?"

"Don't forget you're the mother of my daughter," he said, trying to control himself. "I'll be in your life as long as the girl is alive. The girl has to be raised properly. Her mother has to be respectable. If you don't know how to raise her, I'll take her and raise her myself."

"You can't!" I screamed. "You can't!"

"I can," he said confidently. "I won't just stay silent."

That day, he left me terrified.

But he didn't try to take my daughter from me. All he did was cut off the support that he was paying me.

He had been giving me fifteen pounds a month. I needed it since my father was only giving me five pounds a month and wouldn't pay more. I couldn't ask my mother's husband to support my daughter. It was enough that he'd taken me in for my mother's sake. Besides, I wasn't spending the whole fifteen pounds on my daughter. I spent a big part on myself, my clothes, and my makeup.

I didn't know what to do.

My mother gave me an additional five pounds after my daughter's support was cut off, but it wasn't enough.

I was furious. I felt 'Abd al-Salam wanted to humiliate me. He wanted to force me to submit to him. But I wouldn't. I wouldn't be humiliated by him.

I told Hashim.

"I'm going to sue 'Abd al-Salam," I raged. "Imagine, he cut off my child support!"

"Please," he said simply. "No one decent goes to court."

"So, what do I do?"

"Nothing," he said with the same simplicity and indifference. "He probably just wants to upset you. The best thing is for you to convince him that you're not upset."

"But I need that money."

"Take it from me," he said, smiling. "Did you forget that I'm responsible for you?"

I'd only broached the subject so I'd get this offer from him.

I didn't say anything.

I didn't refuse or accept.

"I'll give you thirty pounds," he continued as if he was hiring me as a nurse in his clinic. "Half for the girl, half for you."

"Absolutely not, Hashim," I cut him off. "What have I done to deserve this?"

"This will make me feel better."

"No. I don't want it."

"It's better than seeing you in court. Don't forget I'm responsible for you."

I turned my eyes away from him and kept silent.

He put his hand under my chin and raised my face to him.

"Who do you belong to?" he asked smiling.

"You," I said in a low voice.

And I took my first payment from him.

This wasn't the first money that I took from Hashim since he gave me fifty pounds when my daughter was born. He had given me many gifts, all of them cash. He claimed he didn't have the time to wander around the stores and that I had to buy the gifts for myself. He gave me thirty pounds to buy a ring. He gave me fifty pounds to buy something beautiful in gold. He gave me money to take taxis, and on and on. I was weak before his money. I couldn't take my hands off it. I had accepted Hashim's money because he gave it to me as gifts. But that day, I started accepting a salary. I asked myself: why was I accepting this money? In exchange for what? What was I giving him for it?

Nothing.

I didn't feel that I was giving him anything. I always felt I was taking from him. I felt I needed him more than he needed me.

I fantasized that the fixed salary I started taking from him made me like his wife. What's the difference between me and a wife? Nothing. A wife was a woman living with a man supporting her. I was living with Hashim, and he was supporting me. It was the same principle and logic.

It didn't occur to me that this money would get me used to a life that I couldn't sustain without him, and would set me on a path of holding out my hand to men. I didn't imagine that I was selling my body since I'd given my body to Hashim for free for so long. I didn't feel that I was selling my dignity. Hashim had already trampled on my dignity. I no longer had any left to sell.

None of that occurred to me. I felt strong, so strong that I'd dismissed my entire family and everyone else. I was no longer weak. I was no longer afraid. I set out with more courage, more insolence.

That Hashim never tried to give this money any meaning pushed me to my feeling of strength. He was always polite. He was always generous. In reality, it wasn't a big deal for him. He earned a lot. He didn't even notice what I took from him.

Since I started taking my salary from Hashim, I began feeling more afraid about him, afraid that he'd vanish from me. And I became even more jealous of him.

Hashim became both my love and my livelihood.

If Hashim disappeared, I would lose everything.

I began to impose myself on him more and more. I'd try to take more from him. I'd get jealous to the point of insanity. If I couldn't reach him at his house or at the clinic, no matter the time of day, I'd set out like a crazy woman, take a taxi, and go to his apartment. If I didn't find him there, I'd drive around looking for his car. I started asking him about his friends. I'd ask him where each of their bachelor apartments were so I could look for him there. Or, more specifically, to look for his car in front of the building, whenever I couldn't find him.

Hashim changed too once he started giving me a salary. He started ignoring me more, as if he had become more confident that I needed him. He was harsher when he talked to me on the phone. He started leaving his private line at the clinic off the hook so I couldn't bother him there. He started meeting me only when he didn't have anything else to do. It was no longer only his patients he preferred to me, but also his friends, his journals, his sister, everyone else. If we met, he was always in a rush. He'd take me quickly and then leave immediately. He even started declining when I suggested spending the night with him.

We still spent wonderful nights together and shared many sweet kisses. We even spent the weekend in Alexandria a bunch of times. We stayed at Hotel al-'Agami. He'd sign the hotel register: Hashim Muhammad 'Abd al-Latif and wife.

He cut off the title "Dr." and added the name "Muhammad." And I was the "wife." When we were there, I really did feel like I was his wife. I'd see him in his pajamas. I'd see him in the bathroom. I'd see him shaving. I'd sleep in his arms, his breath enveloping me, his heavy arm on my back. I'd wake up in the night and look over at his sleeping face. I'd chuckle at his puffy eyes, which were puffier when he was sleeping. I'd then rest my head on his shoulder and sleep, restful and sated.

When we woke up, I'd play the role of the perfect wife. I'd run a bath for him. I'd clean his shaving supplies. I'd pour tea for him as we had breakfast on the balcony. We'd then go out together to the shore and I'd put my arm in his to tell everyone: This man is my property. Mine!

He'd get annoyed when I did this and I'd feel him trying to pull his arm away gently. He'd act like he wanted to light a cigarette or lean over to play with the sand, just to pull his arm from mine, as if he wanted to tell people: I'm not hers. We met just by chance. But I kept insisting on putting my arm in his.

As soon we started the journey back to Cairo, this beautiful dream began to dissolve. I'd have to face the truth. I'd have to face my loneliness, my ruin, my confusion. The days that followed these trips were harsher and more bitter than the rest, days when my body suffered alone having gotten used to that heavy arm, when I was tortured by the reality that I wasn't Hashim's wife. I was just a fake name in a hotel register in Alexandria.

Fear would oppress me.

Fear that I'd lose Hashim one day.

Lose my love . . . and my livelihood.

Fear is what was made me think that Hashim had changed, that he was ignoring me, that he wasn't seeing me as he did before.

Fear also pushed me to something else.

To greed.

Nothing was enough for me anymore. Everything started to lose its value as soon as my hands touched it. I became like a sieve in which everything I put fell straight through.

Especially money.

The thirty pounds that I took from Hashim was no longer enough. I wanted more. I felt every month that I was about to lose Hashim, so I tried to take everything I could. And Hashim didn't ever refuse me money. He kept giving it to me simply, gently. But I wasn't asking simply or gently. I was lying to him and concocting reasons. I discovered that the best time to ask was when we were in bed, after he took me, and he was relaxed, calm, pleased with his manliness, happy with my femininity. I know now that this wasn't only the best time for Hashim, but also for every man I wanted something from. It was the peak of a man's conceit, his pride in his masculinity.

I started taking about sixty pounds a month from Hashim, thirty pounds as a fixed salary and the rest for odds and ends.

I spent excessively on myself, especially my clothes and makeup. This splurging was compensation for the damage that I was feeling and for my deterioration. I felt this in the eyes of my girlfriends and of all the people who knew my story with Hashim, who knew I wasn't his wife, but only his lover. I knew they were gossiping about me whenever I walked away from them. I wanted to stir up jealousy in these people, and this was the only way to do that.

I was delighted when I noticed looks of envy from my girlfriends and relatives whenever I appeared in a new dress or with a new piece of jewelry. They talked about my insanity, gossiping about my honor and principles, but they still coveted my new shoes.

I started to hate people.

Everyone.

Even those who thought that I really was Hashim's fiancée.

My hatred was making me more anxious and fearful. I tried to flee from fear, so I plunged forward into even more bragging, more insolence.

My mother didn't stay silent as she saw all this. Once day, she took me by the hand to my room and closed the door behind me. She sat down on the bed, her favorite place when she wanted to solve a problem, and she sat me next to her.

"Mitou," she said discreetly. "I can't keep quiet anymore. My husband is constantly making a scene because of you. I can't keep defending you, your behavior. I used to believe you. But now I don't."

"What don't you believe?" I asked indifferently.

"Tell me, where do you get this money from?"

"From Hashim."

She was surprised, terrified.

"Oh my God," she said, striking her chest with her hand. "That's money of sin!"

"Why sin?" I said, laughing at her naivete. "When a man loves a woman and gives her gifts, it's sin?"

"But it's not gifts, it's money!"

"A gift is money. If he buys me a piece of chocolate,

it means he gave me a dime. He doesn't have time to go out and buy anything, so he gives me the money for me to go and buy it."

"That's money of sin," she insisted.

"Why?" I asked, smiling at her. "All girls take gifts."

"Could you tell me why he gives you all this money?"

"Because he loves me."

"No, my dear. It's not for something else?"

"Don't say that, Mommy. There's no other reason. Believe me."

"No. I don't."

"He's a rich man and he loves me. If he gives me a hundred pounds, it's like someone else giving one pound."

"That's how much this rich man gives you?"

"Not always," I said bending the truth. "But he gives me a lot."

"What do you do with it?"

"I buy the things that you see."

"Fine," she said sighing. "But instead of buying these trivial things, spend it on something better for you, like a diamond or a brooch."

Just like that.

My mother yielded to me. She didn't try to fix my life. She didn't try to give me any principles to cling to. She just accepted the situation. I even started giving her the money I was taking from Hashim for her to hold for me. She became my bank. My mother became happier with this money than I was. Maybe I inherited my love for money from her. She even started picking out the gifts that I'd ask Hashim for. She opened my eyes to even bigger greed. For my twenty-second birthday, she wandered around the jewelry stores herself and picked out a diamond necklace that cost two hundred pounds for Hashim to give as a gift to me, and she left the rest for me to arrange. Hashim paid the two hundred pounds in one of the moments of pride in his manliness.

My mother also kept igniting my fear. She made me more and more afraid. She'd remind me all the time that I wasn't Hashim's wife. She'd tell me stories of girls who were pulled along behind their emotions. And then the man vanished, she'd say. He suddenly married another girl. Who knows, maybe I'd wake up one morning and read in the newspapers that Hashim had married another woman.

My heart pounded at the thought.

My nerves were shredded, and I felt like I was suspended in air, a furious wind tossing me around.

Hashim knew about my fears.

"We can't ever get married, Hashim?" I'd ask in hesitation and weakness.

"No," he said resolutely.

"But I can't live without hope," I said, looking at him in grief.

"When you think about getting married, you need to think about someone other than me."

"I can't think about anyone other than you," I said, tears in my eyes. "I love you, Hashim."

"Our love has no future," he said firmly as if discussing a medical matter.

"How do I know you won't marry someone else?"

"I'm not getting married."

"How can I be sure?"

"I've never lied to you," he said. "You can be sure."

But I wasn't.

My fears increased day after day.

I felt as if I was in an incredible battle with the next day. Every day for me was a wild animal that wanted to tear me apart. I'd cling to each day to try to stop it from throwing me to the next one. I started clinging to every hour so it didn't toss me to the next.

I knew I wasn't alone in wanting to marry Hashim. I wasn't the only one he wanted without marriage. There were dozens of girls around him, beautiful girls, girls from important families, rich girls. Every girl I saw at the club or whose picture I saw in the papers, I thought was trying to marry Hashim. And I hated them all. Hatred made me evil and harsh without realizing it.

I insisted every morning, as soon as I woke up, on reading the society page of the newspapers, just to check if he had gotten married. I wasn't reassured when I didn't find anything. Maybe the newspapers hadn't reported it yet. I'd then rush to the phone and call him to make sure he was still mine for at least another day.

One day, I was talking with Hashim on the phone when he told me he couldn't meet me that afternoon because he had to go for lunch at his uncle's. He then asked me what I was doing that afternoon. I told him that I was going to stay home. He asked me again. You're not going out?

His tone made me suspicious. He was gentler than usual.

I tried to get rid of the whispers gathering in my mind. I tried to feel reassured, to be calm. But I couldn't.

At three o'clock, I jumped up and left the house. I took a taxi to Zamalek. I passed by his building, but I didn't find his car. Maybe he parked at a distance so I wouldn't see his car. I circled the building in the taxi, all the streets leading to it, and I didn't find anything. I kept circling and I finally found his car. I told the driver to take me back to the apartment. I was a woman possessed.

I got out of the taxi, almost falling on my face, and ran up the stairs to the fourth floor. I threw all my weight on the buzzer and started banging on the door until my hands burned. I then took off one of my shoes and started hitting my heel on the door.

"Open up, Hashim!" I screamed. "Open up! I know you're inside!"

At that moment, I didn't care about anything except getting that door open. I didn't care about the scandal that I was creating in the building or the voice of the doorman yelling from the bottom of the stairs.

"What's going on? Who's screaming?"

Suddenly, the door opened. Hashim grabbed me and pulled me inside the apartment.

"You're crazy," he said in a low voice. "You want to make a scandal for me? Is this what good girls do?"

Before he could hit me, I pulled myself from him. At that moment, I had enough strength to raze mountains. I plunged forward inside the apartment.

And I saw her.

It was Mervat again.

Before Hashim caught me, I was digging my fingernails into her face, scratching long lines down her cheeks and neck. I then pulled her by her hair and threw her down to the ground. I jumped on top of her.

Hashim grabbed me. He yanked me by my hair, lifted me from on top of Mervat, and threw me on the bed.

"Filth!" I screamed with a crazed look in my eyes. "Lowlife! You're still coming to him? Don't you know he's married to me?"

Mervat fled.

Hashim then raised his hand up.

"Don't hit me! You have no right. You're the one who's wrong!"

He brought his hand down on my cheek. Mercilessly.

"Marry me!" I screamed, my tears flowing. "You have to marry me right now!"

"You want me to marry someone crazy?"

He raised his hand again.

"You have to marry me! I'm not like any girl just because you give me money."

He lowered his hand.

He turned his back to me without saying a word, catching his breath.

I collapsed in a heap on the bed. Everything was being drained away, my love, my dignity, my life, my very being.

He turned to me.

"I don't give you money because you're like any girl, Amina," he said in a serious tone. "I give you money because I love you, because you need it and because I have it. The day you leave me, I'll still give you money for as long as you need it and for as long as I have it."

I felt that he didn't mean what he was saying. He was just defending my honor to himself. He didn't want to feel that he was buying a woman. I discovered at that moment that this money wasn't disgracing just me but him as well. It was wounding his pride and conceit, since men like to think that every woman who shows an interest is actually in love.

"If you loved me, instead of giving me money, you'd marry me. You have to marry me, Hashim. You have to!"

"You know that I won't," he said calmly. "It's better that we leave each other."

I was terrified.

"You're going to leave me after all this, Hashim?"

I turned away and sobbed.

"No, Amina. Let's talk rationally."

Hashim came and sat next to me. He tried to quiet my tears. He began to caress my hair. He then moved his hand over my shoulder. But I didn't stop crying. He then leaned over and kissed me on my cheek.

"Stop, Amina," he said. "Stop, my love. I'm sorry."

I didn't want him at that moment. But another feeling was seizing me. I wanted to be sure that Mervat hadn't taken anything from him, anything that I was used to taking from him. I wanted to make sure that she'd left him to me safe and sound, that she hadn't sucked him up and tossed the leftovers to me.

I turned to him and threw myself into his arms, still crying.

"Hashim," I whispered. "I'm all yours, Hashim."

And I pressed my lips against his.

His hand worked energetically on the buttons of my dress.

"You're going to leave me, Hashim?" I whispered, his breath burning my eyes, his crazed lips roaming my face, his arms squeezing my naked body.

"Never. Never. I can't."

I was reassured.

Mervat hadn't taken anything from him.

I went home with my head throbbing. I didn't hate Hashim as much as I hated Mervat. I wanted to take revenge. I wanted to destroy her. Since I'd caught her that first time, I'd figured out her whole name. I'd also got her phone number.

I called her house and her mother picked up.

"This is the wife of Dr. Hashim 'Abd al-Latif," I told her.

"Hello, ma'am," she said politely.

"Has Mervat come home yet?" I asked boldly and calmly.

"No," she said with uncertainty in her voice. "Not yet."

"Okay. When she gets back, you'll see the scratch marks on her face. I'm the one who did that . . . because I caught her with my husband."

I hung up.

And I felt better. I felt calm.

The pleasure of this feeling lasted for a few days until Mervat's mother discovered that Hashim wasn't actually married.

10

I KNEW HOW BAD THINGS had gotten.

I couldn't bear it anymore.

I couldn't bear my life with him anymore.

I knew I had to forget Hashim.

I tried. I really tried.

Believe me.

I tried to cut him out of my life, cleanly, like I was using a knife.

I believed that it would be enough to decide to leave Hashim. Everything would be over. I'd wake up from this crazy anxiety and fear to live in stability and calmness. Then I'd go back and remind myself of the previous times that I tried to forget Hashim and failed. I'd tell myself, girl, you're in too deep.

I thought about how I'd bet my entire future on Hashim, that I could no longer get married. It wasn't enough that I was beautiful or that my mother and aunts knew half the city and could find me a groom, any time I wanted. My heart was filled with hatred, hatred for Hashim. I'd squandered my future, and maybe my daughter's future, and he hadn't given me anything except a few fleeting memories and some money.

My body ached for him, but I bore it.

I bore it for four weeks. I resisted. The effect of my resistance showed on my face. My face withered. It became sallow. My eyes were dull and swollen.

I started going out to the Heliopolis Club.

That's where I met Muhammad again, the first guy that I had met, before Hashim. He'd grown up. He was twenty-six, a year older than me. He'd gotten a job after he graduated from law school. He had a fine small mustache under his nose. I laughed when I saw him with his silly mustache.

I met Muhammad on the road as I was going to the club. He stopped his car next to me and leaned out.

"Bonsoir, miss," he said politely. "Do you remember me?"

I smiled. Of course, I remembered him. I forget women's faces, but never men's.

"How are you, Muhammad?"

"Good. Would you like a lift?"

"You're still very bold."

"Not at all, miss. I just feel that we're not strangers."

I got in next to him, just like that.

I met Muhammad a second time, then a third. I was impatient to talk to him and meet him, not because I was in love with him, but because I needed him to distract me from my state of crisis.

On the fourth time, I went with him to his apartment. I was surprised to learn that Muhammad's apartment was in Zamalek as well. It was near Hashim's.

Muhammad didn't know anything about my relationship with Hashim even though they lived in similar social circles. I was astonished that there was still anyone in Cairo who didn't know about it with all the rumors that I had stirred up.

I discovered that Cairo wasn't a single city. It was dozens of cities. What was happening in one of them, the others didn't hear about. Cairo was made of closed social circles so that a disgrace in one circle wouldn't reach another. Every circle has its own world, its own interests and scandals. The girl who was virtuous in one could be a sinner in another. One circle might refuse to marry her to one of its members, while another might accept her with open arms. It was only all over if someone's story appeared in the newspapers. And the newspapers hadn't gotten hold of mine.

I went up with Muhammad to his apartment, my knees shaking. I felt like I was going back to my life again, the life that I'd gotten used to, the life of bachelor pads.

I couldn't pretend this was the first time I'd done something like this. I was too weak to feign fear or terror or bashfulness or whatever girls are supposed to feel. I wanted to be free from all that, to be myself.

Muhammad sat opposite me, delighted. He couldn't believe I was with him. He was confused, not knowing where to begin. He seemed about to get close to me, but he was afraid to offend me so held back. He made small talk, to show me that he didn't want anything more than to be in my company.

I looked at him with clear eyes, a small smile on my lips. I tried to ease his confusion, to free him from his fear, to give him short responses to show him I didn't need to talk. I needed more.

Finally, Muhammad made a move.

He leaned over me and put his hand on my cheek, gently, hesitatingly, as if touching something precious and valuable, afraid that he would harm it simply by touching it. I smiled. He was still young. He didn't know me. His confusion and fear delighted my ego. I surrendered my cheek to him. I let his arm creep around me to embrace me to his chest. I let his lips wander until they reached mine. He gave me a shy, sweet kiss. I tried to fall into his kiss, to fall in love in it, but, suddenly, images from my torn-up life began flooding my mind. I felt anxious. I wanted to flee from my life and so I pressed my lips onto his. I kissed him more than he was kissing me. I kissed him in a way he hadn't experienced. He was driven forward with all his youth, all his being, smitten with me, that I was something more beautiful and more incredible than he was expecting.

He raised his eyes, dazzled, pulling me to him, asking me for permission to take more.

Should I give him more?

Why wait for the second meeting or the third? I knew I'd give him everything so why not today? Why are there traditions that a girl shouldn't give herself on the first date? I didn't believe in those customs. I was an honest, realistic woman. I'd be wasting my time pretending to be bashful and shy, when I wasn't. Maybe I could flee from myself.

And he took me.

I felt him panting like a child. I felt his breathlessness inflating my ego, returning my self-confidence to me, my belief in my future, that I could always find a man who would be dazzled by me and would want me so much, a man I could possess.

I was wearing a gold bracelet that I'd bought with Hashim's money. I tried to look away from it.

I centered all my thoughts at that moment on Muhammad. I was imagining a future with him. With him, I could be stronger than Hashim.

Muhammad was something else. He was different from the men I knew. I was confident that he loved me more and wanted me more, that I was stronger than him with my experience and intelligence. I could control him and make him move as I wanted. Muhammad made me feel the strength of my personality more than any other man.

Would I marry him?

This kind of guy doesn't marry a girl like me. He was from a well-known, rich family. He was his mother's only son. He had three sisters. I was divorced, I had a daughter, and I was his age too. He'd eventually hear about my adventures. All that would end any hope of marrying him. I knew all that. This kind of guy only married as a kind of transaction—a young girl from a rich family with a good reputation. No doubt his mother was working on that transaction at that moment.

But marriage didn't matter.

What was important was that I kept him.

He was a catch, even without marriage.

I decided to confess to him. Confession wipes away sin and inoculates people against gossip.

I began to confess my relationship with Hashim. I confessed to Muhammad with tears in my eyes. I didn't reveal all the details. But I confessed enough to inoculate him against people talking. Anything that he heard about me after that wouldn't be new to him.

Muhammad heard my confession with a sad expression in his eyes. He felt my scorn for Hashim. He promised to compensate me for all my suffering, to provide me with a new life, a sweet, amazing life.

That day, we left the apartment with me not regretting what I gave him. When I rode next to him in his car as he took me home, he turned onto the street where Hashim's apartment was located. I thought I saw Hashim's car.

I couldn't ask Muhammad to support me. He still thought that I was a girl from a well-to-do family whose father was supporting her. He couldn't imagine that I needed a man to support me. Maybe if he could, he'd be afraid of me and run away.

I kept meeting Muhammad.

Instead of forgetting Hashim, it only weakened my resistance for him. I resisted my love for him, my body's need for him, my desire to take revenge against him. But meeting Muhammad broke the chains that I was trying to jail myself with. It broke my will. My mind set out with all its might, all its desire, toward Hashim. He was something different from Muhammad. He could sate me. He could sate me fully and control every part of me, with his conceit, with his arrogance, and with his neglect for me.

I called Hashim after depriving myself of him for weeks.

I was firm and casual.

"Where've you been?" he asked, happy to hear my voice.

"I have to see you, Hashim."

"No," he said, hesitating. "Let's get used to not seeing each other."

"I need you. You can't leave me alone now. You have to help me."

"Okay."

"But I won't see you at your apartment."

"Why?"

"Because my family is very upset at me. They're keeping tabs on me. They know where your apartment is."

Of course, this wasn't true. But I was afraid that Muhammad would see me when I went to Hashim's apartment, which was close to his.

"So where can I see you?"

"At your friend Ra'uf's apartment."

"Okay. Tomorrow at four."

"No, today. I want to see you. I have to see you."

"Okay."

I made up a lie and left to see Hashim. I knew the address of Ra'uf's apartment from the many addresses, phone numbers, and license plates that I'd memorized to keep track of Hashim.

As I rang the bell waiting for Hashim to open the door, I felt overcome by weakness. I was collapsing before a man who had taken away all my pride, all my dignity, even my beauty and my youth. I was going back to him as a beggar.

Hashim opened the door.

I tried to cover my face with a stamp of sadness and grief, but I couldn't suppress the small smile on my lips as I looked at him.

He didn't take me in his arms.

He didn't kiss me.

It was as if many weeks hadn't passed since we last met, since we last touched each other.

"You lost weight."

"Why didn't you kiss me? Didn't you miss me?"

He looked at me for a bit. He then pulled me to his chest and tried to kiss me lightly, but I kissed him back. I drank and drank, but before my thirst was quenched, he pushed me away.

"Tell me," he said, taking a deep breath. "How are you?"

"Don't push me away. I missed you."

We sat on the couch, and I started talking with him, my eyes fixed on his face. I didn't want to talk to Hashim. I wanted him.

Hashim wasn't as he usually was. He was calm, not frantic. I thought he was acting, doing what he had to do to comply.

I didn't want him like that.

I didn't want to be respectable.

I wanted him violent, as I'd gotten used to.

I dug my sharp fingernails into his bare shoulder. He yelled out . . . and he hit me.

I took from him more than any other man could give me.

It was habit.

Not love.

Believe me.

It wasn't love.

Those days, I hated Hashim.

My life went back to how it was.

But now it was torn between two men, Hashim and Muhammad.

11

BACK THEN, MY MOTHER FOUGHT with me all the time.

I kept insisting that Hashim was planning to marry me, but she didn't believe it anymore. She cried constantly and cursed Hashim.

"This Hashim of yours has ruined our life and torn our family apart!" she'd scream at me.

My mother's husband was worse. One day he lost it.

"I'll divorce your mother if you stay in my house any longer! You think I don't know what you're doing? You're deviant! You have no place in a decent family. You belong on the street! In a cabaret! I have daughters. I'm afraid for their futures. Get out of my house! Out!"

My mother screamed. She threw herself on his chest.

"Shame on you! She has no one but you. She's your daughter. You've raised her since she was only three years old. Please!"

"I swear I'll divorce you," he continued. "Understand? If this daughter of yours isn't gone today. Shame on you. Aren't you afraid for our other daughters? For our family? Our reputation?"

I couldn't bear it anymore. I didn't cry. I didn't beg.

I grabbed my daughter roughly like I was picking up a sack of potatoes.

My mother clung to me, tears running down her cheeks.

"Wait, Mitou, please! Leave Huda," she said, reaching out to my daughter.

I gave her my daughter. And I left.

I was kicked out.

I went to my father.

I didn't go back again to my mother's house. I started only seeing her secretly, like we were two lovers, fearful that her husband would find out about us meeting and divorce her. We'd meet at the house of one of my aunts so I could see Huda. Sometimes we'd meet at the tailor. Sometimes at one of the stores on Qasr al-Nil Street.

I entered a new phase of life. My father rented another apartment in his building for me so he could have his fun with his wife and his cognac alone. He'd come by in the evening sometimes to sit with me.

He never kept tabs on where I was.

For the first time, I felt that I had my own home. When I was married, I was living at my mother-in-law's. When I was with my mother, the house belonged to her husband. But now, I had my own place.

I was alone.

I loved it.

I was free.

I'd go to meet Muhammad whenever I wanted.

I was even free from my daughter. 'Abd al-Salam came and took her from the maid when my mother wasn't home. He was insisting on me not seeing my daughter until I got married and lived a respectable life.

I had dark moments when I was afraid of facing life alone. I'd force myself out of this mood and remember that I wasn't alone. I had both Hashim and Muhammad.

I need not worry about my future, whether I built it legitimately or not. I had two men. If one of them left me, I'd still have the other. Both were rich. If neither married me, either could support me financially.

I then told Hashim about Muhammad. I told him a quarter of the truth, as usual.

"I've gotten to know someone named Muhammad," I said. "The son of Mahran Pasha, who passed away. Do you know him?"

"No," Hashim said curtly, turning his lips in annoyance.

"He's a very decent guy."

"Where'd you meet him?"

"In Heliopolis. At the club. You can't imagine how decent and polite this guy is."

"Everyone who meets a girl is decent and polite," he retorted. "At first."

"You're upset," I said, putting my head on his shoulder. "He's only twenty-six."

Hashim let out a loud laugh.

"You don't think there's anything between me and him?" I asked coyly.

"No, I don't believe you," he said, looking at me with pity.

He was conceited. I wanted him to interrogate me, to hit me. But he didn't, that cold conceited man.

Hashim's coldness increased day after day as if he'd given up on me. We started meeting only for one thing, to be done quickly, neglectfully, as if performing a duty, like brushing his teeth. If we had any time afterwards, we didn't have anything to talk about.

When I talked to him about Muhammad, Hashim began telling me about Nagwa. I never saw her in the flesh, but I saw a lot of her in Hashim's eyes. One day I found him sitting in the apartment with his eyebrows knitted, a sad look in his eyes. A long time passed before he said anything or got close to me.

"What's wrong?" I asked him.

"Nothing."

Another period of silence passed.

"Imagine," he said suddenly. "A girl who's nineteen, beautiful, lovely like a rose, with a heart condition? Why? Why didn't I get rheumatism in my heart? I'm old and I've lived life. But her? She's only nineteen."

I knew Hashim was tortured by his patients, but I hadn't ever seen him so sad, so compassionate. I felt this Nagwa was more than a patient for him.

"Why are you so upset? Aren't there a million girls with rheumatism in the heart?"

"Not like Nagwa. If you saw her father and her mother, what they're like. They're both old. They don't have anyone but her."

"God willing, she'll die," I said, a tempest of hatred tearing out of me.

He looked at me in disgust.

"You're inhuman," he said in a voice as sharp as a knife, after a cold silence. "You're heartless."

He then went silent, not wanting to talk about his patient to a monster like me.

I too was quiet, feigning indifference, jealousy eating away at me.

I became jealous of Muhammad too.

But my jealousy for Muhammad was born more out of anxiety. I knew there wasn't a woman more beautiful than me in his life. And I was still new, so I wasn't afraid he was bored with me. I'd already confessed to him about Hashim. I even told him that Hashim was the one who supported me financially, that he'd done it for six years. I painted a tragic picture where I was the victim of a man I once loved, who now abused me.

The day I told him, Muhammad was at a loss.

"I'm ready to support you," he said.

"No, Muhammad. You're the only love in my life. I thought I loved Hashim. But after I met you, I realized that I was deluded. I don't want you to bear responsibility for me, for my bad circumstances. I want to love you like any girl who's in love with a man without any financial burden. That's my right, my right to be like any other girl."

Muhammad was touched.

He thought I was a victim.

The victim of Hashim.

"Mitou," he said, his voice filled with agony, "I'm ready to save you from your life, to save you from Hashim, that criminal. I'm ready to marry you after . . ."

"No, Muhammad," I cut him off. "Don't bring up marriage."

I didn't love Muhammad, but I was propelled forward with him. Hashim's ignoring me pushed me to him more and more. I started to despise Hashim. I wanted to humiliate him, to take revenge against him.

I was no longer careful. I'd go to meet Hashim at his apartment at four o'clock, give myself to him, and then, after he left, I'd walk out in plain daylight and go over to Muhammad's apartment in front of all the neighbors. I'd then give myself to Muhammad and stay with him until nine o'clock. I'd go back home and call Hashim, telling him that I'd been home since I left him.

This became my life.

I was tortured by anxiety. My face became paler and my body was numb. I had to fake it. I faked passion. I faked my screams. I did it so well that neither of them felt they were taking a body that was already dead. I started needing more violence, to escape the chasm I was living in. I needed to suffer so that I could scream, so that my senses and my body didn't dry up and die.

Then something else happened.

Some of 'Abd al-Salam's friends intervened to let me see my daughter. They thought everything that had happened to me and all my insane behavior was because my daughter had been taken away from me.

'Abd al-Salam agreed to let me see my daughter, but only at his house in Suez. I went there for the first time with a friend of his and his wife. I felt I was stepping back in time, to when I was still a girl intoxicated by her youth, her beauty, her love.

His mother refused to see me. I sat with the friend and his wife for more than half an hour before 'Abd al-Salam came in holding my daughter's hand. I fell to my knees and hugged her to my chest.

As he was saying goodbye to me, 'Abd al-Salam told me he'd agreed to let me see my daughter every week in Suez.

Two days passed in which I tried to reform myself. Alone in my apartment, with only my father's brief evening visits, it wasn't long before I went back to Hashim and Muhammad.

The following week, I went to see my daughter in Suez. I couldn't bear going on the train or the bus, so I asked Hashim to drive me. It was a Friday, but he refused. I tried to tempt him by saying that we could go to Ain Sokhna afterwards, that he could relax after his long week at work. But he still refused. I shifted my efforts to Muhammad, who was delighted. I should have gone to him from the start, but somehow, I still considered myself property of Hashim.

Muhammad dropped me off just as we entered Suez so that 'Abd al-Salam wouldn't see me with him. I told Muhammad to pick me up at the same place in two hours. Then I got in a taxi and went to 'Abd al-Salam's house. I saw my daughter. It was so hard to leave that I stayed for three or four hours.

I went back in a taxi to find Muhammad waiting for me. He was furious with me for being so late so I decided to make it up to him. When we got to Cairo, I went to his apartment and spent the night with him.

Maybe it was the first time Muhammad had spent all night with a woman. His mother found out and was terrified. She declared me her enemy. I'd spoken with Muhammad's sisters on the phone just as I spoke with Hashim's sister. I'd even met his mother. All sisters have a fake, delicate way of talking to the girlfriends of their brothers. All mothers too. But after Muhammad spent the night with me, their treatment changed and became malicious.

I started spending the night with Muhammad every week when we went to Suez. I felt a malicious joy about it, but also grief because Hashim didn't ever spend the night with me in Cairo. I would tell Hashim I was sleeping at my cousin's. I wasn't sure if Hashim believed my lie or not, but I loved lying to him. Every lie was a victory over him.

After a while, my daughter was no longer the primary reason for traveling. Seeing her became ordinary and boring as if she were living with me. I started traveling to be with Muhammad, to feel that I was far from Hashim, independent from him, even if for a day or two.

My nerves got more and more frayed, though.

I started thinking about suicide. I'd cry, hoping God would save me, save me from myself, from my insanity. No one could save me except for Hashim. If only he cared about me more, if only he felt jealous of me, if only he expressed what he was really thinking, if only he threatened me or reassured me of his love. I thought about confessing everything, that there was another man in whose arms I spent entire nights. But I was afraid that I'd lose him. He became colder and more neglectful. I felt him moving away from me with his heart and his mind. I felt there was another girl in his life. Perhaps it was Nagwa. He refused to talk about her, but I saw her in his eyes, in his distraction. All I knew about her was that she lived on Haram Street.

"How's it going with Muhammad?" he surprised me once.

"Muhammad who?" I asked, not looking him in his eye.

"You don't know someone named Muhammad?"

"I know ten Muhammads," I said. "Which one do you mean?"

"None of those ten. I mean the eleventh."

"Don't play games with me. Tell me what's on your mind."

"Whatever I ask, you'll deny it. You'll swear on your daughter. You'll swear on the Qur'an. I know you. You refuse to accept that I'm not your husband no matter how much you lie to yourself. You can be with someone else whenever you want, and you and I will stay friends. Maybe that would be better for us."

"I'm not lying to you. The day I meet someone, I'll tell you."

"You just don't get it. Our love has gone sour."

"I still love you, Hashim. I love you like I did at the beginning, and more."

"Fine."

And then he left.

He didn't try to save me from myself. He didn't try to intervene to limit my freedom, my freedom that was killing me.

My nerves were becoming more frayed.

I felt anxious whenever I lay down in Hashim's bed or in Muhammad's bed. I wanted to escape my own my skin.

Then, one weekend, Hashim had had a constant

headache all week and he decided to get away to al-'Al-amein, which was on the Mediterranean outside of Alexandria. I managed to convince him to take me with him.

We stayed in a small hotel with only four rooms. It was quiet and classy, overlooking the road to Marsa Matruh and the World War I cemetery of white grave-stones that extended out in front. A wide stretch of salty land separated it from the sea, glittering with what looked like stars or tiny diamonds. Country girls in their splen-did clothes and their sweet naive smiles stood around outside the hotel. The color of the sea was a clear blue that you wouldn't see anywhere else. It was magical. I felt like I was in a movie.

When we arrived, Hashim wrote his name in the hotel ledger as he usually did: Hashim Muhammad 'Abd al-Latif and wife. He didn't use "doctor." We went up to our room, took off our clothes, and put on our bathing suits. I put on the one with blue stripes, which Hashim had bought for me. We then went walking on the salty ground, on the stars, on the tiny diamonds, until we got to the sea. No one was there. He and I were completely alone. Hashim was calm, distracted, silent. Maybe he was thinking about his patients. I was happy, in love with everything around me. The fresh air on my skin caressed me tenderly and sweetly, like a gentle lover's hand. I was looking at Hashim and feeling that I wanted to live inside him. I wanted to love him.

I remembered Muhammad and felt his fingerprints on my skin. I felt that I wouldn't ever be able to give to Hashim a clean body, that I wouldn't ever be able to enjoy him unless I shed my filthy skin and put on clean skin.

I was suffocated.

I turned to Hashim.

"Let's go walk around a bit."

He got up from the sand and walked next to me. There was no one around at all except for the two of us. I was overwhelmed by this feeling that I wanted to be free of my skin.

We got to a bend hidden by boulders.

I took off my bathing suit and tossed it away.

I was naked.

Totally naked.

I felt free, free from the prison of my own skin. I felt I'd taken it off, gotten rid of a heavy weight. I felt a delicious calm.

I lay down naked on the sand, my eyes imploring Hashim to come to me.

He looked at me annoyed and grumbled something that I didn't hear. He then turned his back to me and sat on one of the boulders.

I got up and then I threw myself in the sea, naked, a new person from when I arrived there in my bathing suit.

"Come, Hashim," I screamed. "The water is wonderful!"

He ignored me. He then got up and walked off.

I left the water, running after him, naked, screaming. "Hashim! Hashim!"

I caught up with him and clung to him.

"Don't do this, Hashim," I begged him.

He looked at me with such pity.

He wasn't upset. He didn't hit me. No. He only pitied me. In his eyes, I was only . . . a crazy woman.

That day I felt I took on a new skin, that I had cleansed myself. But no, some stains can never be wiped away.

12

MARRYING MUHAMMAD BECAME MY BIG hope. It was the only thing that could restore my life, restore my reputation, my respect before my family and friends, and the social circle that I lived in. Marrying someone like Muhammad was as good as any of my friends could hope for. His mother was trying to engage him to girls from other well-known families in Egypt. If I was the one who married him, it would mean I was better than them all. And Muhammad was the one who could compensate me for my love for Hashim. The only one who could make a respectable girl of me, heal me of my jealousy, liberate me.

I knew Muhammad wouldn't be able to marry me unless he defied his family. They wouldn't ever agree to him marrying me. They knew more about me than even Muhammad knew himself. They brought him stories about me, but he didn't believe them since he loved me. Could Muhammad defy his family and sacrifice them for me?

I wasn't so sure.

He promised me he would.

He swore that his mother would eventually give in because she couldn't sacrifice him. He was her only son.

He wanted me to give up Hashim entirely.

I couldn't. Not yet. Hashim was the only weapon I had to push Muhammad to defy his family. I wouldn't give up this card until the last moment, until I saw the marriage official with my own two eyes.

So, I stayed with the two of them.

Hashim and Muhammad.

I was tired.

I was torn up. I couldn't go on for much longer. My body couldn't take it and neither could my nerves.

They each had time to relax during the day. I was the one who didn't have a break.

Hashim would meet me during the daytime, and he'd sleep at night. Muhammad would sleep during the day and meet me in the evening. As for me, I didn't sleep. I had to be sure that one of them was asleep before I went to meet the other. I even sometimes met both on the same night. I'd spend the night with Hashim until one o'clock, and then he'd bring me back home. I'd call Muhammad and ask him to come. I'd go out with him until five. I'd ask permission from each of them every time I went out to prove that he was my man.

Each of them felt responsible for me. I'd consult with each about everything, and they'd each give me lots of advice. Of course, I wouldn't listen. Either could leave me at any moment without saying goodbye. Why didn't one of them marry me instead of giving me endless advice?

Muhammad would see the bruises that Hashim left on my body. He'd get angry and go crazy with jealousy.

Hashim would see the bruises that Muhammad left on my body, and he'd be disgusted. He'd look at me as if

I was something that nauseated him, even though I kept swearing to him that I'd bumped into a table or tripped going up the stairs.

"You know my body is delicate," I'd tell him.

He'd look at me as if he didn't believe a word I said.

Hashim didn't take up my time as much as Muhammad did since he was always busy with his patients or he was just ignoring me. Muhammad was free. He'd go to the company where he worked in the morning and leave at one o'clock in the afternoon to have lunch and nap until the evening. He'd then be free for me until the following morning, either with me or talking with me on the phone.

I didn't try hard to dupe Hashim since he'd still kiss me even if he discovered a lie. He was pushing me down this road. Each of us knew our love was withering. As for Muhammad, his love was new and it still had all its heat. It took a lot of effort to keep duping him.

I was more afraid of Hashim. I was afraid that he'd leave me suddenly and before I'd married Muhammad. And besides, I wanted to be the one who left him. I knew I'd go crazy if he left me first. All that pushed me to chase him more, to always be sure he was at his clinic or at home or out with his friends, to be sure some other woman hadn't taken him from me.

Until one day, I called around for Hashim as usual and I didn't find him. I went out like a madwoman. I took a taxi and searched for him. I didn't find him at his apartment. Then I remembered Nagwa, that sick girl who made him so dreamy, and that she lived on Haram Street. I told the driver to go there. As we came out of the tunnel, I saw Hashim on the other side of the road, driving back in his car. He was driving slowly, smoking a cigarette with a sleepy smile on his lips, as if he was the happiest man in the world.

I told the driver to turn around and follow Hashim's car. As we caught up to him, Hashim saw me and pulled over.

I stopped the taxi, paid the fare, and jumped in Hashim's car.

"Where were you?" I demanded.

"Don't ask," he scowled. "You don't have any right. We broke up a long time ago. You can do whatever you want. All I ask is that you let me do what I want."

"Are you serious, Hashim?"

"Of course I'm serious."

"We've broken up?"

"You know we broke up a long time ago."

"No. I didn't know. I didn't leave you. You don't have the right to leave me. You can't after all you did."

Hashim didn't respond.

I was sobbing and I started slapping my cheeks and stamping my feet on the floor of the car. Hashim wasn't moved. My tears didn't have any effect on him.

"Could you stop crying?" he asked coldly. "We're in the street."

"You care about nothing but yourself! You want me to scream so people can see how the famous doctor treats good girls?"

"Good girls don't scream in the street," he said in an icy tone.

My heart filled with malice. I wanted to hit him, to tear up his face with my fingernails. But I could only cry.

Hashim took me back to my apartment.

"Goodbye," he said as I got out of the car without turning to him.

"May God make you pay for what you've done to me," I said, slamming the car door behind me.

He took off before I got to the building door.

I quieted my tears as soon as I went into my apartment. Some were real, but I had a stock of tears I could squeeze out whenever I needed them. I didn't believe Hashim when he said he'd left me. I knew he only said that because he was embarrassed that I caught him coming back from Nagwa's. I knew I could always get Hashim back.

I called Muhammad and he said he'd come get me at nine. I went to shower, standing under the water and thinking about how I could make up with Hashim and get him back. I got out of the bathroom and started getting dressed. I wore a black dress that revealed my shoulders. I put my hair up. I put on long diamond earrings, which Hashim had bought for me. I'd decided to make it a big night with Muhammad, to take revenge on Hashim.

Before I finished getting ready, an idea came to me.

I squeezed my eyes to make my tears flow. I brought my years of pain out of my storehouse. I picked up the phone and called Madiha, Hashim's sister. As soon as I heard her voice, I broke out into sobs.

"Madiha, this is Amina. I want to tell you that if anything happens to me, your brother is to blame. I've had it. I can't live anymore. I've put up with enough. I have no one left but God. I'm going to our Lord. Tell your brother he won't be able to live after me. He won't be able to. Our Lord will take revenge against him for me."

"Don't talk like that, Amina!" Hashim's sister screamed. "Just calm down and tell me what happened."

"It's no use," I said. "I've had it. I've given up. I've put up with your brother for six years. It's enough. There's nothing left after this. Tell your brother I'm dead. I'm free of him."

I hung up.

I went back to my mirror, wiped my tears away, and finished putting on my makeup.

I knew Madiha wouldn't be able to get in touch with her brother until the following morning or at least not until late at night after he came back from his evening out. Hashim would try to call me and then I'd convince him that I tried to commit suicide, but my father saved me. No doubt, he'd take pity on me and make up.

That was my plan.

I finished putting on my makeup. I put on the mink stole that Hashim bought me and I went out to meet Muhammad.

Muhammad got out of his car to meet me as usual.

And suddenly a car pulled up next to his.

A breathless woman got out with a man next to her.

I was stunned.

It was Madiha and her husband. They came to save me.

Madiha stood in front of me aghast, looking at me and then at Muhammad as if she didn't understand what was happening.

"I'm sorry," she then mumbled. "I came to make sure you're okay."

She looked at me again and then at Muhammad.

I collected myself.

"I'm good, thank God," I said calmly. "I recovered. I found there was another way."

I kept my calm, I didn't even tremble.

Madiha shook her head. She and her husband then got back in their car. They watched as I got into Muhammad's car next to him.

I began to wake up from the shock. My heart began to beat fast.

"You know who that was?" I asked looking ahead into the black night.

"Who?" Muhammad asked, disinterested.

"Hashim's sister."

"Really?"

"I decided this morning that I'm leaving Hashim. I've had it. I can't bear it anymore."

I then broke down in tears.

I was crying real tears. I was crying in rage at the failure of my plan. I was crying for fear of losing Hashim. A sharp siren of hatred for Hashim's sister set out from my heart. I hated her. I hated her for believing me and coming to save me. I hated her because she had exposed me. I hated her. I still do, even today.

My mind began to spin. Maybe this could be a good thing. I could tell Muhammad he was the reason for my split with Hashim and make him bear responsibility for me. His conscience and his decency wouldn't let him flee from this, no matter how much his mother and sisters opposed it.

"That's it, Muhammad," I said in the voice of the martyr. "I have no one in the world but you."

Muhammad reached out, took my hand, and squeezed it tenderly.

"We'll get married, Mitou," he said. "I promise."

I spent that night with him, crying until five in the morning. I told him stories about Hashim's despicableness and the torture that he made me suffer. I gave myself to him, as if I was bribing him to marry me. That night, I didn't ever want to part from Muhammad.

As soon as Muhammad brought me home, I fell into the well, the deep well that Hashim had dug in my chest. I forgot immediately about the night I had spent with Muhammad. I found all my mind, all my heart full of Hashim, looking for a way to get him back. Every part of me was tortured longing for him. My chest was tight. I was overcome by fear as I imagined life without Hashim. He alone was my man.

There were still some threads of hope. Maybe his sister wouldn't tell him what happened, or she'd think it was only a mistake because I was angry at him.

I didn't sleep.

I was awake until Hashim arrived at the clinic. Then I called him.

"Good morning," I said, trying to sound calm.

I didn't start off by apologizing. I was still clinging to hope that his sister hadn't told him.

"Good morning, Amina," Hashim responded, his voice pained.

He was quiet.

"Are you free today?" I asked, my voice shaking. "Can I see you?"

"There's no need for us to see each other."

I imagined a bitter smile on his lips.

"Your sister told you," I said in a trembling servile voice. "Right?"

"Of course."

"Your sister hates me," I said, raising my voice. "She should've let me tell you myself. I was planning on telling you everything."

"You were planning on telling me what?"

"That you're the reason. You think I can catch you coming back from a girl's house and then you tell me that you've left me? See, you wanted me to kill myself. That would be better for you!"

"Regardless, we really have broken up."

"But I don't want to leave you. I can't leave you."

"I left you because it's best for you. You don't know what you're doing. What you're doing to yourself, being with two men at the same time, is the worst thing possible. If you get used to that, I'll find you standing under some streetlamp. As long as you're with someone else, it's over."

"But I don't love him. I love you, Hashim."

"So, why go out with him?"

"Because you drove me crazy. You made me do it. You're the reason."

"A decent girl doesn't do that, no matter what. You're not decent. You've never been in love. You just needed me. Goodbye."

He hung up on me.

I went insane.

I tried to call back, but he took the phone off the hook. I tried to call the main clinic line, but he didn't respond. I spent the whole day trying to call him. I tried more than thirty times.

The world narrowed before my eyes. I imagined that I really was standing under some streetlamp.

I ran to Muhammad for him to save me from myself. I spent another night with him.

The anguish, the insanity, my longing for Hashim all rushed back as soon as I left him. I was surprised at myself. Why all this longing, all this love, only now that Hashim was about to leave me? When I felt like Hashim was mine, I'd despise him and play games. I was like a little child who could go too far when she was next to her mother, sure of her protection, but when the mother goes away, she stops playing. She's afraid and cries.

I was able to get in touch with Hashim the following day.

He refused to meet me.

I became crazier. I could no longer stand to be alone for a single moment, so I ran to Muhammad. I met him in the morning, in the evening. I ate lunch with him and dinner. But Hashim still filled my heart and mind.

Five days later, I was coming back from Muhammad's apartment in a taxi when I spotted Hashim in his car. He saw me. He gave me a blank look.

I smiled at him. It was a fearful, trembling smile.

He drove off quickly. I told the driver to follow him. He looked at me in the mirror and started going down one street and then turning quickly to another. The taxi driver kept following him.

I knew Hashim would eventually stop because he was afraid of a scandal. He was afraid that people would notice that there was a girl chasing him in a taxi.

He finally stopped at an isolated spot on the same street where Umm Kulthum lived.

I jumped out of the taxi, and I got in next to him. My blood ran cold. My face lost its color.

"What do you want?" he asked in a stern voice.

"I want you," I said trying to smile.

"Lord, I'm being tortured by you," he muttered to himself. "I must've committed a big crime, a very big crime."

"Against me," I said calmly.

"How do I atone for this crime? Tell me what to do. What do you want from me?"

"Marry me."

"Again?" he said mockingly, looking at me like I was crazy. "This again? After all you've done?"

"I didn't do anything."

He let out a deep sigh of disgust.

"Listen, Amina. You know we're not ever going to get married. And you know you can't live with me without getting married. The only way forward is for you to leave me."

"Hashim, that was the first time I went out with that guy your sister saw me with. I know his sister. I called her when I was upset, and he picked up the phone. I asked him to come and take me out."

"I know you've been with him for a long time. I know you go to his apartment. There are people who've seen you. I've seen him right by my apartment in Zamalek."

"Lies!" I screamed. "You heard that from girls who are jealous because I'm with you, because I love you."

"Amina, I'll stand beside you until you marry him. You know you're beautiful. Don't believe that your reputation is lost. And don't think you can't marry a guy like Muhammad because he's from an important family and won't marry a divorced woman with a child. What's important is that he loves you. You just have to know that there's a difference between a woman who goes out with a guy to marry him and one who goes out with a guy knowing he won't marry her. There's a big difference."

I felt Hashim's words like pins pricking my heart. I couldn't bear it. I couldn't be so cheap for Hashim that he agreed to give me to another man. I felt like I was worth nothing, I was just some cheap woman to him.

"Hashim. I'm not with him. I don't want to be with him. I only want to be with you. If I'm going to get married, I'll marry you or I won't get married at all."

Hashim looked at me in disgust.

13

I STARTED TAKING MORE MONEY from Hashim. I wanted at least to have saved enough to take care of myself. I told him that, point blank. I told him that I wanted to ensure my future. I wanted to guarantee that I wouldn't be destitute. I begged him. He told me he'd bear financial responsibility for me until I got married. He agreed to open a bank account in my name. He gave me a hundred pounds to put in it. Then another hundred. In a few months, I managed to save seven hundred.

Muhammad kept offering to support me.

"I want to feel that I'm your man," he'd tell me. "I want to feel that I'm responsible for you. I don't want to see you wearing a dress bought with Hashim's money or holding a purse that I didn't give you."

"Soon," I'd say smiling. "When we get married. No one is responsible for me except my father. Don't think that my father isn't supporting me financially."

I didn't want Muhammad to give me money because I knew the day I accepted it from him, I'd be excusing him from marrying me.

Muhammad compensated me with a lot of gifts. He gave me a chic handbag with a gold handle. He gave me a ring decorated with small diamonds and one large pearl. He gave me another gold ring with a turquoise stone. I always had one of his gifts on me when I went to meet Hashim. I don't know why. Maybe I was savoring going to him with a piece of Muhammad on me, so he knew Muhammad was giving me expensive gifts.

Then, I got pregnant.

I was more disgusted at myself than ever. I felt that this entire mess was sitting in my stomach. I felt exposed, not to others but to myself.

Whose child was this in my belly? I tried to work out when I could've gotten pregnant. In the end, it didn't matter. It was still a child conceived in sin. Its fate was inevitable: abortion.

My psychological state got much worse.

I tried to convince myself this wasn't anything new, but it was different. The first time, one of the two men was my husband, and there was always hope that the child would be legitimate. This time, I didn't have any hope to cling to. This child would be born in shame, one hundred percent. There were other times I had gotten pregnant when I was only with Hashim and I kept telling myself that the baby would be the offspring of love, even if it was fantasy. But now, this baby would be the offspring of whose love? Hashim's or Muhammad's? No. It was the offspring of insanity, my insanity.

I called Hashim and asked him to come visit me in the morning to have a cup of coffee with me. When he came, I couldn't face him as I had when he'd gotten me pregnant in the past. I couldn't be coy with him about my pregnancy or ask him to give me an extravagant amount of money. I couldn't. I was weak.

"I'm pregnant," I told him, my head bowed.

Hashim looked at me and hesitated for a bit. He then put his hand in his pocket and took out twenty pounds, the fee for the doctor who would carry out the abortion, and tossed it in my lap.

"Didn't I tell you to be careful?" he asked coldly. "You're going to hurt yourself like this. Any more of these operations will affect you later, when you're older."

He said goodbye and left.

I then went to see Muhammad at his apartment.

I was stronger with Muhammad than Hashim. I let Muhammad hug me to his chest and squeeze me in his arms, kissing me with the heat of his love. Then, suddenly, I moved away, and sat on a chair. He came up behind me, worried.

"Leave me now, Muhammad," I said in a sad voice. "Please."

"What's wrong, Mitou?" he asked, his breath hot.

I put my head in my hands. Muhammad enveloped me in his arms.

"What happened?"

"I don't want to tell you, Muhammad."

"You have to tell me."

"No," I said, hesitating a little.

"You have to tell me."

"I'm pregnant, Muhammad," I said in a choked voice.

His eyes grew wide.

"Impossible," he said, terrified. "What are we going to do?"

"I don't know, Muhammad. I'm scared of the operation. I'm afraid."

"I'm ready to do whatever you say."

"There's nothing to do but the operation," I said. "But I'm afraid I'll die during it."

I didn't even bother mentioning getting married. I learned from Hashim that if I asked to get married at a moment like that, the natural response of men would be that getting married had to happen before getting pregnant.

I just let Muhammad soothe me.

Muhammad was the one who went with me to the doctor, but I didn't let him go up with me to the clinic. I left him waiting for me on the street. He insisted before I left on paying for the procedure. I could only refuse for so long. I was weak before money.

"Why not?" Muhammad insisted. "I'm the father!"

He then gave me another twenty pounds.

I went into the doctor's clinic. This was the fourth time that I went to him. The nurse and the doctor weren't the only ones who couldn't hide their disgust at me. I was disgusted at myself.

I lay down on the operating table without any fear, like I was sitting down on the hairdresser's chair, with an incredible determination to end this life.

I went back down four hours later.

I found Muhammad waiting for me, his face eaten up by anxiety.

I felt a tremendous determination. I had to marry Muhammad. But first, I had to give up Hashim.

Muhammad was my only hope if I wanted to get out of this misery, to have a house and kids, to live a good life that I could be proud of.

I began to press Muhammad. We no longer talked about anything but marriage.

I started threatening him. If you don't marry me, I'll leave you.

"You know who called me today?" I asked him one day.

"Who?"

"Hashim."

"What does he want from you?" he asked sharply.

"He wants to marry me," I said in a serious tone. "He keeps begging me to make an appointment for him with my father. He wants to meet him soon."

"What did you tell him?"

"Nothing."

"You can't marry him, Mitou. He's a scoundrel."

"I have to get married, Muhammad," I said resolutely. "I can't live like this. If you don't marry me, I have to marry Hashim."

"You know we're going to get married," he pleaded. "Bear with me until I convince my mother."

"I can't bear it anymore," I said with stronger resolve. "We've been together for two years."

"Trust me," he said, his eyes resting on my face. "Believe me. You know how things are."

I kept pressing him, emotionally blackmailing him, stirring up his jealousy, toying with his need for me.

Finally, he told his mother. He told her that he wanted to marry me.

His mother tore at her clothes as if she'd prefer that her son commit suicide in front of her instead. His sisters slapped their cheeks. His entire family turned against him, all his friends too.

I began to live in a state of war against them. I was strong. The secret of my strength was that Hashim was still with me. Whatever happened to me, I could always get strength from him.

I took Muhammad away from them all. I took him from his home, from his mother and sisters, from his friends. His entire life became mine. He started being unable to live except with me. If his mother wanted him back, she had to agree to marry us first.

I insisted that I'd only marry him with the agreement of his family, with a big wedding. I imagined everyone who had talked about me all these years surrounding me and congratulating me for my marriage to one of the most eligible bachelors of Cairo. I was confident of Muhammad's love, confident of his promise, confident that he loved me, and that he couldn't break his promise.

My devotion to Muhammad made me see Hashim less, but I still found a way to talk with him at least twice a day. I always found a way to meet him too, whether he came to have morning coffee, or I went to meet him at his apartment.

I didn't tell Hashim anything about what was happening between me and Muhammad. I was still pretending that I didn't have a relationship with anyone but him. And he didn't ask any questions.

I spent New Year's Eve with Muhammad, alone in his apartment. It was the first New Year's that I spent with a man. Hashim would usually host a New Year's party at his house. During the seven years I was with him, he never invited me to this party. He'd leave me alone to spend the evening with some of my relatives or alone at home. I usually spent the night miserable, tears in my eyes, wondering what Hashim might be up to with another woman, and then I'd look up when the clock struck midnight and blow Hashim a kiss.

As soon as I woke up the next afternoon, I called Hashim.

"Happy New Year," I told him, yawning and stretching.

"You too."

"What'd you do?" I asked.

"Nothing," he said. "I was asleep by one o'clock."

I was surprised. Like every year, I imagined Hashim dancing and laughing and flirting with women. These thoughts pushed me to give even more of myself to Muhammad.

"How's that?" I asked, feeling disappointed.

"I was tired. I didn't feel like going out so I went to bed."

A period of silence passed as if we were each keeping something from the other.

"Listen, Amina," Hashim said, calm and serious. "What do you think about us turning over a clean slate?"

"What does that mean?"

"Start getting yourself used to being only with Muhammad," he said. "Only be with one man. Stop seeing me. Stop calling me. We'll stay like that for a year, and next year, on the same day, call me. God willing, you'll tell me the good news that you got married."

"I know what you want," I yelled, jumping up out of bed. "You want to weaken me. You know that if you leave me now, I'll crumble. No. I won't let you leave me. You can't leave me until after I marry Muhammad. One of you has to marry me before the other leaves me."

"Amina, be reasonable. A woman who's with two men can never be strong. A strong woman has strong principles. And there is no principle that says a woman should be with two men at the same time."

"That's ridiculous. Principles are worthless these days. I've grown up and I've become practical. If principles were useful, you would've married me by now."

"Amina, you know we have to leave each other. We've tried a hundred ways to leave each other. There's nothing left but for us to cut it off. We have to."

"Not now!" I screamed.

"It's over, Amina. I'm leaving you with a clean conscience. I'm leaving you enough money for two years. I'm leaving you things you can sell and live from for five years. I'm leaving you with a good man who loves you and you can rely on."

"You're a scoundrel!" I screamed. "You don't have the right to leave me."

"Sorry. I've decided."

"You decided? You think you can do without me? You're forty. You won't meet anyone like me, anyone who loves you like me."

"Goodbye, Amina. Take care."

And he hung up on me.

I went crazy.

I called him back.

"I told you not to call until next year," he said furious as soon as he heard my voice.

He hung up on me.

He took the phone off the hook.

The phone was off the hook for two hours. I called his number every minute, expecting him to pick up, sure that Muhammad wouldn't notice that my phone was busy because he was still asleep at home.

Hashim eventually put the phone back on the hook. As soon as he did, I got through.

"Don't hang up, please," I said as soon as he picked up. "I'm not playing around. I want to talk to you about something important."

"What?"

"The money."

Money wasn't the only thing, but it was a pretext to convince Hashim to meet me. Maybe after I met him, I could convince him to stay with me.

"You're now with a man who can support you. Go ask him."

"You're just like other men. You don't pay except for what you take."

"I'm better than the rest of them. You'll learn that soon."

He hung up.

Had I lost my dignity to that degree?

I kept trying to call Hashim for five days. Every day, I dialed him more than twenty times. He'd hang up in my face or not pick up. I even tried to find him in a taxi. I was afraid. I was afraid of Muhammad. I was afraid he'd catch me chasing Hashim, and he'd leave me too. This was the first time that I was so afraid of Muhammad leaving me. Weakness began to overcome me.

One night, Muhammad brought me back at one o'clock in the morning. As soon as got home, I picked up the phone and I dialed Hashim.

He picked up.

I heard the ring of submission in his voice.

"Shame on you, Hashim, driving me crazy by not answering."

"I had to do that, Amina," he said sighing.

"But not like that, Hashim. People have to come to an understanding before they break up."

"I've given up on coming to an understanding with you."

"But there are a lot of things that I have to tell you. We've been together for a long time, Hashim. Not just a year or two."

"What do you want to say?"

"Can you come by?" I asked.

He hesitated a little.

"When?"

"Now."

He hesitated again.

"Fine. I'll be there in half an hour."

"I'll be waiting for you," I said happily. "Don't ring the bell. I'll open the door for you as soon as you get here."

I put the phone down. I got up with my heart beating with happiness, the happiness of victory. I went into the bathroom to freshen up. I put on my silk nightie and the perfume that Hashim loved. I waited at the door. As soon as I heard his steps, I opened the door for him. I didn't turn on the light. I took him by the hand into the bedroom.

"Don't make a sound," I whispered.

I lay down on my bed, my nightie revealing my skin, my hair falling across the pillow, my perfume pulling Hashim to me.

A long period of silence passed as Hashim looked in my face for the girl he used to know.

"Are you happy now?" he asked.

"Happy because I got you to come. I want you to kiss me."

Hashim looked at me for a long time. He then sighed as if he was performing a heavy duty. He took me in his arms and kissed me.

For the first time, I felt that his lips were truly lost, as if he didn't know where to kiss me, the kiss that he'd gotten me used to through all those long years.

He was faking it. He wasn't like Muhammad whose arms I was in less than two hours ago. He was cold, ice cold. He couldn't make himself care.

I started to fake it too. I faked my enthusiasm, faked being consumed, faked my moans.

He got up and put his clothes on quickly.

"Everything I've done was for you," I told him.

"Not for me, Amina," he said calmly. "You never did anything for anyone but yourself."

"I sacrificed my entire life for you."

"If you could've been good, I would've married you," he said in a cold voice.

"If you'd have married me, I would've been good long ago," I said, consumed by my own weakness. "I don't want to marry you now, Hashim. I know you won't marry me. But stay with me until I marry Muhammad."

He gave me an empty smile and turned to leave.

I ran after him to the apartment door, clinging to his neck and kissing him. He pushed me off his chest gently. He looked at my face and then hugged me again. He pressed his cheek against mine for a bit and kissed me on my brow. He then moved me away from him.

"Hashim, when I call you, pick up."

"God willing," he said.

And he left.

I felt that he had left my life forever. I tried to dispel this feeling. I'd always thought I could get him back whenever he was about to leave me. But a wave of weakness washed over me.

I threw myself on my bed and cried.

14

THE NEXT DAY, I CALLED Hashim, but no one picked up. I kept calling. There was no answer.

I figured out that he changed the number of his private line.

The scoundrel.

I tried to call him at the clinic, but the nurses knew my voice. They kept making excuses and must have received instructions to get rid of me when I called.

I tried to call him at home, even at three in the morning. But he never responded. It was his sister who always picked up. She hung up on me as soon as she heard my voice. Despair began to consume me.

More than a month passed without me finding Hashim. At least hearing his voice on the phone used to keep alive the hope that he was still mine. Now Hashim deprived me of even that. He denied me any hope.

I felt I'd lost him, and I yearned for him. I was bound to him by habit. My mind and my body had got used to him. And habit is stronger than will. Just ask any addict.

I discovered that Muhammad wasn't enough for me to quit this habit. He couldn't help me quit Hashim. Now that Hashim had really left me, my habit dominated me with all its tyranny, all its brutality. When I rode next to Muhammad in his car, my eyes scanned the road looking for Hashim. Whenever I was with Muhammad, my mind drifted toward Hashim. When I slept in Muhammad's arms, I still couldn't forget Hashim. As soon as I was alone, I would be under attack: his voice was in my ears, his scent was in my nose, his touch was all over my body. It was agony.

I didn't stop trying to get Hashim back. I sent him a letter.

Hashim, my love,
You know I love you. I still love you. More than my soul, more than my daughter, more than anything in the world. I sacrificed everything because I love you. I sacrificed my daughter, my family, my future, everyone. Then I made a mistake. I admit that I made a mistake. Please be merciful and remember that you're the one who pushed me to it. I've forgiven you for what you did to me, so forgive me for what I did to you. I promise you that as soon as I return to you, I'll atone for my mistake. You'll find me as someone else, a girl who loves you more, who desires you more. The saying goes: the broken plate lives longer. Our love was broken, but it will live longer. I beg you. Let me come back to you.

I sent him the letter by registered mail.

But Hashim didn't write back, and I sank even more in my misery.

I called his friend Ra'uf. I cried to him on the phone. Just hearing the voice of someone close to Hashim released my tears. I told him Hashim left me because I was with a young man who wants to marry me, but I was ready to leave that guy. I even told him I already left him. I only wanted Hashim. He had to come back to me. He had no right to abandon me.

Ra'uf took pity on me. He almost cried with me. When I told my story, I could always get people to feel sorry for me.

He promised me he'd call Hashim and get back to me.

I didn't hear from him for three days, so I called him again.

"Sorry, Amina," he told me in a sad voice. "Hashim won't budge. The truth is that he convinced me this is best for you."

"It's best for me that he stays with me for seven years and then tosses me away like a piece of trash?" I screamed.

"You know, Amina, Hashim isn't going to get married," he said gently. "You've suffered so much, pointlessly. It's best you end this here."

"Okay, but, please give me his personal number."

"Sorry. I can't give it to you. I'd have to ask his permission."

"Forget it. I don't want it."

I hung up.

I went back to my broken heart, my broken mind, my broken body, to the cracks through which the pain flowed, from which my will, my strength, my dignity poured out.

I spent four months unable to reach Hashim. I didn't even see him by chance. I couldn't believe that Cairo was so big that Hashim could escape me in it. Then, finally, I saw him in his car on the road to Heliopolis with a girl next to him. It had to be Nagwa. I was more beautiful than her. But was I? I didn't know. I'd lost confidence in myself, in my beauty. I was devastated. At that moment, I didn't want to ever see Hashim again.

I had to give up hope, hope that he'd come back to me. To do that, I had to hate him with everything I had. I had to detest every day I spent with him, to blame him for every catastrophe that happened to me. He was the one who ruined my life. He was the one I left my husband for. He was the one who made me lose my daughter, my family, my reputation, my friends. He was the one who exposed me to all those men who would pass through my life and over my body. I lost everything, but he didn't lose a thing. I left him just as I found him. He'd only become more successful, even better paid, as a doctor. I had paid the entire price. I hated him. Hatred consumed me to the point that I wished he were dead.

I had no way to take revenge, so I raised my head to the sky and screamed with everything I had: "Lord, take revenge and make him pay for what he did to me!" I pushed Muhammad to talk about him so I could fill my ears with his insults. But I discovered that hatred was like love. Each is a climax of emotion. Each makes you obsess about the other person and tortures you with their memory. I discovered that I hated Hashim because I still loved him. As my hatred increased for him, so did my love.

I had to forget him instead. I started holding my tongue at the mention of his name. I pretended to ignore the things that filled my house and reminded me of him. I looked at them with dead eyes. I distanced myself from all my girlfriends who might talk to me about Hashim. I didn't go by Sulayman Pasha Square where his clinic was so I wouldn't see the sign with his name hanging outside and so I wouldn't see his car. I worked to ignore my emotions, as if they belonged to another girl I didn't have anything to do with.

I fought this battle with myself. Hashim was millions of images that invaded me one after the other, all hot and alive. I'd remember a word that he told me, his striped pajamas, the way he used to comb his hair, the smoke of his cigarette coming out of his big nose, his long fine fingers, the green ring on his right hand, his laugh, his teeth, the way he ate his food, and on and on and on. Unending memories, millions of little things that I had to kill so they didn't come back and shut down my life.

During this time, Muhammad changed. Maybe because he felt I needed him more, because he felt my weakness after Hashim. I tried as hard as I could to hide my growing need for him and to maintain my ability to control him. But day after day, I started to discover that Muhammad wasn't naive as I'd thought. He wasn't weak. He wasn't decent and polite. He was despicable. He had the despicableness of a conceited young man. And I was the one who filled him with that conceit. I gave him more than he expected and he became arrogant. He started talking to me about our marriage in a new tone.

He started holding me accountable for my relationship with Hashim. He started distancing me from his friends and their wives after he'd gotten me used to hanging out with them. He was hiding me now. Our relationship was becoming separate from his social circle.

I wasn't always quiet about what was happening. I sometimes resisted violently. I fought with him. A couple of times, I went completely crazy. In my insanity, I tried again to call Hashim, calling out to him for help. I dialed the old number, but then I remembered that the number had changed. I called him at home.

"Get your brother!" I screamed at his sister. "Let me talk with him!"

"I'm very sorry," his sister responded as if she didn't know me. "The doctor isn't here."

I hung up. And I screamed. I screamed and pulled at my hair and slapped my cheeks. I screamed at my misfortune, my stupidity, my weakness. I screamed because I'd lost Hashim and I hadn't married Muhammad.

Finally, I gave in.

I accepted I wasn't going to marry Muhammad. I didn't need to marry him or anyone else. It was better that way. I wasn't lacking anything. I had a house and a man. All I lacked was a piece of paper, a piece of paper with no value. It was a piece of paper that produced the coldness and boredom of every man and woman who had it. It couldn't do anything for me. It couldn't protect me. A man could rip it up at any moment and then pay the balance through alimony.

I started taking money from Muhammad, but he didn't pay with the same ease as Hashim. He kept track of every pound. He'd do a full audit, demanding I account for every cent.

I made Muhammad move from his apartment near Hashim's. He rented a place in Heliopolis.

I left the apartment that my father had rented for me. I cut the last thread that tied me to my family and moved into Muhammad's apartment. I lived there. I went back to Heliopolis, the neighborhood that I had lived in when I was a girl from a respectable family. I went back without a family, neither dignified nor respectable.

I lived in a fantasy: this house was mine, this man was my husband, and his estate and money were mine. I bought a diamond wedding ring, etched Muhammad's name inside it, and put it on my finger. I wasn't trying to convince people that I'd married Muhammad. No. I didn't care about people anymore. I was trying to convince myself. I was trying to dupe myself.

Despite all this, I still kept pressing Muhammad to get married. I hid my misery and the fact that I'd submitted to this situation. And more than our getting married, I didn't want Muhammad to marry someone else. I made sure that all of high society knew about our relationship so Muhammad's reputation was ruined. There was no way any respectable family would give one of their daughters to him. His mother was frantic trying to get him engaged. I'd hear about her trips from house to house, begging for a girl to save her son from me. I'd tell Muhammad about it.

"Let her do what she wants," he'd respond coldly. "You know I can only marry you."

I wouldn't let it go. I demanded that he guarantee my future, to marry me despite his mother and his family. But he didn't marry me. He found another solution. He wrote me a check for five hundred pounds to reassure me. If he left, I could cash it.

He wrote me another check. And a third. The amount came to one thousand five hundred pounds, more than the bank balance of any girl from any important family.

I was still afraid. Fear was my constant.

I was afraid that I'd lose Muhammad. My experience with Hashim only increased my fear. I lost Hashim after thinking I'd never lose him. I could lose Muhammad too. This fear made me faithful to Muhammad, especially since Muhammad wasn't like Hashim. Hashim was too busy for me. I didn't live with him. And he was always telling me that I was free and I could do what I wanted. Only my desire to be with him had tied me to him. But Muhammad wasn't too busy for me. I filled his day. And he demanded all of me in exchange for the money he gave me.

I was able to contain my fear and go out with another man once.

I met him by accident. He was Lebanese. I met him when I went to visit a friend, Samah. That day, I asked Muhammad's permission to go out shopping. I passed by Samah's on Ma'ruf Street and this guy was there. He started teaching me the twist. I laughed a lot. Samah then left me with him so she could go to work. She worked as a model. I needed to laugh, and dance. I felt liberated. I can't remember his name now. I never saw him again.

There was nothing more than that. I was faithful to Muhammad, faithful for two years. My love for Hashim shrunk and turned to stone until it became a pebble in my heart. It only hurt when I pressed down on it, like a pebble under foot.

Then, Muhammad got married. I read the news in the newspaper. He was with me the day before he got married. He had slept over. That morning, he told me he was going to his family's farm. And the following day, I found the announcement in the paper.

It hit me cold as ice. I went crazy, but it was different this time. It was cold, the most dangerous and severe kind. At that moment, I thought about committing suicide for real. Then I thought about killing Muhammad.

I lay on my back, my eyes fixed on the ceiling. I could feel my blood in my veins, its speed and color changed.

I didn't try to call Muhammad or look for him. After two days, he called me.

"Congratulations, Muhammad," I said, my lips feeling like pieces of wood.

"I'm sorry, Mitou." He sounded like he was crying. "You know how much I resisted. I resisted until my mother was about to die. I had to do it. I only love you. I only wanted to marry you. The girl they married me to isn't divorced. If you knew my situation, you'd know I'm tortured about this more than you."

"Poor thing."

"Don't be like that, Mitou. Insult me. Curse my father, but don't be like that."

A moment of silence passed between us.

"Mitou," he continued. "I have to see you."

"Fine," I said indifferently.

"I'll be right there."

I didn't care about making myself up. I'd been in bed since I woke up.

"You brought the fifteen hundred pounds?" I asked him coldly when he arrived.

He was shocked.

"That's all you care about, Mitou?"

"You think there's anything else between us now?"

"Our love," he said, sitting on the edge of the bed.

"Let's talk first about the money."

"I want to assure you, Amina, nothing will change between us. We'll go on as we are. I'll continue being responsible for you. My getting married doesn't mean that I've left you. Not at all. The girl I married will never be important in my life. I'll come to you every day. I'll stay overnight. We can get married, even if I don't divorce the other one, but I will."

"Pay the money first and then we'll talk," I said in a voice even I wasn't used to from myself.

He looked at me in astonishment as if stunned by the new woman in front of him.

"But you know I don't have money these days," he stammered.

"You don't have anything left after the dower and engagement present?" I asked sarcastically.

"I didn't pay for those things. My mother is the one who paid."

"I don't care who paid," I said threateningly. "I only care about the money. Give me any less than the fifteen hundred and I'll take you to court."

"You'd never go to court, Mitou," he said spitefully. "And the court won't rule in your favor. This is an unnecessary scandal."

"What do you mean?"

"I'll pay you five hundred pounds now," he said, with a deep sigh. "We'll talk about the rest later. But that's not important. What's important is that we stay together. I can't live without you. Believe me. I love you. Forgive me for what I did. I couldn't let my mother die."

"When will you bring me the five hundred pounds?"

"Tomorrow morning," he said, lowering his eyes.

He then raised his head and looked at my face for a long time.

"Can I kiss you?" he pleaded.

"Go ahead."

I let him kiss me. I let him take what he wanted. I didn't feel it at all. All my feelings were dead. All I saw in my mind was Muhammad's bride. My chest filled with malice for her.

Muhammad only paid me five hundred pounds. He paid it out of fear of a scandal. He took back the three checks. Five hundred was better than nothing. He kept coming to see me. Every day. But only at those times when husbands go to see their lovers. He paid for the rent and my expenses.

I couldn't bear my life with Muhammad for long. I moved out of the apartment and went to live with my friend, Samah. I thought I'd work like her as a model, but I had to follow a particular diet to lose weight and I had no energy for that. I started staying out all night at the club dancing. And then waking up at three o'clock in the afternoon.

Marlo, the maître d' of the club, is a good friend now. He introduces me to lots of his friends. They're all foreign: Americans, Brits, French, Saudis, Lebanese, Kuwaitis. He knows the whole world. He takes somewhere between ten and twenty pounds from each of them. He keeps twenty percent and gives me the rest.

This is better than getting used to just one man. I'm no longer so dumb that I'd get hooked on one man. Muhammad still visits me. He doesn't pay by the month anymore. He pays by the night.

Hashim's gold bracelet is always on my wrist.

My friend Samah and I laugh a lot. All day long. And I love dancing. I can say that I've become the queen of the club. I dance better than all the young girls even though I'm thirty now. I tell everyone I'm twenty-five. And I dance like a fifteen-year-old.

No one does the twist anymore. The new dances are the chicken and the limbo.

I love dancing the chicken. Everyone gets together on the dancefloor in a circle. Every guy stands next to a girl. They raise their hands in a circular motion and . . .

The Second Eye

1

I'm Nagwa. Nagwa Tahir.

My mother thinks I'm beautiful. She never stops talking about how beautiful I am or boasting about me to her girlfriends. My hair is the color of copper, she says. My happy wide eyes are like two delectable, freshly peeled almonds. My full lips like two roses.

My mother finds a thousand descriptions and a thousand songs for every part of me. She used to have me stand in front of her and look at me with servile eyes as if she was seeing God in me. She gave me a tiny copy of the Qur'an and a blue bead to wear around my neck to protect me from envy. I couldn't leave the house until I stepped over incense seven times in front of her.

Despite all that, beautiful or not, I have no interest in beauty. All I wanted was to be something, to be my own person and make something of my life. I was the top student at school. I participated in everything. I was the head of the acting club. I was on the basketball team. I was my class representative and the representative of my school at the council of the union of high schools. I loved being important and special. I loved being loved, loved by my classmates, my teachers, my mother's friends.

And, of course, loved by my mother and father. I was their only child. I tried to make every minute a sweet song for them. I felt more responsible for their happiness than my own. I made myself everything in their lives. I was the laughter on their lips, the beating of their hearts. I was their entire life. I was happy with them, with their love, and they with me, with my love.

Love is everything: happiness, well-being, comfort. It is intelligence. It is success.

I'm amazed at the girls who deny the existence of love. Love is the one firm truth in life.

What makes a girl love one guy in particular and not another?

Circumstances? No. Circumstances could bring a girl together with dozens of guys, but she'd only love one. Circumstances brought friends together but could not on their own get two people to love each other.

Marriage? No. Marriage might produce a family, but it isn't enough to create love, no matter how long it lasted. A marriage might last so that both spouses preserved the life they shared, like two partners joined by a single interest, but that doesn't mean they loved each other. Life isn't an interest, and we sometimes sacrifice our own interests along the path of life.

So, what is love?

It is finding yourself in another person, finding in them your mind and your heart, your now and your tomorrow, your laughter and your tears, your life and your body. It is discovering that your body isn't something isolated, but that your mind and your heart are part of it too.

There are some who think love is weakness: submission of the woman or the man.

No. Never. Love isn't weakness. It is strength. Love can withstand any catastrophe. Love needs strength, the strength of faith, a strength bigger than ego, bigger than caprice, bigger than life itself. A strong man is a man who is in love, who can protect being in love from his own self.

I found this man. A strong, wonderful man: Dr. Hashim.

I found him while standing on the edge of hopelessness. He returned life and love to me. He returned my faith, faith that life could include men like him.

But let me start from the beginning.

I was the happiest child in the world.

When I was in elementary school, my father was already an old man. He was in his sixties. He was good-hearted and tender, submissive to my mother. My mother was around fifty. She rarely smiled, determination and harshness hiding the traces of her former beauty. She was active, more active than me. She was strong, stronger than me. She held the reins at home. It was her word that mattered. She managed my father's money. They didn't have much, only twenty acres of land and my father's pension, but no one could dupe her for even a single piaster.

I never wondered why my mother and father were so old when I was young. I didn't notice their age and thought all mothers and fathers were as old as mine. I was attached to them to a strange degree. I slept in their bed, even though I had my own room. My mother would go with me to school every morning, after I stepped over the incense seven times and after she read verses from the Qur'an over my head. She wouldn't let our maid take me or bring me home from school. She did it herself. She did everything herself, from feeding me to changing my clothes. She used to love me like a child loves a doll, playing with it and not letting anyone touch it.

My mother made friends with the school principal as well as the teachers. She'd ask them about every minute that I spent at school, every move I made, every word I said. I couldn't hide anything from her, ever. I was amazed at her ability to find something out before I told it to her. When I came home, I'd escape from my mother and sit on my father's lap. I'd tell him the stories the teachers told us at school and I'd show him my books and notebooks. I'd teach him the songs I memorized so he could memorize them too. He'd laugh, happy like a child. I loved my father, more than I loved my mother.

I had one aunt. Her husband had left her with six kids. She was poor and her life was hard. We saw her rarely, but I loved her. Whenever I saw her, I'd cling to her and throw myself on her chest. I'd laugh when my mother was jealous of her. My mother was really possessive of me, especially around my aunt.

My mother had friends who got together at her house every week. They all wore a white veil that hung down to their shoulders and a coat, whether in winter or summer, that covered them from their neck to their feet. I later learned they were members of the

Nour al-Huda Association for Muslim Women. My mother wasn't a member, but she was friends with them and believed in the goals of the association. I couldn't think of my childhood without remembering the women of Nour al-Huda, who floated through my life like ghosts.

One day, when I was seven, the superintendent came into my class. She started calling out the register, going through the names until she reached the name Nagwa 'Abd al-Hamid.

No one responded.

"Nagwa 'Abd al-Hamid?" she called out again.

No one responded.

The superintendent looked around until she got to my face.

"You're not Nagwa 'Abd al-Hamid?" she asked sharply.

"No, ma'am," I said raising my little eyes to her in surprise and fear. "I'm Nagwa Tahir."

"No," the principal snapped. "You're Nagwa 'Abd al-Hamid."

"No, I swear, ma'am," I said, tears starting to flow from my eyes. "I'm Nagwa Tahir."

The superintendent flipped through the papers she was carrying.

"Isn't your father's name Raghib 'Abd al-Hamid?" she continued.

"No," I said. "My father's name is 'Uthman Tahir."

The superintendent stared at me.

"So, who's Raghib 'Abd al-Hamid?"

"My aunt's husband," I said.

The superintendent stared right at me.

"Fine, come with me."

She took me by the hand. I walked with her to the principal's room, sobbing, my little heart trembling.

I stood at a distance while the superintendent leaned over and whispered something to the principal, showing her the papers. Through my tears, I saw the principal shake her head a bunch of times. She then turned to me with a big smile.

"Come here, Nagwa," she told me. "Why are you crying, my dear?"

She took me in her arms and pulled me to her. I lowered my head to her chest but I kept sobbing.

"My dear," the principal said tenderly, "don't cry. We don't want to upset you."

She then opened her desk drawer, took a piece of candy, and gave it to me.

"Take this, my dear. Now go back to your class. No need to be upset."

I looked up at her as I took the candy and wiped my tears with my sleeve.

"My name is Nagwa Tahir. Right, ma'am?"

"Of course, my dear," the principal said with a tender smile. "Now, go on, back to your class."

As soon as I left the principal's room, my tears flooded me again. I couldn't put candy in my mouth. The trembling of my little heart increased. I was afraid. I felt something was going to happen to me, something I didn't want. I kept crying in class until the teacher had to call the superintendent to take me and sit with me in the courtyard to try to comfort me.

After a while, the office assistant came to call me to the principal's office again. The superintendent took my hand.

"Your mother must have come," she said.

I pulled my hand from hers and ran to the principal's office.

I found my mother there. I threw myself in her arms. I kept crying as she tried to console me.

"My dear. Don't be upset."

"Did you hear what the superintendent told me?" I asked, raising my head to her sobbing.

"I know," my mother said, her face pained. "I know everything."

She then got up, my hand in hers.

"I'll get back to you tomorrow," she told the principal.

She then turned to me.

"Come, Nouga, let's go home. You can wash your face and play."

We took a taxi even though our house wasn't more than a ten-minute walk from school.

At home, I began to feel something was very off.

"Come, 'Uthman Bey, I want to talk with you," my mother said, looking at my father.

He went into the bedroom behind her and closed the door.

I was anxious. I still felt something big was about to happen to me.

At noon, the women of Nour al-Huda came and encircled my mother in the salon. When I went in, they gave me strange looks, perhaps pitying, even mourning. I wasn't at an age that allowed me to understand what their looks meant. But I remember I was unsettled by it. Each of the women took me in their arms and kissed me. I walked over to my mother and sat on her lap, seeking protection from the ghosts in white sheets.

The ghosts left the house.

My mother's wrinkled face looked even harsher and more determined.

She pulled me to her chest as if she was trying to protect me from this big thing that was about to happen.

"What's your name?" she asked.

"My name is Nagwa."

"Nagwa what?"

"Nagwa Tahir."

"What's your father's name?"

"That isn't necessary now, 'Aziza," my father cut her off. "Don't upset the girl."

My mother fell silent.

She gave in to my father, unlike usual. Her resolute face had a cloud of sadness and pain.

In the evening, I was surprised to find my aunt and her ex-husband had come to visit us. My aunt only visited us on special occasions. My aunt's husband had never visited us before. That day, he sat me on his knees and kissed me a lot.

My aunt looked at me, clearly uncomfortable. She kissed me too. Her ex-husband then picked me up and lifted me up in the air.

"Up and away!" he said, letting out a big laugh.

My mother's face was severe. My father smiled goodheartedly. My mother pulled me from him.

"Listen, Nouga," she said, sitting me next to her. "I'm going to talk to you, and I want you to pay attention to what I'm saying."

"Be quiet, you," my father cut her off again.

My aunt looked at me with pity.

"Come here, Nouga," my father said tenderly.

He sat me on his knees as I was looking at him trembling.

"I'm going to tell you a story," he said in his calm voice. "But before I do, you have to give me a big kiss."

I kissed him.

"And where's your sweet smile?"

I smiled without feeling sweet.

"Look, my dear. There was once a husband and wife. Our Lord gave them everything except kids. No boys, no girls. They went to many doctors. They visited wise men and saints. They went on the pilgrimage. But it was no use. It was the will of our Lord. One day these two people, who were old by then, went to visit their relatives and they found lots of boys and girls there. And there was a toddler. She was so sweet. There was no one sweeter than her in the whole world. They sat and begged the mother of this sweet little girl to take her for themselves, for her to live with them and keep them company in their loneliness, to fill their lives with light and hope. The mother agreed to give them the girl because she had so many."

"I understand," I said.

"What did you understand?" my father asked, surprised.

"I understand that my real name is Nagwa 'Abd al-Hamid," I said, sobbing and kicking my feet forwards. "But I don't care. I'm Nagwa Tahir. You're my father. I don't have any other father. I don't want any other father."

I began to scream. My aunt got up, looking worried, but I screamed even more. I knew she was my real mother.

"Leave me alone!" I shouted at her. "I don't want you. I don't know you!"

She sat back down silently.

"But Nouga," said my father who wasn't my father. "Don't be silly. You must be the happiest girl in the world. All girls have one father, but you have two. All girls have one mother, but you have two."

"Really, my sister 'Aziza has more right to her than me," my real mother said. "I cared for her until she was a toddler, but she's cared for her since. I'm not part of her life."

"I don't care," I screamed again. "The only father I have is you."

"That's it," my father said, his face brighter. "We're finished. So, tell me, what's your name?"

"Nagwa," I said, calming down.

"Nagwa what?"

"Nagwa Tahir."

"What's your father's name?"

"'Uthman Tahir," I said.

"And what's your mother's name?"

"'Aziza."

"Okay. Now go to your room and wash your face, Nouga," my mother said as if nothing happened.

I got up from my father's lap.

I turned and stared at my aunt, my real mother.

Then I stared at her ex-husband, my real father.

And I ran to my room.

My mother came after me. She started kissing me. She kissed me all over my face and hands.

Since that day, I knew my mother was my aunt and my father was my aunt's ex-husband, but I've tried to ignore this truth. I continued to call my birth mother "aunt" and my biological father "uncle." My mother and father were the ones I lived with. I don't know what official steps were taken, but from that day, my name was always Nagwa Tahir, even on my birth certificate.

Back then, I didn't wonder why my real mother gave me up like that. With time, I realized it was because she loved me and she wanted me to have a better life than she could offer me as a single mother with six kids, living in a two-bedroom apartment. She gave me up me so I could live a pampered life with two old parents who needed me as much as I needed them. My mother didn't hate me the day she gave me up. She loved me.

We started seeing my aunt and uncle even less, and now I knew my mother was distancing me from my aunt so I didn't get close to her. My mother, with all her love for me, couldn't forget that I wasn't her daughter. This feeling created for her a complex of fear that she would lose me. That's why she worked so hard to impose her control on me. She tried to control every minute of my life, every last detail. She was always there with me, always trying to get into my thoughts, to share in every one of my emotions. I didn't have any freedom, even in my sleep. She got me used to me sleeping with her, between her and my father. It was a control motivated by love, but it was a strange love.

My mother loved to pretend that she was from a big rich family. She always made up family links that extended to one of the pashas. She always insisted on calling her husband "'Uthman Bey" and insist that he call her as his wife "Madame 'Aziza," even though families at our socio-economic level don't use "Bey" and "Madame."

My mother was always trying to form friendships with rich families. One of these families lived in Helwan. It was an important family, old and well known. They weren't super rich, but they had more money than us. My mother met them through the ladies of Nour al-Huda. Before I knew it, we started visiting them every week. She always took me with her and I'd play with their girls. I got along with them great.

Then, something strange happened.

I was twelve.

We were visiting this family and I was playing with the girls when my mother called me over.

"Kiss her hand, Nouga," she told me, pointing to the mother of the family. "You're engaged to Adel."

I stood there, dumbfounded, not understanding a thing.

My "mother-in-law" pulled me to her, hugged me to her chest, and kissed me.

"I'm the one who kisses her and her hand," she said. "How could I find a bride prettier than this for my son? Such beauty, morals, and good roots."

I didn't understand a thing. I couldn't even really remember what Adel, my "fiancé," looked like. I saw him come and go from their house, but I never got a good look at him. At that age, I didn't look closely at men. At the time, he was twenty-three. He was a student in business school.

I thought it was a joke. Just chit-chat.

But, no, they were serious.

I was engaged at twelve years old.

2

MY MOTHER WAS AFRAID I'D rebel against her one day. She was afraid that my heart would burn for a man that she didn't like. She was afraid my beauty would mature to the point that she couldn't monopolize it for herself. She was afraid someone would steal me from her, so she put me in a safe and kept the key in her pocket. The key, so she thought, was Adel.

She loved me to the point of complete lunacy, but it was a love that differed from maternal love. It was a love driven by the desire to possess me. She felt she owned every pound of my flesh and bones as if she'd paid for me. No one else had any rights to me.

In those days, I didn't feel any of this and I didn't even wonder why my mother engaged me to Adel at such a young age. Instead, I was happy with my engagement as if my mother bought me a new pair of shoes. I was even happier when I felt that I'd become someone different among my classmates. I was the only girl engaged in the entire school. I had a man. There was a ring on my finger.

At such a young age, I began to think about men.

I didn't lose my childlike appearance. I still ran around and played blindman's bluff, jumped rope, and laughed as kids laugh, cried as kids cry. Behind these outward appearances, I was living in a more grown-up world. My mind was opening up to thoughts and fantasies that shouldn't belong to a girl at that age.

I began to see Adel regularly.

He would stir up feelings and make me blush, as if he'd tossed me into still water and woke me up, ripples encompassing all of me.

I felt his small, neat mustache tickling my nose without him getting close to me.

I felt the weight of his tall broad body even when he was far from me.

I began to look at all men in a new way. I started looking for beauty, strength of character, masculinity, and then comparing each one to Adel.

Adel was mine.

It's true, I didn't pick him, but he was my man, just as I hadn't picked my mother and my father either.

I started drinking up Adel's features day after day. My heart bloomed in his love day after day. My heart fluttered in my ribs like a baby bird trying to break the shell of its egg to get out to life.

Adel continued to treat me like a child. He didn't imagine that my chest could hold all these feelings since I was still twelve. Without meaning to, he was misjudging me. The way he looked at me wasn't any different from the way he looked at his sisters who spent their days skipping rope.

"How are you, Nouga?" he'd ask. "How's school?"

He'd sit next to me for a while, his mother and my mother with us, and then get up and go to his room. One day, I finally got the courage to sneak off behind him and follow him into his room. I stood in front of him like an idiot, not knowing what I wanted from him, even though I felt that I wanted a lot of things from him. I felt that I wasn't like the rest of the girls my age. I had more rights over him. I had demands that I couldn't make out, the demands of love. Even my idea of love came from the fairy tales my mother would tell me before I went to sleep.

Adel looked at me that day as if he was weighing every piece of me for the first time. I felt his eye fall on my neck, my chest, my waist, my thighs. He then shook his head, as if he decided that I hadn't matured yet, and leaned over and kissed me on top of my head.

"Go play with my sisters, Nouga," he said smiling at me like I was a child.

I left his room lost in a thick fog filling my heart and mind.

Maybe those days, it would've been possible for me to be oblivious to all my feelings, to let them fall into the pit of my heart or crumple them up in the back of my mind and devote myself to my childhood. But my mother didn't leave me alone. She kept stirring up feelings that I had grown up and trying to make me bear new responsibilities. She'd tell me "Don't run like that, Nouga. Don't forget that you're no longer a kid. You're engaged." Or "Cover your knees or I swear I'll tell Adel." Or "Why are you standing at the window? Aren't you afraid Adel will find out and think you're looking at the guy who lives opposite us?" Adel . . . Adel . . . Adel. My mother would repeat his name a thousand times a day. I started not doing anything unless I had

Adel's permission. If I told my mother that I wanted to go out to play with a friend, she'd say coldly: "Ask Adel first."

If I wanted to go on a school trip, she'd tell me she was no longer responsible for me.

"Ask Adel's permission."

Adel wouldn't say no unless my mother wanted him to. He told me what my mother wanted to tell me. His opinion was hers. She was controlling me through Adel, even increasing her control over me.

Adel would believe her and respect her. He'd sit with her more than with me. She'd talk with him on the phone whenever we didn't see him. She'd talk with him for a long time, much more than I did. Sometimes she'd talk with him without me knowing, and then I'd be surprised by Adel's orders as if they were coming from my mother's lips.

My mother's insistence that I was bound to Adel hurried me to love him. I started loving him when I was twelve. I acknowledged this love to myself. It was a naive love with the innocence, fantasies, and purity of childhood. And this love increased my submission to my mother since she was the one who owned Adel.

I started imposing myself on Adel. Whenever we went to visit his family, I went to his room. I played with everything there. I sat on his bed. I talked to him, and he talked to me. I looked at him as if he was everything, my entire future. But still he treated me like a child.

One day, I opened his desk drawer and saw a girl's picture. Before I'd looked closely at it, Adel saw me.

"Don't open my drawers!" he yelled.

He hurried over and slammed the drawer shut. It almost closed on my fingers.

"Why?" I asked looking at him, feeling something I couldn't understand.

"Because it's not appropriate."

"I saw a picture of someone," I said innocently.

"That picture belongs to one of my friends. He left it with me."

"Why?"

"Why what?"

"Why'd he leave it with you?"

"It has nothing to do with you." He was annoyed. "You're still young and it's not appropriate for you to ask about these things."

At thirteen, I started feeling jealousy with all its pain and harshness. I thought Adel was with other girls because I was young. This pushed me to try to get ahead of my age, to seem older. I tried to get my mother to let me wear high heels. Through one of my classmates at school, I managed to get a lipstick. I started flipping through magazines, my eyes stopping at the pictures of the girls who were older than me. I started liking clothes that weren't appropriate for my age. My mother didn't understand fashion, so she'd yield to me and let me dress how I wanted. She let me put on lipstick once or twice. She was happy with me like a girl with a doll.

Adel came to visit us one day. He sat with my mother and my father.

I stayed in my room, preparing a huge surprise for Adel. I stood in front of my mirror, brushed my hair, and tied it up like older girls do. I put dark eyeliner around my eyes. I put on lipstick. I put on a new dress and undid the top so that it revealed some skin. I put on stockings and high heels.

I was beautiful, even though I didn't know how to do my hair right, the eyeliner was shaky around my eyes, and the lipstick was sloppy.

I went out to Adel.

And he was stunned. He kept looking at me as if he was seeing me for the first time.

I smiled at my mother. She smiled at me like I was the most beautiful girl in the world.

"What happened?" my father guffawed. "Did you grow up overnight?"

"Please, daddy," I said, trying to appear twice my height. "Don't say that."

"Since when do you wear lipstick, Nouga?" Adel asked.

"Mommy let me," I said shrugging my shoulders.

"What's wrong with that, Adel?" my mother asked. "As long as she's engaged to you, she has the right."

The look of surprise remained in Adel's eyes. After that day, he started showing me more interest. He lowered his kiss from the top of my head to my cheek.

I still remember his first kiss on my cheek. I went into his room when we were visiting his family. I was wearing high heels. My dress was tight, open at the chest. My hair was parted in the middle and hanging down around my face. Adel stared at me. There was something new in his eyes. His face was gleaming. He tried to busy himself by shuffling things in his desk drawers. He then got up suddenly, got close to me, and took me by my shoulders.

"You've grown up, Nouga," he said. "I didn't think that you'd grow up so quickly."

He kept gripping me, his eyes on mine.

All my feelings were roused and confused as if under a strong light that they couldn't bear.

He leaned over and kissed me on my cheek, the first warm lips to touch me there. I felt a violent rush of blood. I felt my heart fly between my ribs like a bird breaking through the eggshell and becoming free in a world that it didn't know yet. I felt my knees tremble. I felt that I needed a lot of strength, that I didn't have yet, to bear all of this.

I tore myself from his grip and ran off, my hand on my face where he had kissed me as if I was afraid that it would fly away from me.

I went into the salon, and no one was there. I stayed there by myself, perplexed at my feelings, my sweet feelings, my hand still on my cheek.

I stayed alone in the salon until I heard my mother's voice calling me for us to leave.

We rode the Helwan train, me next to my mother, silent, intoxicated, confused.

My mother looked at me, trying to reveal my secret.

"What's wrong?" she asked.

"Can I tell you something?"

"Is everything okay?"

"Adel kissed me."

She suddenly looked worried and pulled me to her.

"Where?"

"In his room."

"I mean, what part of you did he kiss?"

"My cheek," I said, smiling.

My mother was quiet for a little as if she was swallowing something painful.

"How many times?"

"Just once."

"Were you sitting or standing?"

"Standing."

"How did he touch you?"

"I don't remember. He was holding me by my arms."

"And what did you do?"

"I ran and sat in the salon."

My mother was silent for a bit, her face becoming more severe.

"It's nothing," she said as if talking to herself. "He's already your fiancé, but he doesn't have the right to more than a kiss. Understand?"

"I understand," I said, still confused about my feelings.

After that day, my mother always asked about the details, the most precise details. She didn't care whether something was right or wrong, she only wanted the details. And I got used to telling her everything. I didn't feel any embarrassment. I knew that was all she cared about.

My love for Adel grew. Everything in me grew with my love for him. My chest grew, my body, my mind, my feelings. Everything got bigger in Adel's hands. Every part of me that he touched got bigger. My mind got bigger with every word he said. My heart got bigger with every moment with him.

I was deeply in love. It played out in my imagination, with the naivete of childhood mixed with the intoxication of a young woman. I loved him like a girl driven by love. I loved him like a young woman preparing herself for marriage. I loved him like a woman picking the names of her children before seeing them.

Adel loved me. He loved me as much as I loved him. His love was growing as I grew and the lust in his eyes increased day after day.

We got to the point that neither of us could do without the other. I was writing a letter to him every day, even on the days I saw him, letters full of the sweet words that I read in stories and which I transferred to the reality that I was living in.

Adel wrote me a letter every day too, even if only a few words. His words were naive, the attempts of a conceited young man trying to prove to himself that he was a writer and a lover. I thought his letters contained the most refined words that a man could write.

I loved the whole world with him. I sang along with every song on the radio. I memorized the lyrics of songs by 'Abd al-Wahhab and 'Abd al-Halim, as well as the songs by second- and third-rate musicians. I found love in every word.

How happy I was those days.

But there was pain too. Adel had some adventures with women. I once found some lipstick on his kerchief. I found another picture of an older woman in his drawer. I'd explode and cry. But Adel would convince me quickly that he needed these relationships to live out his youth. Once we got married, he'd atone. He always convinced me that they were flings that didn't leave any traces on him, relationships that every man needs before getting married.

Moments would come when I started thinking about giving to Adel what he was getting from these women even before we got married. No. They weren't love. I was above these fleeting relationships. I was bigger than the passing needs of men. I couldn't lower myself to that. I was love. I was all of life. I was Adel's love, Adel's life. I'd repress the pain of jealousy in my little heart. I'd drive away the image of Adel kissing and embracing an older woman. But I started hating older women. No, I didn't hate them. My heart wasn't big enough for hate. I was afraid of them. I imagined that any of them could pounce on Adel and take him from me, even if it started as a passing pleasure.

Our kisses had moved on during this time. Adel's kisses landed on my young, virginal lips. And I melted in his kisses.

My mother directed our kisses like she was a conductor, directing the notes of two birds whispering to each other.

She'd give us the right to exchange kisses, but under her supervision. When Adel would come to visit us, she'd sit with us like a security guard as we'd exchange sweet words and hot glances until my mother got up suddenly to do something in another room. She'd then go sit with my father and leave us alone. As soon as her back was turned, our thirsty lips would meet. We'd live in a single long kiss as if each of us was holding our breath for as long as possible to make the most of it. Then, suddenly, my mother would come back and our lips would part, still thirsty.

When we went to visit Adel's family, the same thing happened. We exchanged looks of enormous desire. Then

Adel would get up and go to his room. My mother would keep talking to me until she decided to let me go join Adel. That's when I'd run to him and we'd kiss, until I heard my mother's voice calling me, pulling me from paradise.

Not leaving me alone with Adel was the harshest punishment that my mother could inflict on me. The amount of time that she left me alone with him would depend on how pleased she was with me. Sometimes she'd leave me to him for fifteen minutes, sometimes five minutes, sometimes one minute.

My mother would pretend in front of Adel that she didn't mean to leave us alone, but the situation was obvious. Once we left, she'd tell me directly that she was purposely leaving me as a kind of threat that she might not do it again the next time. And, of course, she'd demand the details, all the details.

"What happened?" she'd ask with an excited greed in her eyes.

"We had to hurry," I said, being coy with her. "You were away for barely a minute."

"Don't worry," she said. "You'll get your fill of him soon enough."

"I know," I said shamelessly. "He kissed me."

"How naughty! And what else?"

"Nothing. What else is there?"

"Did he embrace you?"

"No."

"Did he put his hand on your chest?"

"Mommy! I won't let you talk to me like that."

"Don't let him put his hand on your chest," she said resolutely. "He doesn't have the right."

She kept pressing me, looking at me closely, inspecting my body and my mind. Maybe he took a part of me or maybe he left something of himself.

I wasn't annoyed. I loved these exchanges. I loved that it went on for so long, as if I was revealing to my only girlfriend my deepest secrets.

But those sweet days didn't last long.

When I was sixteen, my father got sick. Half of his body became paralyzed and he lost the ability to speak. He could no longer move unless we carried him from place to place. He was reduced to nothing.

I lost him and felt that I had lost the anchor in my life. I hadn't realized that my father was so important in my life until there was nothing left of him. He was the guardrail against my mother's tyranny, against her caprices. He loved me like I was his real daughter.

My mother's tyranny escalated after my father got sick. Her egotism became as sharp as a knife. We started constantly fighting with each other. We'd yell at each other and then I'd run to my father in his bed. He'd look at my mother with all the anger and scorn he could muster and try to gesture with his healthy arm. He'd let out broken, pitiful sounds that sounded like the lowing of a wounded deer. He'd then look at me with tears in his eyes and a weak smile on his lips. He couldn't do more than that.

My father's illness impacted my love for Adel too, which moved into a new phase. It was no longer a love with the happiness, freedom, and naivete of childhood. It became serious and deep, heavy with responsibility.

Adel became my only strength, my only support. We no longer accepted my mother's supervision or her stage directions. Our love began to take on a personality that was independent from my mother. Our conversations, plans, and dreams became ours alone. I no longer welcomed the long debriefing from my mother after I met Adel. Adel and I started talking about my mother. We wanted our independence.

My mother noticed this change immediately. She noticed that I had become more attached to Adel than to her. I was influenced by him and what he said more than by her. She began to feel that Adel wasn't the key to the safe that she put me in and which she was keeping in her pocket. Adel became too big for her pocket. Her fear that she'd lose me one day began to stir inside her. She began to fight with Adel, to fight my love.

She began to reduce our visits to Adel's family. If Adel came to visit us, she met him in a formal way like he was a stranger. She sat with us like a prison guard. She didn't leave us alone for a moment.

She then started relaying news of Adel's affairs with other women, dripping them into my ears like poison.

"I know," I'd scream in her face. "You can't tell me anything about Adel that I don't already know."

She kept testing me. She contacted a forty-year-old divorcée that Adel had been seeing. She put this woman on the phone and had her tell me her story with Adel, swearing that she had been giving him money.

"Do you know the brown suit that he wears?" she asked me. "I'm the one who bought it for him."

I was tortured by rage and jealousy, by my impotence before my mother's oppression. But I persevered.

Finally, Adel decided that the only way out was to speed up our marriage. He talked to my mother about it, but she refused. She said that we had to wait until I finished high school. When Adel promised to let me finish school after we sign the wedding contract, she set up other obstacles. She asked for an unreasonable dower, made unnecessary stipulations for the apartment that Adel had to find for us to live in. The situation developed very quickly. There were lots of talk, lots of fights between my mother and Adel's mother. The ladies of Nour al-Huda would try to mediate.

I became lost. I wasn't seeing Adel. I'd talk with him on the phone in secret. I'd cry on the chest of my paralyzed father. Once or twice, Adel would rush in to see me to spite my mother. But she'd toss him out, even threatening once to call the police.

My mother lost her mind when she learned that Adel was up for an important position in Kuwait. Adel wanted this job to build his future and save money for us. But, of course, this meant that he'd take me far from my mother.

No one could take me far from her. She owned me. She owned every pound of my flesh. She wouldn't let anyone take me from her. Not Adel nor anyone else.

I screamed like a crazy person. I smashed things up. My mother showed no mercy. She declared war. And she was used to being victorious.

She pressured every member of the family to convince me to forget my love for Adel. Even my real mother came to convince me to break off the engagement, saying that Adel wasn't appropriate for me. Everyone was denouncing Adel and his family. My mother even went to his boss to complain about him and convince them that he was trying to corrupt and steal me.

Adel was furious.

"I'm going to marry her no matter what!" he screamed at my mother on the phone. "If you were really her mother, you wouldn't be doing this to her."

My mother accepted the challenge.

I was trying to be patient. I was trying to see the light at the end of the tunnel. But there wasn't any light in my mother's steely face.

So I fled.

I'd never thought about running away. My mother took me to school one day and, as usual, she told the principal and teachers not to leave me alone. I spent the whole morning distracted. I couldn't take in anything from the lessons.

During the afternoon break, I was in the school yard. I noticed that the school gate was open. In a daze and almost involuntarily, I walked toward the gate and left.

I didn't realize what had happened until I was already far from school. I paused for a moment in the street, having been driven forward unconsciously to that point. I ran to the nearest phone and called Adel at work.

He arrived in a taxi fifteen minutes later. I was standing on the street wearing my school clothes.

I ran over as soon as I saw him and jumped in.

We didn't talk.

Neither of us were expecting this moment. We hadn't concocted a scenario to flee together. Adel took my hand in his and told the driver to head to Agouza.

We were both quiet the entire trip, my hand in his. Our hearts were pounding.

Adel took me to his oldest brother's place. He lived alone in an apartment in Agouza.

Adel opened the door with a key that he took out of his pocket. I didn't think about asking why he had the key to his brother's apartment already in his pocket.

"I don't want to take you to my house in case your mother tries to come and catch us there," he said as we went in.

I nodded my head in agreement.

Adel closed the door behind him.

I didn't try to look around me at the apartment. My eyes stayed on Adel's face.

"We'll wait until my brother gets back from work at five o'clock," Adel said. "Then we'll send for the marriage official, and we'll get married."

At that moment, I wasn't thinking about marriage. I was only thinking about being alone with Adel, alone after this long torture, after all my longing for him. For the first time, we were together alone, far from my mother's iron grip.

"I'm so tired, Adel," I said sighing, leaning my head on his chest.

"That's it," he said resolutely. "After today, no one can separate us."

He then raised my head to him. Our lips met and we lost ourselves in a long kiss. I felt it would never end.

"You're my wife, Nouga," Adel said sitting me on the couch. "My wife before our Lord and before everyone. My wife of six years, since the day we got engaged."

"My love, my husband," I whispered, clinging to him.

We didn't wait for the marriage official to come. We couldn't wait after all this torture, all this deprivation.

I submitted. No. We submitted to each other. Adel didn't want anything more than what I wanted. I didn't feel that I lost anything. I didn't feel that I sacrificed anything. All I felt was that I didn't want to lose Adel again. I didn't want anything to stand between us. I didn't want to go back to the torture of longing for him, of being deprived of him. I wanted to spend the rest of my life right there, in his arms.

There was no pain. It wasn't as I'd imagined. Life at that moment flowed on its own, without any will from me or him, as if we weren't in control of our actions.

Afterwards, I lay down in Adel's arms and closed my eyes. I wasn't sleeping. I was in love, relaxed, the smile of victory on my lips, victory over my mother.

We were lost until Medhat, Adel's brother, came back. Adel jumped up as soon as he heard the key turn in the lock. I sat up too, pulling down my school uniform over my knees. A look of surprise appeared on his face when he saw me.

"Nagwa," he said, aghast. "Why are you here?"

"We're going to get married now, Medhat," Adel said cutting him off. "We were waiting for you so you could bring the official and be a witness for the contract."

"Isn't it better for us to tell your mother first and bring her?" Medhat asked looking at me like I was crazy.

"Mother won't be happy that we're getting married."

"But when she finds out that it's gotten to this point, she'll have to accept it," he said.

"It's pointless, Medhat," Adel snapped. "You know 'Aziza."

"That's why," Medhat said. "If she finds out that you eloped, she'll turn the entire world against you. She might even drag you to court."

"There's no point talking now," Adel said, about to lose it. "We're getting married means we're getting married."

Medhat shifted his gaze between Adel and me. He saw the determination on our faces.

"Okay. But let me at least tell our mother so you two aren't fully eloping."

"If your mother finds out before mine," I told Medhat, "my mother will go even crazier."

"Leave that to me. You two aren't thinking clearly."

He then hurried to the phone and called his mother.

"My mother will be here in ten minutes," he said happily. "She'll be here for signing the contract."

"She agreed?" Adel asked.

"She seemed happy when I told her," Medhat said.

We sat and waited.

It wasn't even ten minutes before we heard a number of people approach the door.

The door opened.

I saw my mother before me with her harsh, wrinkled face.

My aunt was with her as well as my cousin, Adel's mother, his father, and another person that I didn't know.

My mother stared right at me. She didn't look at anyone else, not at Adel or Medhat.

She grabbed my arm.

"Let's go, girl," she said harshly. "You're going home."

I tried to pull my arm from her, but her grip was strong and I was weak and exhausted. I was trembling. Everyone around me was silent as if they were witnessing my execution. This silence only increased my fear, my weakness, my trembling.

My mother pulled me toward the door.

"We have to get married!" Adel screamed. "We're getting married. That's it!"

My mother turned to Adel's parents.

"Look at your son," she shot out.

She took me down to the street and put me in a taxi.

"What a waste after the way I raised you," she kept repeating on the ride. "Is that how you treat your mother, Nouga? What will people say about me? They'll say I didn't raise you right. Me! I gave you my whole life. Is this how it is, Nouga? Is this it?"

I was silent next to her, trembling, a thick cloud filling my eyes.

"Listen, girl," she said firmly as soon as we walked in the door.

"Stop," I cut her off, harnessing my remaining strength. "I'm not a girl anymore."

"What do you mean?" she asked, her eyes wide with terror.

"I mean that I'm a woman now," I said, leaning on the edge of the table so I didn't collapse. "That's it. Your daughter is a woman."

She lifted her hand and brought it down on the side of my face with all her might.

She tried to collect herself.

"So what?" she said after thinking about it for a moment. "You still aren't going to marry him. You think you and your boy can make me? Never. A simple operation and you'll be back to being a girl again."

"You're not my mother!" I screamed as loudly as I could. "You're not my mother!"

This was the first time that I confronted her with the truth, a truth that we had never spoken of before.

3

I OPENED MY EYES THE next day to find myself in my bed, my mother next to me, her wrinkled face watching over me. I felt a sharp pain in my stomach, in my chest, and in my throat. It was a terrible pain, a pain that I'd never felt before, as if everything in me was being strangled. There was a pain in my head, an incredible pain.

A doctor came, but he wasn't sure if the problem was my stomach, liver, or gall bladder. He wrote a lot of prescriptions and with each new drug, I got worse. The pain tore up every part of my body. Every muscle was tense, pressing down on my heart, my throat. It was torture.

"Please, I want to see Adel," I pleaded with my mother, staring her in the eye. "Send for him. Let him come."

"Get better first," my mother would respond. "Then we'll see about Adel."

"I won't get better unless I see Adel," I said shaking my head on the pillow as if I was trying to get free from a chain around my neck. "Bring me Adel."

"Adel won't heal you."

"Shame on you, mother," I whispered, tears running down my cheek.

"Tell me," she leaned over me, her voice low. "How'd it happen?"

She wanted to know the details, the details of the moment I became a woman. All her pain, all her anger and worry for me couldn't restrain her deviant craving to know the details, the hunger to know exactly what happened between me and Adel.

"I won't tell you anything until I see Adel!" I screamed.

My mother took me in her arms and hugged me to her chest tenderly as if she wanted to compensate me for Adel's love, compensate me for Adel's arms with her arms.

"They bewitched you," she whispered, tears running down her face. "They cast a spell on you. May God punish you, Khadija, you wicked woman."

My mother really was convinced that Khadija, Adel's mother, had put a spell on me. She started meeting with the women of Nour al-Huda to ward off the spell. They would all gather next to my bed every morning after the dawn prayer and every evening after the evening prayer, their faces framed by their white veils. They stood in front of me like ghosts, reading the Qur'an and reciting spells. I was going crazy. My head was burning, my ears were ringing. The white ghosts gave me vertigo. I'd jump up from my bed and run to my paralyzed father. I'd throw myself on his chest, crying in terror. My father would wave his healthy arm at my mother. His eyes would flash with all the anger and scorn left in him, but he couldn't do anything. My mother would always take me back and put me at the mercy of the white ghosts.

My state got much worse. Was it love? Could it have been black magic? I didn't know. I didn't know anything anymore.

The women of Nour al-Huda decided to make use of a certain Sheikha Zein to ward off the spell. She was a strong fat woman with penciled-on eyebrows. She sat in my room burning incense and reciting spells. I could only catch some of the words, as if it was a hallucination. She then put a veil under my head, swearing that it could break the spell and make me hate Adel after three visits.

A few days later, Sheikha Zein came back and she declared that my case called for writing spells on an eggshell and then burying it in an abandoned grave.

My mother asked one of her friends from Nour al-Huda to go with Sheikha Zein to bury the egg.

After another few days, Sheikha Zein came back to announce that I had to walk on top of soil taken from under a dead person's head who hadn't been dead for more than two nights.

I walked on the soil.

My state worsened.

The council of Nour al-Huda decided that my condition was too serious for the abilities of Sheikha Zein and that the spell that Khadija had placed on me had to be a Christian spell. It therefore required seeking the help of Sitt Victoria.

"This is all nonsense!" I'd scream. "I don't believe in any of this. Bring me a real doctor."

"How is it nonsense, Nouga?" they'd respond. "Black magic is mentioned in the Qur'an."

"Didn't I bring a doctor for you?" my mother would add. "What are all these medications on your dresser?"

It continued. Sitt Victoria came. She was an old ugly woman, but she was lighthearted. She could make me laugh. When I laughed, my mother thought Sitt Victoria was her secret weapon. Sitt Victoria looked me over. She decided that my situation was serious and that she had to spend a night with us in the second half of the Islamic month when the moon began to wane. She then took one of my combs and dug some symbols on it with a nail. She ordered me to comb my hair with it every day seven times. My mother insisted on carrying out these instructions precisely. She was the one who brushed my hair with the magic comb seven times a day.

On the appointed day, Sitt Victoria came back at sunset. She sat with my mother and me, telling us the secrets of families who came to her for help to expel spells or to set spells. She was indiscreet and mentioned the families by name. My mother egged her on, her ears open, hungry for details. I'd doze off and wake up to find Sitt Victoria still talking, my mother still listening eagerly.

I opened my eyes again late at night, after midnight, and I saw Sitt Victoria take off her clothes. She took them all off. She was naked as her mother bore her. She then took a candle and lit it. She went out to the balcony and closed the door behind her. My mother watched her with respect and veneration.

"What's this crazy woman doing?" I whispered in terror. "Someone should keep an eye on her."

Sitt Victoria stayed on the balcony until dawn began to break. She opened the door and came back to us still naked, the candle in her hand extinguished.

"That's it, madame," she said smiling happily. "Everything will go well from now on."

My mother paid her ten pounds.

It seemed like my mother was spending half her savings on black magic and sorcerers.

All for me to hate Adel. But I didn't. Every day, I became more insistent for my mother to call him. I still begged her to let us get married. But she kept refusing on the pretext that Adel was a scoundrel. She kept repeating stories about his scandals. She kept saying he didn't love me and that he had duped me.

"Listen, Nouga," she said one day, looking me in the eye. "There's something that I didn't want to tell you until after you got better. But I'm going to tell you now since you're still insisting on this Adel."

I raised my eyes to her.

"You know who Adel wanted to go out with?" my mother continued, her face ironclad.

"Who?" I asked, annoyed.

"Your cousin."

I jumped up in bed as if I'd been stung by something.

"Liar!" I screamed. "Nothing but lies!"

"Fine. I'll bring her and she'll tell you everything herself so you know whether I'm lying or not."

I kept on screaming, pulling my hair and hitting the pillow.

"Liar! Liar! You hate him and you want me to hate him. You don't care that I'm dying because of this!"

My mother wasn't affected.

She sent the maid to Wailiya to get my aunt—my real mother—and my cousin, Samira, who was my real sister.

She was a year older than me. She was beautiful, maybe more beautiful than me, despite the poverty that she lived in.

I clung to her hand.

"Tell me the truth, Samira," I said with tears on my cheek. "Adel came on to you?"

Samira looked at my mother and then at her mother and hesitated for a long time.

"Forget it, Nouga," my aunt said. "What difference does it make?"

"No," my mother said. "Let her talk."

"Last year," she stammered, "when he saw me here at your house, he heard that I was looking for work. He gave me his phone number and asked me to call him. He promised me he'd get me a job at his company. I didn't mention it because I thought he'd tell you."

"And then?" I asked, feeling my chest contract.

She looked again at my mother and her mother.

"I called him two months later. He asked to meet me. We arranged to meet outside his office."

"And you went?" I screamed.

"Yes. I thought you knew. I thought he told you. I met him at the door of the office building. As soon as he saw me, he took me by the hand and called a taxi. I asked him, where are we going, Adel? He said, just come, it doesn't matter. He took me to an apartment in Agouza."

"Liar!" I screamed. "It's not possible. You're all lying. You want me to hate him, to leave him. I won't!"

"At any rate," Samira said. "I haven't talked to him since then, even though he kept waiting outside our apartment, waiting for hours for me to come down. I know what he's after."

"Liar!" I screamed again. "I don't believe it."

"Let her call him on the phone in front of you," my mother suggested.

She then took the phone and put in front of Samira.

"Call him," she continued, "so she knows she's been duped."

My aunt—my real mother—was in a corner of the room, crying silently.

Samira lifted the receiver with a trembling hand and dialed the number. My mother then pulled her over to me and put her head next to mine so I could hear everything Adel said.

As soon as Adel heard Samira's voice, he yelled out. He clearly knew her voice.

"Samira! How are you?"

"Fine," Samira said, bringing the receiver closer to my ear.

"When will I see you?" he asked enthusiastically.

"I can't, Adel," Samira said looking at my face. "It's better if we don't see each other."

"Why?" he said shocked. "Didn't we agree . . ."

I couldn't bear any more. I grabbed the phone from Samira's hand, pressing my other hand to my broken heart.

"Really, Adel?" I yelled. "Really? It's like that?"

The receiver fell from my hand.

"Nouga! Nouga!" I could hear him screaming my name.

My mother took the receiver off the bed and put it back in the cradle.

I lay back down, my head spinning, a sharp pain in my stomach. The last thing I heard was the voice of my aunt, my real mother.

"Really, shame on you," she said.

I passed out.

I learned more than three years later that this was all nothing more than a play directed by my mother. My cousin and aunt participated in it after my mother convinced them that Adel wasn't suitable for me and that he had duped me. I learned that Adel had been visiting my aunt's house, not to hit on my sister but to ask about me and to try to get my real mother to intervene.

But at the time, I believed it. I believed that Adel had been hitting on my sister.

I fell to pieces completely. The illness that I couldn't find a drug for tightened its grip on me. I could no longer stand. My face was sallow, almost tinged with green. Whenever I looked in the mirror, I cried.

During that time, Adel kept calling, but I refused to talk to him. My mother would pick up instead.

"Adel," she'd tell me, her eyes on mine.

I'd shake my head on the pillow.

"I don't want to talk with him," I'd say in a weak voice. "I don't want to hear what he has to say."

My mother's eyes sparkled with victory.

"Sorry, Adel, my dear," she'd say into the phone. "Nouga's tired. She can't talk."

Adel gave up hope and went to Kuwait to take his new job. He sent me letters from there, but I didn't get a single one. My mother intercepted them all.

I was broken. I'd lost the father who had raised me and in whose embrace I grew up. And I'd lost Adel. My lips were orphaned, my chest, my neck, my waist. Every part that Adel touched was crying for him. I was consumed by these feelings and couldn't imagine that there could be another man in my life after Adel.

Sorcerers and charlatans kept coming to the house.

Doctors too.

One of them said I needed an operation on my intestines. This made me happy. I wanted anything to distract me from my torture, to get me out of this house, even if to the hospital, to pass out under anesthesia and have my stomach opened up, to find another kind of pain to distract me. I wanted nurses, bouquets of flowers, all the attention.

But my mother hesitated. She was afraid of cutting open my stomach.

That was when I first heard Hashim's name. I mean Dr. Hashim 'Abd al-Latif. We heard about him and the miracles that he had performed for a lot of important families. My mother called him for a second opinion.

It wasn't easy. He was always busy. His appointments filled up way in advance. But my mother didn't give up.

Hashim came.

He had a presence that filled the entire house. His manner soothed my nerves. I smiled as soon as I saw him.

Hashim pulled a chair over and sat next to my bed like he was an old friend.

"How are you, my dear?" he asked, smiling and looking into my eyes.

"I'm tired, Doctor," I said. "Tired. I feel like I'm suffocating . . . and . . ."

"We'll see now," he cut me off, smiling at me.

"Can I make you a coffee, Doctor?" my mother asked, standing at the head of the bed.

"Medium sugar, please," Hashim said quickly without turning to her.

My mother hesitated. She didn't want to leave me alone with the doctor, but she couldn't ignore the doctor's request. For the first time, I felt my mother to have the weaker personality, overshadowed by someone else. She went out to tell the maid to make coffee for the doctor and came back quickly to stand next to me.

From his pocket, Hashim took out a small notebook with a nice pen attached to it and he started asking me dozens of questions, writing down my answers. He then put the notebook back in his pocket and started examining me. He knotted his brows, concentrating his entire mind into his fingers with which he was examining me. My pain fled under his slender, gentle fingers. Wherever he touched me, I felt that part of me was healed. I was confused about what to tell him. I'd tell him about the pain in one spot, but then I didn't feel it anymore after he'd examined me there. A heavy silence surrounded us. The entire house was silent. My mother almost held her breath. I thought all of Cairo was silent as Hashim examined me.

Hashim finished and he looked at me for a long time. He seemed confused. He then started flipping through the prescriptions of the doctors who had examined me before him. He shook his head.

"I'm going to tell you something, but don't be mad at me," he said, smiling, about to render his verdict.

I looked up at him.

"There's nothing wrong with you. You're in excellent health. The pain in your stomach and chest is the result of a nervous crisis."

I looked at him as if he'd revealed my secret.

"But I'm very tired, Doctor," I said.

"I know. Our nerves wear us out more than a physical illness. I'll write you a prescription for a sedative to relax you. But the drug isn't enough. You have to help yourself."

"So, no operation, Doctor?" my mother asked.

"If she wants to do an operation for fun, that's up to her," he joked. "But no, no operation."

He looked at his watch and then smiled at me again.

"I have fifteen minutes," he said. "Time for me to have a coffee. I can be your psychologist. Talk to me."

"About what?" I asked searching his face.

"About anything that's bothering you," he said calmly.

I looked over at my mother. He followed my eyes.

"Let's talk alone," he said. "Please, ma'am, leave me with Nagwa. Could you get the coffee?"

Hashim was talking with a surprising simplicity and tenderness. My mother couldn't oppose him, but she hesitated for a moment. She looked at me and then at him.

"Okay, Doctor," she said finally leaving the room. "May she be healed in your hands."

I stayed with him alone. I felt embarrassed. I don't know why. I was confused about what to tell him. I was confused where to begin.

"You want me to help you get started?" he asked. "It seems to me that you, my dear, are in love with someone . . ."

"He was my fiancé," I cut him off.

I began to tell him the whole story. I told him lots of details, small details that I'd been bottling up. I tried to empty myself. I began to feel better. He listened calmly and patiently and with great interest as if my story really did concern him.

Still, I hid things from him. I hid from him that my mother wasn't my mother. I hid from him that I wasn't a virgin. I hid from him that Adel was hitting on my sister. It wasn't because I didn't trust him, but because I felt ashamed. I felt already that Hashim wasn't just my doctor.

"Your pains are psychosomatic," he said gently. "Emotional blows can have a big effect on the digestive system and the chest. The pills will relax you but aren't enough on their own. You have to face your problem and solve it. Make a decision and take responsibility for it. But the first thing you should do is get up out of bed."

Hashim paused.

"Look, Nagwa," he continued softly. "This isn't therapy, not only because it's not my specialty, but because you don't need it. You need to regain your health and then your anxiety will go down, and you'll feel like yourself."

I felt very close to him, that I'd known him for a long time.

He stood up and reached out to the bed cover, pulling it from on top of me.

"Stand up," he said, smiling. "Show me."

I reached out quickly and pulled my nightshirt over my thighs. I felt the blood rush to my cheeks.

"I can't, Doctor," I whispered.

"Yes, you can," he said. "Call your mother so she can see too."

I raised my voice weakly, calling out to my mother.

My mother was standing outside the door. Maybe she'd listened to every word that I'd said to him. She came right in.

"Nagwa is getting out of bed," Hashim told her. "I don't want her to get back into bed unless it's time to sleep."

My mother reached her arm out to help me get up.

"Let her do it herself," Hashim said in a commanding tone.

My mother pulled her arm away.

I got up. I'd been lying in bed for more than a month. As my feet touched the ground, I felt dizzy. I was about to fall. My mother then held me and pulled me to her chest.

"Sit her down on the chair," Hashim ordered.

My mother sat me down on the same chair that Hashim had been sitting on. Hashim sat on the edge of the bed. He brought his face close to mine.

"Listen, Nagwa," he said. "Until you regain strength, it will be difficult. You have to take care of yourself. I can't treat you without you helping me. Eat well, sleep well, laugh, go out of the house as soon as you can. Walk around, smell the air. You'll feel better."

"Yes," I said weakly, nodding my head.

He turned to my mother.

"I beg you, ma'am," he said. "Don't let her sit around by herself. Call her friends over, do whatever she wants."

"That's it, Nagwa," he said, my hand in his. "Promise me you'll take care of yourself."

And then he left. I felt a shudder run through me.

I wanted to move, to go out. I wanted to be free from my thoughts and my illness.

I could go back to school. I had been preparing to get my high school diploma. It was only a few months until the exam.

But I was a coward. I felt I wasn't strong enough to face my classmates. I thought everyone would discover instantly that I wasn't a virgin. I wasn't like them. I wouldn't be happy like them. I wouldn't be able to talk like them. So I didn't go back to school.

The next day, I braced myself and told my mother: "I want to go out."

"Where?" she asked.

"I don't know. I just want to go out."

"You're not going out unless I'm with you. God willing, even if you go to a cabaret, I'm going to be with you."

I started going out, but I didn't go anywhere without my mother by my side.

We went far, to a place more abominable than any cabaret.

We traveled down a long road.
The road of desperation.

4

"LET'S GO TO ZIZI'S," MY mother announced a few days later.

All I wanted to do after my month in bed was to call some friends my age and go out shopping with them. As for Zizi, she was something else. She was a married woman. Her husband had an important job in Beni Suef and she lived in Cairo alone, completely free. She lived the high life. She had a big Chevrolet and another car just for her kids. She lived in a luxurious apartment in Heliopolis and bought her clothes by the dozen. She had so many clothes she seemed to have a different outfit for every day. People talked about her, but Zizi couldn't care less.

My mother had known Zizi for a long time. She knew her mother and sister. She made up some family link between us, as usual. Our family tree seemed to connect us to everyone she wanted.

My mother loved Zizi, but she tried not to show it. She admired Zizi because she thought she was a smart woman who could play with men and get from them the wonderful life she was living.

My mother believed that the role of women in life was to exploit men. Nothing more. She didn't believe there was anything women could offer men besides their bodies. Women therefore had to haggle to get the highest price. Even marriage for my mother was nothing more than a simple transaction: buying and selling. That's why she liked Zizi, because she knew how to haggle.

The women of Nour al-Huda also liked Zizi because she volunteered a lot for the organization and because she called on them for their magic from time to time.

My mother, before my collapse, had kept me far from Zizi. That's why I was surprised when my mother suggested that we go see her.

"Why Zizi?" I asked.

"Because she likes to have fun," my mother said. "Maybe she can make you laugh and help you forget what happened."

I got up and put on my clothes, almost holding my breath. I still felt weak.

My mother had put on her black coat and black turban and stood at the door of my room.

"Let's go, Nouga. Hurry it up."

"Don't rush me!" I yelled.

She went away but then came back a few minutes later holding a metal tray with burning incense. She put it on the ground for me to step over seven times.

Without thinking, I turned from in front of my mirror and kicked it over.

"I don't want to be covered in incense! Enough of this! Do you think anyone will envy me? For this miserable existence?"

My mother rushed over and picked it up off the ground before it lit the room on fire.

From that day, I got used to screaming at my mother, and she got used to putting up with my screaming. But putting up with it didn't mean that she submitted to me.

We left the house. We took a taxi to the station and then we rode the metro to Heliopolis.

We arrived at Zizi's. Her house was luxurious. The floors were covered with enormous rugs. The furniture was all modern and looked new. Zizi changed the furniture every year or two. There were chandeliers and statues, extravagant pieces in every corner of the house. Despite that, I wasn't comfortable there. There was something missing. Maybe it was too ostentatious. No doubt it was full of valuable, expensive things, but they were laid out in a way that made it look cheap, and made you feel cheap for being there.

"I'll make you a house that is a hundred times better than this," my mother said as she noticed me staring.

"I wouldn't want a house like this," I told her. "It has no taste!"

"This is like the house of a princess," my mother informed me.

Zizi came in to welcome us.

Even though it was two o'clock in the afternoon, she was wearing a silk embroidered robe, open at the top to reveal her nightie and, under it, her full body.

"Welcome, 'Aziza," she said, kissing my mother on both cheeks. "I've missed you!"

She then turned to me with an astonishing happiness sparkling in her eyes.

"Nouga! I can't believe it. You've grown up so much. I haven't seen you for a year. No one grows up this much in one year."

She hugged me to her chest and started patting me on my back.

"We have to marry her right away, 'Aziza," she said, turning to my mother. "That's it. The time has come."

"She's the one who's refusing," my mother said, happy with Zizi's delight. "She wants to continue her studies and go to university."

"Is that forbidden?" Zizi said and let out a ringing laugh.

She took me by the hand and sat me next to her on the couch. She then started examining my face.

"What's wrong, Nouga?" she asked. "Something's wrong, I can tell."

"You know she was sick," my mother said quickly.

"Your hairdo isn't right," Zizi said, looking at me. "This is the hairdo of an old lady, not a pretty girl like you. Come, let's give you a new one."

She stood up and pulled me by the hand, nearly skipping along as if she were a child. She brought me into her bedroom, my mother behind us.

The bedroom was all brown: brown shades, brown covers on the bed, brown upholstery on the chairs, and dark brown wood.

Zizi sat me in front of her mirror. There were dozens of expensive glass perfume bottles and makeup brushes. She stood behind me, doing my hair as she talked and laughed.

Her energy was infectious. I found myself coming back to life. I laughed with her. I quickly forgot myself and all my worries.

My mother sat at a distance, happiness plastered across her face.

Zizi then began to show us her new clothes.

She opened a wardrobe that extended the length of the entire wall. I could see dozens of dresses, coats, furs, shoes. I'd never seen so many clothes in one place.

She got undressed without any hesitation and put on one of her new dresses to show me. I felt embarrassed.

She then insisted that I take off my clothes for me to try one of her dresses. I tried to refuse, but she insisted. My mother insisted with her.

"What's wrong, Nouga?" she asked. "Why so shy?"

Zizi grabbed me and started taking my dress off. She looked at me in my undershirt as if through the eyes of dozens of men.

"What's this?" she said, surprise flashing in her eyes. "Your chest is amazing!"

I wrapped my arm around my chest as if protecting it from leering eyes. I was so embarrassed.

She put me in her dress. It was delicate chiffon blue. She tied it from behind so that it was tight because the dress was too big for me. I turned to the mirror and looked at myself. The dress revealed my arms and was low-cut. It clung to my body and was the color of the sky. I felt I could fly in this dress. Zizi made me feel like a woman. I hadn't ever truly felt that way, despite what happened with Adel.

"'Abd Allah, my husband, is coming from Beni Suef this afternoon and we're going out to the Auberge tonight," Zizi said. "What do you think about coming with us?"

My mother hesitated and then looked at me as if she was asking me.

"Come on, time to get out of your prison," Zizi said. "Nouga needs to see the world. How long are you going to hide her for? Girls her age are out every night."

"I don't have any objection," my mother said. "But . . ."

"But what?" Zizi kept going enthusiastically. "No buts. We'll be with my husband. Nouga, what do you think?"

"I've never gone to the Auberge," I said shyly.

"That's it, then. You're coming. We'll see you at ten o'clock."

At ten thirty, Zizi arrived to pick us up. She left her husband in the car and came up to get us.

"What's this you're wearing, Nouga?" she exclaimed as soon as she saw me. "You look like you're going to school!"

She pulled open the top of my dress to reveal part of my chest and my shoulders. She started doing my hair, and then she took a lipstick out of her bag and put it on my lips. She fixed the kohl that I'd put around my eyes.

I gave in. So did my mother. It was as if both of us were women from the countryside who'd come to Cairo for the first time and had given themselves over to a swindler.

Zizi wasn't interested in my mother. She didn't say a thing about her black coat or her turban, as if they didn't have anything to do with us.

We left.

Zizi's husband wasn't alone in the car. There was a young man with him. He was younger than Dr. Hashim. Maybe he was thirty-five. Everything about him was fine and precise.

The young man got out of the car to greet us.

"Khairy," Zizi said, presenting him to us.

She didn't bother giving us his last name.

"Sit next to 'Abd Allah, Khairy," she ordered. "The ladies will sit in the back."

She turned to my mother as if to reassure her that no man would get close to her daughter, that everything was above board.

Her husband greeted us. He was at the wheel. He was broad and fat. His laugh was loud. He looked happy, like he didn't have a care in the world.

We went to the Auberge.

We walked in with my mother at my side. I felt at that moment that I really did need her protection. I was filled with terror. I didn't notice that my mother was nervous too. We both stuck close to Zizi, like two kids afraid to lose their mother.

Zizi led us to a table. Two men and a woman were already there. The two men were jubilant as they greeted Zizi. They then went quiet when their eyes fell on me. They exchanged questioning glances with Zizi and went back to looking at me. They were both well-mannered and urbane, but with wide, smarmy smiles on their lips.

I sat between Khairy and one of the two men we found at the table. His name was Sami. They were both staring at me. Their smiles floated around me like butterflies, each of them doing their best to make me laugh, to attract my attention.

The third man devoted himself entirely to Zizi. They were whispering to each other words that I could barely make out.

As soon as he sat down at the table, 'Abd Allah filled his glass and devoted himself to consuming the meze. From time to time, he made a comment that no one heard or laughed at. It was like he wasn't with us, as if his wife wasn't there.

My mother sat in her black coat and turban at the end of the table. She looked like an old chaperone. That's probably who the men thought she was. Probably none of them realized she was my mother. Maybe they thought she was in business with me. 'Abd Allah, Zizi's husband, was the only one who paid her any attention.

"Would you like a pickle, 'Aziza?" he'd ask in his thick hoarse voice.

My mother would give him a weak smile. Her eyes were centered on me, keeping watch on every movement, every touch, every look. She was wide-eyed, trying to catch every word, every whisper. She sat at the end of the table like a radar, her face reflecting everything that was happening to me. She'd smile when I smiled, and she'd look frightened when one of the men at the table would go too far with me.

This wasn't her place.

She wasn't that kind of old woman.

She was doing this for me because she wanted me to forget Adel, because she was still afraid she'd lose me to him.

Despite that, I didn't know if I was embarrassed by her, dressed all in black with her wrinkled old face at a table covered with bottles of whiskey, or if I felt pity for her.

"Why are you so quiet, Nouga?" Zizi asked. "Watch out for Sami. Don't trust what he says. That one's a devil!"

I don't know why I gave her a defiant look. I decided at that moment to prove to her I wasn't some country girl who'd never seen Cairo before. An incredible stubbornness gripped me. I decided to show this group that I had a strong personality.

I pushed away my fear and decided to attract all the attention to me. I started talking. I told stories. I made sarcastic comments. I stirred up laughs.

In just a few minutes, I became the queen of the table. Even the man sitting next to Zizi turned to me. 'Abd Allah forgot to eat the meze. Instead, he started eating up every word that came out of my lips. My mother was watching it all, and it clearly made her nervous. Zizi was surprised, and she gave me a piercing stare as if she discovered that I wasn't the simple naive girl she'd thought I was.

Khairy filled a glass and gave it to me.

"Merci," I said, refusing with a big smile.

"Why?" he asked.

"You're enough for me," I said loudly. "You're intoxicating!"

The laughs rang out. Khairy drank the glass himself. Sami tried to draw me into a heated conversation with him alone. But I turned his whispers into words that everyone could hear. He seemed embarrassed, but he kept going, giving up trying to whisper. He started pretending to touch me by accident. He was acting like he wanted to get the plates of meze from the end of the table, but he kept brushing against me, getting close to my ear, his face almost touching mine. Before I knew it, I felt his hand on my thigh. I took his hand and held it up where everyone could see it, like I was lifting up something filthy.

"Look what I found on my leg, Zizi!" I announced.

Everyone burst out laughing. I tossed Sami's hand away, turned to him, and gave him a long look.

My mother was watching the whole scene, her lips trembling, not knowing how to act.

"We have to go too," my mother said as if she couldn't bear any more. "Nouga is still recovering from her illness, and she shouldn't stay out late."

"We have to go too," Zizi said quickly.

We all got up.

"We have to see each other again," Sami said, squeezing my hand and saying goodbye.

"I guess . . ." I said.

We got in Zizi's car. Khairy was with us. This time, Zizi didn't bother trying to protect me. She sat next to her husband in the front seat and let Khairy sit with us in the back. But I outsmarted her, putting my mother between me and him.

"We have to see each other again," Khairy said, saying goodbye to me in front of the house.

"I guess . . ." I said, playing hard to get.

I went up to my room. My mother was behind me. She sat on the edge of the bed as I took off my clothes. Before she asked anything, I satisfied her curiosity and told her all the details, every word, every touch, every glance. After she had her fill, she left me alone to sleep. Black clouds of confusion swallowed me up. Why had I done all that? Why had I set myself on this road? I wasn't naive. I knew how this would end.

My confusion poured out as tears on my cheeks. I cried myself to sleep.

I woke up the following day feeling weak again, so I stayed in bed. Zizi called to ask about me three times. She talked with my mother for a long time on the phone.

When I did get out of bed, we went to spend the evening at Zizi's. I found Sami and Khairy there, as well as a third man, Murad. Lots of other men and women came and went. All the women there were like Zizi. I was the only girl among them, much younger than the others. I was much more beautiful too. I was a flower in a forest of women swaying in depravity like old, worn-out trees.

The evenings flew by at Zizi's house, at the Auberge, at the Arizona, at the Shagara.

No man got anything from me, not a single touch or even a word of encouragement. Despite that, all the men loved me. I was a breath of fresh air in their stale old lives.

My mother knew what was happening. She became friends with the men we met, friends for me, of course. My mother felt more comfortable being friends with the men than the women. She knew their interest in her was only to get close to me. And with that, she could exploit them, put them at her service.

I remember the day when the treasures of this new social circle opened up in front of us.

Khairy called one morning to invite us to an evening out. My mother told him she was going out shopping with me. Even today, I don't know if she had planned this or not, but Khairy offered to go with us. And my mother agreed.

We spent more than twenty pounds. Khairy paid for everything.

And after that, the gifts came pouring down, from Khairy and the others. There were gifts for special occasions, and gifts for no reason at all. I was delighted. I didn't know there were people who gave such expensive gifts that easily. I got three radios, a television, rings, dresses. My mother was even more delighted than me. She locked everything in her closet and kept the key. I couldn't touch anything without her permission.

One day, I was surprised when Sami proposed to me. I had no idea they got married in this social circle. I thought it was all fun and nights out, that they thought getting married was for idiots. Maybe Sami understood me and realized that I was in this group by mistake and that their corruption hadn't reached me. He was going to save me as he knew that no one had gotten to me yet.

I appreciated Sami as a man. I didn't love him, but he was handsome, and he had an important job. He was a husband that any girl would be proud of.

My mother didn't refuse. But she didn't accept. She left him hanging.

I didn't care what she thought. I didn't want to get married. It wasn't marriage I longed for. It was love. And I didn't feel any love for him.

Khairy too came forward to propose. My mother left him hanging as well. That made me realize that my mother didn't want me to get married. She wanted me to have many suitors, so I'd have to stay with her. She didn't want any one man to take me from her. That's how far her selfishness went.

Dozens of men came to our house. They kept coming without their wives or sisters. Incredibly, we didn't lose our reputation in the neighborhood. Not at all. My mother managed to keep up appearances. The women of Nour al-Huda still came regularly. The incense still burned in the morning and evening. My mother didn't let any man visit us except at appropriate times. Maybe some rumors were stirred up about us, but it was quiet, restricted to our neighborhood. And none of our friends lived in our neighborhood.

I was miserable. I wasn't happy with these gifts or parties. But I didn't have any choice but to accept the gifts and pretend that I was happy. I got tired of all the parties and I started to hold back from the men, being stingy with entertaining them. But what was I going to do? I couldn't go back to school. So I just kept going along with it, becoming colder and more distant.

Soon, 'Abd al-Fattah Bey Rif'at came into my life.

He was forty-eight years old and married with kids. One of his daughters was older than me and married with her own kids. He was a millionaire. Even after nationalization, he managed to keep most of his money. Maybe it made him only a half millionaire.

Of course, I never saw his wife or daughters. I met him at Zizi's house, not at a party but for tea. Zizi called us and invited my mother and me for tea. She told us not to be late because she had an important guest waiting for us.

"Have Nouga wear her green dress," she told my mother. "Don't forget."

What made my green dress special was that it revealed my shoulders, which Zizi thought were the most beautiful she'd ever seen.

I put on my green dress and went to Zizi's with my mother.

'Abd al-Fattah Bey Rif'at was the only guest that day.

He stood up to greet us with great politesse, giving me a calm look. Despite that, I felt that he was trying to take all of me in, that he studied me all at once, every part of me, with the look of a connoisseur.

He then turned around and greeted my mother, exaggerating his attention toward her. He presented the center chair in the room to her and gave her the first glass of tea. He directed most of what he said to her, but without ignoring me.

He talked to me like I was his daughter, respectfully, tenderly. I felt he was trying to show me that he wasn't like the rest of Zizi's friends and that he didn't want from me what Zizi's other friends wanted.

This made me feel calm. I felt I could be myself with him, like I really was his daughter.

As usual, my mother shifted the conversation to the subject of family ties. She quickly discovered a link between us and him.

"You know, Nouga," she said turning to me, "this 'Abd al-Fattah Bey really is your uncle. He's the son of the aunt of the niece of your father. In other words, your uncle."

"How are you, uncle?" I asked laughing.

'Abd al-Fattah turned to me with a serious look in his eyes.

"I want you to consider me your uncle for real," he said.

I felt embarrassed by the way he looked at me.

"Yes, uncle," I said lowering my eyes.

I don't remember exactly how the conversation went after that.

"What's that ugly pin on your shirt?" I remember Zizi asked me at one point.

"Oh no, Zizi," I said. "It's fabulous. I bought it for three pounds from Mounaz."

"How could you put a three-pound pin on such a beautiful dress and such a beautiful bosom?" Zizi scolded me.

"Don't worry, Zizi," 'Abd al-Fattah said, letting out a small laugh. "She'll have a different pin there tomorrow."

"You don't like it either?" I asked.

"I do. But let's put something new there to make Zizi happy."

At seven o'clock, 'Abd al-Fattah got up to leave. We stayed with Zizi as she went on talking about all of 'Abd al-Fattah's assets and factories, his manners and taste.

"His only fault is that he never stays out late," she said. "He has to be home right after seven. And he's very strict at home. Imagine, no one has ever seen his wife."

The next day, 'Abd al-Fattah sent his personal driver to us with a small package. My mother opened the package and found a small box of red velvet. As soon as we opened the box, we were both stunned. There was a diamond brooch in it. It was a real diamond.

The brooch had a card with the name 'Abd al-Fattah Rif'at. Above his name, he had written three words: "From your uncle."

That same day, my mother rushed to the jewelry shop to get an estimate for it. It was worth at least 350 pounds.

My mother was salivating.

Our relationship with 'Abd al-Fattah developed quickly, and strangely, after that.

'Abd al-Fattah was my mother's friend more than he was mine, even though I knew for sure the only thing that tied him to her was his desire to get to me.

He'd talk with her on the phone twice a day and for a long time. My mother only told me half of what they talked about. I wasn't interested in asking about the other half.

Then he started visiting us. He didn't come every day, but two or three times a week to have coffee with me and my mother in the living room.

He soon became everything in the house. He became the man of the house. He was the one taking care of everything, of all our needs. He was the one who bought my clothes. Not himself, of course. He gave money to my mother to buy them for me. He got two of my cousins a job at one of his companies.

The formality disappeared between us, even though I kept calling him "Uncle 'Abdu."

Sometimes he'd try to kiss me on my cheeks, but I'd squirm away and run off, playing the role of a little girl. And then I'd indulge him and sit on his lap. As soon as he wrapped his arms around my waist, I'd jump up and yell out something like: "Let me show you my new belt, uncle!"

He'd smile patiently. I knew there were limits to his patience and that 'Abd al-Fattah wanted to reach his goal. How and where, I didn't know, but I began to get scared. I was afraid of the day that he'd get there. I sensed he was more intelligent than me, with a determination that was stronger than my insistence on maintaining my purity.

What remained of my purity.

I began to fear those long discussions between him and my mother. I began to get extremely anxious. I'd shout at my mother, accusing her of hiding things from me. I started breaking things. I'd smash plates or vases. Once, I broke the television. I threw an ashtray at it.

But my mother put up with me. And Uncle 'Abdu put up with me with the patience of a man who knows he will get everything he wants.

Everything around me changed quickly, too fast for me to grasp what was happening. We didn't go to Zizi's anymore. We forgot about Khairy and Sami. My mother didn't encourage other men to visit us anymore. She seemed to have decided she was more pleased with 'Abd al-Fattah than any of the others. I started to feel that there was a force pushing me into a tight corner to tear me up, a mysterious force that I couldn't see or resist.

I was afraid. Confused. Anxious.

I was deprived of the fantasy of love.

I'd cry.

Then, one day, the phone rang. I happened to be next to it while my mother was in the kitchen.

I picked up.

I heard Adel's voice. I recognized it immediately even after such a long time.

"Adel!" I exclaimed.

I then lowered my voice so my mother wouldn't hear me.

"When'd you get back?"

"Half an hour ago," he said breathing heavily. "Why didn't you respond to my letters, Nouga?"

"What letters? I didn't get any."

"How's that possible? I sent you a letter almost every day. I couldn't believe that you just went on with your life without responding to me . . ."

"Where are you now?" I asked cutting him off.

"Home."

"Can I see you?"

"Of course. I came back just to see you."

"Not at your house."

"Where?"

"Somewhere no one can see us."

"What do you have in mind?"

"Your brother's apartment," I whispered quickly. "Right now."

I hung up. Without looking behind me or changing my clothes, I tiptoed over to the door and opened it quietly. I closed it without a sound.

I left.

I went to him.

5

I WALKED QUICKLY, ALMOST RUNNING. I looked behind me afraid that my mother would catch me. I looked around for a taxi. And then I remembered that Adel had called from his house in Helwan and that he wouldn't get to his brother's apartment in Agouza for at least twenty minutes. I then realized that I didn't have any money with me. I forgot to take any. Even if I'd remembered, I would've had to take it from my mother since she didn't give me my own money. I never had my own spending money. She was always with me and paid for whatever I wanted.

I decided to walk from Giza to Agouza.

I went by the back streets so my mother wouldn't see me if she tried to come after me.

I walked for a long time, lost in thought, barely noticing anything around me. I was thinking about what would happen when my mother discovered that I'd disappeared. I was thinking about the kind of life we were living, about Uncle 'Abdu and Zizi. I wasn't thinking about Adel. I wasn't confused at all about going to meet him after he'd been gone for more than a year. I didn't feel like I was driven to him, or desiring him, or in love with him. All these emotions were absent.

I tried to focus on Adel. I tried to picture what he'd look like after all this time. Did he fill out and put on weight? Did he still have that heedless smile and that confident sparkle in his eyes? I tried to fill my chest with the feeling of love, to be aroused about it, to be happy. But it wasn't long before I found myself thinking about my mother again.

I was fleeing my mother and the life she was planning for me. I wasn't running to Adel. I was running away from my mother. I was escaping the life that she was preparing for me, not fleeing to a life that I wanted.

I began to doubt that I was still in love with Adel, but I tried to dispel this doubt. I was afraid I'd discover that I didn't love Adel anymore. I hoped I was wrong, that I needed his love, that I needed someone's love to save me from the fate that I was being driven to, to give me the strength to face my mother and Uncle 'Abdu.

There was no doubt I'd figure out how I felt about Adel the moment I saw him.

I walked for more than an hour. I went down one street and then the next without feeling tired. I was lost in thought.

I reached Adel's brother's building. I began to walk around it until I was sure that Adel must have gotten there from Helwan.

I went up to the apartment. I wasn't nervous, I was still distracted by my worries about my mother.

Then the door opened.

I saw Adel in front of me.

It was as if I woke up suddenly, as if I returned suddenly from a distant world with no Adel.

I couldn't take him in with a single look. He appeared before me like a blurry picture. Before he came into focus, he pulled me toward him and closed the door.

"Nouga," he whispered as he held me in his arms.

He squeezed me so hard it was as if he was trying to pull me in under his ribs.

I tried to relax against his chest. I leaned my head on his shoulder and closed my eyes to forget everything except my feelings for him.

Adel moved me away from his chest. He began to look at me, his eyes gleaming. I looked at him too, searching for my old love.

It seemed that he'd changed. His eyes didn't have that confident sparkle. There was still a glimmer, but it was duller with a harshness to it. They were the eyes of a man who'd plunged into the battle of life. He had a calm and settled smile, that of a man who no longer played around.

He'd put on weight, too, and he seemed shorter. His face was browner and there were deep lines around the sides of his nose and cheeks, battle scars left behind by his life over there in the desert of Kuwait.

There was a small mustache above his lips. It looked like it was dusted on with the sand that the wind blew at traveling tribes.

"I missed you so much," Adel whispered as he clutched my hands, giving me a big smile.

"Me too," I said coldly.

"How could you leave me without a word?"

"Let's sit down first, Adel," I said as a kind of hope-lessness crept into my chest. "I'm so tired. I walked all the way here from my house."

"Really?"

"I ran away from Mother. I didn't have any money to take a taxi."

He took me by the hand and sat me on the couch. It was the same couch where he took my virginity. I looked at it before sitting down as if searching for something precious that I'd lost there. I then sat down on the edge like I was trying not to sit on another person sleeping on it, as if this other person was me.

"I'm sure your mother is the one who hid my letters from you," Adel said sitting down, pressing himself against me.

"Maybe," I said.

I was lost in the memory of that distant day.

"I learned a lot of things about you that upset me," I continued, turning to him. "Maybe if I'd gotten your letters, I wouldn't have responded to you."

"What did you learn?"

"That you hit on my sister, and you brought her here, to this apartment."

"Complete lies! Whoever told you that is lying. They want to break us up. I went to your sister to find out what was happening with you, for her to help me with your mother."

I looked at him. I didn't care if he was telling the truth.

"Maybe," I said tepidly, feeling exhausted.

"Don't say 'maybe.' Believe me, Nouga. Those are lies."

"I believe you."

A heavy silence passed between us. It seemed at that moment that we were each struck by the other. I wasn't the only one. Adel felt that I'd changed as well.

Despite that, we each wanted to be sure about how we felt. He wanted us to try to rekindle our broken love, the love that I lived so passionately. He came closer to me.

"We won't leave each other like that ever again, Nouga," he said, his warm breath on my face. "No one can separate us."

"I've been so tired, Adel," I said lowering my eyes.

"You'll never be tired again."

I shut my eyes. I wanted his kiss. I wanted to confirm that it was still the kiss of my memory from so long ago. His lips got closer. I felt them touch mine. My eyes were closed. I threw myself into his kiss like I was tasting food to see if it needed more salt.

No. His kiss was missing something. I felt like my lips were strangers from his. They didn't remember and had strayed.

I let him kiss me more. I tried as hard as I could to kiss him back. But I was a stranger to him.

I let him continue. He squeezed me to him as if seeking shelter in me after the months spent in the Kuwaiti desert. His hand was stroking my back and then crept around to my chest.

My body was cold as ice. My heart murmured anxiously. My chest didn't recognize this hand that had raised and matured it. I didn't feel anything except my long months of deprivation. I still submitted. I wanted to find my love in Adel.

He leaned me over the couch, his hot breath on my face. One of his hands was buried in my hair while the other moved over every part of me. His entire weight was on top of me. I couldn't bear to close my eyes. I couldn't bear to open them. His hand reached the side of my dress and started to lift it up. I was going to submit to him. It was his right. He was the only man who'd had my body. He owned my body. He was the man who made a woman of me. He's my husband, even if we haven't gotten married.

But I couldn't. I couldn't bear any more submission. Disgust grew inside me. I reached my hand out, grabbing the sides of my dress so he couldn't lift it up. I pulled my lips away from his.

"That's enough, Adel," I whispered.

But he didn't want to stop, which disturbed me. I thought he was tender, that he was concerned with not taking more from me than I wanted to give.

I was forced to resist.

"Don't be crazy, Adel," I said nervously, trying to get him off me.

He gave me a look of surprise as if he couldn't believe it.

"I don't want to, Adel," I pleaded, whispering. "I'm tired."

He got off me. I sat up straight, trying to catch my breath. I could feel where the hairs of his mustache had been pressed against my face.

"We have to get married, Nouga," he said, panting. "We have to."

"You think Mother will let us?" I asked, smoothing down my hair.

I looked at the door as if hurrying my mother to come and catch us.

"We won't wait for your mother's permission. We have to get married."

"You know it's not that easy."

"It doesn't matter. We're worn out by all this, Nouga. You don't know how hard it was in Kuwait waiting for you. Every day was like a year. The only thing that kept me going was that I was making money so I could come back and marry you."

He then started telling me about his life in Kuwait, about the money he saved working there. I kept looking at the door, waiting for my mother. Why was she late? Enough time had passed for her to discover that I'd run off. She had to know that I went to Adel. Surely, she didn't think that I'd forgotten him. She had to realize that Adel had come back from Kuwait for the simple reason that I'd run off. Maybe she'd called his house looking for me. She had to know that I'd meet him at the same apartment where she caught me with him when I fled the first time.

She was smart. She had the nose of a hunting dog. She could track me wherever I went. So, why was she late?

"I feel you've changed, Nouga," Adel said, his voice bringing me back.

"How?"

"I don't know. But you have. You're not the same. I feel like you didn't miss me."

"That's not true. But I gave up on you. I thought I wouldn't see you again. And I've been sick."

"With what?"

"Anxiety."

"You've suffered a lot, Nouga," he said taking my hand and pressing down on it.

I lowered my head. I had suffered a lot. And I'd changed. I suddenly felt all the change that had happened to me. I was no longer the girl who felt that adolescent love for Adel. I felt at that moment that I really was a different person, not the one I'd imagined myself to be. I felt a new mind in my head, a new heart in my chest, a new world surrounding me. This new world had become my world, no matter how much I wanted to deny it or refuse to acknowledge it.

But what had changed me? Was it just the passage of time? Did I love Adel as a girl and now I couldn't love him as a woman? Or was it my despair when my mother tore me from him and destroyed my love? Or that I'd realized there were men other than Adel? All these men liked me. They all wanted me. They all had their own way of expressing their desire, each different from the other, and different from Adel.

Or was it the luxury, extravagance, and gifts that had distracted me?

Or was it Dr. Hashim? Why was I even thinking about him? He had passed through my life like a cloud overhead. I hadn't thought he had left anything behind, but I had been thinking about him, about his kindness, his tenderness, his manliness. He was a distant dream, but maybe I was looking for a man more like Dr. Hashim than Adel.

Adel got near me again and tried to kiss me. But as soon as his lips touched my cheek, I moved away.

"No, Adel," I whispered sternly.

Adel backed away. He had a sad smile on his lips.

I turned again to the door. Why was she late?

Then, finally, the doorbell rang.

A feeling of vindication erupted in my chest.

"That must be Mother," I said as if talking to myself.

"I won't open the door," Adel said.

"If you don't, she'll just keep ringing the bell and make a huge scandal for you in the building. She could bring the police."

Adel's face darkened as if getting ready for war.

"Fine. Get up and go in the other room. I'll tell her you're not here."

"It's no use, Adel. We have to face her."

I looked at Adel for a long time.

The bell kept ringing.

I turned to the door and then to Adel, imploringly. The ringing filled my ears like the horn of a fire truck on the way to put out a blaze.

Adel groaned and then got up to open the door.

It was my mother.

She was wearing her black coat and black turban. Her shriveled face seemed even more severe than usual. She had a terrifying look in her eyes, but I could see that she was anxious. She had brought three women from Nour al-Huda in their ghostly white veils.

As soon as I saw her, my chest filled with defiance, almost malice.

"Nice job, Miss Nouga," she said with a hoarse voice. "This is a childish game you're playing."

I leaned back against the couch.

"I'm free," I said indifferently. "No one can tell me what to do."

"No, you're not," she screamed.

The Nour al-Huda women looked like they were ready to abduct me . . . or kill me.

"We're going to get married," Adel declared. "No one can stop us. You've already wasted a year of our life together. Shame on you!"

"If you were serious, you would've come to her family to ask to marry her," my mother said. "Good girls don't get married in the street."

She then turned to me.

"Get up, Nouga," she said sternly. "Enough scandals. Come with me."

"No, I won't," I said, trying to infuriate her. "I don't want to go back to your house ever again."

"It's as much yours as it is mine."

If she'd left at this moment, I would've run after her. But she didn't.

"Come with me, my dear," my mother said with a sigh. "Adel can visit us to propose. I swear I won't object. We'll do what you want."

I looked at her in surprise. Her submission enraged me. She didn't know that I didn't want to marry Adel. She didn't know that I'd discovered my love had faded, that it had become like a flower I'd put in the pages of a book. There was nothing left of its scent, it was just a memory.

"Fine, let's go," I said, jumping up angrily.

"Are you serious?" Adel asked looking at my mother in disbelief.

"Of course," my mother said without looking at him. "All I want is for Nouga to be happy."

"Can I come tonight?" Adel asked excitedly.

"Leave it till tomorrow," my mother said.

She then put her arm around me and pulled me to the door.

We left without me looking back at Adel. The three women in white veils came after us.

In front of the building, I found Uncle 'Abdu's car waiting for us, his chauffeur at the wheel.

We got in the car. I was in the middle, right next to my mother, with the women from Nour al-Huda around us, like I was a criminal, under arrest, on my way to prison.

I didn't say a word the entire way. Not one word. A torrential feeling of hopelessness filled me, hopelessness about everything, about love, the future, happiness, myself. This hopelessness peaked and then dissipated into indifference. I didn't care anymore what was happening or what could happen to me.

We got home.

I went to my room expecting my mother to come ask about the details of what had happened. But she didn't. She stayed away, talking on the phone for a long time with the women of Nour al-Huda next to her.

Around three o'clock in the afternoon, I heard the doorbell ring. I then heard Uncle 'Abdu. I expected my mother to call me to welcome him as usual. But she didn't. And I didn't leave my room.

More than an hour later, my mother came in with a stern look on her face.

"'Abd al-Fattah Bey wants to see you," she told me.

"Why?"

"You can get up to see what he wants."

I shrugged. I got up in my nightshirt, put a robe on, and started to leave the room.

"You're not going to put on something nicer?"

"It's not necessary. Uncle 'Abdu isn't a stranger."

'Abd al-Fattah stood up to greet me with a big smile on his thick lips.

"I'm mad at you, Nouga," he said with an artificial tenderness. "We were so scared about you. All these tricks!"

"Sorry," I said, sitting down next to him.

He looked at my mother and she looked at him. She then turned to me, showing me a piece of paper on the side table.

"Take this and sign here," she said.

"What is it?"

"This, my dear, is a piece of paper to make sure you don't try to get married behind our backs again."

"I don't understand."

"I can't bear any more of this," she continued. "I can't live afraid that you'll run off at any moment and get married behind my back. This paper prevents you from getting married without us knowing. When you want to get married, we'll tear it up and we'll marry you to whoever you want."

"What is it?" I asked again.

"A marriage certificate," my mother said firmly.

"So, I'm getting married?"

"Only like this, until you get married for real."

"And who am I marrying, God willing?" I asked sarcastically.

"'Abd al-Fattah Bey," my mother said seriously.

I let out a loud laugh.

"May God preserve this man," my mother continued. "You have nothing to worry about. He and I have agreed on the contract. It's what you call a temporary marriage, but there's nothing more to it than the contract."

"You're really going to marry me, uncle?"

"I wish, Nouga," 'Abd al-Fattah Bey said with a calm smile.

I took the paper and grabbed the pen.

"See, done," I said signing without reading a word of it.

My mother took the paper, folded it carefully, and slipped it into her shirt.

"You have to understand that if you marry someone else now," my mother said, "before we tear up this contract, you'll go to jail. It'd be like you're married to two men."

"Don't worry," I said indifferently.

"Take this too," 'Abd al-Fattah Bey said.

He handed me a check.

"What's this?" I asked.

"It's the dowry. Doesn't someone who gets married pay a dowry?"

I looked at the check. It was for two thousand pounds, addressed to my mother.

I smiled at 'Abd al-Fattah Bey.

"Thanks, uncle."

I leaned over and gave him a quick kiss on the cheek.
I tossed the check at my mother.
I ran to my room.
And Uncle 'Abdu came after me.

6

It was a piece of paper that I signed and did not read. My mother called it a marriage contract, and it made all her hopes and dreams come true.

All she ever wanted was to marry me to a man who wouldn't take me from her, a husband who would give away all his rights to her, except for that one right reserved for him.

'Abd al-Fattah Bey Rif'at was that man. He didn't want to marry me. Marriage in the normal sense was the farthest thing from his mind. He wanted simply to take me, at any price. He knew he couldn't get me by my heart. His mentality and way of life wouldn't accept that. He knew this path was barred before him. He didn't have anything he could open my heart with. All he had was his money. The only way was to buy me. From who? Me? No. He knew that I wasn't free. He knew I belonged to my mother, whether I wanted to or not. He decided to buy me from my mother. With a view to making a deal, he began negotiating with my mother. He put up with her haggling for a long time. And all this went on behind my back.

My mother wasn't easy. She knew how to bargain. She wasn't open about what she was doing and found a way to cover up this deal she was working on. She knew the whole time that they had a joint interest. 'Abd al-Fattah Bey wanted to take me, but he didn't want to take me from her. On the contrary. He insisted on keeping me with her. He was married with grown children, and he had social standing that required certain appearances. All of that forced him to keep our relationship secret. No one knew about it. And to make sure that no one knew, I would stay with my mother and live as a girl who hadn't gotten married yet, even if that meant suitors still came to see me.

This made my mother happy. She could make sure that I'd remain hers forever, remain her personal piece of property, in her house, right in front of her. She alone had a claim over me. There was no man sharing control.

Negotiations ended with them agreeing to write out this piece of paper, which my mother called a marriage, or a temporary marriage. But in reality, it was a sales contract. It was a single copy of a sales contract, which my mother kept. She refused to write another one for 'Abd al-Fattah Bey to make sure he couldn't threaten her with it, to make sure she'd be the one with the power over him. And 'Abd al-Fattah Bey was pleased. He didn't want any more rights than what my mother had agreed to.

This paper was the cover my mother used to ease her conscience, to convince herself that she wasn't selling me, that she wasn't giving me to a man in sin, that it was marriage, recognized by the law and Islam.

Despite that, my mother kept putting off telling me about this scheme. She was afraid that I'd flee or resist. Once I'd run off to Adel, she was afraid that I was still in love with him and that I'd try to marry him behind her back. That was when she decided it was time to execute the agreement between her and 'Abd al-Fattah Bey, to "marry" me to him.

I didn't understand any of that when I signed the paper. I didn't give myself a moment to think. I had fallen into the depths of despair, gripped by a horrible emptiness filling my heart when I realized that I didn't love Adel anymore and that everything I felt for him was only a delusion, only the memory of an adolescent love, a love that didn't grow with time. It had been left behind in my childhood.

'Abd al-Fattah Bey came into my room behind me. My mother let him. She stayed in the living room. My paralyzed father was in his room. He didn't know anything about what was happening in his house.

I threw myself on the bed, still wearing my robe on top of my nightshirt. I looked at 'Abd al-Fattah indifferently. Maybe with a little scorn.

He sat on the edge of the bed and started talking. I didn't care what he was saying, but I wanted to hear anything that would make me feel there was something happening in my life, anything that would pull me out of this stagnation, this weariness, this emptiness.

I looked at his face. I saw the wrinkles of his brown face, a brown tending toward blue, from the fifty years surrounding his eyes. And I looked at his short thick fingers.

A question occurred to me at that moment. Did 'Abd al-Fattah Bey actually love me? It was strange that I was asking myself that. The thought had never occurred to me before. Why was I assuming that all there was between us was this contract of sale? Maybe he bought me because he loved me. And maybe I sold myself because I found something in him that I loved. Maybe I felt his strength, his influence, his patience all these months, his ability to get me, his desire for me. I didn't feel any of this from Zizi's suitors as strongly as I did from him.

"Do you love me, uncle?" I found myself asking, almost talking to myself. Even at this moment I called him "uncle."

"So much, Nouga," he said, with the smile of a man who had been waiting patiently for a long time. "I love you so much. Whenever I look at you, I feel like I'm twenty-five years old. Whenever you laugh, I feel like the entire world is laughing, laughing for me."

I was distracted. I tried to feel the echo of his words in my heart. I needed love, any kind of love.

I looked into 'Abd al-Fattah's eyes. They were rapacious. He loved me in his own way, the way of a rich man. He loved me like he loved his jewels and his buildings, a love on which the egotism of ownership had triumphed, just like my mother's love.

I came to as 'Abd al-Fattah brought his lips close to mine. I didn't try to escape. There was no point. I had signed the paper. The man had paid two thousand pounds. My mother said this was marriage. And I wanted something to happen to me, to enjoy something, anything. I didn't care what.

Then a violent feeling took hold of me. I wanted to watch 'Abd al-Fattah Bey Ra'fat, the rich, famous man, the man with influence. I wanted to watch him as he was making love.

So, I watched. I watched his lips as they moved onto mine with a violent, greedy lust. I watched his eyes sparkle and then I watched his eyes close. I watched his thick dry hands as they picked spots to grope on my body. I watched as he took off his clothes in a comical rush. I watched his face as it got red and flushed. I watched him as he hissed and panted.

I watched.

I felt I was watching a movie, a movie for adults only, and that this body wasn't mine, everything that was happening wasn't happening to me. I was far away.

I didn't tell him at that moment that I wasn't a virgin. It didn't occur to me. 'Abd al-Fattah didn't say anything about it and he didn't seem surprised when he discovered this fact. Maybe because he knew that the relationship between us didn't stipulate it. It didn't give him the right to hold me accountable for my past.

When it was over, 'Abd al-Fattah put his clothes back on and went out to have a cup of coffee with my mother.

I started to feel something new. I felt that I was absurd. Everything that had happened was just absurdity. My submission was absurd. My ideas were absurd. The movie that I watched was absurd.

But I didn't regret it. I wasn't happy, of course. But I didn't want to cry. And I didn't want to smile.

The feeling of absurdity was filling me, running through my veins. It was painful. I felt something draining from my heart. I felt my nerves chattering. But I couldn't do anything. I had no tears to soothe me. Absurdity is an icy torture. I became deaf, like wood, like I had an iron stake in my chest. I was writhing in my bed. I hid my face in my pillow. I hit it with my fist. My chest became tight.

After Uncle 'Abdu left, my mother came in to hear all the details.

"Leave me alone, Mother," I said quietly.

My mother left. She came back later to spend the night next to me, still hoping to hear the details.

After that, our lives changed thanks to 'Abd al-Fattah's generosity.

We moved from our little apartment in Giza to a villa on Haram Street. We got new furniture for the whole house. We got a cook and a butler. On my birthday, 'Abd al-Fattah bought me a white Opel Kapitän, but my mother didn't let me learn how to drive. She was too afraid. Maybe she thought I'd flee in it. So, 'Abd al-Fattah gave us a driver too.

My relationship with 'Abd al-Fattah stayed secret. People thought that he was a family friend or maybe some relative of ours. I still called him "Uncle 'Abdu" in front of people, including my father. He didn't come to visit us more than twice a week. He usually came at three in the afternoon and left at seven. My mother got ready for his visit by getting everyone out of the house. The cook left. She sent the driver on a long errand. She told the butler to take my paralyzed father in his wheelchair to the park on Haram Street. Once everyone was gone, 'Abd al-Fattah came into my room while my mother sat waiting by the door.

When my father got back from the park, 'Abd al-Fattah would be finished, sitting with my mother in the living room, having a cup of coffee. My father didn't like or hate 'Abd al-Fattah. He had accepted 'Abd al-Fattah's presence in the family. Maybe he felt some pride that one of our family friends was such an important man like 'Abd al-Fattah Bey Ra'fat, but I didn't ever know how my father really felt about him. His paralyzed tongue prevented him from saying what he really thought. His eyes were silent, almost dead, whenever he saw 'Abd al-Fattah or when we talked about him.

Despite all this, I was still living the life of an ordinary teenage girl. In front of people, my mother treated me like a teenager, taking me to visit families and encouraging people to talk about me getting engaged. She still welcomed suitors. It was strange. I had a lot of suitors, all of them eager. My mother refused them, every one of them.

Adel was still trying to get in touch with me, but in vain. I wanted him to keep trying. He was the only weapon that I had to threaten my mother with, to make her think that I might run off and marry him. My mother was still convinced that I loved him. And I wanted her to keep thinking that so she'd be afraid. I'd pick fights with her, threatening to flee to Adel, to make her more scared.

But I felt ridiculous. It was a feeling that never left me, the ridiculousness of my entire life, of the drama that I was living. I tried to flee from this feeling, to fill my time with trifling things. Every day, my mother and I would go out shopping. I'd buy tons of things. 'Abd al-Fattah 's money was endless. Every day, I'd go to the movies or to visit someone. Then I suggested to my mother that we go back to visit Zizi, but she refused. She was finished with Zizi after 'Abd al-Fattah. But I insisted. I was weary and I wanted something to distract me from myself. I wanted parties, something loud, but my mother refused. She complained to 'Abd al-Fattah, but he didn't refuse me any request.

"As long as you're with her, 'Aziza, I have no objections," he told her.

"You know, 'Abd al-Fattah, that I don't agree with Zizi's lifestyle," my mother responded. "People talk a lot about her. Nouga's still young and we don't want to encourage people to talk more."

"My dear," 'Abd al-Fattah said as if he was entering, with my mother, into a competition of hypocrisy. "People say all kinds of things. The truth is that Zizi is a fun woman, and she loves Nouga. As long as you're with her, there's nothing to worry about."

'Abd al-Fattah really wasn't worried as long as my mother was with me. He was confident my mother was working on his behalf. She became an employee of his. Her position was to save me for him, even to jail me for him.

My mother and I went back to Zizi, but she no longer treated me like the new girl. I was no longer a young naive girl for her. She knew that we had picked 'Abd al-Fattah. It's true that she didn't know the extent of the relationship between us. She didn't know the details of the contract. But she knew everything else, even on the first day we went back to see her.

"How's 'Abd al-Fattah Bey?" she asked, letting out a loud laugh. "No one has seen that one since the last time I saw you. Isn't he a generous man? Didn't I tell you? There's no one as generous as him, the way he tosses money around."

As she talked, she was looking at my dress, the watch on my wrist, and the ring on my finger.

Zizi welcomed us. She needed every pretty face she could get to embellish her evenings and please the men there. I began spending the evenings out again. Zizi's friends went out at a particular level of places, like the Auberge, the Shagara, the Arizona. There was another type of place that I didn't go to with Zizi's clique, big hotels like the Shepheard, the Semiramis, the Hilton. She went to those places with a different group of people.

If I didn't spend the night out, I went to the private parties that Zizi's friends put on. All of them were hosted by married women. Their husbands were all idiots.

Men still stared at me. I was still the youngest and most beautiful woman in the group. I enjoyed the stares at first, but I became nervous and unsure how to behave. I started picking clothes that revealed more of my skin. I was putting on lots and lots of makeup. Sometimes I'd blurt something out and offend someone unintentionally. My mother was always next to me in her black coat and black turban like the gendarme, guarding me for 'Abd al-Fattah Bey. She'd let men look but not touch.

I'd go back home to writhe in my bed. I'd hide my face in my pillow. Nothing soothed me from this feeling that I was ridiculous. I felt a vast emptiness, as if I was living inside a bag with holes in it and whenever I tried to fill it, it became empty again.

I began to feel physical pain, which I hid from my mother. I didn't complain. But it got worse, it moved and spread. I felt pain in my chest, and suddenly I came down with a fever and my temperature skyrocketed to 104.

I collapsed.

I submitted silently, immersed in the pain, melting in my fever. I didn't want anything. I didn't want to recover.

'Abd al-Fattah brought a doctor with him. Then another. Then four doctors came to examine me.

It was my heart. Rheumatism had reached my heart. The doctors came every day, whispering to each other, then whispering in my mother's ear. No one was telling me anything. Sometimes I felt as if my heart stopped. I closed my eyes waiting for death.

"Get Dr. Hashim," I whispered to my mother.

My mother's sad eyes sparkled. She'd been relying on the doctors that 'Abd al-Fattah was bringing, but 'Abd al-Fattah didn't know Dr. Hashim. She rushed to the phone as if she'd suddenly decided to be liberated from 'Abd al-Fattah 's control.

I felt some hope through the forest of pain that I was living in. I thought about Dr. Hashim not as a doctor, but as a calming drug.

Hashim came. He came that same day at two o'clock in the afternoon, right after his clinic appointments. No doubt my mother had told him about the seriousness of my condition.

He stood at the head of my bed with a cloud of worry on his face. He then gave me a big smile.

"I'm angry with you," he said. "You only think of me when you're sick."

I filled my eyes with him. He hadn't changed, except for a bit more white hair. He still had those kind, wide eyes. He had the same imposing nose and smiling lips. A clean scent wafted from him like the scent of pure air.

I relaxed simply by seeing him. I felt that I wanted him to get close to me so he could examine me. No. I didn't want him to examine me. I wanted him to get close to me so I could put my head on his chest and sleep.

He came over, took a chair, and sat down next to my bed. He then took my hand to measure my pulse.

"We don't know what to do, Doctor," my mother said.

"Please, ma'am, could you bring me a coffee?" Hashim cut her off in a decisive tone.

My mother looked at him then left to tell the maid to make the coffee.

I turned to him. I didn't want to say anything. I only wanted to look at him.

"Don't say anything, Nagwa," he said, his brows knitted as if he was collecting his thoughts.

He began to examine me. He took out his stethoscope and listened to my heart for a long time. It was like my heart was having an extended conversation with him. Suddenly, he raised his head and looked at me smiling.

"One doctor isn't enough for you," he said. "You need two."

He then stood up.

"Where's the phone?" he asked.

"Outside, in the hallway."

I reached out to press the bell on the side of my bed for the maid to bring me the phone, but Hashim left to look for it himself. He walked in a leisurely manner, as if this were his house.

I heard his voice as he talked to the other doctor.

He came back. My mother came in behind him carrying a cup of coffee. He took it and put it aside.

"Could I see the prescriptions?" he asked my mother.

My mother showed them to him, as well as the reports and X-rays from the other doctors.

While he immersed himself in them, I found myself wondering if he knew about my relationship with 'Abd al-Fattah. I thought that he might have discovered it as he was examining me. I was afraid that he might have seen 'Abd al-Fattah's fingerprints on my thighs or noticed the scent of his breath on my chest. I wanted to run to the shower so that I could clean myself of 'Abd al-Fattah's scent and fingerprints for Hashim.

Hashim tossed aside the papers that were in his hand. He looked at me with troubled eyes and then smiled.

"I still don't know. I should know in fifteen minutes."

I felt him very close to me. I felt him in my sick heart. He was confused like me. He didn't seem like a doctor who was just saying things to reassure a patient. He was genuinely concerned.

"Let's chat until Dr. Rushdi comes," Hashim said. "Tell me, what have you been doing all this time since I saw you?"

"I've been living," I said, smiling.

"Who's the one who wore out your heart?" he whispered, looking at my mother quickly and then back at me again.

"No one," I said in my weak voice. "It was exhausted on its own."

"That has to be because it was alone."

"Maybe."

"How could you be sick?" His voice was tender. "How does a young pretty girl like you let herself get so sick?"

Dr. Rushdi arrived carrying a heart monitor with him. Hashim stood up and welcomed him as if it was his house. He then helped him set up the monitor, tying nodes to my arm. I looked at his eyes as he followed the paper coming out of the machine, recording the beats of my heart. His brow was tight, and he looked anxious watching the paper scroll out.

He and Dr. Rushdi got up after they'd finished and went out of the room. My mother was with them. They were gone for a long time, fifteen minutes or more. Hashim then came back with my mother behind him. The other doctor had left.

Hashim sat at the side of my bed, a warm smile on his face. He took my hand in his.

"Look, my dear," he said. "The doctors who saw you said that you have rheumatism of the heart, but I say no. The rheumatism still hasn't reached your heart, but it's very close."

He pointed directly under my heart.

"The rheumatism has reached all the way here," he said. "And it's trying to reach the heart. You and rheumatism have entered into a battle. I have to know—will you stand with me or the rheumatism?"

"With you, of course."

"Okay. We're agreed. You have to want to win this battle. You have to think about what you want to live for. What are your hopes and dreams? What do you want to achieve? You have to decide that you're going to live for these things, that you have a will to live."

I looked at him and his words made my blood flow faster through my veins. I felt something rush forward inside me, quenching the thirst of my dried body that illness had crushed.

I locked my eyes on his face. I realized that his face had been with me since I saw it the first time.

"Yes," I said again.

"It won't be easy," Hashim continued. "The war between us and rheumatism could take a month. We have to bear it. Maybe two months. We have to bear it laughing, all the while sure that we'll be victorious. Are we agreed?"

"Agreed."

"Don't move from your bed. It's not enough that you don't get up. Try not to move at all. We don't want to stress your heart at all. Any movement could tire it. When it's tired, it's weak and then it can't resist the enemy at its door."

He once again reviewed the prescriptions that the other doctors had given me and told me to stop taking half of them. He then looked at his watch.

"I'll call to check on you at eight o'clock tonight," he said. "You should be asleep at nine. Tomorrow morning, I'll come by before I go to the clinic."

He looked at me with smiling eyes.

And he left.

7

WE DEFEATED MY ILLNESS TOGETHER.

Hashim and me.

My heart is now healthy, and it can bear double the love of any girl's heart. But I'm still afraid for it. I don't waste its beats running and skipping. I keep them all for love, for life.

I don't believe that Hashim healed me as a doctor. Any other doctor could've prescribed the treatment he did. He healed me with his will, with his stubbornness in fighting the illness, his insistence that I get better. He transferred to me this will, stubbornness, and insistence. He released in me his zest for life, his faith in it, his love for it. He released rays of hope into my heart.

Maybe all this was part of Hashim's skill as a doctor, the secret of his success and fame. I thought that Hashim was interested in me as just another one of his patients. But surely, he couldn't give all his patients the attention he gave me. His very presence filled the entire house, breathed fresh, clean air into it. We all submitted to it. My mother, my father, and me. My mother wasn't entirely convinced, but she went along with him because of his ability to heal me.

Our entire life started revolving around Dr. Hashim. Everything changed, even the times when 'Abd al-Fattah would visit us. He no longer came at three o'clock in the afternoon because Hashim usually came at that time. He started coming at five after Hashim went back to his clinic.

Hashim would visit me in the morning before he went to his clinic. He'd visit me in the afternoon, after his clinic. He often came back in the evening. At first, he would examine my heart when he came, then he started to sit next to me and explain my condition to me, detailing the development of the rheumatism in my chest and the effect of the drugs that he was giving me. I came to know every vein in my heart, every muscle, every one of its beats. Through my heart, I came to know Hashim. He knew my heart like the back of his hand. Soon, he didn't have to examine me when he came.

"I've listened to your heart so much that I can hear it from far away. I hear it in my clinic. I hear it at home. I hear it when I'm out with my friends."

I looked into his kind, smiling eyes.

"You must be troubled," I said.

"I was at first," he said laughing.

That day, I was confused as to what he was saying. I was afraid that I'd fly away with his words, feeling that Hashim loved me. At that same time, I was afraid to embrace hope. I fled from my confusion into the sweetness of his words and the looks that lingered between us.

I didn't need him to love me. It was enough that I loved him. I loved his words, his eyes, even his big nose.

Hashim began to talk with me about his patients. He gave me hope with the stories of patients who made a full recovery after it seemed all was lost. His patients were his whole life. He lived their lives, suffered their pain, gave them medication as if he were giving it to himself, feeling its bitterness and its aftereffects. All their feelings were his.

I didn't feel jealous of his patients. On the contrary, I began to share this feeling with him and to live in the same world as him. I came to know his patients. I had a picture of each one in my mind.

"How's Mr. Marwan now?" I'd ask him.

Mr. Marwan was sick with liver disease.

Hashim smiled as if I had reminded him of someone dear to him and he started talking about Marwan with much emotion.

My interest in his patients was genuine. I wanted to share his world with him. But there was something else. I found a more decent life in the lives of these patients. I could flee from my life to theirs. I could escape my worries by preoccupying myself with theirs.

Hashim was happy with me. I could feel it. I started feeling that I wasn't simply one of his patients.

"What's going on with school?" Hashim asked me one day.

I was surprised at this question. I felt many years had passed since I left school. It was a distant memory. I almost laughed at his question. He still thought I was the young innocent girl he had met when I was overcome by the shock of first love.

"Nothing," I told him, lowering my eyes. "Last year, I didn't take the exam. And I didn't go at all this year."

"Why?" he asked, raising his eyebrows in surprise.

"I was worn out."

"That's no reason. Your mother is spoiling you. Why did she allow you to stop going?"

"All that Mother cares about is that I stay by her side."

"What year were you in?"

"My last year. I was really very smart."

"That's it. You'll go back to being very smart again. You'll start studying again today. And you'll go to university. You're not getting married this year, you're getting your degree. Unless you want to get married."

I raised my eyes to him, and I thought I was about to cry. He didn't know anything. He didn't know about all the change that had happened in our lives. He could see we had moved from our tiny apartment in Giza to this villa on Haram Street, full of new furniture. We now had a cook and a butler and a driver. He had no idea what all this change meant. My mother kept lying to him, telling him that she sold land from her farm and that she bought a piece of land in Heliopolis . . . and . . . and . . . she kept fabricating stories and exaggerating the family's wealth to defend herself and our new life. He didn't pay much attention. He assumed we were respectable people.

"No. I don't want to get married."

"Then you're going to get your degree."

He was quiet for a bit. He gave me a fixed serious look.

"Do you know what your new treatment is?" he asked, smiling. "Studying. Starting today, go back to studying.

Take the exam this year. I know you'll pass. Where are your books?"

"I don't know," I said, feeling like he was bringing me back to my childhood. "Mother took them."

"'Aziza," he said, calling to my mother. "Nagwa will begin studying again today. Bring her the books and let her study in bed."

"Why is that necessary?" my mother asked as if she'd been slapped. "We left these things behind a long time ago."

"This is her treatment," Hashim said, laughing.

And he left.

"That Dr. Hashim is in love with you," she said.

"Please stop, Mother. Why would he love me? Just like that?"

"Believe me. He's been in love with you since the first day he laid eyes on you."

My mother fell quiet, her eyes looking off into the distance as if she was hatching a new plan.

I turned away from her. I didn't want to hear any more. But my mind totally drifted away trying to believe what she said.

'Abd al-Fattah was coming to us at his new times two or three times a week. He changed his times so that he didn't run into Dr. Hashim. He didn't want anyone to know about his relationship with me, even if I called him "uncle."

He was starting to get annoyed with me. I was preoccupied with my illness, and I was no longer submissive. I no longer cared at all about all the gems that 'Abd al-Fattah gave me. I discovered there were many things more important and more beautiful, more important than our villa, my white Opel, and my many dresses. There were more important things, like my health, my heart whose beats were defective, and, of course, Hashim.

But how could I backtrack? Could I convince my mother that I no longer wanted 'Abd al-Fattah? And ask her to free me? It seemed impossible.

I knew even thinking about this would exhaust my heart. I tried not to think about him in the new hope that Hashim would get rid of him. To a certain degree, I could put it out of my mind, especially as 'Abd al-Fattah wasn't asking anything from me when I was sick. He was afraid for me. When he came, he would sit with me for a little while and then go to drink coffee with my mother.

I threw myself into studying as if it would bring back my old life, far from Zizi's world, the nights out at the Auberge and the Shagara, and the stares of men. I started imagining living among my old classmates, laughing with them, whispering rumors, loving like them with a clean innocent heart. I started feeling as if I was regaining something that had been lost, something of myself. I could one day be a person of value, be the best student in the school, the head of the drama club, my class representative in social activities, the representative of the entire school in the union of high schools.

There were moments when I'd be hit by reality. Despair would overrun my imagination. I'd look around the room. This wasn't a student's room. This was the room of a rich girl. I was the wife of a rich old man. My heart would pound anxiously, and my throat would constrict. I was afraid, afraid for my heart. I resisted my feelings of despair and clung to my image of Hashim like I was gripping a lifejacket. No doubt there was a way to reach the shore. I just didn't know the way. But I was confident that it was there, and that Hashim would lead me there.

All I did was study and wait to see Hashim.

I started calling him every day, sometimes twice a day.

He couldn't talk long at his clinic. His words there were quick and rushed, but gentle and sweet.

Hashim took me and my mother in his car to the pyramids. It was the first time that I left the house since I got sick. We all got out of the car and walked around. Hashim sat me on one of the boulders under the pyramid's mount. My mother pretended that she wanted to walk around and left us alone.

Hashim and I got into a long conversation. There was something big between us, something that I could recognize. It was love. Hashim seemed like he couldn't believe it. He couldn't believe that he loved me and that I loved him. As soon as his eyes met mine, he looked away. As soon as his words began to express his emotions, he cut them off. I felt his hesitation, that he was holding down something in his chest that wanted to come out. I was tuned into every one of his gestures, every blink of his eyes, every sigh.

We realized that we were holding hands. He didn't mean to take my hand. I didn't mean to put mine in his. We didn't even notice until we got close to the car. I noticed a pulse run between our hands. I didn't know if he was the one who squeezed my hand, or I was the one who squeezed his. We stopped at the car. He looked at me. My eyes were raised to him, imploring. Our eyes met in a long conversation.

"I want you to put up with me, Nouga," he whispered.

"Put up with what?"

"A lot of things. But you have to put up with me."

"A long as you're beside me, I don't feel like I'm putting up with anything."

"You're something else," he said. "You're a lot younger than me and . . ."

"Not at all," I said, cutting him off. "I'm twenty-one now."

"I'm forty-one," he said sadly.

He doesn't know. He doesn't know that I'm older than my age. He doesn't know what I've done with my life.

As we drove back, I sat next to him with my mother in the back seat. There was silence between us. Hashim and I were listening to the beats of our hearts.

My mother sat in my room as I changed my clothes.

"You know better than me that he loves you," she said.

"I wish," I said, distracted.

"But do you think he'll come to do it?"

"What's that?"

"To marry you."

"How's that? Haven't you married me off to 'Abd al-Fattah?"

"And what of it?" she asked, her wicked intelligence flickering in her eyes.

I hated her. I hated her for Hashim. I couldn't let her do with Hashim what she could do to any other man. He wasn't just another man.

Despite that, I didn't say anything. I needed her. I couldn't defy her now. If I defied her, the first thing she would do was to distance Hashim from me.

"But it's obvious he's not easy," she said.

"Please, stop."

"Why?" she asked sharply. "You think he's too old for us? Or because he's famous, he's not interested in you? If you want him, I'll marry him to you."

I didn't respond.

"Why don't you say something? You think I don't know what's in your head?"

I hesitated a little.

"I love him, Mother," I said. "I love him."

I had to do it. I had to confess my love to her so that she didn't forbid me from him, so that I didn't make her feel that I was hiding anything from her.

She patted me on my shoulder, happy with my confession.

"That's it," she said. "Leave it to me."

At that moment, 'Abd al-Fattah arrived. I heard his voice outside my room, so I hurried to put on my nightie, and I threw myself onto my bed.

"I'm still sick," I told my mother. "Very sick. Don't leave me with him for a single moment. If he gets near me, I'll kill myself. Understand?"

"Fine, be quiet," my mother said.

I evened out the blanket around me. 'Abd al-Fattah came in and looked in my face. He then looked at my mother as if he was suspicious of what we were talking about.

"What's wrong with Nouga?" he asked.

"The doctor let her go out of the house," my mother said. "He took us in the car and we drove around for fifteen minutes. I saw her face go pale like she was going to pass out. I brought her back right away."

"Wasn't she feeling better the day before yesterday?" 'Abd al-Fattah asked, his hopes dashed.

"How should I know?" my mother responded.

"That doctor is an idiot," 'Abd al-Fattah fumed. "How could he take her out?"

'Abd al-Fattah got near me and took out a small box from his pocket. He opened it before my eyes. There was a pair of pearl earrings in it.

I sighed as if I couldn't talk.

"We have to bring another doctor," 'Abd al-Fattah said.

"No!" I snapped suddenly. "I'm fine, uncle. I'm just tired. It was the first time that I've been out."

'Abd al-Fattah put the earrings in my ears with his short thick fingers. He then leaned over my face to kiss me, but I turned away. His kiss fell on my hair.

"Don't worry, Nouga," my mother said. "You'll feel better now, my dear."

'Abd al-Fattah sat next to me, disappointment all over his face. He brought the pearls hoping they would help end his long deprivation.

He bore his disappointment and left to have coffee with my mother.

I started talking with Hashim at his house after he got home from work, long endless phone conversations. We always found things to talk about. And he continued to visit us regularly.

My mother arranged the visits with him and 'Abd al-Fattah. Whenever 'Abd al-Fattah came, I pretended to be sick. Whenever Hashim came, I sat with him in the salon, my mother sitting with us and then leaving us for a bit. Sometimes she was gone for ten minutes, sometimes fifteen. But Hashim never tried anything in my mother's absence. All he did was hold my hand as we talked. Our conversation was sweet, almost compensating us for the lack of kisses. When my mother knew that he hadn't tried to kiss me, she started staying away longer and longer, to give him more opportunity. But he didn't kiss me, and I didn't push him to. I knew that a day would come when our lips would meet. But not here and not because my mother left us and went into the other room.

It was during this time that I passed the graduation exam.

I finished secondary school.

8

MY PROBLEM BECAME HOW TO convince my mother to let me go out with Hashim alone. I went out with him a lot, but always with my mother. He'd take us on a tour in his car. Once or twice, he invited us for tea at the Mena House. It was very uncomfortable having my mother there with us. Perhaps it was the clothes she wore, the black coat and black turban, or the way she acted and the look of her wicked eyes. Or maybe it was my lack of respect for her. I was more annoyed with her when I was with Hashim than ever before. I was ashamed of her. I felt like her presence was proof of my dirty secret. I would search Hashim's face for any hint of my secret.

Hashim never showed that he was annoyed by my mother. He was a good man. He lived in a clean world. He thought everyone was good like him, clean like him, with good intentions. He didn't presume ill of anyone. He believed what he saw with his eyes, and he believed what he heard from me and my mother.

Hashim didn't try to ask me to go out with him alone. He seemed to be completely satisfied with things as they were, talking on the phone and meeting under the watchful eyes of my mother. He didn't reveal his love directly, but I caught glimpses of it in his eyes, the quick movements of his hands, and moments of confusion on his lips. We sometimes talked about love, but it was like we were reviewing an academic subject, as if it had nothing to do with us.

Confusion started eating me up. Maybe he really was satisfied with how things were. Maybe it was just friendship.

My mother was dumbfounded. She couldn't believe that she could give a man—even Dr. Hashim—all these opportunities, but he didn't demand anything from me. He didn't even try to kiss me. She became suspicious about Hashim's intentions. She began to feel like he was stronger than her and her plans. She was using the same playbook that she used for all men. She brought him into our life and told him our problems, most of which were fabricated. She even made up fights between me and her so that Hashim could patch things up between us. She always presented herself as an old weak woman whose husband was paralyzed and who bore the responsibility of raising and protecting me alone.

"People are trying to take advantage of me and Nouga because they know we don't have a man," she'd tell him, tears in her eyes. "I'm so tired, Doctor. I can't bear it anymore. At my age, I can't bear all this."

I didn't try to warn Hashim about her schemes. I was afraid my mother would think that I was standing with him against her. I was afraid she'd block me from him.

"Don't believe her, Doctor," I'd tell him weakly, not looking at him. "Mother always exaggerates."

I was still calling him "doctor."

Hashim seemed to believe my mother. He seemed to listen to her fabricated problems like she was one of his patients.

"Listen, Nouga," he'd tell me when we were alone. "You have to placate your mother. She loves you and she has no one in the world but you. Make her feel better."

I didn't say a thing. He clearly didn't understand my mother.

"Listen, 'Aziza," he told her one day when she was complaining to him. "I beg you to stop thinking that you're alone in the world. You've been three. You, your husband, and Nouga. Now you're four. I'm the fourth."

She smiled broadly. She thought these words were as good as Hashim proposing to me. She even started planning our life after Hashim married me as if there was nothing that could ruin her plans, not my truth as a woman, not my relationship with 'Abd al-Fattah, not the sinful money that we were living on. Nothing could stand in her way.

But Hashim didn't take another step forward. And he didn't confess his love to me. He didn't ask me to get married. All he was interested in was my future and that I go to university.

I couldn't stand it anymore. I loved him. I didn't care if I went to university or not. I didn't care if he married me or not. All I cared about was that I loved him. I wanted us to go out alone, a world just for us, without my mother or 'Abd al-Fattah.

I started getting angry at Hashim. How could he bear this long deprivation?

One day, Hashim came to visit at nine in the evening. I was ready for him that day more than any other. I was wearing a low-cut lace sky-blue dress that revealed my arms. I had a scarf the same color draped around my neck. I had on black patent leather shoes with three-inch heels. I put on Femme perfume. I put a lot more perfume on than usual. I put on my diamond ring, the brooch, and the earrings, all gifts from 'Abd al-Fattah. I put on bright red lipstick. I put shades of Ombre on my eyelids, and kohl, and mascara. I let a lock of my hair hang down on my cheek. It was as if I was heading to one of Zizi's parties.

He met me in the salon.

He looked at me in delight and disbelief and asked: "What's all this? Where are we going?"

"Nowhere," I said, strutting in front of him, trying to see myself in his eyes. "Why? Do I look like I'm going somewhere?"

"You look like you're going to a big party."

"Not at all. You *are* the party."

He smiled and seemed to be holding himself back from taking me in his arms. He then greeted my mother warmly.

My mother sat with us for a while, her eyes on Hashim as he looked at me. After she had pleaded some of her usual worries, she got up to leave us alone.

Hashim was sitting on the couch, smoking his cigarette. He seemed nervous. I was sitting opposite him, my back straight, my head held high as if I was a bride on the dais.

"Do you want to look at pictures of me when I was little?" I asked him.

"Sure," he said looking closely at me.

I ran to my room and brought down my big photo album. I threw myself next to him on the couch. I opened up the album on our knees. We started flipping through it. He leaned over and my cheek almost touched his. My knee was touching his under the album. My perfume mixed with his clean scent. Our warm breath mixed. Everything around us was getting hot. I felt a new sensation. It wasn't simply love, but an excitement running through my body. I felt that I was a woman. It was the first time. Neither Adel nor 'Abd al-Fattah had made me feel this way.

Our voices got lower and then we were silent. We flipped through the pages, and I waited for something, anything. I waited for him to pull me to him, to turn his face to meet my lips, to pull me by my hair, to hit me, anything, anything.

Suddenly, Hashim looked at his watch and took the photo album off his knees. He jumped up as if he was fleeing from a fire.

"I have to leave," he said. "I'm meeting a bunch of friends at the Semiramis."

I couldn't believe it.

"It's still early," I said in a hoarse voice.

"I can't. I have to go."

He then reached out, took my hand, and pulled me to stand up next to him.

"It's better that I go now," he said tenderly, still holding my hand.

I bent my head as if I was about to cry.

"As you wish."

He put his other hand under my chin and raised my face up to his.

"By the way, I forgot to tell you. My sister wants to invite you to her house for dinner on Thursday."

I thought that I hadn't heard him correctly.

"What?"

"My sister is inviting you to dinner on Thursday."

"But I don't know her."

"You have to get to know her. You can't know me if you don't know her."

"But she doesn't know me."

"She's known about you since the day I met you."

"You talked to her about me?" A mysterious happiness filled my heart.

"A lot."

I was quiet for a bit to catch my breath.

"Where'd your mother go?"

He then raised his voice before I could respond to him, filling the entire house.

"'Aziza! 'Aziza!"

"Mother's invited?"

"If she comes, I'll be annoyed," he said quickly. "Because everyone coming is young. But, of course, she's invited."

My mother came into the room.

"My sister has invited Nouga over on Thursday," he told her simply. "I'm asking that you let her come."

My mother looked at him with her wicked eyes and wrinkled face.

"Why not?" she said. "We'd be honored."

"Merci, madame."

I was stunned.

"Madiha will call tomorrow to invite you herself," he said, turning to me. "Good night."

He shook my hand goodbye, squeezing it as if he was pressing hope into me. He then said goodbye to my mother and got up to go. Before he reached the door, I woke up from my stupor and ran after him.

"What should I wear?" I asked.

"Anything," Hashim said, laughing.

I ran to my room and threw myself on my bed. I pushed my head onto my pillow, and I cried.

My mother came in behind me.

"Why are you crying?" she asked, terrified. "Did he say something?"

"Leave me alone!" I screamed, hitting the bed with my hands and feet. "Get away from me! Please, leave me alone."

"Why?" she said sitting on the bed. "You're not going to tell me why you're crying?"

"This is the first man I've met since Adel who wants to introduce me to his family," I said through my tears as if talking to myself. "No one else offered to introduce me to his mother or sister."

"What's wrong with that? What does that mean? Isn't that what you wanted, to meet someone's family?"

I didn't respond to her. She wouldn't ever understand.

"You know what the meaning of this invitation is?" she asked. "Marriage. If he wasn't planning on marriage, why would he introduce you to his sister? But we still have to be careful."

Why hadn't I been honest with him? What had happened to me wasn't my fault. He'd forgive me.

If he loved me, he'd still love me as he imagined me, as innocent, pure, virginal. But he didn't love me as a woman, as the lover of a rich man.

I couldn't reveal the truth to him. I couldn't lose his love. But if I built my love on deception, Hashim would break it off after he discovered the truth.

"We'll go forward until we see how this ends," my mother said.

My mother kept talking and talking. I was distracted, only half listening.

"You need to know that if I go, you're not coming with me."

"No?" my mother said, surprised.

"Listen," I said to her sharply, with a new strength. "Hashim isn't like other men. He hasn't even tried to kiss me. They're modern people. They don't have any problem with him inviting his girlfriend to his house . . ."

"I don't know modern or not modern," she cut me off. "Aren't modern men still men? What I know is that once he takes you to his house, he'll do what he wants with you."

"And what's that?" I snapped.

"Listen. If you think you're free, you're wrong. Everything here has a price."

"Except for me," I said, cutting her off.

She looked at my face, searching for something.

"Don't try to shame me," she kept talking. "Or think that I'm not at the level of your Dr. Hashim and his sister."

"Not at all, Mother," I said with a hint of pity. "But he told me everyone coming is a young woman. You'll be out of place. You have to understand."

"No," she said stubbornly.

"Please let me sleep. I'm tired."

I got up and took off my clothes. I kicked off my shoes and went back to my bed.

My mother insisted on sleeping next to me. I gave her my back. I let her speak, but I didn't respond to her. My eyes were closed, but all of me was awake, my mind, my heart, my nerves.

My mother fell asleep. I didn't. I couldn't. I got out of bed and walked barefoot to my father's room. I wanted to sleep next to him. My father was the only pure thing in this house. I wanted to take refuge in something clean.

My father opened his eyes. He looked at me as if he could understand all my problems without me telling them to him. A slight smile appeared on his paralyzed lips to console me.

After a while, my mother came and shook me gently, thinking that I was sleeping.

"Fine," she whispered in order not to wake up my father. "You can go alone. Go back to your bed."

The following morning, his sister called. I was waiting for her call, sitting next to the phone, stiff like wood. I heard her serene voice, balanced in its goodness and happiness.

"Nagwa," she said as if she'd known me for a long time. "This is Madiha, Hashim's sister. I'm calling to invite you for dinner tomorrow at my house. I'd love to see you after how much I've heard about you. I really hope you can come."

"Merci, thank you very much," I said.

I accepted the invitation.

It was the first time I went out with Hashim alone.

Alone with him, I felt my age, that I was twenty-one years old. I felt all my emotions, a free liveliness, shyness, fear, alarm, hesitation, anticipation. Every movement of Hashim was stirring something up in me, as if I was still a girl, naive and innocent, as if my love was still clean and pure, as if my mother's wickedness hadn't stained me.

We were quiet in the car.

Before we got to Maadi, Hashim stopped suddenly on the side of the road next to the Nile. I looked at him in surprise. He turned to me. As soon as I met his eyes, shyness overcame me and I lowered my eyes.

"I want to tell you something before we arrive," he said.

"Is everything okay?" I asked in a low voice trembling with my emotions.

"I was seeing someone, but it's over," he said, setting his eyes on the surface of the Nile.

I was surprised. Maybe he had made me endure this long deprivation so he could finish things with this other girl. He didn't want to have me and another girl in his life at the same time. Maybe he didn't invite me to his house until after it was over with the other girl. Maybe now he'd give me all his love, all his life. How wonderful he was. I couldn't believe there were still men in the world like this.

"When did it end?" I asked.

"A week ago. Her name was Amina. I had to tell you, so you know everything about me, just like I know everything about you."

"What happened?"

"I couldn't respect her. I never respected her. She didn't have dignity for me to respect. Love that lacks respect is unsuitable for marriage."

I felt a knife was cutting into my heart. He didn't know anything about me. He didn't know I wasn't an innocent girl who loved him. He didn't know I was the lover of a rich old man.

I swallowed, looking at 'Abd al-Fattah's diamond ring on my finger.

"Show me your eyes," I said.

"Why?"

"So I can see if there's still something of her in you or not."

"Don't worry. There's nothing at all left of her."

He took my hand, raised it to his lips, and kissed me on the palm of my hand. This was the first touch of his lips. It flowed all the way to my feet. The blood rushed to my face. Then he turned on the ignition and we went on to Maadi.

My heart was pounding. I made every effort to be confident with his sister. At dinner, I was able to get complete control of my nerves and my smile. I felt calm and composed.

On the way home, I rode next to Hashim in his car, my heart full of happiness. I had succeeded. His sister liked me. Her friends liked me.

He then stopped the car on the side of the road and turned to me.

My eyes were fixed on his face. I didn't know what to say or do.

Hashim was quiet.

My eyes were searching in his for something. He then brought his face close to mine. Before he reached me, he wrapped his arms around me. He squeezed me to his chest, his cheek against mine, his breath on my neck. I wanted to sleep on his chest, on his cheek.

His lips were very close. I felt them on my cheek, then on my lips. My eyes were closed. His first kiss was gentle, from the heart. I felt his heart, his tenderness, his goodness, his raw masculinity. It was a safe, sweet world.

He opened his eyes. I opened mine.

"We're late, Hashim," I whispered.

He drove the car with one hand, his other hand holding mine, squeezing it the entire ride as we sat in silence.

We reached our house in Haram Street. I woke up from my beautiful dream at the sight of my mother as soon as I walked in the door, her hair disheveled like a lunatic.

"Why are you late?" she yelled. "I was about to call the police. This is the last time you go out by yourself."

I didn't want to talk to her. I didn't have the energy. I wanted to be alone to think about Hashim's first kiss. I turned to her and kissed her to placate her.

"Please leave me alone, mother."

My mother sat on my bed, her head on her palm.

"Tell me," she demanded.

I told her quickly, but she wasn't satisfied. She asked for a lot of details. Even my right to be alone in my room, she was taking from me.

I wanted to be alone, to relive his kiss, his words. It was like a dream.

Then, suddenly, a terrible thought struck me.

He doesn't love me. He loves another girl, a virgin, a university student, not me.

I got up the next morning exhausted. Happiness, love, and fear had worn me out.

My mother kept asking me the same questions she asked last night.

"When do you think he'll come to propose?"

"I don't know, mother. He only just introduced me to his sister yesterday."

"All I want is to be sure, Nouga. We have to know where we're going with him."

I didn't respond.

"'Abd al-Fattah is coming today at three o'clock."

I turned to her in horror.

"Why didn't you tell me before?"

"What's the problem? Is it strange that 'Abd al-Fattah is coming?"

"I'm sick," I said, taking my shoe off and throwing it across the room.

"No," she said calmly. "He doesn't believe that story anymore. Yesterday, he talked with me for an hour on the phone. The man smells a rat. He's no fool. He knows something's going on. We can't trick him."

"I don't want him anywhere near me."

"Listen, Nouga. A bird in the hand is worth ten in the bush. I'm not tossing 'Abd al-Fattah away for your Mr. Doctor. When we know exactly what he wants, we'll act."

"Not one bird or ten, I can't stand 'Abd al-Fattah anymore."

"But you can stand his money?" she asked calmly.

"I don't want his money!" I screamed. "He can take it and get out of my face."

"When Hashim learns we're living in a villa that costs fifty pounds a month, what will you tell him?"

"Don't be crazy," she kept going. "Don't forget that 'Abd al-Fattah is your husband."

"Don't say that! He's not. You know he's not. You sold me to him. You trafficked me. You're living off my body!"

She looked at me in shock.

"May God forgive you, Nouga. Did I force you to do anything?"

I ran from her to my room, but she followed me.

"Get it in your head that he's coming at three. I don't want this spoiled behavior. Understand?"

"I don't want to see him!"

"And what will we live off?"

"I don't know. We could live in a cheap neighborhood and live off bread. What's wrong with us going back to live in our apartment in Giza? What's wrong with living like we did before we met 'Abd al-Fattah?"

"Don't be a child," she said calmly. "You can't live like you did in Giza. I'll tell you what. You want to marry this Hashim, right?"

"I love him," I said, still angry. "It's not important if I marry him. Besides, I'm not a little girl anymore. I have the right to come and go as I wish."

"So, you want to meet him alone?"

"Yes."

"You know you can't do that unless I agree. You can run to the end of the world, and you'll find me right behind you. I won't leave you for a single moment, not with Dr. Hashim or anyone else. Unless we agree . . ."

"To what?"

"I'll let you go meet the doctor."

"Thank you very much," I said sarcastically.

"But on one condition."

"What?"

"That you're nice to 'Abd al-Fattah. I promise you the day the doctor marries you, you won't see 'Abd al-Fattah again. You know 'Abd al-Fattah doesn't object to you getting married. Only two months ago, he promised me that the day you get married, he'll prepare you a dowry that is better than the one he gave for his daughter."

"But there's a catch."

"What? The man doesn't have any conditions."

"That I remain nice to him even after I get married."

"At that point, our Lord will solve it. Don't worry about that. So what do you say?"

"I agree."

She looked at me as if she wasn't expecting that I would agree so quickly and easily.

"So, can we agree that 'Abd al-Fattah will come today?"

"No. Later."

"Why not today?"

"Because I want to meet Hashim."

"But 'Abd al-Fattah will go crazy."

"Let him."

"Fine, my dear," she said, sounding worried, getting ready to sleep next to me. "I hope this Dr. Hashim works out."

"Please, leave me alone!"

He eyes widened in terror. She then swallowed the wound and left my room.

I threw myself on my bed crying.

9

Days passed.

I met Hashim. I received 'Abd al-Fattah.

My life was becoming more difficult, more complicated.

Hashim would meet me in his car. We'd go to the Mansuriya Canal or the airport road. Sometimes we'd have tea at the Mena House or the pyramids. He took me many times to the club at the beginning of the road to Fayoum for lunch. Sometimes he'd invite me to spend time with his sister. He was always gentle with me, good-hearted, tender. He'd treat me like an angel, as if I was made from delicate glass. He was afraid that a word or a touch would break me. Nothing more happened between us than kisses that would take my heart and transfer it to his clean, pure world. I felt that I was a woman. He was the only man who could make me feel that way. I'd sense his strong arms losing their tenderness and tightening around me, but his will was stronger than his urges. He'd get control of himself quickly and then give me an apologetic look. That would only make me feel the crisis I was in more deeply. I almost confessed everything, but I was afraid I'd lose him.

"You know, Nagwa, the more I know you, the more I get lost in you," he told me once. "When I learn something about you, I think that there are a lot of things I want to know."

I looked at him with terror in my eyes. What did he mean? Did he doubt me? Had he heard something about me?

"You know everything about me," I said, my throat dry. "There's nothing I haven't told you."

"Of course," he said, smiling. "But I'm talking about my feelings. I always feel like I'm waiting for you to tell me something new."

"Like what?"

"I don't know."

"Ask me about anything and I'll tell you."

"You still don't understand. I'm talking about my feelings, just feelings."

He then raised my hand to his lips and kissed it. He leaned over and kissed me on my ears. He was so sincere. Maybe this sincerity was making him hesitate to define his relationship with me. He didn't know what I was suffering. He didn't know that I'd be happy with any relationship he chose. Any relationship. His tenderness was torturing me more than 'Abd al-Fattah was.

'Abd al-Fattah felt that I'd changed, that I'd changed a lot. I wasn't playing along anymore. I couldn't fabricate my feelings anymore. I could no longer feel that the body I gave him wasn't mine. 'Abd al-Fattah didn't demand love from me. All he wanted was an hour of pleasure, an hour of torture.

He became suspicious of me. He started believing that something had happened to me, that there was another man in my life. He expressed his suspicions to my mother.

"Not at all, I swear," she told him. "There's no one. But since the day she got better, she's changed. She's like a different girl."

'Abd al-Fattah didn't believe that the reason for my change was my illness. He started questioning me, taking me and my mother to task.

My mother was losing it waiting for Hashim. She kept trying to push him by suggesting to him that I'd be getting married to someone else soon. Every time he'd visit us, she'd claim there were many suitors.

"What do you think, Doctor, about 'Abd al-'Aziz Rahmi?" she asked. "Do you know him?"

"No," he said calmly.

"He's a well-known engineer. He's thirty and has two buildings. He keeps coming to ask for Nagwa's hand. His mother too. She keeps calling. I don't know what to tell her."

"Whatever Nagwa wants."

"Nagwa is being coy. But I see the time has come. We have to convince her to get married."

"I agree," Hashim said. "Nagwa has to get married. But who and when, this is what she'll decide on her own."

"You don't have an opinion?"

"No," Hashim said, his calm smile on his lips.

My mother was silent as she looked at him angrily.

After Hashim left, I yelled at her.

"Don't talk about marriage to Hashim again! That's how they do it in the countryside. It's embarrassing. Hashim isn't an idiot. He knows what you're trying to do."

"If he understands me," she snapped, "why hasn't he committed yet?"

My mother felt she was starting to lose me, to lose her control over me. She felt that even if I married Hashim, I wouldn't come back to her. Hashim would take me to a world far from her, far from her influence. She started to lose her mind. I'd come back to find her semi-crazy, not caring what Hashim did with me. All she really cared about was that I'd been liberated from her control for an hour or two. She became jealous, jealous of Hashim, more than 'Abd al-Fattah, as if she was my lover. It was a deviant possessiveness, not that of a mother.

She knew I was in love with Hashim. She tried to stop me from going to meet him. She started setting up some barrier every time I went to meet him. We yelled at each other. I started threatening her. I would cut off my relationship with 'Abd al-Fattah by telling him the truth about my love for Hashim. She was forced to let me go out alone with Hashim and to cover up for me so that 'Abd al-Fattah didn't know anything.

One day, she came and lay down next to me with a smile. She pulled me to her chest tenderly. She told me she'd been able to save three thousand pounds, all from 'Abd al-Fattah's money, of course. She had decided to use this money as a down payment on a building that she was buying and putting in my name.

"Merci," I said to her, giving her a kiss on her cheek. My mother was silent for a bit.

"Listen, Nouga," she then said. "We have to talk about something."

"What?"

"This doctor of yours . . ."

"Go ahead."

"He isn't the marrying type. This man is forty-two and he still hasn't married yet. Why would he get married now after all this time?"

"So what type is he?"

"He's the type who likes women."

"If he's that type, why hasn't he asked anything from me yet?"

"Okay, so he's the romantic type. There are many like this, dabblers in love."

"What are you trying to say? What do you mean?"

"I mean we can forget marriage with him. Enough."

"What does that mean?" I asked, looking at her in disgust.

"It means he can come to see you here at home. Instead of you having to go out in public. That way, your reputation is still intact. Suitors can still come to visit."

"I don't understand," I said, pretending not to know what she meant.

"I mean you can be alone with him here." She thought she was on the verge of convincing me. "God willing, he'll come every day. What you do is up to you."

"Like 'Abd al-Fattah? Right?" I asked in bitter derision.

"Isn't Hashim a man and 'Abd al-Fattah a man? All men are the same. They all want the same thing from women. The smart woman is the one who knows how to take advantage of it."

I did everything I could to contain my rage.

"You're horrible, Mother," I said calmly, suppressing the fire in me. "Horrible. I love Hashim because he convinced me that I could be good. But you insist on making me bad. You insist that I continue my whole life like this."

"That kind of talk doesn't serve any purpose. We're speaking logically . . ."

"Leave me alone!" I exploded. "Get out of my room! I don't want to hear a single word from you! Get out! Get out!"

I picked up the pillow, put it over my head, and covered my ears with it so I didn't hear what she was saying.

My mother left. She left me crying. She didn't try to come back that night. She was calm the next morning, her face frozen. She didn't try to continue the conversation from the previous night. She didn't even seem like we'd fought about anything.

I called Hashim as I usually did every morning.

"Listen, Nagwa," he said in a hesitating tone. "There's something bothering me. I spent all night thinking whether to tell you or not. I still don't know, but I feel I have to tell you."

"Is everything okay?"

"Your mother called me last night. She asked to see me alone, outside of the house. She begged me not to tell you."

I gasped. I knew what my mother wanted.

"What did you tell her?"

"I told her to meet me today at four thirty in front of the Giza tunnels."

"Don't go," I pleaded, almost crying. "Don't go, Hashim. Please."

"Why?"

"I'll tell you later. You don't know Mother."

"But I promised her," he said, surprised by my reaction.

"Apologize. Tell her you can't go. Please, please."

"But why?"

"I'll tell you later. I'll meet you today instead of Mother. Not at four thirty. Let's make it two thirty, right after the clinic."

"What do I do about your mother?"

"Just excuse yourself. I'm hanging up. Call her now and tell her you have an emergency."

"Okay."

"I'll meet you at the same place, in front of the tunnel on the Haram Street side," I said. "Don't come to the house."

"Okay."

He hung up, not knowing what was going on.

I knew what my mother wanted from him.

She wanted to sign with him a contract like the one she signed with 'Abd al-Fattah. She wanted it in writing. She wanted him to pay two thousand pounds. She was selling me to him. And there was nothing stopping 'Abd al-Fattah's contract staying in place too, nothing stopping her from selling me to two men instead of one.

After a bit, the phone rang. My mother answered. I let her answer. I saw her face change.

"Thank you very much, Doctor," I heard her say.

She hung up. She looked over at me and looked away quickly, not saying anything. She couldn't tell me that she tried to come to an agreement with Hashim about me behind my back.

"Who was it?" I asked, innocently.

"Dr. Hashim," she said. "He was in a rush, so he didn't have time to talk with you."

She went into the kitchen.

I went out without telling her.

I decided to put an end to this farce that I was living. I decided to shine a light on myself so I could appear before my love as I really was, no matter what that truth was, no matter how much of a risk it was, no matter my fate.

I couldn't bear this deception anymore, this deceit, this lie.

Hashim looked at me as I got into his car.

"Do you want to go to Saqqara?" he asked.

"Where would you meet Amina?"

Hashim was surprised. He looked in my face trying to work out what I was thinking.

"Why does that matter? I thought we talked about that already."

"I have to know," I said, feeling that I was about to scream. "Where would you meet her?"

"At the apartment," Hashim said, regaining his calm, looking back at the road.

"You have an apartment?"

"Yes."

"Why didn't you tell me?"

"I was going to tell you."

"I want to see it."

"God willing, you'll see it one day."

"I want to see it now. Right now."

"Why?"

"Because I have to know everything about you."

He looked in my face, examining me like one of his patients.

"Okay," he said.

He turned the wheel, and we headed toward Zamalek.

As I went into Hashim's apartment, I took nothing in, not the color of the walls or what the furniture looked like. I only saw what was going to happen next.

Hashim showed me all the rooms. I stood at the door of each room and looked over it distractedly. We then went back to the outer salon. I decided to sit on the couch. Hashim sat next to me, very close to me.

"Do you feel better?" he asked. "This is the apartment, my dear."

"I see your entire past here."

"No, not all of it," he said, laughing. "Only half."

"Where's the other half?"

"In another apartment," he said. "The one I had before this."

"Because your past is too big for one apartment."

He laughed again. His laugh resonated all over the apartment. He then brought his face close to mine.

"I don't have a past anymore," he said in a serious tone. "I've swept it away. I only have a future. You're my future."

I lowered my head, unable to bear all his love and the promise of a future.

A period of silence passed between us. His face was very close to mine.

"You know that I sometimes don't believe it," I said in a low voice, breathless. "I'm suspicious of you. I think you're with a lot of girls."

"If there was another girl," he said, stretching his arms out along the back of the couch, "you would know."

"How so?"

"It would be obvious. I wouldn't know how to hide it."

"So why do you still have this apartment?"

"To make coffee. Speaking of which, would you like me to make you coffee?"

"No, merci."

He got up from beside me.

"I make the best coffee."

I grabbed his hand, so he wouldn't get up.

"Really, I don't want any, Hashim."

"I'm sorry, I don't have anything to offer you except coffee."

"That's it?"

"Just me."

He then fell on me. His kiss here was different from in the car. He wasn't afraid or hesitant. He wasn't thinking about who might pass us on the road.

Our kiss went on longer than we were used to. I felt it take off. I took off with it. His arms squeezed me to him. His hands were on my back. Everything else left my mind. I only wanted him to kiss me, to kiss me more, without reservation, without limits.

Suddenly, he pulled away from me. I opened my eyes as if I woke up from a dream. He started trying to light a cigarette.

"Are you sure you don't want coffee?" he asked without looking at me.

"Yes."

He took off his jacket slowly. He took it off because it was hot. Everything around us was hot, everything was on fire.

"Aren't you going to tell me?" he asked, a bit breathless, not wanting to look at me. "Why didn't you want me to go meet your mother?"

I looked at him wide-eyed. I could no longer play the role of the virgin, of the angel. I was a woman. He had to know that and forgive me.

"It's nothing. I don't want her to see you alone."

"Why?"

"Because she's jealous of you."

He stayed silent for a moment, then took me in his arms.

I clung to him.

"Kiss me, Hashim," I whispered. "Kiss me. Don't leave me."

He laid me down on the couch. He no longer tried to resist. He gave in to his desire.

He tried to take me as a girl, as a virgin.

But I gave him myself as a woman.

I'm the one who gave him myself.

I felt love at its peak, its climax. I felt love flowing in my body, calm and beautiful. My tears rushed out, silent tears, perhaps tears of happiness, a happiness that I hadn't felt before.

We remained silent. The beats of our hearts blurred together and our breath became one.

Hashim sat up on the edge of the couch next to me. He knew I was not a virgin. I closed my eyes, waiting to hear what he was going to say, waiting for the verdict of fate.

Hashim put his head in his hands.

"I don't want you to tell me anything you don't want to," he said in a low voice.

I didn't respond. I didn't know what to say. My heart was trembling. My tears ran onto my cheek. These were new tears, they bore a different feeling, a different meaning.

Another period of silence passed.

"We'll get married," Hashim then said in a low voice.

I was stunned. I couldn't believe what I heard. I turned around. I raised my face, wet with tears. His head was lowered with a sad smile on his lips, as if he had been hit by a sudden catastrophe, as if he'd lost something very valuable to him.

I began to sob. I turned over again. Hashim turned to me.

"You're crying because we're going to get married?"

"We can't," I said through my tears, looking up at him. "We can't."

"Why not?" he asked stunned.

"Because I'm married."

His eyes widened as if a hand had reached out to his neck and was choking him.

"What?"

"I'm married!" I blurted it out again. "I'm married."

He was silent.

"I should have told you before."

He got up from beside me and threw himself down on the wide chair next to the couch. He put his hand on his chest and took a deep breath.

I sat up, took my bag, and pulled out a tissue to dry my tears. I looked at him. He looked like he'd aged ten years in a single moment.

My heart ached for him. I was afraid for him. I didn't think that he'd be so shocked. I didn't know what to do. Or what to say.

At that moment I realized what I had done. How harsh it had been to hide the truth from him, and then how I had revealed it to him. I felt like a criminal.

"I think I'll make that coffee now," he said.

He got up and left me trying to work out what I was going to say to him. I didn't plan on hiding anything from him, but I wanted to pick my words carefully so as not to wound him further.

Hashim came back with his coffee and sat on the wide chair. He lit a cigarette.

"Let's start from the beginning. You're married?"

"Yes."

"Tell me again."

"I'm married."

"Since when?"

"About a year and a half ago."

"Since before you were sick?"

"Yes."

"So why haven't I seen your husband?"

"Because we were married in secret."

He raised his eyebrows.

"Why? What made someone like you get married in secret?"

"Because he's married to someone else."

"So why did you marry him?"

"For his money."

"I can't believe that! Don't talk about yourself like that."

"That's how it is. We're not rich. Haven't you noticed how we live on Haram Street now? Didn't you notice? Didn't you see that I have a car, so many dresses, a villa, a butler? All that is from 'Abd al-Fattah."

"Who's that?"

"'Abd al-Fattah Rif'at. Do you know him?"

"He's the one you married?"

"Mother says I'm married."

"Your mother says you're married?"

"She made me sign a contract. She said it was a marriage, a temporary marriage."

"What you're talking about isn't marriage."

I swallowed this insult. He had every right to be harsh.

Hashim was silent. He turned his back to me. He took a sip from his cup of coffee and then a deep drag from his cigarette.

"Mother is the one who made me do it," I said after a bit, pleading for his understanding.

"Don't say that. You're not a little girl. You're stronger than your mother. If you did something, you did it because you wanted to, not because your mother was stronger than you, not because she made you do it."

"I didn't know what I was doing. Mother is the one who agreed on it with 'Abd al-Fattah. She drew up this contract so I couldn't get married behind her back."

My tears flowed freely. They were silent, sad tears. I was crying for myself.

There was a long period of silence between us. Hashim seemed like he'd regained his control over himself. He turned to me with a sad smile.

"I'm sorry," he said in a low voice with a rattle of tenderness. "Forgive me. You surprised me. I know everyone has their own circumstances. People do wrong when what's wrong is stronger than them, when their circumstances push them to it against their will. You're a good person. I'll always be convinced that you're a good person. If my sister or my mother were in your position, they might have done the same. I'm sorry."

He sat down next to me. He took my tissue from my hand and started drying the tears on my cheeks.

"Where's your smile?" he asked.

I couldn't smile.

"I don't know what to do, Hashim," I said, my head on his chest meekly and ashamed.

"You can do anything you want."

"What does that mean?"

"You can continue with this man. Or you can leave him whenever you want."

"And Mother?"

"You're stronger than her. No one in the world can impose their will on you."

"You don't know Mother. She could do anything."

"She can't if you insist on what you want."

"I'll leave him. I'll rip up the contract. I'll go to live with my birth mother."

Hashim was silent. He then got up and started pacing in front of me.

"But there's something I have to say."

"What?" I asked, raising my face to him.

"If you leave him, I don't want you to leave him for me."

"What does that mean?"

"You have to leave him for yourself. You have to be convinced of it, even if I wasn't in your life. You should leave him to regain yourself, to affirm to yourself that you're stronger than these circumstances. No matter how much you hide from people, you can't hide from yourself. No matter how much you lie to people, you can't lie to yourself."

I looked at him, trying to follow what he was saying.

"Since the day I met him, I've been trying to leave him."

"I won't help you," he said, still pacing in front of me as if he was talking to himself, as if he didn't hear my words. "This is a decision that you have to carry out on your own."

"I'm not asking anything from you, Hashim."

He stopped pacing and stood in front of me, a line of pain cutting through his brow, his eyes dark and worried, his lips taut like an angry child.

"I haven't loved anyone in my life as much as I love you," he said. "But now, now is different. I feel like I don't know you. I feel like I have to get to know you all over again. I have to start loving you from the start all over again."

"All I know is that I love you," I said. "All I know is that I've become a different person since the day I fell in love with you."

"How could you hide all of this from me?" he asked, pained.

"I was afraid. Not afraid of you, but of your love. It wasn't possible for me to hide forever. I couldn't because I love you."

"I've never been stunned like this before," he said.

"I'm strong with you, Hashim."

He looked me in the eye.

"You don't need anyone, Nagwa. Not me or anyone else. You can go to university and graduate and get a job. You can get married any time. Don't say that you're strong with me. You're strong because of your intelligence, your youth, and your will, strong because of who you are."

He paused.

"I can't leave you," he said. "I won't help you, but that doesn't mean that we're breaking up. Please be patient with me until I figure things out."

"I never felt like I'm putting up with you," I said, smiling. "All I feel is that I love you."

I stood up and kissed his worried lips. I kissed the line of pain traced on his brow. I kissed his dark, tortured eyes. I looked at my watch.

"It's five thirty," I said. "Time for the clinic, Hashim."

"I don't think I'll go back today," he said. "I can't work."

"You have to."

"Okay."

"Promise me."

"I'll try."

He then took me in his arms, pulling me to his chest gently.

"Don't forget you're strong," he said, his voice raspy.

"I've never felt as strong as I do today."

I then kissed him on his lips, his sad, tired lips.

"You're not leaving?" I asked.

"I'm staying a little," he said, bringing me to the door. He opened it for me and I left.

I held my head up high. I felt strong, that I wasn't ever as strong as I was at that moment. I felt whole. I felt as if I'd been liberated, that I'd been released into a new world which I was controlling. I was its master.

On my way home, I planned what I'd say to my mother, my mind filled with strong, decisive words, the words of fate, my fate.

I found my mother sitting in the salon, her head in her palms.

'Abd al-Fattah was sitting next to her.

I went in feeling strong. I looked each of them in the eyes.

"That's it!" my mother screamed, looking up at me. "I want nothing to do with you. You'll drive me crazy. You'll kill me. And here, 'Abd al-Fattah knows!"

"Where were you?" he said in a nervous voice.

"It has nothing to do with you," I said.

He raised his eyebrows, surprised at my boldness. I'd never snapped at him like that. His eyes narrowed as he looked in my face, trying to work out the truth.

"I know where you were," he said. "You were with that Dr. Hashim, right?"

My mother looked at me.

"I told him everything," she said, almost wailing. "That's it. I can't bear the responsibility for you by myself anymore."

I looked at 'Abd al-Fattah. I was still standing at the door.

"Yes," I said. "I was with Dr. Hashim."

"How well do you know this Hashim?" he said. "You know he's been with a hundred girls before you? You know he was going out with a girl named Amina? He destroyed her and her reputation. And then he left her like a stray dog . . ."

"And what will you leave me like?" I cut him off.

"How dare you talk to me like that?" He was losing his self-control.

"I'm the one who wants to understand. What right do you have to hold me accountable?" I asked, looking at him in defiance.

He hesitated. He looked at my mother, as if he was consulting with her, and then turned his wretched face back to me.

"I'm your husband, Nouga," he said.

"This isn't marriage. Marriage means a house and children. If you wanted to consider yourself my husband, you should've married me in front of people, like you married your wife, the way your daughter got married. Go take your money and don't show your face here again!"

My mother screamed out.

"That's what you want?" 'Abd al-Fattah raised his voice. "Or is that what Hashim told you?"

"That's what has to happen," I said.

I left the two of them flabbergasted.

I took the phone, brought it into my room, and locked the door behind me.

I called Hashim at the clinic. I wanted to check on him after I left him in such a state of shock. But the nurse told me he'd called and said he wasn't coming because he was sick.

It might have been the first time Hashim had skipped his clinic. And it was because of me.

10

I WANTED TO BE SOMETHING else, something clean, innocent, sinless, something that deserved Hashim's love.
I was strong. Hashim gave me this strength so I could
become clean.

But the road to a clean life was difficult. I plunged into
battle.

'Abd al-Fattah and my mother were on one side. And
I was on the other, all alone. Hashim refused to stand
beside me, refused to intervene, refused to do anything
that would lighten the burden. He insisted that it was my
battle alone.

My mother and 'Abd al-Fattah didn't give up. 'Abd
al-Fattah started coming to the house every morning
before going to the factory and every evening before
heading back home. My mother yelled. 'Abd al-Fattah
yelled. I yelled. The yelling consumed me like a fire. I
was resisting. I was insisting. I only asked for one thing,
which was to get 'Abd al-Fattah out of my life, to tear up
the contract that I'd signed, for him to free me.

"Listen, Nouga," 'Abd al-Fattah said with a forced
calm. "Listen to me well. I'll buy you this villa that you're
living in. Wait a month or two until all this nationalization

is finished and afterwards, I'll marry you properly. You know I've put everything I have in my wife's name so if I marry you right now, I won't have a piaster. What do you think?"

"It's no use," I said, looking at him in disgust and defiance.

"Unbelievable!" my mother screamed. "That Hashim has eaten the girl's mind. May God cut short Hashim's years. I curse the day we met him."

"If I hadn't met Hashim, I would've died a long time ago."

"Be reasonable," my mother kept wailing. "Listen to what 'Abd al-Fattah is telling you. He'll buy you this villa. You don't deserve even a room. Who do you think you are? You think you're an English queen. Use your head, girl."

"The villa isn't important," 'Abd al-Fattah cut her off to try a new approach.

He then turned to me.

"What's important is that I love you, Nouga," he said, grabbing my hands. "I love you so much that I can't imagine life without you. I have nothing but you."

I looked at him. A moment of weakness passed over my heart. I almost took pity on him. He gave me a pathetic smile. But I regained my strength quickly, my determination. Even if he loved me, it wasn't decent or respectable. He hadn't offered anything he'd want for his daughter.

I pulled my hands from his and looked him straight in the eye.

"Sorry, uncle," I said calmly.

He looked at me sharply.

"What does 'sorry' mean?"

"It means there's no use. It's over."

"If you think your doctor will marry you," he yelled, "you're a fool!"

"You think I'm your slave girl?" I shouted back, my blood boiling. "You think you bought me with all your money?"

'Abd al-Fattah stood there with his short fat body. He then raised his thick hand and brought it down on my cheek.

"Why do you think you can speak to me like that?" he screamed. "Since when are you so rude? I won't let a little runt of a girl like you play with me, understand?"

I shook under the impact of his slap, but I didn't scream. I didn't cry or put my hand on my cheek. I took control of myself quickly. I held his scornful gaze. At that moment, I hated him more than ever before. I hated him and felt nothing but complete disgust for him.

"Do what you want," I said, my head held high.

I turned my back to him and walked with firm steps to my room, locking the door behind me. I stayed in my room for an entire day. I didn't care about eating or drinking. My mother was on the other side of the door begging me to open it for her, but I refused. I only opened up when she brought my father in his wheelchair. I threw myself on his chest and I cried, letting go for a moment.

My mother set the Nour al-Huda ladies on me. Whenever 'Abd al-Fattah was gone and my mother was busy, they tried to convince me that my relationship with 'Abd al-Fattah was legitimate, that the contract that I signed permitted him to demand my obedience, and on and on. They were trying to scare me. But I knew them. 'Abd al-Fattah was paying them to do this in the name of piety and devotion. A lot of men paid them to dupe good girls.

All this I could bear. What I couldn't bear was that I was no longer seeing Hashim or even talking with him on the phone.

I refused to tell my mother the details of what had happened between me and him when I went to his apartment. She was convinced that Hashim was stronger than her now, that he had more influence, that I loved him to the point that I'd sacrifice her and hide the details from her.

She declared war on him. She decided that Hashim would never enter our house again. She blocked me from talking with him on the phone. She always had the phone next to her and carried it around with her from room to room. If I insisted on calling one of my friends, she'd dial the number herself. She jailed me in the house, and she jailed herself with me. I spent long days seeing only her wrinkled face, 'Abd al-Fattah's bluish face, and the faces of the ladies of Nour al-Huda, cold as ice. I'd fight with them and then I'd go to my room and lock the door.

I longed for Hashim. Sometimes, I'd blame him for what was happening. Why did he leave me alone? Why wasn't he doing anything to save me? Then I'd return to the warmth of his love, Hashim's love. I knew he couldn't do anything. He couldn't call or visit, even if he wanted to. Maybe he was suffering as much as I was, maybe more.

Maybe he was suffering in confusion, shock, and deprivation from me. The path was clear before me, the straight path. I was doing all this not so I could be Hashim's wife, not for marriage, but so I could be a woman who deserved Hashim's love. It was easy to picture myself as this woman with a strong personality, who went to university and then graduated and worked. After that, I could love my husband completely, without complications, without cracks.

My mother resorted once again to magic and witchcraft, as she did when she destroyed my love for Adel. But this time, I didn't submit. I refused to deliver myself to the magicians and sorcerers. She'd steal the comb I used to brush my hair and give it to Miss Victoria for her to plant her magic spells. She lit a candle in the bathroom immediately after I showered on one of the days of the last half of the Islamic month and left it lit all night, and on and on. She did a lot of things thinking that the magic would wipe Hashim's love from my heart.

I didn't say a word. I just looked at her with disdain and turned my back on her, trusting that my love was stronger than her magic, but she reached the point of doing more than that. My mother set up an exorcism for me without me knowing. Sheikha Zahra recommended it to her. She secretly put a veil under my pillow before I went to sleep. The next morning, my mother came and asked me tenderly what I'd dreamed about the night before. I told her that I had dreamed I was running down a staircase. I fell and then I tried to get up, but I couldn't. I discovered that my foot was broken. I really did dream that. My mother asked me again with great interest if I'd seen my own blood in the dream. I said I had, without realizing why she was so interested. My mother took the dream to Sheikha Zahra and the sheikha told her that a black billy goat had to be slaughtered for me. A few days later, my mother called me to a room next to the kitchen that we were using for storage. As soon as I stepped in, they slaughtered the goat at my feet. I screamed. I looked around me and I saw Sheikha Zahra and three women from Nour al-Huda with my mother, all of them covered in white veils, even my mother.

"What are you doing?" I screamed. "Stop this madness!"

Sheikha Zahra and the women of Nour al-Huda stayed in the house for three days and nights, casting their spells on the blood of the black billy goat.

I decided to flee. I couldn't put up with it anymore. I pretended to be calm so my mother wouldn't keep close watch on me. When she was busy with something, I went into her room and took three pounds from her drawer. My father was lying in the bed looking at me with his smiling eyes full of love, like he didn't understand or suspect anything. I threw myself on his chest and kissed him many times, holding back my tears. I felt like I was saying goodbye to him and that I wasn't ever coming back. My father was the only thing that I loved in this house.

I left my mother's room.

"Go fill the bathtub," I told the maid. "I want to take a bath."

My mother heard me.

I went into my room for a moment until I heard the water filling the tub and I was sure the maid was in the bathroom.

I left. I tiptoed out of the house. I ran down to the street and found a taxi.

"Zamalek, please," I told the driver.

I got out near Hashim's apartment. I then called him from a grocery store nearby. He was about finished with his clinic for the afternoon.

"I'm ready to see you now, Hashim," I told him impatiently as soon as I heard his voice.

"Where are you?"

"I'm calling from the street, next to your apartment."

"I'll be there in ten minutes."

"We'll meet in the apartment?"

"Yes."

"What's the number?" I asked. "I forgot."

"Third floor, number thirty-one."

"Don't be late, Hashim."

I hung up. I started walking slowly around the block where the apartment was located until more than fifteen minutes had passed, then I went up.

He opened the door for me.

I stood looking at him, drinking up the sight of him after a long thirst. The line of pain still cut through his brow. Worry had left dark imprints under his eyes. His smile was sad. I thought his face was thinner, his nose bigger. The look in his eyes was hesitant. He seemed to have more white hair.

I tried to keep my eyes on his face, but I couldn't. I felt everything slipping from me. As much as I felt strong with my mother and 'Abd al-Fattah, I was weak before Hashim. I lowered my eyes and stood opposite him silently.

He pulled me to him and embraced me, resting his face on my head silently.

We relaxed into each other and held our breath.

He moved me away from him gently, then he took me by the hand and sat me on the couch.

"I missed you," he whispered.

"Me too," I said, looking away.

"You've lost weight."

"You too," I said, looking at his face. "I'm very tired, Hashim."

"What happened?"

"I fled."

"Where to?" he asked, raising his eyebrows in surprise.

"Here."

He let go of my hand.

"But this isn't a solution."

"I didn't find any other solution," I said, about to cry. "You don't know what they're doing to me."

I started telling him about what had happened.

"What do you plan to do?"

"I plan to stay here from now on."

"This isn't a solution," he said again, looking me in the eye.

"So, what's the solution?"

"The solution is that you go back home and stay there until you get what you want."

"And not see you?"

"Your problem isn't whether we see each other or not. The issue is that you choose the life that you want."

"Hashim," I said, my heart pounding. "Tell me the truth. Do you still love me?"

"I don't know."

My heart trembled like a terrified bird.

"How don't you know?"

He got up and started pacing up and down front of me.

"I don't know anything," he said nervously. "I don't know if I love you or not. I'm not confused about you, I'm confused about myself, confused about every day that's passed since I met you. I love the you I thought you were, a strong, innocent, young girl. That girl is the one I love. But all of a sudden, I found another girl before me. I found a woman with a man who takes care of her, who gave her a house, a woman who could hide all that from me for a whole year. I started doubting every day we spent together, every sweet word you said to me. I can't believe that when I'd leave your house, another man would come in after me. I can't believe that your mother knew, that I was such a fool, that you are the one who duped me. Maybe if you'd told me everything from the start, I would've loved you anyway, I would've loved you without having to discover that I'm a fool. But now, I don't know who I love. Do I love the innocent girl or the woman who has another man? It's driving me crazy. I can't work. For the first time ever, I'm distracted when I'm with my patients. For the first time ever, I need a drink to be able to sleep."

I cried silently. He was hitting me with the whip. I couldn't complain or oppose him.

"Make me understand, Nagwa," he said, tormented, gripping my hand. "I loved you in a way that meant marriage."

"And now?"

"I don't know."

"I want to stay here until you know. I'll stay a day, a month, a year. I love you, Hashim. I can't do without you. I don't want anything from you but your love."

"No."

"No, what?"

"Don't stay here. You'd be living here as you live with 'Abd al-Fattah. If you love me, don't act with me as you did with him. If you love me, your love has to turn you into another person, a completely different person."

"I can't be with you like I was with 'Abd al-Fattah. I . . ."

"I don't believe it. All I'll feel is that you got used to that way of life."

I felt as if he'd stabbed me with a cold knife in my heart. I rocked in my seat and straightened my back against the couch, so I didn't collapse.

"You don't want me, Hashim?" I asked, in despair.

He came beside me, putting his arm around my shoulder.

"I wish I felt that way. There isn't a day that's passed where I've felt I didn't want you."

"You can't forgive me?"

"I can't forget," he said, squeezing me to him gently. "I've tried."

"Forget, Hashim," I whispered. "Forget."

My lips were close to his.

He leaned over to touch my lips. He gave them a light touch and then pulled me to him roughly. He kissed me with all of his lips. Then he went back to being gentle.

He pulled away from me.

"Don't torture me, Hashim. I've suffered enough."

He looked me in the eye, and then he kissed me forcefully. His fingers crept across my back, plunged into the folds of my hair, and then pulled it harshly. I submitted to his violence and his harshness. I wanted to forget myself. I wanted to forget my life.

Suddenly, he got up from next to me, his face flushed, panting.

"No . . . No . . . No . . ." he repeated.

I sat up, straightened my dress, and fixed my hair. I then put my head in my palms.

"This isn't a solution," Hashim said, calming his beath, turning to me and standing with his back to the wall.

"Is there one?" I asked.

"There has to be."

"What?"

"That we start to get to know each other from the start again."

"How?"

"Let's not meet here in the apartment," he said. "Let's meet anywhere outside. We'll give ourselves time for me to love you as you are, not how I imagined you."

We were silent. Hashim sat down again beside me.

"All this is because I love you, Nagwa," he said, taking my hand.

"I know."

"All that's happened is that my love was shaken. It was stunned. Wait for it to get over the blow and go back to how it was. I promise I'll try to go back to how I was."

"Promise you won't hate me."

"I love you. How could I hate you?"

I gave him a sad smile, then got up and headed to the door.

"Where are you going now?" he asked, getting up with me.

"I don't know."

"Back home?"

"I don't know," I said. "I'll call you and tell you where I am."

"Go back home for me."

"Let me decide what to do, Hashim."

"As you wish."

He opened the door for me.

I looked at him in pity. I touched his cheek with my lips, and I left.

11

My mother was livid.

"You think I'm going to spend my entire life running after you!"

I went into my room refusing to engage her.

At that moment, I was sure I was stronger than her, stronger than her need for me.

She tried to get me to come out of my room, but I refused. I told her my conditions. She had to tear up the contract that had my signature. 'Abd al-Fattah had to leave my life. She had to let me be free, let me go to university, and not intervene between me and Hashim.

My mother refused. I insisted. I needed all my will to resist her. She kept pleading for me to come out. She'd remind me of my paralyzed father and manipulate me with him. Sometimes she'd threaten me. But I insisted. She had to agree to my conditions first. I noticed how she became more fragile. I felt as if I'd dug holes in her heart from which she was bleeding.

After days of this, my mother finally gave in.

"Please," she said in a shaky voice from outside my room. "I'll do what you want. I'll do it for your father.

You won't see 'Abd al-Fattah anymore. He doesn't want to see you either. Take the lousy contract."

She slipped the sheet of paper under the door. I began tearing it up nervously into little pieces. I didn't even read it.

I opened the door and I looked at her. I was afraid to believe her.

I threw myself in her arms. I cried. She cried with me. Seeing her cry was like seeing a mountain made of stone collapse.

I went to my father and threw myself on his chest.

"I'm sorry, Daddy," I repeated. "I'm sorry. Forgive me."

He pulled me to him with his good arm and started to stroke my hair slowly, his lips resting on my cheek.

I stayed next to him all day, talking to him. He looked at me as if he understood everything, but he couldn't articulate it.

My mother was moving around us, pretending to be busy. Her steps were no longer so certain. Her looks were no longer so commanding. Her voice was shaken, like she no longer knew what she was saying. She looked emaciated and exhausted. She came and sat on the couch in my father's room.

She didn't speak. She stayed silent as if nothing had happened between us that deserved any discussion.

That night, after my father fell asleep, she came to my room. She didn't sit on my bed as usual, but she sat on the chair at the side of the mirror and looked at me with a trembling smile.

"Listen, Nouga," she said. "I'm worn out. I have nothing left. From now on, you're in charge. I saved three thousand pounds. And you know there's income from the land and house as well as your father's pension. You take care of how we live. I don't have anything to say about it anymore. You're grown up."

A long time passed without me calling Hashim. Whenever I thought about it, my wounded dignity got the better of me. I told myself we weren't meant to be. I wasn't suited for him. I wasn't suited for his love. The best way forward was not to contact him.

I started calling my old classmates from secondary school again. I told them I'd been sick all this time and that I got my diploma from home. We started spending time together again. I began to regain my old life with them. I started getting ready to go to university. I decided to enroll in the college of economics and political science. The road was clear before me. It was brilliant and clean. My mother started to be proud of me before her friends, proud of the path I was taking, not of my clothes or appearance.

"What will you do after you graduate?" she asked.

"I'll work in the diplomatic corps. I'll rise through the ranks until I'm an ambassador, and then I'll become a minister."

"Okay, we'll see, Miss Ambassador," my mother said, happiness sparkling on her face.

As for 'Abd al-Fattah, I was afraid a day would come when I'd need him and his money. I was determined to always be stronger than that. To make sure, I had to be careful about our living expenses. We'd have to leave this villa, do without the butler and driver, and live within our family's means.

But what would people say? What would my friends say when they saw we'd suddenly moved from a villa on Haram Street, from the high life, to an apartment like the one we used to live in? It didn't matter. I didn't care what people said when I moved to Haram Street and I wouldn't care when we left.

I started to convince my mother that we had to move somewhere more modest, to downsize our life. It wasn't easy to convince her. She'd lived her whole life clinging to appearances. Her fear of losing me made her submit in the end. Living with me somewhere less fancy was better than living alone. I was her life. I was her laughter. I was the focus of all her attention. I was the pivot around which her world and my father's world rotated. I was all that was left for her.

We began to look for a small apartment near the university.

One day, I went out to visit a friend of mine. I saw Hashim driving by slowly with a girl next to him. She was beautiful in a way that I hadn't seen before. Maybe she wasn't Egyptian. She was young, probably younger than me. She was fair with black hair. It was very black with the sun reflecting off it in streaks of almost blue. Hashim was turning toward her and talking. He was talking enthusiastically and waving his hands.

During this break from Hashim, I imagined him with other girls. I tried to convince myself that I didn't have any right to be jealous. It was enough that his love had saved me. But imagination is more merciful than the truth. I could bear seeing him in my imagination, but I couldn't bear to see him with another girl in real life.

I tried to continue to my friend's house, but I never got there. I walked and walked, completely distracted. I tried to convince myself, to make myself understand, but a jealous fire burned inside me.

I went back home after a few hours. I found myself picking up the phone and dialing his clinic.

I heard his voice.

"How are you, Hashim?" I asked hesitatingly.

"Nagwa?" he exclaimed as soon as he heard me. "Before people break up, don't they at least say goodbye? You left me without a word."

"I didn't leave you, Hashim," I said, the fire dying down.

"It's been over a month. Why haven't you called? Tell me what happened."

"I can't. But everything's changed."

"Where are you calling from now?"

"Home."

A moment of silence passed.

"I saw you today," I continued, trying not to let my voice betray the trembling of my heart.

"Where?" he asked in surprise.

"On Haram Street. Who is she?"

"A friend from Lebanon."

"Just a friend?"

"So far."

I was quiet for a moment.

"What's her name?"

"I didn't think you were the jealous type."

"Why wouldn't I be jealous of you?"

"If you were, you wouldn't have left me alone for so long, no matter what happened to you."

"I thought it was better for us not to talk to each other."

"Why?"

"Because you told me the only solution was for us to get to know each other again from the start. When I thought about that, I knew it was impossible. We can't forget what has happened. If we were together, you'd wind up losing your respect for me, like you lost your respect for Amina."

"I was trying to forget, but I couldn't. I still can't."

I didn't respond. I didn't know what to say.

"You didn't tell me. What's her name?"

"Rihab."

"An odd name," I said, suppressing the pain erupting in my chest. "But nice. She's pretty. The color of her hair is amazing. She must get it dyed in Beirut."

"Her hair is dyed?"

"Of course. There's no natural black color like that. It's incredible that such an important doctor like you can't tell dyed hair from natural hair!"

"No," he said confidently. "Her hair isn't dyed."

"Ask her, then."

"I will."

I realized I was saying goodbye to him.

"Do you love her?" I whispered.

"I don't know. I don't know anything these days. I don't know how to act or why I'm doing anything. I feel unstable. There's nothing stable in my life, even my work."

We ended the conversation soon after that.

I never saw him again.

There was always something pulling me to him, but I resisted it. I love him and maybe he still loves me. It's a love that changed me into a better person, but it made Hashim confused and suspicious. He could never forget that I'd lied to him for so long.

It is love that saved me. It's what changed my life. It opened the doors to university for me. It raised my head up high and brought me stability and strength. I started to believe that my entire life was love. Even my mistakes were mistakes that came from love.

Before, I was weak. I couldn't choose the kind of love that I wanted. But all of life is love. Every road is love. What's important is that I choose the road that I want and that I'm convinced of where I'm going. Hashim came and gave me this love, a love that I wanted. I regained my strength, the strength of who I was. I could choose my road. I could free myself from 'Abd al-Fattah and my mother.

It was Hashim that did this. Hashim was incredible. He was a real man.

I'm now a student at university. I'm the head of the drama troupe and the representative of our social club. My classmates love me. We have lots of fun together.

I've been pardoned from military service because of my heart condition. I wish I could have done my military service.

I got honors this year.

Ibrahim passed too.

Who's Ibrahim?

That's another story.

The Third Eye

1

I'm Rihab.

My friends call me Rolly, sometimes just Ro.

I don't know what brought me to Cairo. Just a week before, I was getting ready to go to London. My good friend Hind lived there. I liked her so much that I thought I could bear the cold and fog of London. But, when the time came, I started feeling the cold creep into my bones and the fog cloud my vision.

I had to leave Beirut.

Beirut had started to disgust me. Everything about it, its guys and girls, its streets, the mountains that overlook it, the stores in the long market and the Starco, its thick laughs, harshness, cars, tears, and its lira. Whenever I touched a lira, I started to feel as if I was touching something sticky and disgusting like the stomach of a lizard. Boredom and exhaustion were choking me. I felt like I was going around and around in circles. Violent headaches would overcome me, a thousand hammers pounding in my head. I would be suffocated and feel that my blood had ceased to flow to my throat.

I had to leave Beirut. I was going to flee to London, but I suddenly decided to go to Cairo instead. I wanted to avoid the cold and fog, but there really wasn't anything to take me to Cairo. I had no ties there, no friends there. I didn't love ancient relics. I didn't want to see the pyramids or the Sphinx. I had no understanding of politics and couldn't pretend I picked Cairo out of faith in Arab unity. Not at all. I just chose Cairo and that was it, like I would pick out something to wear without giving it much thought.

I went to my father before he left for work.

"I'm going to Cairo," I informed him, as if the decision was out of my hands.

My father was used to my whims. Nothing I did surprised him anymore. He smiled at me patiently.

"And London?" he asked.

"Fog and cold."

"And your friend Hind?"

"I'll write to her. We don't fight when we write to each other, but we fight a lot when we're together."

"But we booked everything for you there, and we exchanged lira for you."

"Cancel the reservations and exchange the money again."

He looked at me, trying to figure out what I was really thinking.

"Why Cairo?"

"Because. No reason."

"I'm afraid for you. The men there are terrible."

"Ugh," I said nervously. "The way you talk to me! Hajj 'Abd al-Rahman, don't be afraid for your daughter."

He laughed. He trusted me. His whole life he had trusted me despite all my whims.

"I mean," he said, his big belly still shaking with laughter, "I'm afraid for the men of Cairo. They're Muslims, they're Arabs. It's shameful that we send them a devil like you."

"So, it's agreed," I replied.

He thought for a moment.

"The Muhi al-Dins still live there. You can stay with them. They're our relatives. And he still owes me ten thousand lira."

I jumped up and kissed him on the cheek.

"You're the best father, Hajj 'Abd al-Rahman!"

His cheeks trembled from happiness. These moments always made him happy. He loved me, more than all his other kids. I was the most beautiful, the smartest, the youngest. Actually, no, not the youngest. I have a younger sister, but I don't like to mention her. I don't like that I have a sister younger than me. I don't like to be in the middle, the middle of anything. The middle has no color, no taste, no character. People can never describe the middle. You find character at the peak of something, the peak of intelligence or the peak of stupidity, the peak of chaos or the peak of order, the peak of beauty or ugliness, the peak of happiness or misery.

I always lived at the peak, I felt all those extremes. I'd be happy one moment, miserable the next, crazy one moment, calm the next, smart one moment, stupid the next. My life wasn't years or months or days, it was moments. Even my appearance changed from one moment to the next. People were confused about it. I'd go out wearing pants and a blouse, flat shoes, with my black hair loose, falling into my eyes, as if I was straight out of *Elle*. I'd go to Café Dolce Vita and sit among the young men there, smoking cigarettes in a black holder, like one of the existentialist girls in the Latin Quarter in Paris. Then I'd jump up, go back home, put on a dress of fluffy organza and high heels, pull my black hair back and put a tiara with pearls on my head. I'd look like Queen Elizabeth. I'd invite some of my girl-friends over and we'd go and sit on the balcony of the Phoenicia Hotel and have orange juice.

I'd always been like that. The reality was that my feelings controlled me. No one could control me, not my father, not my mother, not my brother, only my feelings. Any action that didn't come from real conviction was hypocrisy or cowardice. I was not a hypocrite and I was not a coward. My feelings controlled even the connection between me and God. One moment I'd feel close to God and put my golden Qur'an on my chest and another, I wouldn't.

I'd always submitted to my feelings. Yet, most of the time, I was incapable of explaining them because I was incapable of understanding them or expressing them.

I'd been like this since I was born.

I remember when I was seven, we spent the summer at Dhour El Choueir, a mountain town outside of Beirut, and I woke up one morning and told my mother I was going on a trip. I asked her to get some food ready for me to take with me. My mother was surprised. She tried to ask where I was going and with who, but I couldn't answer. I myself didn't know. I only felt that I was going on a trip. When my mother opposed me and insisted that I not leave the house, I became possessed. I couldn't break the spell until my mother prepared the food that I asked for and put it in a picnic basket. She let me go out and had our driver keep tabs on me. I ended up not going further than the garden. I sat under a stone pine tree, the travel basket next to me. I sat there from nine in the morning until six in the evening and talked to the big black ants. I was the queen of the ants for a day.

My family left me alone, afraid that the spell would take hold of me again. They waited until I came back of my own accord, carrying the basket as if I really was coming back from a trip.

"Are you back from your trip?" my mother asked, welcoming me.

"You know I wasn't on a trip," I responded. "I was in the garden this whole time."

My mother didn't say a word.

These impulses only got stronger as I got older. I'd insist on joining a different class in school. After a few weeks, I'd insist on going back to the first class. I went to a French school and then I insisted on going to the American school. Then I went back to the French school, and on and on. My mother thought that there was something wrong with me. She took me to a psychologist, but he didn't understand me. I was a normal person who simply always gave in to their feelings.

My mother was sad. She didn't understand me. Life for her was a series of steps, done in order, one after the other. You follow the steps and the result is a rich husband. There was no place in her life for feelings.

She was a young mother. She wasn't yet twenty-eight. Beautiful, chic, one of the chicest women in

Beirut, from a well-known family in Tripoli, the house of Kamal al-Din. She was virtuous with good manners. She had married my father because he was rich.

My father was more good-natured and sweeter in the way he treated us, maybe because he was always so occupied with his work. He was one of five big Muslim traders in Beirut. I didn't know exactly what business he was in. I wasn't interested. It seemed that everyone in Beirut was the same. They were all traders, all standing in a single shop. I felt like all of Beirut was a single shop with a single man standing in it with drawers and shelves all around him, drawers full of cloth, spices, politics, different kinds of religion, and on and on. Everything was for sale. The trader might be my father, or my uncle, or Anton, or Selim, or a saint, or a minister, but they were all the same man standing in the store of Beirut, selling things.

My father and mother tried to apply to me and my siblings the steps through which they were raised. They arranged everything for us, a big house in Achrafieh, the best schools, cars, servants, endless advice, and so on. The math worked with my oldest sister. She was the image of my mother in her moral standing and her hypocrisy. It was successful with my youngest sibling too. He was not like my father or my mother. He was dumb and smoked nargileh. It was enough for him that he was the son of the big trader Hajj 'Abd al-Rahman. Stupidity wasn't an obstacle in this system. As for my older brother, he was crazy, at least in my mother's eyes. He'd stir up Beirut every night with a scandal, and then suddenly he disappeared. We found out he'd left for South America. My father was shocked. It was the first time I saw him cry. He was crushed. He loved his oldest son. There wasn't any reason for him to emigrate. We were rich, so why go look for opportunity somewhere else? This was my father's logic. A year later, he was hit with another blow when his second son left for Belgium, also with no reason except that their math didn't wind up working for him either.

My father only had his stupid son left, and his daughters, my sisters and me.

I noticed I was beautiful when I was fourteen, when Andre started staring at my face like an idiot. He waited for me every morning in front of the house and then he'd follow me in his car to school.

I stood in front of my mirror and discovered I was beautiful. I looked like Audrey Hepburn. My hair was black and so shiny it seemed to emit moonlight. All my features were fine. My eyes were round and full of life. My lips were delicate. My nose was small. My cheekbones were high. No one who knew me thought I was Lebanese. They thought I was Parisian. Ghassan thought my face was like an apple, but let's leave him aside for now. He wasn't the first man in my life. The first one was Andre, who I met when I was fourteen.

Andre was an old twenty-one-year-old. His mother was French. His father was a Lebanese Maronite. His hair was blond, his eyes light, his face always flushed, and his ears stuck out. I laughed whenever I looked at his ears.

"Go to your mother," I'd tell him. "Ask her to stick your ears back with tape."

There was nothing between me and Andre. There wasn't anything between me and any man up to that point. Unless kisses are considered something. In Lebanon, it was different. In Egypt, every step led somewhere, it was all about sex. Maybe because of the hot climate. But in Lebanon, we didn't think much about sex. Not in my clique, at least. We were happy, we laughed, we went out on trips. We went to the movies, always in small groups. Sex was for wives to worry about. Sex life started after marriage.

Andre thought I was his girl. I thought he was my guy. We'd go out in a group of friends. Every guy had a girl. We'd go to the movies, to the mountains, to the sea. He kissed me for the first time under the trees of the Bois de Boulogne, not in Paris, but in Dhour El Choueir.

He kissed me on the lips.

I hated it. I was hit by a dizzy spell afterwards, not of intoxication but nausea. I spent many years hating anyone kissing me on the lips. They could kiss me only on my cheek. When I liked it, I'd let the kisses go down my neck.

At fourteen, I started putting kohl around my eyes. I was obsessed with kohl. It made me look older than I was. Even now, I don't wear any makeup except for kohl. Even lipstick, I only use it rarely. I'd leave home only carrying a kohl stick and a pack of Kleenex, not a handkerchief. I never took a purse. I couldn't stand carrying a purse. I'd put money in my pocket. If there wasn't a pocket in my clothes, I'd hold it with the kohl and Kleenex in my hand.

Soon, I left Andre. I felt that I was older than him. I could no longer stand him. Every one of his simpering words got on my nerves.

Andre followed me around for a long time. He couldn't do without me. In those two years, I'd filled his whole life. I'd set his daily schedule. I moved him from place to place. I made him laugh and cry. I let him show me off in front of his friends. He didn't have a personality without me. I was everything to him. But, sorry, I couldn't stand him anymore. I belonged to my feelings, and my feelings could no longer stand him.

Nizar came after him. He was nothing either, just a few kisses on my cheek that I sometimes let move down my neck.

Then Hazim came along. He was also nothing.

I picked these guys only to fill out my circle of friends, for us to have fun. We'd bathe in the sea. We'd go climbing in the snow. We'd drive around in our cars. None of them could seduce me away from my girlfriends. I always preferred to be with them. No man could capture my heart or leave a mark on my body.

Never.

It was friendship, just a particular kind of friendship.

I took up dancing. I got good at it. I danced the cha-cha and the merengue better than any girl, more smoothly. I made up my own new steps. The clubs in Lebanon would open at two in the afternoon for boys and girls our age. Every day at three exactly, I'd go to the club. I'd wear pants, flats, my hair down, my hand gripping my kohl and Kleenex. In my other hand was always a boy's.

My family didn't know anything about my life out of the house. They thought I went out with my girlfriends. My mother probably thought there were both girls and boys in our group, but no one knew the details, not even my sister. I had big fights with my mother about going out. When she'd insist that I stay home, I'd go crazy, really crazy. I'd feel a wave of suffocation come over me. I'd tear up my books. I'd attack my mother's dresser and toss all her clothes on the ground. She'd stand there trembling, afraid to get near me in case I started ripping up her clothes. The insanity and suffocation wouldn't leave me until after she finally gave in and let me go out.

We stopped discussing my comings and goings. I started going out in the morning and not coming back until eight in the evening. I was never later than eight, not purposely, not out of fear of my family, but because I'd be tired by then.

At seventeen, I found myself moving into another social circle. There were writers, artists, journalists, some crazy people, young people who talked enthusiastically about politics, literature, and philosophy. They'd get together in the cafés around the American University, especially Faisal Café and Uncle Sam, and then going to Dostoyevsky Café in the evening.

I was delighted with this circle, by every word I heard. I felt that the doors of a new world had opened up before my eyes and new horizons had come into view in my mind. I felt that I'd grown up.

The people of this new world welcomed me. I could win people over easily. My appearance seemed to stir up innocent admiration.

I quickly became part of this new circle. My life started moving between Faisal, Uncle Sam, Negresco, and Dolce Vita. I quickly took on the things they were saying. I started talking like them. I talked about literature and politics without understanding anything about either. I thought I was an existentialist without trying to understand what existentialism was. All I understood was that I could speak as I pleased, do what I wanted, and wear my hair loose, hanging over my eyes.

The circle became hostile toward everything. They mocked the whole world for its politics, religions, and God. I hated being a rich girl or, more specifically, the daughter of a rich man, because they mocked the rich, so I started pretending I was poor. Poverty in Beirut wasn't like poverty in Egypt. Poverty in Beirut meant not having a car. I no longer went around in our family's car. I started taking the bus, the tram, walking, and eating falafel and hummus.

I wasn't the only young girl in this circle. There were lots of others, rebelling against the prison, without walls or jailors, that they lived in. They sought to liberate themselves from the complexes that raged inside them, ever since Islam gave every four of them a single man, and Christianity gave them an image of a virgin without a man.

I was the most sparkling of these girls. The sweet looks of delight from the men started to turn to lust. Every one of these genius artists started to want me for himself. They were all men, after all, whether they were sitting in a café with us or loitering in Burj Square.

They were men, not the boys that I'd known before. Some of them were thirty, thirty-five, thirty-eight.

Despite that, I wasn't afraid. I found these men safer than the younger guys. I started to pick from this new circle.

The first was Sami.

He was short. His eyes were wide but narrow, kind but confused. He was a painter. He didn't sell his paintings because those who wanted to buy them didn't deserve them and those who deserved them couldn't afford them. That's how he talked about his work. Sami drew me more than a hundred times. He drew me on a box of matches, on a tablecloth, on the glass table of the café that we went to meet at. He'd draw me whenever he saw me.

Sami was afraid of knives. If there was a knife on the table, he'd take it, his fingers trembling, and toss it on the ground or out the window.

We always met at the Eagle's Nest. We always sat at the same table, talking while he drew me. Nothing more. Never anything more. After two years of friendship, and after I left for Cairo, Sami wrote me in a note: "I don't know why I didn't try to kiss you, why I didn't try to hug you. Oh, Ro, you are delectable!"

I pitied Sami. He was a lot older than me, but my pity made me feel responsible for him. I couldn't stand to see him angry or confused or in one his bouts of insanity. Just fresh out of childhood myself, I could wipe away his anger and take hold of his confusion. I often felt I was his mother.

But Sami wasn't the only one who'd stir up my pity.

Talal deserved pity too. He was a poet. I could never understand his poetry, but he had to be a great poet because Talal believed it to the point of hallucination. He was also broke. His father was rich and lived in Africa, but he left his father and came to Lebanon to live with nothing. He didn't want to be rich. He detested wealth. He was a complicated guy. His complexes sometimes got the better of him and he'd cry like a child. He'd take off his shoes and toss them into the street. Talal became my friend too. I met him at the same café where I met Sami, the Eagle's Nest.

And then there was Ghassan, who was thirty. He studied psychology. He insisted that he was a psychologist, a doctor without a clinic. He was hit by a car when he was young. He'd walked with a cane ever since and had a constant tremor in his right eye. He'd come every day to Faisal to have lunch, and he'd sit with his legs stretched out.

I became friends with five guys. I met them one after the other at the same place, even at the same table. The waiter knew me and reserved the same table for me.

I took pity on them all. I felt responsible for them all. Then I started feeling overwhelmed by this responsibility, that I could not get free from them, from these strange friendships. I needed something else. Maybe I needed love.

Whenever I arranged to meet one of them, I'd feel my chest tighten and tears collect in my eyes. I'd cry a lot. Boredom and exhaustion started to envelop me, collecting in thick clouds before my eyes and pressing down on my chest, choking me. I started to feel that my life was stagnant, that nothing in it was moving. The cars stopped. People stood like rocks strewn out on a dry riverbed. Faces were frozen like candles, with deadened looks. Everything was dead. The sidewalks were dead. The cafés were dead. Our houses, the sea, the mountain was all one big graveyard. I stood in the branches of a dead tree like an owl, looking down onto all this death.

I was a broken record, saying one day whatever I had said the day before. I'd tell Sami the same thing I told Talal and the same thing I'd told Ghassan. I said the same thing to each of the five, to everyone I knew. It was the same thing I said last year, the same thing I'd say tomorrow and next year. The tone of my voice didn't change. It didn't rise or descend, like the hoot of an owl.

I almost went crazy. I was on edge the whole time. My father and mother didn't know what to do with me, so they gave in to everything I asked for. My mother fed me fish oil and vitamin B, and two cups of yogurt every day. I'd toss them out the window of my room.

I decided to get a job. Every place I went to work, the owner met me with a big welcome, maybe because I was beautiful and maybe because I was the daughter of Hajj 'Abd al-Rahman. In Beirut they don't ask for your qualifications, just the name of your father.

I worked at a radio station, a clothing store, and a bank.

They'd always set my salary before I started working, a salary much bigger than I deserved. I got to five hundred lira a month, simply because I was beautiful and the daughter of Hajj 'Abd al-Rahman. Everyone wanted me to work for him even if I didn't do anything. They could pin me on their chests like a rose, hang me on the door of their offices like a picture. They'd invite me to cocktail parties just so they could show me off to their colleagues.

It took a toll on me to put up with all this flattery, all the fawning looks that followed me from office to office, all the vile old men. I found myself forced to play the hypocrite, to pretend not to notice all the deference. I started hating myself, being disgusted at myself.

I quickly abandoned working in Beirut.

That was when I met Taysir.

I'd seen him around before. He was always wherever I was. I'd meet his eyes sometimes, but he never tried to create an opportunity to introduce himself. Even when I'd be sitting with some of his friends, he didn't try to force himself on me. He was a handsome guy, about twenty-one. His father was Syrian and his mother Lebanese. His father had died, and his mother brought him back to Beirut to live with her family. Taysir was forced to work. He worked in one of those tourism companies for a meager salary and he was completing his studies at the American University.

I knew all this from talking to his friends about him.

Then they introduced him to me at one of the parties at the university. I found myself wondering, as I reached out to shake his hand, could he be something new? Could he stir up a new feeling that would save me from this exhaustion?

Taysir looked me over. He was arrogant. He talked a lot about politics. I didn't like politics, but I liked his enthusiasm as he talked about it.

Taysir became my friend. We met every day. I got to know him. And he got to know me.

That didn't mean I abandoned my five original friends or my responsibility for them, and Taysir didn't object. He wasn't the jealous type. My friendship with him made the burden of my other friendships easier to bear.

I wondered if Taysir could be something more in my life. Could I love him?

One day, he was dropping me home and stood looking at me at the door of my house for a long time. Then, as if he'd made a decision, he pulled me to him, held me against his chest, and started kissing me all over my face. I turned my head so his kisses went down on my neck.

"I love you, Ro," he whispered in a hoarse voice. "I love you."

I slipped away from him and ran inside, my face and neck still tingling with his kisses.

I hadn't kissed anyone for months, but I didn't feel like there was anything new in his kisses. No deep feelings rose up to the surface. I needed to feel something new, so I faked it. I started convincing myself that Taysir wasn't like the others, that his kisses were something new.

Taysir started kissing me all the time and I submitted to his attempts to kiss me on my lips even though I didn't like it much.

I was faking it. I was faking being in love.

Whenever I'd go out with Taysir, each of us paid their way. This was always how I went out. I felt more independent when no one was paying for me. One day, Taysir dropped me home in a taxi and I gave him a twenty-five-lira bill to pay for the taxi and told him to give me the change the next day.

I didn't think much of it since I was the one who had called the taxi.

But Taysir didn't give me the change. I didn't notice. I didn't care.

Another time, he didn't give me the change either. I also didn't care.

Then he borrowed one hundred liras from me. And I started to notice.

I wasn't angry at him. I didn't blame him, and it didn't shake his image for me. Not at all. I appreciated his situation. He was poor. His salary wasn't more than two hundred and fifty liras, and he was responsible for his mother. I even liked it. I liked his struggle in life and his struggle to get an education. I really did.

I started giving him what I could take from my father and mother. I gave it to him without wounding his dignity. And he became more tolerant with me, tolerant of my whims, my moods. I became stronger than him. My personality was stronger than his.

All of Beirut was talking about me and him. He was happy about that, but he didn't show it.

I didn't care.

Soon, he asked me to marry him.

"But we're still young," I told him.

"Our love is bigger than our age," he replied.

"It would be a shame to jail our love in four walls."

"I fear we'll set our love free if we don't get married."

"You believe in freedom. You can't demand freedom for the country and then ask for prison for me."

"It's not a prison. I'm asking for stability for both of us."

"I don't feel like I want stability. I don't want to get married."

"It's as if you don't love me."

"I do," I said. "But marriage is something else."

"Marriage is the throne of love."

"I don't want to sit on a throne. I don't want to sit at all. Don't talk to me about marriage. It makes me feel like you're just any other guy, and I hate that."

But Taysir didn't stop talking about marriage.

Long weeks passed, and his words were like a siren in my ears. We'd fight. We'd get angry at each other. We'd make up and the siren would start up again.

One day, Taysir borrowed a friend's car and invited me to go to the mountains. I wasn't paying attention to the route he took. He was silent. There was a strange desperate look in his eyes. We stopped at the entrance to a village called Hammana, on the road to Bhamdoun. He turned to me.

"We're going to visit some of my friends. I told them we've come today to get married." His voice was manic. "They've arranged everything."

"Have you lost your mind?" I screamed.

"I have not," he said, with a crazed look in his eyes. "But I know you love me, and I love you. We have to get married."

"Take me back to Beirut!"

"After we get married."

"You don't want to marry a girl who doesn't want to marry you."

"She does. She's just stubborn."

"Wait until she's over her stubbornness."

"I've waited a long time."

"Wait some more, if you're a man."

"Men don't wait. They take."

"You mean thieves."

He raised his hand and tried to slap me, but I dodged him. I opened the car door and ran. I don't know for how long, but I felt like I rolled the whole way down the mountain. Everything was rolling, my heart, my head, my stomach, my tears.

He found me on the road and stopped the car next to me. I heard his voice, it sounded distant, like it came from very far away, from the inside of a wadi.

"Get in. We'll go back."

But I ran. I couldn't stop. A nervous violent spell took hold of me.

He got out of the car and ran behind me. He grabbed me by my shoulder. He started shaking me.

"We'll go back. We won't get married," he kept repeating.

I was screaming and screaming. I was shaking.

He grabbed me and carried me back to the car. He brought me back to Beirut.

I stayed for some days at home. I didn't go out. I just lay in bed. Taysir called many times, dozens of times a day. Whenever my mother or my sister or the maid brought me the phone, I refused to speak to him. My family was worried.

Doctors were happy to prescribe me sedatives.

I started taking Librium to calm my nerves. And I slept.

I woke up. I started to regain myself. And I went out.

I went back to Hamra and the streets and clubs around the university.

But exhaustion and boredom still suffocated me.

I no longer had any choice but to leave Beirut. No one could dissuade me.

I was going to go to London. But suddenly I picked Cairo.

"Why Cairo?" my mother asked when she heard the news. "All the big families have left Cairo. You'll only find that people have nothing there. You won't even find a single dress worth buying!"

My mother couldn't fathom why I'd travel except to find a husband among the expat Lebanese families or to buy new clothes.

I insisted on Cairo. My feelings led me to Cairo.

Everyone submitted to the crazy girl.

My father began getting me ready for my life in Cairo, exchanging money for me, arranging things with the Muhi al-Din family who would host me.

Everyone started saying things to protect me from Cairo. They gave me the phone numbers of Lebanese girls who went to university there. My uncle gave me a letter to give to a doctor named Dr. Hashim 'Abd al-Latif. He told me he was a famous doctor, cultured, from an important family, with influence. He could help me if I needed anything.

My uncle was a doctor too. He was using my trip to Cairo to deliver a letter to one of his friends. I tossed the letter that he gave me in one of my bags in total disregard.

I blocked my ears to all the advice that rained down on me.

My ears could only pick up the sound of the airplane engine.

My father came to say goodbye to me at the airport. He hugged me to his chest, his eyes wet with tears.

"Don't stay away too long," he said in a choked voice. "Three weeks only."

He was afraid I wouldn't be coming back, like his son who went to South America and his other son who went to Belgium.

2

My first days in Cairo were a disaster.

The Muhi al-Din family consisted of Auntie Nazli, who was an old woman. She was seventy years old, maybe older, and lay in her bed like a corpse. She never got up. Her face was pale and drained and most of her hair had fallen out. She'd scream every five minutes in a hoarse voice, "Saniya! Saniya!" Saniya was one of the servants. She was enormous like a jailor. Then there was Auntie Mimi, Auntie Nazli's daughter. She was ancient too. All she did was shuffle around the house hunched over an ebony cane with a chic golden handle. With every step, she issued an order, but no one paid attention to her, not even the servants. Then there was Auntie Lola, Auntie Mimi's daughter. She was the ruler of the house, even though her hair was already going white. She'd stomp around with decisive steps. There was a harshness in her eyes and her smile was forced and fake. Her husband was the head of the family, Muhammad Muhi al-Din. He was a broken man. Everything in him seemed to have collapsed, his eyes, lips, nose, stomach, and even his crooked legs. Finally, there was 'Aida, or Dudi, the daughter of Auntie Lola. She was thirty. She considered herself something of a writer. She wrote stories in French. She fancied herself a sculptor too. She had a room on the roof where she kept piles of clay and stood among them wearing a white coat, making statues with no clear shape whatsoever. They were all horrible and scary, the kinds of things you'd see in a nightmare. Her husband didn't know what to do with her. He'd disappear for days. His name was Rafiq.

This family of four generations all lived in a single grand house with a view onto the Nile, packed with horrible pieces of dark old-fashioned furniture.

The family made a big deal of welcoming me. They met me at the airport. They gave me the nicest room in the house, overlooking the Nile. They threw a big party for me and invited the big Lebanese families. Dudi invited me to dinner the following night with some of her friends at a nightclub in Haram and she insisted on inviting some guys about my age to dance with me. Nonetheless, I felt their generosity wasn't natural. Their welcome wasn't from the heart. Maybe they thought my father had sent me to them to remind them that they owed him a lot of money.

From the first day, Muhammad Muhi al-Din talked to me about how bad his financial situation was. He owned a big factory that the government had confiscated. They took everything. All he had left in Egypt was a building overlooking Tahrir Square. The entire family was living on the income from that building. I had no interest in any of it. I didn't come to Cairo to understand what was happening in Egypt, or what was happening to Lebanese families living in Egypt. I felt that Muhammad

Muhi al-Din was telling me all this by way of an apology to my father for not paying him back. He was a boring man, incapable of stirring up my sympathy.

After two days, I felt like I couldn't breathe in this big house.

I couldn't stand that the balcony of my room overlooked the Nile. I'd always imagined the Nile as a pure river with palm trees leaning over it to wash their branches in it. It was a dream, a philosopher, an old man. But I saw it now as a terrifying drunk, its dark black waters unsuitable for what was in its depths. I saw it as a wild bull and imagined it was trying to pull me in by my feet to swallow me up.

I started to feel I was turning into Auntie Nazli, the same age and with the same pale face. Then, whenever I laid eyes on Auntie Mimi, I felt I needed a cane to lean on too. I felt I was becoming harsh and hypocritical like Auntie Lola. I started taking on the characters of the house, one after another, all of them wretched, miserable, and broken. Gone was the character of a happy young girl.

The family was still doing all it could to please me. They charged Dudi with showing me around since she was the youngest, but Dudi kept complaining about me. She accompanied me as if she were in charge of a tourism bureau and I was some boring tourist who was wearing her out and costing her a fortune. She was a complicated woman and maybe she was jealous of me. I don't know, but she didn't like me at all.

She'd drive me to the pyramids.

"These are the pyramids," she'd say, bored, pointing at them from inside the car.

She then drove to the Sphinx.

"This is the Sphinx," she'd then inform me in the same bored tone.

I left her in the car and got out to walk around the pyramids and the Sphinx. I looked at them and felt exhausted. What did they want, these massive pieces of stone? That was all they were. What's the difference between stones that are a million years old and stones that are just two days old? Who cares if there's a king like Khufu under these stones or just a lizard? The people who came to Cairo to see the pyramids were idiots.

I went back home to the dark house.

All they talked about was Lebanon and the families of Lebanon. The food they made was all Lebanese. Oh, Lord. Where was Egypt? Where was Cairo? I left Lebanon only to imprison myself with a crazy Lebanese family. I'd dreamed of a wider world, of more freedom, and woke up to find myself stuck in the most annoying corner of Lebanon. I'd been freer living with my mother and father than I was in the house of the Muhi al-Din family.

After a few days, 'Issam called me. He was a Lebanese student at Cairo University. He knew our family and some of my friends in Lebanon wrote to him with news of my arrival in Cairo and let him know that I was staying with the Muhi al-Din family.

It was afternoon. He offered to come pick me up.

I accepted quickly.

I went out wearing pants and flats, carrying my kohl, Kleenex, and some Egyptian pounds in my hand. I almost forgot to ask Auntie Lola's permission. I wasn't used to asking permission to go out. She asked me about 'Issam's family, his age, and some other things.

There was another friend with 'Issam. Hisham. He was also Lebanese.

"Should we go to the pyramids?" 'Issam asked me.

"No! Any place but there. I haven't seen Cairo yet."

'Issam took me to the Hilton Cafeteria. Within a few minutes, I found myself sitting with seven Lebanese guys. Some of them were students studying in Cairo. Others were visiting. I felt I was in Snack Bar Starco in Beirut. The same characters, the same faces, the same topics of conversation. All that was different was the accent. It wasn't pure Lebanese or pure Egyptian. As soon as the Lebanese got to Cairo, they tried to pick up the Egyptian accent. A lot of my friends who went to Cairo came back to Beirut speaking with an Egyptian accent like they were proud of a new dress they got there. In Beirut it was a sign of political and cultural solidarity. Some people spoke French, some spoke English, some spoke Egyptian. French meant you loved France, English meant you loved America, and Egyptian, of course, meant you loved Gamal Abdel Nasser.

That day, we had lunch at the Hilton Cafeteria, me and the Lebanese guys, then we went to the movies. We wandered around on Qasr al-Nil Street and Sulayman Pasha Street and I loved how lively and noisy they were.

I went back home to the dark house. Auntie Lola met me with her forced smile.

"I asked you to let me know if you wouldn't be home so that we don't wait for you for lunch," she said with feigned gentleness.

"Sorry," I said, trying to hide my irritation. I didn't like it when anyone tried to take me to task. "Don't wait for me next time. I hate it when someone waits for me."

Auntie Lola was quiet, breathing deeply as if she was counting the days until she could get rid of me.

I started going out every day with 'Issam's clique. We'd have lunch at the cafeteria. We'd go to the movies. Sometimes I'd go with them to parties at the American University. We'd stay up late at a nightclub or at the Shepheard Hotel and we'd dance. I'd laugh at Egyptians when they danced. They didn't know how to dance, and they were way behind the times—Cairo was still dancing the twist. People were shocked when they saw me dance.

Day after day, my group of friends got bigger, all of them Lebanese, Jordanian, Palestinian, and Syrian. I chose Hisham to be my friend. He was charged with picking me up from home to wherever we all met up. He was the one I picked to come with me to the movies alone. He was the one who called to let me know what was going on that day. He was just a friend, nothing more.

I once again started feeling like I hadn't seen Cairo yet. I hadn't set foot into an Egyptian home, I hadn't made friends with an Egyptian guy or girl. I felt like I was living in a distorted, smaller Beirut. It was a closed society, shutting the door on itself and not letting anyone but Jordanians, Palestinians, and Syrians in to complete the picture of Beirut society. I didn't know if it was Egyptians who isolated the Lebanese, or if the Lebanese did it to themselves, moving only between the Hilton

Cafeteria, the Sharqi Club, the American University, foreign student apartments, and a nightclub in Haram.

I didn't know how to find a road that would lead me to Cairo, so I could feel that I had left Lebanon. Exhaustion and boredom were closing in on me again. I started thinking about going back. It was better for me to live in Lebanon than in a disfigured image of Lebanon. I should have traveled to another country, one without a Lebanese community determined to keep me inside it.

One day, I was in my room in the dark house, digging through my bags, when I found the letter that my uncle gave me. I'd completely forgotten about it.

I read the address: Dr. Hashim 'Abd al-Latif, Sulayman Pasha Square. Then a phone number.

I gripped the letter in my hand, thinking. I didn't care about doing a small favor for my uncle, I was curious about this Dr. Hashim. He was Egyptian. My uncle had told me so. Maybe he was an old man. But he was Egyptian. That was enough for me. Simply seeing an Egyptian doctor would be something new for me.

I took the letter over to the phone and dialed Hashim's number, feeling like I was embarking on an adventure. A polite and cultured voice answered.

"Is Dr. Hashim there?" I asked, trying to lighten my Lebanese accent, knowing how foreign I sounded to an Egyptian.

"Who shall I say is calling, ma'am?"

"I'm from Lebanon. I'm bringing him a private letter."

"One minute, please."

I waited for more than a minute.

"Who is this, please?"

"I'm bringing you a letter from my uncle, Dr. Shams al-Din."

"Welcome. How is he?"

"Good. When can I bring you the letter?"

"Any time you'd like. Or, if you prefer, I can send you someone to get it."

"I prefer to bring it to you myself," I said quickly.

"Thank you. I'll be waiting for you."

"I'll be half an hour at the most," I said. "The address is in Sulayman Square?"

"Yes," he said. "Sulayman Pasha Square. Many thanks."

I hung up. I ran to put on a dress and a small black fur hat that I'd gotten as a gift from Paris. It accentuated the paleness of my skin and made my face look rounder. With the hat on, I looked like a cat. I picked up my kohl and Kleenex, and I left. I took the family car, and I went to Dr. Hashim's clinic.

The nurse met me with great interest. He led me through the rooms of the clinic, jammed with women and men, and into an office, where he left me alone. I looked for my uncle's letter and suddenly realized that I'd forgotten it. I thought about going back home to get it, but decided I'd just tell him I forgot it.

The door next to me opened and Dr. Hashim came in.

I looked at him. The first thing I saw was his white hair. It was the color of smoke, as if there was something in his heart that had burned and smoke from it set out through his hair. His eyes were good-natured but had a certain bleakness and exhaustion to them, like the eyes of an orphan. His nose was prominent. He was old, at least compared to me, but I found in him something human. I found myself looking at him for a long time. I examined his features closely as if I was seeing the face of Egypt for the first time. He stood before me, with a confused smile on his lips. Then he came over, extending his hand out to greet me. I realized I was staring at him, so quickly I averted my gaze.

"Rihab," I said, reaching out my hand to him.

"Welcome," he said, his smile widening.

He sat down at his desk, and we started to talk. I felt he was trying hard to maintain a respectful distance from me. He was careful with where he looked and what he said so as not to seem too forward. He seemed to be resisting reaching out his hand to touch me. I felt all of this. Maybe every girl can feel her position with a man simply by looking in his eyes. I felt he was delighted with me and trying very hard not to show it.

Talking to him made me feel for the first time that I was in Cairo. He had a refined Egyptian accent. His questions made me feel that I was in a foreign country, that I was on a trip. He had naive questions about Beirut that every foreigner would ask. He asked about the places that I'd seen in Cairo. The conversation paused between us for a moment, and I thought he was about to ask me about the letter.

"I'm sorry," I said quickly. "I forgot my uncle's letter."

He laughed loudly.

"No problem," he said.

"I forget a lot of things," I said, the echo of his laugh on my lips. "But I'll bring it to you."

"Tomorrow?"

"No. The day after."

I didn't know why I'd said that. I didn't have anything to do the following day. Maybe it was simply a spontaneous reaction to my feeling that he liked me.

"The day after tomorrow," he said.

"I'll call you to figure it out," I said.

He looked at me hesitantly and then grabbed his pen, wrote a number on a piece of paper, and handed it to me.

"Call me at this number."

I didn't know why he seemed so hesitant and shy.

"It's so I answer it myself," he continued. "It's the private line."

I nodded and got up.

"Can I do anything for you while you're in Cairo?" he asked, shaking my hand goodbye.

"No. Thanks."

"Are you here with the family?"

"No. Alone."

"Perhaps I can invite you out?"

"I don't know. Let's figure it out later."

He smiled.

"If I saw you somewhere, I wouldn't think you're from Lebanon," he said, opening the door for me.

"Why?"

"You seem like you're Parisian."

"A lot of people say that."

"I'll wait for a call from you."

"God willing."

I left with a smile of pride, pleased with myself and my self-confidence, feeling that I'd finally opened the gates of Cairo.

I went to meet the Lebanese clique at the Hilton Cafeteria and had lunch with them. They noticed that I was happier, more confident. I was leading the conversation, laughing, and making jokes. I felt that I'd been able to leave this narrow circle I'd lived in since I arrived in Cairo.

When I got back home, I started looking for the letter. I looked for it next to the phone, in my room, in my bags, in the closet, but I couldn't find it. I asked Auntie Lola. I asked all the maids. But no one had seen the letter.

I shrugged my shoulders. No matter.

I lay in bed, still in my clothes, the image of Dr. Hashim filling my mind. He wasn't that old. Maybe forty. Maybe a little more. He was older than Sami, Ghassan, and the rest of my friends in Beirut. He seemed worried, confused, and weak, like a lost child. He had that broken look in his eyes.

Despite that, he was something new for me, a new character, exciting, mysterious. He had the mystery of Cairo that I hadn't yet encountered.

The following day, I decided to go out alone. The car took me to Qasr al-Nil Street and I walked around by myself. I purposely went into the side streets that I hadn't gone into before. Then I went to Opera Square and 'Ataba Square, areas I hadn't seen before. I walked down a packed street. I learned later that it was al-Azhar

Street. I walked and walked. I hoped I'd get lost. I really hoped I'd get lost in Cairo or have some kind of adventure that would move the stagnant water I was immersed in. But I didn't get lost, and no adventure happened to me. I walked, observed the brown faces that I passed, and I felt like each face was a steel wall behind which I couldn't see anything. The scent of Africa filled my nose, the scent of sweat, the crowds, the sun. It was pungent and exciting.

I got tired of walking, so I got in a taxi and asked the driver to take me to the Hilton Cafeteria. No one can ever get lost as long as there are taxis.

I was happy that day because I went out alone, but it was a lusterless happiness. As soon as I settled down among the Lebanese clique at the cafeteria, boredom and exhaustion came back. It was the same vapid conversation. I knew what Hisham would say after half an hour, when 'Issam would let out his boorish laugh, when Suzette would come, what Layla would order.

I suddenly got up, went to the phone booth, and looked for Dr. Hashim's clinic number. I had forgotten to bring his private number with me.

"This is Rihab," I said as soon as I heard his voice. "Can I pass by this evening?"

"When?"

"Five."

"I'll be waiting for you."

I went to him at five o'clock. I put my hair up to seem older.

"Where's your hat?" he asked as soon as he saw me.

"Do you like it?"

"You look like a cat in it."

I didn't like that he compared me to a cat, for no reason except because dozens of men before him had done the same thing.

"I came to apologize. I lost the letter."

He laughed as if he was indulging a little girl.

"Don't worry. I don't think it was anything important."

"I'm pretty sure it was a letter of introduction. Nothing more. But I'll call him to ask if there was anything else."

"Let him call you if he wants to be sure about his letter."

"My father will call me in any case. Sorry again."

I was about to go. He got up from behind his desk and came over to me.

"Can I invite you to lunch?"

"Why?"

"No reason. Only to get to know you."

"I have a friend who wants to go out with an Egyptian. Should I introduce you to her?"

He laughed again, shyly, as if he was wounded.

"I don't want to go out with just any girl. I want to go out with you."

"Would it bother you if my friend came along?"

"No, it wouldn't bother me, but conversation between two is more enjoyable than between three."

I hesitated for a moment.

"You're right."

"Tomorrow?"

"Tomorrow."

"One thirty?"

"Agreed."

He smiled widely.

"Should I take you home?"

"I'm not going home. I'm meeting some friends."

"Girlfriends?"

"And guys."

"Do you have a lot of guy friends in Cairo?"

"Lots."

His face changed, suddenly, as if a pitcher of worry had been poured over his head. He swallowed.

"Tomorrow, one thirty, then. Where?"

"At the Hilton Cafeteria. It's the one place I know how to get to."

"Agreed."

I left.

There was a feeling in my chest that I'd begun an adventure. An adventure in Cairo.

Yes.

I thought it was just an adventure.

3

I DON'T KNOW WHAT DREW me to Hashim. I had new feelings that I hadn't experienced before.

Hashim was older than the other men who'd entered my life. He told me he was forty-one. A few days later, he told me he was forty-three. Then he confessed that he was forty-four. He was giving me his age to drink sip by sip so that I wouldn't gulp it down in one go and be shocked. It had never occurred to me that one day I'd be with a forty-four-year-old man. The number forty represented another world that I couldn't live in, a distant world, very distant from my heart, my mind, my imagination. Despite that, when I got to know Hashim, I felt he was closer to me than all the guys that had filled my life, that his way of thinking was closer to mine. I even sometimes felt like he was younger than me. His words sometimes had the naivete of children. His emotions were instinctive and honest as if they were those of a child.

I felt afraid of this child. I hadn't ever felt this kind of fear before. I'd always plunged forward in life without fear. But since the day I met Hashim, fear had started to creep into my heart. Looking at his peppered hair, I felt like I was drowning in a sea of smoke. Looking into his eyes, I felt that I could get lost in them.

I didn't know why. Maybe because I felt like Hashim was trying to take me from my life to his. I was nineteen and, until that time, I'd been living the life of a fifteen-year-old. I loved that life. I dressed like a fifteen-year-old, wore my hair in a style that made me look fifteen, had the innocent outgoingness of a fifteen-year-old. I wore pants and flats always. Once I met Hashim, I started to feel my age. I then started to feel older than my age. I started to feel something waking up inside me. I started to feel my femininity.

From day one, I resisted. I wasn't resisting Hashim. I was resisting myself. I was resisting these new feelings that had started to sneak up on me.

I became more attached to the Lebanese guys that I met. I tied myself more to my friend 'Issam. I became very outgoing, boisterous like a fifteen-year-old. I tried to remain as I was.

I remember Hashim once invited me to the movies. I went out wearing pants, my hair loose, hanging down onto my face. I knew it wasn't appropriate for me to go with him to the movies like that. I knew I'd look like his daughter. But I was stubborn. I stood before the mirror for a long time and in the end my stubbornness won out. I went out to him as I was and I saw him wearing a dark suit, complete with collar, tie, and jacket, like he was going to a funeral. The difference between me and him was enormous. He was older than his age and I was younger than mine.

As soon as I sat down next to him in his car, he gave me a certain look and asked:

"Do you have to wear pants?"

"Do you like it?"

"I love it. But it makes me feel my age and yours."

"Then wait," I said, taking pity on him. "I'll change."

"No. But we won't go to the movies. Let's go somewhere else."

"I want to go to the movies. Wait for me. Five minutes."

I got out of the car and went back into the house. I felt that he'd defeated me and made me change my clothes.

I put on a brown dress with gold stripes. It was tight. I put on heels, and I put my hair up. I went back out to him, and he met me with a big smile, the smile of a happy child.

Hashim was resisting too. I could feel it.

Maybe he felt the difference between our ages more than me. I felt him talking with me like an older friend or like my uncle. Our conversations would be cold and polite and superficial. Sometimes he'd try to talk to me on my level. He'd pick topics that he knew would interest a twenty-year-old. When he did this, conversation would be forced and cold. Then he'd forget my age and his and talk freely, naturally and we'd have sweet, deep conversations with new ideas, new experiences. These conversations would open my mind to a world I didn't know, a world filled with truth and happiness.

"It's strange," he told me once, looking at me. "Before we met, I liked a twenty-year-old girl. She's now twenty-one, two years older than you, but I didn't ever feel the age difference between me and her."

"Egyptian girls are more mature than Lebanese girls," I said, feeling a lump in my throat. "Your weather is hot. Girls grow up faster here than in Lebanon's weather."

"I don't think so," he said. "Maybe it's physical. She was taller than you, heavier. There wasn't this youth in her face that you have."

I felt angry. I hated that he was comparing me to another girl. It wasn't actually anger. It was jealousy. Maybe this was the first time I'd felt jealous of another girl.

"Were you in love with her?" I found myself asking, the words coming out despite myself.

"Who?" he asked, turning to me in surprise.

"This other girl."

"Yes," he said, lowering his head.

"Where'd this love go?"

"I resisted it."

"Why?"

"Because she lied to me. She hid who she really was from me. Then all of a sudden, I found another girl before me, not the one I was in love with."

"Was it easy for you to forget her?"

"No. We're still friends."

He smiled.

"She saw us together," he said. "She thinks you dye your hair."

"Dye my hair? Why? Am I so old that I dye my hair? Feel it, touch my hair. Is it dyed? She must dye hers."

"I didn't believe her," he said, smiling happily. "You have to forgive her."

"Why's that? I don't know her."

The smile stayed on his lips.

I hated myself at that moment. I felt that I'd grown up suddenly. I was jealous like any other woman.

I didn't like him enough to be jealous of him. I had to remember that he was over forty. He must have had many experiences, many women. He was not some eighteen or twenty-year-old where I'd be shocked to find out he was in love with a girl before me.

I went back to resisting. And so did he. Despite this, we were meeting almost every day. Something was pulling me to him more and more.

My Lebanese friends knew that I'd met an Egyptian guy. I told them his name, but I didn't tell them how old he was.

"Watch out for Egyptian guys," my friend Mona whispered in my ears. "They want everything from girls. And they'll feed you a pack of lies. They all have bachelor pads."

I didn't pay attention to her. Mona didn't know Hashim. He wasn't some young guy. He was a man. He couldn't be that kind of Egyptian guy.

I started to see Cairo with him as I hadn't seen it before. We'd go to Muqattam, to Fayoum, al-Qanatir, the pyramids, *Sayyidna* al-Hussein. We walked together in the moonlight in the narrow streets with the many calls to prayer rising up around us like they were trying to reach God. I discovered Cairo was more than the Hilton Cafeteria and Qasr al-Nil Street, it was different from Beirut. It had another personality, another scent. The meaning of everything changed. The pyramids were no longer simply pieces of stone. The Nile was no longer a wide stream of mud trying to pull me in by my feet and swallow me up. It seemed that you can't see Cairo and feel it except with an Egyptian.

I felt like there was a drop of the Nile in Hashim. There was the strength of the Nile in his prominent nose. There was the goodness of the Nile in his calm eyes. There was the arrogance of the pyramids in him. There was the faith of the call to prayer in him. There was the tumult of 'Ataba Square in him and the calm of Gabalaya Street. Hashim was all of Egypt walking on two feet.

I loved Cairo with Hashim.

I had finally gotten away from Beirut. Every week, I decided that I'd go back to Lebanon the following week. Then I'd postpone my return. A month and a half passed, and I was still in Cairo. My father was calling me every other day for reassurance that I was eventually coming back. Every morning, I wrote a letter to my mother or to one of my sisters or one of my friends. They were quick letters, just a few lines long. I hated writing letters, but I liked getting them. To get letters, I had to write them.

I was afraid that the Muhi al-Dins were getting annoyed about my staying with them, so I decided to move to the Hilton or the Shepheard. The entire family objected. Maybe they were afraid that if I stayed at a hotel, my father would ask them to settle part of the debt they owed him. My father also refused to let me stay at a hotel by myself.

So I remained with the Muhi al-Dins.

They had given up on me. None of them tried anymore to know where I was going or with whom. They just gave me a key to the house.

Every day, I went out with Hashim.

Every day I met the Lebanese clique and my friend 'Issam. I had lunch with them and dinner with Hashim or the reverse.

One day, I was with Hashim in his car on the Muqattam mountain. We were warming ourselves in the afternoon sun.

Hashim looked at me for a long time. It was a look that stirred up this new feeling in me. Then he was silent for a long time. Suddenly, he turned to me.

"Rihab," he said, "we can't continue like this. We're deceiving ourselves."

I gave him a quick look and then lowered my eyes.

"What do you mean?"

"We're resisting. I'm resisting. I feel that you're resisting too. This resistance will ruin everything between us. We have to define our situation and then give in to it."

"What do you want?"

"Honestly," he went on, "I can no longer be content with this friendship. I'm resisting a lot of things. I'm resisting words that I want to say to you. I'm resisting the feeling that I want to touch your hand. I'm resisting, resisting. I want to kiss you right now, but I'm resisting."

"But I don't want to kiss you," I said in a light voice.

"What am I to you?"

"You're a friend," I said, feeling that I was resisting the honesty that I usually lived by. "I'm happy with every minute that I spend with you."

"Only a friend?"

"A dear friend."

He lowered his head, defeated.

"I think that we can be more than friends," he said.

"I don't think we need to be more than friends," I said, trying to be cold.

"You're right. I made a mistake. Forgive me. I felt that I needed you, needed more than your friendship."

I felt as if my heart was split in two. Still, I resisted.

"Are you not happy with my friendship?" I asked.

"Happy," he said sarcastically. "Yes, happy."

"So, let's be content with this happiness. I too am happy with your friendship."

I felt I was the more mature one.

He knit his brows.

"But we're going down a path that will put an end to our friendship. We're going down a path that will end either in love or in the abyss. If we don't get to love, our friendship will fall into the abyss. We have to protect our friendship from falling, from being destroyed. We have to find another path."

"What do you mean?"

"We have to stop meeting every day," he said, clenching his teeth, collecting his will. "We have to not meet alone. I have to introduce you to my sister. You have to introduce me to the family you're living with. If we meet, we have to be in a family atmosphere to protect our friendship from heading somewhere else."

"But I don't want to have family visits. I didn't come to Cairo to visit people's families."

"But this will keep our friendship intact," he said bitterly.

I felt like I was going to cry.

Silence hung between us.

A thick silence.

He drove his car to my house.

When he stopped the car, he didn't turn to me. He kept looking in front of him. His face was flushed as if he was in a battle with himself. I looked at him, filled with both impatience and pity.

"When will I see you?" I asked in a low voice.

"I'll talk with my sister about inviting you to lunch or dinner and then I'll call you," he said, not looking at me.

"Is that what you want?" I asked, looking directly at him.

"That's what you want," he snapped.

"I don't want to be invited to your house for lunch or dinner. I don't want to meet your sister. She's not my age."

He didn't respond to me.

I kept looking at him. I had a lot of feelings swirling in my chest. Rage, stubbornness, fear, compulsion, hesitation. Then, suddenly, I closed the car door before getting out.

"Where do you want to kiss me?" I asked.

He turned to me in surprise.

"What'd you say?"

"Kiss me. If your whole problem is that you want to kiss me."

"I . . ." he opened his mouth to speak.

"Do what you want," I cut him off. "I've never seen a man ask a girl for permission before kissing her or ask for permission to love her. Don't ask. Show me what you want."

His eyes filled with hesitation. He then turned on the ignition.

"You're right," he said.

He drove off.

My heart was beating fast. I felt regret for setting him free in what he wanted.

He was driving silently.

I wanted to ask where we were going, but I was stubborn and wanted to appear indifferent, as if nothing mattered to me. But I couldn't keep it up.

"Where are we going?"

"To a nightclub," he said, not turning to me.

"Which one?"

"An apartment that we call a nightclub."

"Why do you call it a nightclub? Why don't you call it an apartment?"

"Maybe because the word nightclub is nicer than the word apartment."

"But the word apartment is more honest."

"Apartment, then. If you don't want to, we won't go."

"No, let's go," I said defiantly. "You'll kiss me there, right?"

"I don't know. But I'll feel you're closer to me there."

He was quiet. The words of my friend Mona were ringing in my ears: "Watch out for Egyptian guys. They want everything from girls. And they'll feed you a pack of lies. They all have bachelor pads."

I was full of defiance, a defiance bigger than being afraid, bigger than Hashim.

I hated this feeling of defiance. I hated my fear. And I hated this feeling of being a woman, of being drawn to a man. It made me feel weak. All I wanted was to feel that I was Rihab, not a man or a woman, that I was a person who existed on my own and didn't need the opposite sex to complete me.

Why did I agree to go with him to the apartment? Why didn't I go back? What didn't I jump out of the car and run? I wanted to be free, to dance, to laugh. I wanted nothing serious, nothing that scared me.

He stopped in front of a building in Zamalek.

We got out of the car. I walked next to him, almost stamping my feet, my eyes wide.

I didn't speak. Neither did Hashim.

We went up in the elevator.

Hashim opened the door. We went in. I sat on the first seat that I found.

It was the first time I'd been inside a bachelor pad. Despite that, I didn't try to look around, to take it all in. I didn't even look at Hashim. At that moment, my feelings were concentrated on waiting for what would happen. I was expecting something would happen and I was ready to resist.

Hashim was talking. He was talking a lot. He was moving around in front of me nervously like a lost child who didn't know where to begin. He turned on the radio. Then he turned it off. He put on a record. He kept talking. Then he got near me and leaned over and touched my cheek with his lips. I didn't move. I didn't look up at him. I stayed frozen. I felt the warm touch of his lips, fire like the rays of the Cairo sun on me. I felt my entire face was on fire. But I stayed frozen. Hashim touched my cheek with his lips again. Then a third time. I felt he was trying to melt me with his fire. But I was stiff, stiff like wood. I pursed my lips. I hid them inside my mouth. He tried to get to them, but I resisted. I was stiff and frozen.

Hashim moved away. There was a shy look in his eyes as if he felt that he'd made a mistake.

"I'm sorry," he said in a weak voice.

"Don't apologize," I said, fixing my hair and feeling my cheeks to put out the fire that he'd lit. "I let you."

"You don't want my kisses."

"Maybe I'll want them one day."

He then busied himself with playing a record.

I started to feel disgust. My feeling of fear went up in smoke, as did my curiosity for the new experience.

"I have to go back now," I said resolutely, getting up.

He looked at his watch.

"It's seven o'clock," he said, letting out a whistle of surprise. "I'm very late for the clinic. Am I going to see you tonight?"

"No," I said. "I'm meeting some friends."

"Guys?"

"Yes. And girls."

"Suppose you don't go out without me."

"Why?" I asked, surprised.

"Because you let me kiss you."

"What does that mean?"

"That I've become your man."

"I don't like my man to be selfish. It's not my man's right to block me from my friends."

"Would you like it if I went out with another girl?"

"If you feel that you want to go out with another girl, then go ahead. I don't want you to be polite with me or play the hypocrite. I always want to feel that you're being true to how you feel."

"You feel that you want to go out tonight with your friends?"

"Yes. I'd hate not to go out with them just to please your ego. I'd hate to call that faithfulness. In fact, it's because I am faithful to my feelings that I'm going out with my friends tonight."

"You'll dance with them?"

"Yes."

"And one of them will put his cheek on yours while you're dancing?"

"I usually don't like anyone putting their cheek on mine while I dance," I said. "Dancing is feeling the music, not feeling a man. But if I feel like I want one of them to put his cheek on mine, I won't hesitate. Because if I didn't do it, I wouldn't be faithful to what I'm feeling. If I wasn't faithful to what I'm feeling, I wouldn't be faithful to you. If I cheat how I feel, I'd be cheating you. I'd be a hypocrite. I don't want to deceive anyone or be a hypocrite. Understand me. I belong to my feelings before I belong to anyone."

He looked at me, incapable of responding.

He got up and opened the door for me.

"You're right," he said.

We were silent the entire ride back. I thought he was suffering. There was pain in his eyes.

I went out with my friends that night. But the ember of fire that Hashim left on my cheek kept burning all night. And the look of pain in his eyes stayed with me.

I went to bed thinking about the moment I'd meet him the next day. I felt I'd been hard on him, and I promised myself that I'd make up for it. I didn't know if I was deceiving myself, if I was justifying to myself letting him kiss me again. I wanted him to kiss me, but only kiss me.

We met in his car. We went to our favorite place on top of Muqattam. All of Cairo was at our feet, as if it was submitting to us. I'd make fun of Hashim whenever he mentioned Muqattam mountain.

"A mountain?" I'd tell him. "This would be a little hill in Lebanon."

But that day, I didn't try to joke with him. All I felt was that I was waiting for the moment when he'd kiss me. But the pain was still in his eyes. He was talking and acting like an angry child. I got tired of waiting.

"Don't you want to kiss me today?" I asked suddenly, unable to bear it anymore.

"You don't like my kisses," he said, looking at me in surprise.

"Let me try them out again."

Hashim brought his lips near but before he reached mine, I moved my head away.

"No," I said. "Don't kiss me if you don't want to."

Hashim took my hair suddenly and he brought me closer to him.

"You're talking a lot," he whispered.

Then he fell on me.

I submitted to him completely.

It was the first time I didn't mind being kissed on the lips. I was calm as if I had been running my whole life and had stopped only now that I'd reached this point. There was something beautiful flowing in my veins.

Hashim pulled back from me.

Our eyes met as if they'd met for the first time, and then he kissed me again.

The days that followed were more incredible and beautiful. But we didn't go to the apartment.

I did not like that apartment. I hated its walls and I felt suffocated by it. I spent my entire life fleeing from walls, the walls of our house in Beirut, the walls of the schools that I went to. I didn't put myself between four walls except to sleep. Hashim felt all that. He felt how nervous and tortured I was whenever he invited me to his apartment. So he stopped inviting me. I went out with him in the gardens of al-Qanatir, the fields of Mansuriya, the sands of Muqattam. Our kisses didn't lose their magic, they floated like clouds and weren't choked between four walls.

We always disagreed about one thing. Every day we had a fight about my right to meet my friends and go out with them. I insisted on keeping this right.

One day, he came by with his car to pick me up.

"I can only stay with you for ten minutes," I told him as I got in.

"Why?"

"A friend from Lebanon is coming. I promised that I'd go out with him tonight."

"Why don't you get a job as a guide to take Lebanese tourists around Cairo?"

"Don't yell, please."

"I can't love a girl who goes out with other men every day."

"I'm going out with friends," I said sharply. "Not with men. I don't hide anything from you. You want me to deceive you like Egyptian girls do? You want me to tell you that I'm going to the hairdresser or visiting a girl-friend and then go meet a man? You can't bear me being honest with you about going out with a friend. Do you know why girls deceive men? Because men can't han-dle the truth. They don't want to understand that girls aren't simply sex, that the relationship between men and women isn't always sexual. Women are human beings who have the right to have friends, whether they're men or women. They have the right to act as they want. Women are working now and if it's their right to meet a man at the office or at the factory, why isn't it their right to meet him at a café or a garden? Hashim, under-stand me. I can't lie to you and deceive you like Amina or Nagwa did. I won't do it. Not for your sake, but for mine. I'm faithful to my feelings before I'm faithful to you. But this makes me faithful to you."

"Your feelings!" Hashim yelled out angrily. "You're always talking about your feelings. Don't I have feelings too? Do you think I'm made of stone? A donkey with-out feelings? You can't just follow your feelings, it leads to chaos. You might feel that you want to take off your clothes in the street, so why don't you? I sometimes feel that I want to kill someone, so why don't I just do that? Humanity can only advance when people resist their impulses. Human history is the history of resisting impulses and controlling feelings. People made laws to control their impulses and feelings, to set principles, to call people to respect each other. The prophets, the philosophers, the intellectuals, all of them resisted human impulses and got control of their feelings so they could protect human society and advance it."

"You're talking as if my meeting with a friend is a crime," I yelled back at him.

"It's a crime against me. It's an insult to me. If you want to submit to your feelings, you have to live in a world by yourself because other people have feelings that you have to take into account and respect too."

He was silent for a moment to catch his breath.

"I'll go out with a girl so you can feel what I'm feeling."

I felt my heart tighten, but I was stubborn. I opened the car door.

"I have to go, or I'll be late."

He didn't respond.

I got out of the car and turned to him.

"Do you know what's torturing you?" I asked. "Your ego. All you want is that people don't see me with someone other than you. A woman has to be a private possession, like your car, like your shoes. It's the egotism of an Eastern man. It's ignorance. I'm not a car or a pair of shoes. I'm not a flower you put on your lapel and then show off to people. I'm not your property. I belong to myself, even if I love you, even if you're the only man in the world."

I left before I heard his response, feeling like I was about to cry.

Hashim called me the next day.

His voice was weak and defeated with a ring of apology about the previous day's fight.

I smiled. He couldn't do without me. I wouldn't give up my right to have guy friends and to go out dancing. I started feeling that my Lebanese friends were the guarantee of my freedom, my protection.

All of Cairo was talking about me and Hashim as people saw us together. The Muhi al-Din family started whispering to each other about my relationship with Hashim. They started talking about him in front of me. None of them chided me. Maybe none of them could define the type of relationship I had with Hashim since it wasn't easy for them to imagine that Hashim loved me or that I loved him because of the age difference between us. They talked very highly of him to me. They kept saying that he had a lot of influence, that he knew everyone in Egypt. Dudi, Auntie Mimi's daughter, didn't hide her jealousy at my friendship with him. She'd purse her lips whenever she heard Hashim's name and then go up to the roof to work on her statues. But her husband, Rafiq, started to become more interested in me once he heard about my relationship with Hashim. Rafiq was gone a lot from the house and would come back unexpectedly. No one particularly cared about his absence or was happy about his return. I too got used to not noticing him.

He started to wait for me to have breakfast and ask me if I'd be back for lunch. He invited me once to dinner at the Shepheard Hotel with his wife and some of their friends. He gave me a valuable ring that he bought at Khan al-Khalili. He talked a lot about Hashim, about his influence.

"I don't think that Dr. Hashim is someone whose bags are searched at customs when he travels," he told me once.

"I don't know," I said indifferently.

I didn't understand yet what Rafiq meant.

4

THINGS WITH HASHIM DEVELOPED QUICKLY, quicker than I imagined. He was trying to make himself into a different person. It seemed that he had given up hope of raising me up to his age, so he decided to come down to mine. His main aim was to monopolize me, to pull me away from my young friends. He gave up convincing me that I should be his alone, so he decided to be everything in my life, to give me everything, to occupy all my time, all my thoughts, all my feelings, so as not to leave anything for anyone else.

I was having dinner with him in a restaurant on the Nile, Omar al-Khayyam, when he asked me:

"What are you doing tomorrow?"

"I'm going with some friends in the morning to the pyramids to ride horses."

His face changed suddenly and his eyes glimmered.

"With who?" he asked, gripping his glass so tightly I wondered if he was going to break it.

"'Issam," I said indifferently. "And 'Afaf, 'Aida, Asad, Salah, and I don't know who else."

He lowered his eyes.

"Always 'Issam," he said as if talking to himself.

"'Issam is just a friend. Not more."

"I know. Maybe I'm just a friend too. Maybe what's between me and you is what you call friendship."

"You're too suspicious," I said, giving him a smile to try to reassure him. "It's not your fault."

"Whose fault is it?"

"The girls you were with before me. None of them knew the meaning of friendship between a man and a woman. You got used to that."

"Please. I've had enough of your philosophizing."

A period of silence passed between us.

Hashim's face was flushed. He gulped down his drink.

"I'll go with you," he said, not looking at me.

"Where?"

"To the pyramids. To ride horses."

I felt embarrassed. I didn't know what to say. I didn't want him with me.

"And your clinic?" I asked, looking for something to dissuade him.

"It doesn't matter."

"I don't want you to leave your patients for me."

"If my patients concern you, don't go with your friends. I can't treat a patient while my mind is occupied with you, imagining you with another man."

"I'm not responsible for your patients. I'm not a doctor. You're the doctor."

"If you love me, you'll share the responsibility with me," he said weakly.

"You mean if I love you, I'll become your slave? I'll imprison myself at home for you? No. If you love me, you'd trust me."

"I trust you, but I don't trust your friends."

"Because you don't trust yourself."

"It's not possible for a man to trust himself when he loves a crazy girl like you."

"I'm not crazy. But you have issues. You know what your issue is?'

"What?"

"It's the way you live your life. You can't break it."

"Suppose this is true. Why don't you help me? And how can I break out of this life if you don't do the same?"

"Whatever life I live wouldn't forbid me from having friends."

"Then I'll be with you and your friends."

"But you don't know them."

"Introduce me to them."

"You won't feel comfortable with them. They won't feel comfortable with you."

"If I'm comfortable with you, I'll feel the same way with them. If they're comfortable with you, they'll feel the same way with me."

"It's different for me. My mind is open enough to accept you. But them, their minds are narrow and so are their feelings."

"Why are you friends with people whose minds are so narrow?"

"Because I have fun with them. We need fun as much as we need depth. I need fun and these friends satisfy that. With them, I laugh at jokes you'd never laugh at. I dance in ways you don't like. With them, I scream. I run. We sing the songs of Charles Aznavour and Nat King Cole. Why are you trying to stop me from all that?"

"I don't want to stop you from anything," he said, looking at me with pleading eyes. "But I want to share everything with you."

I didn't respond.

I twisted my lips. I leaned back on the chair and looked off in the distance, far from him.

Another period of silence passed between us.

Hashim let go of his glass and reached out to take my hand.

"Rihab," he said, his voice hoarse, as he squeezed my hand. "I . . . I love you. But I can love you more. I can't believe I've fallen in love again so quickly. There were days when I thought I couldn't love anyone again. I can't believe how I feel. I can't believe that I love you. In the months since we met, I wake up every morning and I try to deny to myself that I love you. But as soon as I see the phone, I discover that I love you more than the day before. I'm waiting to hear your voice. When a forty-five-year-old man is in love with a nineteen-year-old girl, he's gambling with what remains of his life, with when he's fifty, sixty, or seventy. I tried to avoid this adventure. But why? Why should I live in the darkness at forty-five? Why doesn't a forty-five-year-old man deserve to be in love with a nineteen-year-old girl? Love isn't a chemical equation between two appropriate ages, but between two minds, two hearts, and two personalities no matter how far apart or close together the ages are."

I looked up at him breathlessly and my heart pulled me to his lips. I hadn't ever heard him talk so gently before, with this sweetness. I hadn't noticed the sincerity in his eyes or in the eyes of any man as much as at that moment. I felt like I was on the verge of crying. I couldn't find the words to say anything.

"All I'm trying to do is for us to live in the same world, to bring your world closer to mine so that they become one world, a world that includes mutual friends, mutual interests," Hashim continued, still gripping my hand, his voice trembling. "This won't be easy, since what separates my world from yours isn't just friends and interests, but my country and yours. You're in Beirut and I'm in Cairo. I'm afraid, afraid of us failing in building our single world. This fear is making me hate your friends and hate Beirut. I hate everything separating us. But we have to pass the test."

I was lost for words again.

"What are you thinking about?" Hashim asked.

"About what you're saying," I said, not looking at him. "You're complicating the world around me. I didn't ask myself if I was in love with you or not. I don't even believe in the things that people tie themselves down with: love, friendship, hatred, ego. All these words don't mean anything because they're not fixed. They're not a past, or a present, or a future. People are trying to make feelings material fixed things, like iron, stone, wood. Wood was wood in the past, it's wood in the present, and it will be wood in the future. But love? How do you trust that you'll love me tomorrow as you love me today? How do you trust that you love me today as you loved me yesterday? Ego. People might be egotistical at one moment and self-sacrificing the next. You can't say that this person is egotistical, and that person is not. Each of them is subject to the feeling of the moment. And friendship? It changes day to day. Your friend might be your enemy tomorrow. My feelings are made up of moments. I live in the moment. I don't try to tie myself to the moment that follows it. You don't love me, and I don't love you, but each of us loves this moment that brings us together. It's a moment, even if love continues for hours or days or years. As long as you can't control the following moment, you can only live the moment you're in. You can't predict your feelings. You can't observe it like an astronomer observes the sky. You can't say tomorrow love, but after tomorrow, exhaustion, and the day after tomorrow, sacrifice. You can't say to a girl that you love at this moment that you'll love her forever because you're predicting something unknown. People's feelings are deeper and more wide-reaching than that."

Hashim was listening to me with wide eyes.

"My whole life, I've been trying to understand my feelings and arrange them, to file them away. I tried to know am I in love or not? I tried to say, this is love, this is friendship, this is hatred, this is disgust, but I failed. I was more surprised by how my feelings control me than other people were. I thought I loved Taysir, who I told you about before. But then, at every moment, I kept discovering that I had a different feeling toward him. Sometimes I was disgusted, sometimes I pitied him, sometimes I wanted him, and then I was fleeing from him. After all that, I no longer feel anything at all. He disappeared from my feelings. Where did my love for him go if love is fixed and solid? Where? Where will your love for me go?"

"To love is to be human," Hashim said, looking at me confused as if I was a crazy person. "If not for love, people wouldn't marry and have kids, and life wouldn't continue."

"On the contrary. Do you know why people get married? Because they don't trust their emotions, because they believe like me that life can't be based on emotions, because emotions are just moments, not life. That's why every couple ties themselves together by a legal contract, to protect themselves from the moment when their feelings toward each other change. They're bound together because neither of them trusts the other. Each of them knows deep down that love is a moment, and what follows may be something else."

He paid the bill and took my arm as we walked along the walkway between the restaurant and the banks of the Nile. I took my arm from him as soon as we reached the edge.

We didn't talk during the whole trip back. I got out of the car in front of the house without him kissing me as he usually does.

"When will you go tomorrow to the pyramids?" he asked after me.

"Issam will come by at eleven in the morning."

"I'll come by at eleven too," he said resolutely.

He then leaned back and sat up straight at the steering wheel.

"And your patients?"

But he drove off before he could hear me. Or maybe he'd heard me and he didn't want to respond.

I went up to my room feeling something heavy pressing down on my chest. I felt I was dragging an iron chain around my feet. I hated this feeling of being tied down. I hated having someone monitoring my every move. I hated Hashim at that moment.

I slept restlessly.

At eleven o'clock in the morning, I heard the horn of 'Issam's car. 'Issam usually honked to a particular tune that I knew.

After a few moments, I heard the angry sound of another horn, from Hashim's car.

I didn't know what to do. I thought about not going at all, not with 'Issam or Hashim, so that I didn't embarrass myself. I didn't even like riding horses. I just liked wearing riding pants. I once saw Audrey Hepburn in a movie wearing riding pants, so I left the cinema and bought some. In the few times when I had ridden horses, whether in Beirut or Cairo, I had made the trainer take the reins and walk with the horse because I was afraid. But I loved wearing the pants.

That day, I could do without the pleasure of wearing those pants.

Nonetheless, I went out wearing a black shirt and grey riding pants, black leather boots up to my knees, and a black hat. In my hand was a leather whip.

I looked amazing.

But I still felt the heavy weight on my chest and the iron chain dragging along behind me.

I lifted my hand with the whip and waved with it to 'Issam.

"Hi," I called with a big smile.

The rest of the clique—'Afaf, 'Aida, Asad, Salah—was with 'Issam.

I headed over to them. We exchanged hellos. Then I went over to Hashim, finding it hard to maintain my smile.

Hashim was wearing his shirt open, short sleeves, a grey scarf with black spots around his neck. His face was frowning and sallow. He looked like he hadn't slept. His nose seemed bigger. His hair seemed whiter. He looked like an old English lord.

I greeted him, torn up by confusion and embarrassment.

"Should I introduce you to my friends now?" I asked, resenting him for coming.

Hashim didn't respond. He opened the car door and got out. He then took my hand and went with me to 'Issam's car.

"My friend, Dr. Hashim."

'Issam, Asad, and Salah sat up in their seats in the car. They seemed nervous, as if the teacher caught them cheating at school.

'Afaf's and 'Aida's eyes took this in suspiciously, looking back and forth between me and Hashim.

Hashim reached out and began to greet them one by one, smiling at each of them to reassure them that, despite his age, he was one of them.

"My car is bigger," he said in a gentle voice. "Do you want to come with me instead of taking two cars?"

The kids' confusion increased. Each of them muttered something, trying to be polite.

'Afaf looked over at Hashim's car. She then turned to him with smiling eyes.

"Good idea," she said.

"As you like," 'Issam said, looking at me for guidance and then looking at Hashim in confusion.

"Whatever you prefer," I said. "You're the majority."

"The majority agrees," 'Afaf said, getting out of the car.

We all headed to Hashim's car. I couldn't look at him. I was purposely not walking next to him to show my friends I was still free.

I sat next to Hashim. On my right was 'Issam and in the back seat were 'Afaf, 'Aida, Asad, and Salah. 'Afaf sat on Asad's knees and leaned forward, putting her arms on the back of the front seat behind Hashim. Her lips were almost touching his neck.

An awkward silence hung in the air. On Hashim's cheek was a hint of red and on his lips was a silly blank smile. Maybe he was more embarrassed than us.

"I heard a lot about you, Doctor, from my Egyptian friends," 'Afaf said, her lips near the nape of his neck. "You're famous."

"Thanks," he said awkwardly.

"I was about to call you once," 'Afaf continued cheerfully. "I had a sharp pain in my stomach. The supervisor of the girls' dorm thought about calling you. Your clinic is very close to the dorm."

"Thank God we met without an illness," Hashim said as if talking to an old woman.

He turned to me, aware what his words were doing to me, imploring me to save him.

'Issam was sitting politely next to me, very politely. Asad and Salah were whispering to each other.

We felt like we were students on a school trip being chaperoned by the teacher.

'Aida's voice then rose up, singing the Enrico Macias song "Adieu mon pays." She then sang "Greenfields" by The Brothers Four. We all sang along with her, but Hashim was silent. He was whistling along with the song until he lost it and became quiet. I felt like he had almost disappeared. He only responded to us when 'Afaf took an interest in him again and tried to draw him into our conversation.

We reached the pyramids. We got out. I insisted on not walking next to Hashim. I left him to walk beside 'Afaf. I was stealing looks at him. At that moment, he seemed shorter than I'd imagined. I noticed the old-fashioned wide legs of his pants. Maybe if his pants were tighter, he'd seem taller, more elegant. I found myself comparing him with 'Issam. He was older than I'd realized. I saw the wrinkles under his eyes for the first time. I saw the small black spots on his hands and next to his nose that I hadn't noticed before. 'Issam's skin was smooth, free of black spots. Why did Hashim put himself in this position, making me compare him with another man? He was losing me, and himself.

'Afaf got close to me.

"Your friend is fabulous," she whispered in my ear.

I didn't respond, but I wished at that moment that she'd take him and go far away with him to rid me of this deep embarrassment weighing down on my chest, to liberate me from his chain, for me to be freed to go back to being indifferent.

We started riding horses.

Hashim looked at me. He then hesitated a little. He mounted the horse. His way of getting up on the horse showed that he hadn't ridden before.

I smiled at him. It was an empty smile.

I rode my horse and told the guide not to let go of the reins. I told him in a loud voice. I didn't hide that I was afraid of horses.

The horses brought us forward slowly. Hashim was gripping the reins with one hand and the edge of the saddle with the other.

As soon as we reached the desert behind the pyramids, 'Issam started galloping. Asad and Salah galloped behind him, almost racing. The girls shouted with joy. I shouted along with them. We were watching the guys gallop on the horses breathlessly.

The horse that Hashim was riding was getting fidgety and pounding its feet, shaking its neck nervously, wanting to join the other horses. Its owner was standing next to him, trying to calm him down, gripping his reins forcefully.

Hashim turned to me. He noticed me smiling at him. I was giving him a smile trying to convey to him that he didn't have to gallop with his horse like the other the guys. But maybe Hashim didn't understand my smile. He kept looking at me. He then looked at 'Afaf and 'Aida. His face was full of an incredible determination, and he turned to the guide holding his reins.

"Let go of the horse," he instructed him.

The guide let go and all of a sudden, the horse set off like a rocket to join the other horses. Hashim was shaking up and down, bouncing backward and forward.

He looked like a bag of cotton on the back of a car that had lost its brakes.

We screamed in terror.

"That horse is unruly," the owner said.

He then asked me to get off my horse so he could ride it to catch up with him.

I got off. I was about to die from terror for Hashim. 'Aida and 'Afaf were screaming. The horse was taking Hashim farther and farther away. With every passing moment, I thought Hashim would get thrown off and die. Tears were collecting in my eyes, not tears of pity, but tears of anger. Why did Hashim subject himself to all this, to the point of risking death?

Hashim's horse overtook the rest of the horses, which started running from behind to keep up. Everyone hid their eyes.

After more than fifteen minutes, we saw everyone come back. Hashim was still on the horse and the owner was gripping his reins. 'Issam, Asad, and Salah were around him, each of them riding their horse. It was a solemn procession for this near disaster, even the horses seemed to have bowed their heads.

'Issam, Asad, and Salah got down. The guide then helped Hashim dismount. His face was pale. His eyes were pained, his lips dry, his shirt untucked. The scarf around his neck was in disarray.

"Not bad," he said, fixing his shirt and trying to keep his cool. "I beat them."

No one said a thing. We didn't know what to say.

"You were amazing," 'Afaf then said, forcing a smile.

I got near Hashim and walked next to him silently, afraid that he'd do something else just as dumb.

"I was worried about you," I whispered.

"You shouldn't be," he said sharply. "I know what I'm doing."

Hashim insisted on paying for the horses for all of us. He made a point of it, looking for a way to outdo the rest of the guys. He didn't know that we were each used to paying for ourselves, even the girls.

We went to the Mena House to have lunch. Hashim drank beer. He drank a lot. We tried to share one conversation. Each of us was doing their best to talk about something that Hashim could participate in. Hashim too was trying hard to pick subjects he thought would interest us. This effort made our conversation strained and silly. Were they all secretly making fun of him? Maybe his idiocy would be the next topic of conversation at the Hilton Cafeteria.

We got tired of this and soon started talking about things that were interesting just to us. We talked about our friends, our parties, about the news from Beirut. Hashim was alone drinking beer. One of us would try to include him, but we'd quickly find ourselves back to our own conversation.

There wasn't anything he could do to make himself one of us. He was the only one there with white hair.

Hashim insisted again on paying the bill. We let him. And we went back to the car.

I thought this experience would convince Hashim that he shouldn't try to share my friends, convince him that he couldn't live in my world. I thought he'd think the day was boring and childish, but as soon as we got in the car, he started talking about spending the evening at the club. Hashim then invited us. I refused, but the rest of the group accepted. He was more enthusiastic than us. 'Afaf pressed me until I accepted. I accepted because I was afraid to leave Hashim alone with them, alone with 'Afaf.

We went that evening.

I purposely tried to look older, older than the rest of the girls.

We danced. I did all the slow dances with Hashim. When Hashim slow danced with me, I felt like I was melting in his chest. I had never felt that before. He danced delicately, charmingly.

I wasn't the only one who loved doing these slow dances with him. 'Afaf got up to dance with him and I saw her after a few moments almost disappear into his chest. Her head was on his neck. Her eyes were closed as if she was in love.

I forgave her.

I danced the fast dances with my friends as usual: the twist, the bossa nova, the chicken. I noticed Hashim looking at me, with a look of disapproval on his face. I was about to stop dancing. I felt embarrassed dancing the twist in front of him. I tried to forget he was there so I wouldn't miss the steps.

Hashim drank. He drank lots of whiskey.

"When will you teach me the twist?" he asked me.

"I won't teach you," I said, smiling at him.

"Why not?"

"Because it's not appropriate for you. You're better than anyone at slow dancing."

"Because I'm old," he said, sighing.

"No. Only because it's not appropriate for you."

"You always remind me that I'm old."

"You're not old," I said, taking pity on him. "You're a man, a fabulous man. The twist will make you lose your charm. Speaking of which, you have to wear pants with tighter legs."

"I won't. Whether you like it or not."

"I like you," I said, smiling.

I then got up to dance the twist with 'Issam and left Hashim with his glass.

Suddenly, I saw him in front of me on the dance floor doing the twist with 'Afaf.

He was shaking as if afflicted by malaria, his movements out of time with the music. He looked ridiculous, laughable, like a circus jester. He was like Tahiyya Kariokka belly dancing.

Damned 'Afaf was dancing in front of him as if she was his puppet master. I hated people who danced without being good at it. Like those who sing out of tune.

"Hashim!" I found myself screaming at him in the middle of the dance floor.

He turned to me in surprise.

I collected myself and put my hand on my head.

"I'm tired," I said. "Take me home."

This was the only way to stop him from making a laughingstock of himself, a laughingstock to my friends, to 'Afaf.

From then on, I decided to lie to him to stop him from asking me to share my world with him.

I started to hide that I was going out with my friends. I'd pretend that I was invited with the Muhi al-Dins for dinner with another Lebanese family.

I hadn't lied to him before. Hashim taught me that it was better to lie, to save him from clinging to me.

Those days, the Muhi al-Din family never stopped talking about the ruin that they met as a result of nationalization. I didn't know why they were pressing me with this even though they knew I wasn't interested. I didn't care about politics or try to understand why the government confiscated their assets. Perhaps it was because they knew I loved Gamal Abdel Nasser, even though I loved him without trying to understand his politics. I loved his strong brown face. I loved his manliness. He made me picture a world of heroes, closer to the stories I read or saw at the movies.

"Why don't you go back to Lebanon and start over there?" I once asked Muhi al-Din, the head of the family.

"How could I begin without capital?"

"Sell what you have in Egypt and start with it in Beirut."

"If I could move my money, I'd go."

"If they let me take just my jewels, we'd all go to Beirut," his wife, Auntie Lola, said.

"Why won't they let you?"

"Because they don't want us to live," Muhammad said.

"Why?"

"Because we're Lebanese. Imagine, Rihab, you come to this country, create the first aluminum factory, and employ dozens of workers. And then they take everything."

I looked at him as if I didn't believe him. There had to be a reason that I didn't know about.

"Dr. Hashim could help us," Rafiq, Dudi's husband, said, staring me in the eye.

I don't know why I felt at that moment that I was a fly about to land on a spider's web.

"How?" I asked in surprise.

"He could move our money to Beirut."

"He might not want to."

"He wouldn't have to know."

Rafiq brought his chair near to mine.

"Listen, Rihab," he continued in something close to a hiss. "We didn't steal this money. We earned it with our sweat over many years. We didn't rob anyone. We didn't commit a crime against anyone. But this government wants to rob us, to commit a crime against us. All we can do is smuggle out what we have left. Dr. Hashim is the only person we know who could move our money without arousing anyone's suspicions."

"I don't understand," I said, the spiderweb closing in, the eyes of the family on me.

"Didn't Dr. Hashim tell you he's going to Lebanon?" Rafiq went on.

"Yes. He'll come to visit me."

"All we want is for him to carry a suitcase for us."

"With your money and Auntie Lola's jewels?" I was beginning to understand.

"Yes."

"Why don't I carry it?"

"Because you'll be subject to inspection at customs," he said, annoyed at me for asking a stupid question. "They don't have any mercy on the Lebanese."

"But Hashim has to know."

"If he knows, he'll refuse. And he might inform the government about us."

"Then what do I tell him?"

"You'll go to Beirut. You'll then call and tell him that you forgot one of your bags and ask him to bring it for you when he comes. That's it."

I thought about it for a little. I then hit the table with my hand nervously.

"But why?" I asked. "Why don't they let you take your money if you didn't steal it?"

"Because they hate us," Auntie Lola said.

"They detest us," Muhammad said.

"It's a revolution," Rafiq said. "Their revolution doesn't know rights or laws. It only knows what it wants, and it wants our money."

I looked at their miserable faces. I felt pity for them.

And so the fly fell into the spiderweb that Rafiq had spun for it.

Auntie Lola was crying. Muhammad was sighing as if taking his last breath.

I could hear Auntie Nazli yelling to Saniya. Auntie Mimi was leaning on her ebony cane giving out orders.

Dudi was upstairs making her clay statues in her room. Maybe she had gone crazy after they took all her money.

I got up and went to my room. I lay down on my bed, imaging myself as a hero who would embark on a mission to save this family. I pictured myself as the Scarlet Pimpernel. But I wasn't the Scarlet Pimpernel. I was a fly that got caught in a spider's web.

5

I BEGAN TO TAKE ON a new persona, that of the Scarlet Pimpernel who smuggled the members of the royal family out during the French Revolution. I would be the person to smuggle the money of the Muhi al-Din family out to Lebanon.

The word "smuggling" wasn't really in my mind though. I didn't feel I was about to commit a crime. Not at all. I felt like a hero, that I was embarking on a big adventure.

It was a naive feeling, a heroism without cause. I didn't feel like I was opposing the revolution of Gamal Abdel Nasser, or that I was challenging it. I didn't feel like I had a political ideology that was pushing me to this heroism. Even my pity for the Muhi al-Din family wasn't enough to push me into this adventure. Their situation wasn't so bad that they deserved pity. They still had a lot. They lived in a palace. They had two cars. They had lots of money and so many jewels.

This feeling of heroism delighted me. It took hold of me. It was new for me. It was a distraction. I felt a new world bloom before me. I felt that I was playing a new role. I'd felt something similar when I'd discovered the world of intellectuals in the cafés around the American University in Beirut, or when I met a new guy and began to get to know him.

This new role demanded that I use a particular kind of intelligence, a sharp intelligence that was closer to wickedness.

This role required me to be deceitful, too. I was no longer honest with Hashim, nor was I as strong and out-going. I let him love me. I let him be convinced that I loved him. I loved him in his way, not mine. I stopped going out with my Lebanese friends so he didn't get mad. I started talking with him on the phone more than ten times a day. I woke him up to tell him good morning and whispered in his ear before he went to sleep at night, just as the Egyptian girls before me had done with him.

Hashim became even weaker toward me. I could see weakness in his eyes, in his trembling lips. I felt weakness in his kisses where it seemed he could no longer breathe except through my lips.

I no longer loved his kisses. I no longer felt like they were the Cairo sun shining on me. I submitted to them wide awake, my nerves on edge. I played the hypocrite. Lord, what was I doing to this man who loved me? What was I doing to myself?

Hashim sensed that I wasn't in love with him or his kisses.

"Are all the girls in Lebanon cold like you?" he asked me once as we were sitting in his car on top of Muqat-tam mountain.

"I'm not cold," I said, pretending to be mad. "You're just trying to melt me. Kiss me again!"

I gave him my lips the way I would give something to my child to calm him down. I let him pull me to him. He ran his fingers through my hair and stroked my back.

Those days, I refused to go with him to his apartment so that I wasn't forced to give him more and submit to him more. I could play the hypocrite with him outside, but I couldn't do it in his apartment.

"Walls suffocate me," I told him whenever he suggested that we go there.

"It will bring me closer to you."

"It brought you closer to dozens of women. I don't want to be one of them."

"You don't want me."

"I don't want you like some other girl wanted you. I want you for my mind and my heart. Walls suffocate my mind and my heart. All that would be left of me there is my body."

"But your body is here too. When you kiss me, you give me a piece of your body. When you wrap your arms around me, you wrap a piece of your body around me. You're mind and heart and body. So am I."

"Hashim, we went there once and we felt ridiculous. You were resisting something you wanted. I was resisting what you wanted, but here we're not resisting. Here I don't feel like I'm resisting you. You don't feel like you're resisting yourself. Here we're more natural, more beautiful."

"I thought you were more liberated," he said in despair.

"I'm more liberated than you think. Being liberated is that I believe in myself. Trust that I believe in myself when I tell you that walls choke me."

Hashim was silent. Maybe he wasn't convinced. But he was silent.

I plunged forward in my plan to smuggle the Muhi al-Dins' money. I hated myself, and I hated the Muhi al-Din family who had stirred up this naive feeling of heroism. Still, I plowed forward.

"Tell me, why does the government take the money of the Lebanese?" I asked Hashim once.

"What Lebanese?" he asked, surprised at my question.

"The Lebanese whose properties were nationalized."

Hashim laughed.

"The government took the money of the capitalists, whether they were Lebanese or Egyptian," he said. "They didn't take the money of the Lebanese because they're Lebanese, but because they're capitalists."

"But whoever builds a factory builds it with his money, money that he earned from his work."

"No one builds a factory just from work. They build it by exploiting others."

"All I know is that these people didn't steal. They didn't commit a crime. They worked for their money, and then the government came and took it."

"They can work again and take a salary from their work. Whether they're Lebanese or Egyptian, no one is stopping them from working. But they don't want to work. They aren't satisfied with the wage of their work. They want others to work for them."

I didn't respond to him.

"I didn't know you're interested in politics."

"I'm not."

"In Egypt, we're different from you in Lebanon."

"People in Lebanon are happy."

"And they're happy in Egypt."

"No. The government takes people's money here."

"Some people's, to give it to others who need it more."

"That's what you call socialism."

"Yes."

"It doesn't interest me. I don't want to understand," I said, shrugging my shoulders.

That wasn't true. I wanted to understand, but I felt confused by the idea that the Muhi al-Dins had been wronged.

I was pushed deeper into this plan, into the role of the heroine who would save the ill-fated family. And the Muhi al-Dins treated me like Joan of Arc, a saint sent to save them. Even Dudi, who hated me, started rubbing herself on me like a friendly cat.

Rafiq had cast his sticky spider's thread into my imagination. He started working out all the details with me. The plan was to prepare a suitcase with secret pockets where the money and jewels would be hidden. I'd take this suitcase with my other bags and go to the Hilton to stay for two days before leaving for Lebanon. When I left the hotel, I'd forget the suitcase with the secret pockets there. Immediately after I got to Beirut, I'd call Hashim and tell him that I forgot one of my bags back at the hotel and ask him to go there and get it for me. I'd then send a telegram to the hotel to ask them to give the bag to Hashim. Hashim would bring the bag to Lebanon when he came.

The point of going to the Hilton before leaving was to remove any suspicion from the Muhi al-Din family so that no one would discover a link between me and them. And if somehow this link was discovered if the bag was seized, the Muhi al-Din family could claim that the suitcase wasn't theirs. As for me, I wasn't afraid at all, because I'd be in Lebanon, far from the hands of the Egyptian government. Even if they ask me about it in Lebanon, I can claim that this wasn't my bag and maybe another guest in the same room left it behind.

What if Hashim changed his plans to travel to Lebanon?

In that case, I'd just come back to Cairo, take the bag, and give it back to the family.

That was the plan.

It was smart, even if there was some risk. It preserved the safety of the Muhi al-Din family more than mine.

The execution began.

Rafiq prepared a yellow suitcase with secret pockets. He hid cash in it, about twenty thousand Egyptian pounds, three thousand dollars, British pounds, diamonds, and bullion of gold. It was a fortune. We filled the bag after that with other things. Not my clothes, so that it wasn't tied to me in case it was seized. We filled it with items of men's clothing, ties, and random gifts from Khan al-Khalili.

It was time to go to the Hilton. Just to make sure the hotel was aware of the link between me and Hashim, I asked Hashim to reserve my room at the hotel. I called him with Rafiq sitting next to me. I told him that I'd go to the Hilton to stay there for two days before going back to Lebanon because I was tired of the suffocating atmosphere at the house. I told him I was afraid that I wouldn't find a free room, but Hashim reassured me, saying that he knew the hotel director personally and he'd take care of it for me. A few minutes later, he called back and told me that the room was under my name, room 625.

None of the family came with me to the hotel. They all said goodbye at the door of the house. I kissed them one by one with different emotions burning in my chest: pity, hatred, sympathy, anger. I didn't even go in the family car to remove any possible suspicion from them. I took a taxi instead.

I went inside the Hilton, the yellow suitcase behind me on the shoulder of the porter. My heart was pounding. I didn't know that I'd feel all this worry, all this fear, all this confusion.

I turned to the receptionist. I couldn't look him right in the eye.

"I believe that Dr. Hashim 'Abd al-Latif reserved a room for me," I said in a trembling voice.

"When?" the receptionist asked, flipping through the register in front of him.

"This morning," I said.

The receptionist's eyes stopped above the register and then he looked up at me.

"Are you Ms. Rihab Shams al-Din?"

"Yes."

He gave me a big smile.

"Room 625."

He then took my passport and completed the registration. Another employee went with me. I looked at the yellow suitcase before I went into the elevator. I pretended to ignore it, afraid that someone would catch me looking at it. The elevator took me up. My heart was in my throat.

I waited in the room for a few minutes alone. I couldn't sit down or look around. I was lost, miserable. An intense feeling of misery was suffocating me. Then I heard a knock on the door. The porters came in. They were carrying my bags . . . and the yellow suitcase.

I gave them a tip. I don't know how much. It could have been a whole pound. I saw them exchange looks.

I stayed by myself in the room. I paced around looking for a place to put the yellow suitcase where I could claim that I forgot it and no one would find it before I left the hotel. I was confused. I was cursing myself for getting caught up in this. I almost picked up the phone, called the Muhi al-Din family, and told them to come and take their bag and free me from this. But I felt I was already trapped, a fly caught in a poisonous spiderweb.

I decided to put the bag on the floor of the big closet behind the door that didn't open. I tried to carry it with my hands. It was heavy, heavier than I thought. I dragged it along the floor.

When I was finished, I lay down on the bed panting. But I couldn't relax. I felt as if there was a murdered body behind the closet door. I couldn't keep still. I picked up the phone and called Hashim.

"Can I see you now?"

"In an hour."

"I can't wait that long."

"In ten minutes, then."

I put the phone down. I couldn't bear to stay in the room for even ten minutes, so I went down to the reception and asked the receptionist to reserve a seat for me on the flight to Beirut in two days. I sent a telegram to my father giving him the arrival time.

Hashim arrived, but I immediately wanted to leave.

"Don't stop," I said as I got in the car. "Drive quickly."

"You're nervous," he said, turning to me.

"I'm always nervous when I travel," I said looking away. "I always feel like I'm losing something. When I left Beirut, I felt like I lost it, and now I feel like I'm on the verge of losing Cairo."

He drove off slowly.

"I'm afraid I'll lose you in Beirut," he said in a trembling voice. "Your family and country are there. You loved me far from them. I loved you as a visitor here. I'm afraid when you're back home, you'll lose your feelings for me."

"I don't think so," I said somberly.

"Love is embedded in the circumstances surrounding it. If the circumstances change, love changes. Like the man who loves a dancer in a cabaret, if the dancer leaves and becomes a housewife, he loses his love for her."

"I'm not a dancer. Cairo isn't a cabaret. And you're coming to Beirut. When are you coming?"

"In ten days. I arranged everything to be with you in ten days."

"You won't be late?"

"No. I won't. I can't be late."

He didn't go to his clinic that evening. He stayed with me until four in the morning. We roamed together through the streets of Cairo. We sat in one place, only to get up and go someplace else. We both got lost in a kiss. Then we woke up to keep moving. He spent the following day with me. The evening too. We weren't happy, but we clung to each other as fate sought to separate us. Every moment felt like goodbye. We consoled each other. We sat in silence, then we went back to talking. I wondered at every moment: Do I love him? Is this love? I had felt something that I hadn't felt before. I hadn't felt this attachment for another man. Maybe it was love. Despite that, I was in a rush to end the evening and go back to Beirut. I was finished, finished with all this, and ready to rest at home. My father, my mother, and my sisters missed me.

The image of the yellow suitcase behind the closet door like a murdered body suddenly jumped to my mind. I turned to Hashim terrified, afraid that he'd see the image of the bag in my mind.

I decided not to go ahead with the smuggling plan. I felt like a fly trying to free itself from the web that Rafiq spun around me.

I went back to wondering: Do I love Hashim?

My mind was racing, yet I was frozen.

Hashim suggested, as we sat in the Hilton Cafeteria at four in the morning, that we should stay up until we went to the airport. I agreed, not wanting to be near the yellow bag.

"As much as I'm afraid I'll lose you in Beirut, I want you to go," Hashim told me, playing with pieces of sugar in front of him, trying to make a house with it. "So you can be far from me and discover how you really feel."

"No matter what my feelings are," I said, exhausted, "the truth is that I live in Lebanon and you live in Egypt. You can't live with me in Lebanon, and I can't live with you in Egypt."

He looked at me in astonishment.

"Even if we discovered that we really do love each other?"

"What's love for?"

"We'll get married," he said calmly, looking me in the eye.

The thought had never crossed my mind. He was thinking about marriage, that's how much he loved me.

"I'm not thinking about getting married. Not now."

"Even if you love me?"

"Even when I'm in love, I don't think about marriage. It's easier for me to think about living in Cairo than about marriage."

"Why? Isn't this love?"

"Marriage is an end. And I don't like endings."

"It's a beginning."

"It's the end of a period of my life that I don't want to end."

He lowered his head.

"This is the first time I've met a girl who doesn't want to marry me."

"I'm not refusing to marry you, I'm refusing to get married. I trust your love to the point that I don't need a legal contract to tie me to you. Your love is enough."

"You can't decide anything now. In Beirut, you'll see whether you need me to the point of getting married."

"Who knows? Maybe a moment will come when I decide to get married."

"You're deluded."

"When it comes to you."

Hope radiated from his smile.

"Don't write to me after you get to Beirut, even if you feel like you want to."

"Why?"

"Because we need this time to test our feelings. If we write, we'll be cheating. I want you to live with your emotions. I'll live with mine too, so that the day we make a decision, we'll be sure about it."

"Agreed."

It was five thirty in the morning. I went up to my room, washed my face, and changed my clothes. I locked my suitcases and called the porter. He carried the suitcases in front of me and went down with them. Three suitcases. I forgot the fourth. It was locked, and the key was with me, according to the plan.

I went back down to Hashim. He was pacing in the hotel lobby. His hands were in his pockets. His head was lowered and he was looking at the ground. His lips were moving as if he was talking to himself, exhaustion and weariness on his face.

I went straight to the receptionist.

I wanted to pay my bill quickly before any of the hotel employees discovered that I'd forgotten a bag.

Hashim noticed me. He came and stood beside me. He tried to pay my bill, but I refused. I refused with a sharpness that surprised Hashim.

He let me pay. He then took care of the tip for me.

I was hurrying him for us to get in the car before anyone discovered the bag. I was anxious, everything inside me was trembling. I thought people could see what was happening inside me. Every face seemed about to yell at me: Miss! You forgot your bag!

We drove off.

Thank God. No one discovered the bag.

I tried to relax in my seat, to calm down, but I couldn't. My nerves were taut, to the breaking point.

Hashim was silent. He was worn out. His face looked creased.

It felt like we'd already moved farther away from each other than just the distance between Cairo and Beirut.

"I'm afraid, Rihab," Hashim said, looking away as we got close to the airport road, his voice deep, distant, and sad. "I don't know why, but I'm afraid. Maybe I'm afraid for myself more than for you. I've been hit by an anxiety that has made me lose my self-confidence, my self-control. I've ignored my work. I've ignored everything. I've been walking down a path whose end I can't see and now I need to stop and open my eyes. The only sign on this path points to you and I need to know if I am getting closer or moving away from it. Or did I already reach it?"

I felt my tears well up.

"I don't know," I said, in an honesty that was filling my heart. "I'm confused like you. I didn't fake anything with you. I was meeting you because I wanted to be with you. There were dozens of others I could have met, but you're the one who pulled me to you. I came to Cairo to spend three weeks and I spent five months, for you. I can't find a reason that kept me in Cairo all this time except for you. But I don't know what I want from you or what I want you to be with me. There's something inside me that is rebelling against you and there's something inside me that's driving me to you. I don't know which will win."

Hashim sighed. He reached out, took my hand, and squeezed it.

"I give in. I've never given in like I have with you, given in to the point of weakness. I feel so weak it's like a kind of impotence, the same thing I feel when I can't diagnose a patient. Which of us needs treatment? Me or you? Or both of us?"

"No. We're not sick. Don't say we're sick."

"We're suffering."

"We're suffering because the road that separates us is long. The road between your way of thinking and mine, between your life and mine, your feelings and mine. Sometimes, I feel like you look at me like I'm from another world, from the moon, from Mars. And I, too, sometimes feel like you're from a strange world. I feel like you're a Bedouin living in the pre-Islamic era, standing at the entrance of a tent, trying to pull me inside and close the curtains of your tent for me to live in the darkness, the light remaining for you alone. I've really felt that way. I resisted. I don't want to live in your tent or in your darkness. But I keep finding myself driven to you. We've gone a long way on a difficult road. We have to keep going on what's left of the road ahead of us."

"You have time. I don't."

"I'm rushing to be with you. You have to slow down for me to reach you."

We arrived at the airport. The porters approached the car. And suddenly, I remembered the yellow suitcase. I had to follow through with my plan, which meant leaving Hashim outside the airport so none of the customs officers saw him with me.

"Stay in the car," I said, turning to him, trying to hide my nervousness. "I don't want you to get out with me."

"Why?" he asked surprised.

"I don't want you to come with me!" I screamed, trembling despite myself, my nerves choking me. "I don't know how to do goodbyes."

Hashim fell silent, startled.

I leaned over and gave him a quick kiss.

"I'll see you soon."

I opened the car door and got out before he could return my kiss. I rushed inside the airport without turning back. I ran. I wasn't running from Hashim, but from myself.

I stopped before going through customs. I took a deep breath. I wiped away my tears. I put kohl around my eyes again. My heart was pounding as I approached the customs officials. They hated the Lebanese. They searched them. They might take off all my clothes and parade me naked in the customs area. There was nothing in my bags to be worried about, but I was afraid, as if the guards knew the story of the yellow suitcase.

Nothing happened. Nothing at all. The guards met me politely. Each of them gave me a nice smile. They didn't open a single bag. Maybe if the yellow suitcase had been with me, they wouldn't have opened it either.

Within minutes, I found myself through customs.

I sat in the waiting area and tried to calm down. On the plane, I couldn't sleep or relax. I couldn't focus on Hashim or my family that was waiting for me. I couldn't feel that I'd left Cairo or that I was heading to Beirut. My feelings were turbulent, like a sandstorm.

We landed in Beirut.

My father embraced me to his big belly.

"Rihab, Rihab, Rihab," he repeated in his great voice through a trembling laugh.

I tried to rest on his belly, to feel that I'd come back to his love and protection.

But my mother snatched me from him and started kissing me all over my face. She then moved me away while still gripping my shoulders.

"Rolly," she said, terrified, looking in my eyes. "What's wrong with you? Are you sick?"

"No, I'm fine," I said, shaking my head.

"We missed you so much!" she cried out happily, pulling me to her.

I embraced her. I cried. Tears shone in my father's eyes, on my mother's lips, and on my sister's cheeks.

We drove home. I looked around, searching for the things that I had missed: the mountains, the sea, the streets, the faces.

I went into the house and took out the gifts I had brought. Then, suddenly, as if a devil had pinched me in my side . . .

"I forgot a bag!" I exclaimed.

"What?" my mother asked in surprise. "Your bags are all here. All three."

"No," I said. "There's a fourth that I bought in Egypt. I know where I forgot it."

"We'll talk to our friends there to send it to us," my father said.

"No," I said, rushing to the phone. "I have a friend who's coming to Beirut in a few days. I'll talk to him."

I placed a call through my father's office. I asked for Hashim. At the same time, I sent the driver with a telegram to the Hilton that read: "I forgot a suitcase in room 625. Please give it to Dr. Hashim 'Abd al-Latif."

An hour later, I heard Hashim's voice on the phone.

"Rihab?"

"I miss you. Do you miss me too?"

"I . . . I feel as if everything has disappeared from Cairo suddenly. There are no more cars in Cairo, or streets, or people. You took everything with you to Beirut."

"Hashim," I said, my mother standing next to me, staring at me. "I forgot a suitcase at the Hilton. Could you bring it with you?"

"Sure."

"You won't be too long?"

"No. Ten days. Saturday. Maybe before that, if I can't bear it."

"I beg you not to bear it."

"We'll see. How's Beirut?"

"I'm still in Cairo."

"I wish."

The call ended.

The fly had carried out the spider's plan.

6

I TRIED TO FORGET EVERYTHING after I talked with Hashim. The plan had been executed. It was like it had all happened in a movie that I'd watched. Now the film had finished. I had left the cinema. I had to forget the heroine of the movie and go back to my life.

I started reacquainting myself with the house, laughing with my sister, chatting about my stay in Cairo, hearing Beirut's news and what had happened while I was gone. My mother kept her eyes on me, trying to see what I was really thinking because she wasn't convinced by my laughing or the happiness I was projecting. She tried to sit me down next to her to tell her about Cairo, but I couldn't bear it. I couldn't bear sitting in one place or talking about a single subject. I couldn't concentrate my mind or coordinate my words.

I went into my room. I took off my dress and put on a blouse, pants, and flats. I let my hair down. I picked up my Kleenex, kohl pen, and some lira, and I left the house.

"Where are you going?" my mother called behind me.

"To see Beirut."

"Aren't you going to spend some time with us? You've been gone for five months!"

"I'll spend my whole life with you."

"Will you be back for lunch?"

I slammed the door behind me.

I went to Uncle Sam, skipping along in the street, trying to convince myself I was happy to be back in Beirut. I would go back to the life I lived here before going to Cairo, the life of a fifteen or sixteen-year-old. I had lived an older life for Hashim. But Hashim was over. He was one of the heroes of the movie that I saw in Cairo. The film had ended. Cairo had ended. The Muhi al-Din family had ended. The story of the yellow suitcase had ended. Everything had ended. I was Rihab again, the girl who lived in Beirut five months ago, wearing pants and kohl around her eyes and her hair loose, living her life moment by moment, not day by day, month by month, or year by year.

I went into Uncle Sam and I saw everything as it was, as if I was gone from Beirut for only a few moments, as if I'd left a wax museum and gone back to it again. The faces hadn't changed. The looks hadn't changed. The voices hadn't changed, nor had the sounds, the waiter, the smells, Sami, Ghassan, Taysir. Each of them was sitting at the same table in the same position.

I stood at the door, looking into the wax museum until the statues—the wax statues—noticed me and started calling over to me.

They sat me among them and asked me about Cairo. I tried to tell them something about Cairo, but I couldn't think of anything. All my memories of Cairo had disappeared behind a dense fog that I could barely see through.

Our conversation about Cairo ended quickly. They pulled me into another conversation, the same conversation that I left five months ago, the same words that I heard five months ago.

I felt like I was shrinking. I stayed with my friends silent, dejected, then suddenly I asked:

"Sami, do you want to have lunch with me?"

"Why not?" he said, looking at me. "Let's go."

I got up without saying goodbye to anyone and he followed me out.

I didn't pick Sami on purpose. He was just the wax statue that my eyes happened upon as I spoke.

"Where are we going?" Sami asked as we walked along Bliss Street.

"The Eagle's Nest," I replied, distracted.

We turned and went up Jeanne D'Arc Street and I tried as hard as I could to shake off the feeling of being constricted. The Eagle's Nest wouldn't have changed in five months. I was as I was. I had to convince myself of this. But something had changed. I don't know how or why. I was no longer me. I felt like someone else. I felt like an old woman, my steps trembled, perhaps my back had curved too. Maybe my face had even become wrinkled.

We went in the Eagle's Nest. The waiter beamed when he saw me. The owner ran over to greet me. They were friendly and I responded without really hearing them. Sami looked at the knife on the table and his eyes widened in fear. He reached out quickly and tossed the knife far away under some chairs. He was still afraid of knives. He hadn't changed.

Sami looked at me.

"What's wrong?" he asked, looking searchingly at my face.

"Nothing," I said, trying to smile.

"You seem like a different girl. I feel like you're ten years older."

"I'm trying to grow up," I said as if talking to myself.

"Don't try to do anything. Spit on the world."

"If everyone spat on the world, they'd spit on each other."

"That's what they're doing. They're spitting on each other. Smiling is spitting, so is laughing and talking. The most honorable people are the ones who don't hide in a smile or a laugh or in words, they spit it out honestly."

"I know, we don't go to death, but death comes to us."

"Since the day we're born, we're heading toward death. Some of us cross that road at fifty, and some at twenty. Those in a hurry at ten. As long as we know where the road is heading, why are we confused? Why do we worry?"

"Your philosophizing is dull," I cut him off. "Talk to me about something that will make me laugh."

"Tell me about what you did in Cairo."

"Nothing to tell," I said, shrugging my shoulders.

He looked at me as if he didn't believe me.

"Rolly. There's no point in regretting things. We should live in the moment. Forget what's passed and what's coming. There's only the moment we're in."

Our food came. I pushed it aside and got up.

"I can't do this," I said, tossing some money on the table. "I'm leaving."

"Should I go with you?"

"No."

I walked out and wandered the streets. I felt everything, the streets and the sea, was dead. The cars were hearses. The mountain was a big grave. I was an owl again, standing on the branch of a dead tree. My eyes were wide like an owl, my nose small and curved, my face round. I was afraid to speak and discover my voice was the hoot of an owl.

I got home at seven, maybe eight o'clock in the evening. My mother met me at the door.

"We waited for you for lunch," she said angrily.

"Sorry," I said, not looking at her.

"Nothing's changed in you. You're still irresponsible."

"Maybe."

I heard my father laugh.

"Rihab has gone back to her old ways," he said.

I went over and sat on his knee.

"I missed you, Hajj 'Abd al-Rahman," I said.

I tried to relax onto his chest, but I only felt that I was going to cry as I leaned my head on his shoulders. If I cried, he'd ask me why. I'd have to say something. I jumped up and headed to my room.

"I'm going to bed," I said.

"Aren't you having dinner?" my mother asked.

"I already ate," I lied.

"Won't you sit with us for a little?" my father asked.

"I'm tired, Daddy," I said. "Tomorrow."

I ran to my room and sat on my bed, still feeling like an owl. I was trying as hard as I could not to think about anything.

I slept, passed out from exhaustion and sleeplessness, a deep sleep as if I was buried under a mountain of dirt.

Another day. And then a third day.

I shrunk more. I couldn't eat. My nerves were eating me up. I didn't try to leave the house. I cowered in my room. My mother kept offering to take me to a doctor, but I refused. She spent the whole day trying to get me to eat.

Finally, I collected my strength, all I had, and I faced myself.

Why was I suffering so much? Because I'd carried out the spider's plan? Because I'd deceived Hashim and was tricking him into smuggling the money of the Muhi al-Din family?

Hashim wouldn't come to any harm, even if he was caught with the yellow suitcase. He could say it wasn't his. He could ask the employees of the Hilton to give testimony that it was mine. Besides, the money we were smuggling wasn't stolen. It belonged to the Muhi al-Dins. It was their right to transfer it to Lebanon, just as my father transfers his money to London and Paris. I wasn't harming anyone by doing this.

I always submitted to my feelings. So why was I revolting against them now? Why all this anxiety? All this suffering? All this grief?

Then I realized that what was bothering me wasn't the yellow suitcase or the smuggling. I thought, the reason for my suffering was because of the spider's plan or because I had deceived Hashim.

Who was Hashim to me? A friend. Only a friend. Not more than Taysir and Sami and Ghassan and the rest of my guy friends.

But no. This wasn't true. Hashim was more than that. He was not only a friend. Suddenly, it was clear why I'd felt this big emptiness since the first moment that I got back to Beirut.

Hashim wasn't a friend. He was my life. He was every minute of my day. Time apart was spent waiting to see him.

What did this mean? Did I love him? Hashim's face rose up in my mind's eye, his hair the color of smoke, his puffy eyes, his nose like that of an old lion. His lips slightly parted, as if in pain.

No. I didn't love him. I didn't want this love. I didn't want any love. Love was a heavy chain, a bond. I can't stand chains or bonds. I didn't want to suffer all this because of a man, any man. I wanted to be free, to fly.

I was not in love. I was never in love. Love takes everything. It would even take my life. Hashim wanted to take me at twenty and make me forty. No. I wanted my life. I wanted my freedom. I wanted my youth.

I got up to call Taysir. Taysir must still love me. Maybe more than Hashim. I'd find the same thing in him that I found in Hashim.

Taysir was stunned when I asked him to meet me immediately. It was eight in the evening. I went out dressed in pants, my hair loose, my kohl in my hand, as usual. I didn't ask anyone's permission before leaving.

I looked at him. There was still that arrogant look in his eyes. His face was beautiful. His skin was smooth. His hair was black. But what he said was trivial. I tried to put up with it, but I couldn't.

I turned to him suddenly as we walked on the corniche along the Mediterranean.

"Taysir, kiss me," I commanded him.

"What?" he asked, surprised.

"Kiss me. I told you to kiss me."

I still remembered his kisses. I had put up with them. Sometimes I wanted them, but that night, when he brought his face close and I felt his hot breath on me, a pungent stench almost engulfed me. I gasped. His lips pressed onto my cheek like spots of cold oil. I put up with it as much as I could. I even turned my lips to him. As soon as he touched them, I felt like I was going to choke. Then I was actually choking. I pulled back from him quickly and I ran. I ran into the night, not seeing anything.

"Rolly!" he was yelling. "Rolly!"

He ran after me.

I don't know how I found myself in a taxi, but I got one.

"Where were you?" I heard my mother scream when I got home. "It's eleven o'clock!"

"Don't ask," I screamed back. "Get away from me. I'm . . ."

My voice was breaking. The veins in my neck were throbbing. I felt a harsh pain around my neck and in my chest. I had faced this before, I knew it well. I passed out.

I woke up in bed with a doctor next to me. My mother and father were at the foot of the bed. I looked at the doctor, and then at my mother and father.

"What day is it?" I asked as if there was another person inside me speaking for me while I had been out.

"Tuesday," my father said, his eyes shining with tears.

I was silent. My eyes clung to the ceiling. My head was filled with a voice repeating, Hashim will come Saturday with the yellow suitcase. I tried to ignore it. I tried to convince myself that I didn't care if Hashim brought the yellow suitcase or not, but the voice continued, repeating insistently: Hashim will come on Saturday with the yellow suitcase.

I spent the entire day silent. Hashim's image filled my mind, as did the yellow suitcase. It occurred to me that I should tell my father what I did to smuggle the Muhi al-Dins' money. He understood these things. Maybe he'd help me relax, but I didn't say anything. It wasn't about the smuggling. It was Hashim. If it was anyone but Hashim, I wouldn't feel like this.

On Wednesday, I got out of bed. My mother surprised me as I was getting dressed.

"Where are you going?" she asked me, worried.

"To the market."

"But you're still sick. You should be staying home. Doctor's orders."

"I know how I'm feeling better than the doctor," I cut her off.

My mother was silent. She was afraid of arguing with me and causing another episode.

I went to my father.

"I need a thousand lira," I told him, kissing him on his cheeks.

"Going out?" he asked, looking at my clothes in surprise.

"To the market. I haven't bought anything since I came back."

My father looked at me, my mother's confusion reflected in his eyes.

"Your mother is going with you," he said, letting out a small uneasy laugh.

"No," I said. "And neither is my sister. I'm going alone. Don't worry. I'm fine."

He laughed again, took out his wallet, and gave me a thousand lira.

"Give me another thousand," I said sweetly.

"That's too much."

"I want to buy a lot of things. I'll bring you the change."

My father chuckled and gave me another thousand.

I left, and the entire house held its breath.

I went straight to the Arab Airlines office and reserved a seat on the plane going to Cairo the next morning. I sent a telegram to Hashim saying: "I'm coming tomorrow on Arab Airlines. Please reserve a room for me at the Hilton."

And I went back home.

"Didn't you buy anything?" my mother asked in surprise.

"No," I said, not looking at her. "I got an idea of what's out there and I'll buy things tomorrow."

I went into my room and lay down on the bed exhausted. I kept still, afraid that if I moved, my determination to return to Cairo would collapse.

The next morning, I got up early, before anyone in the house. I prepared a small bag with a single dress and nightshirt. I then wrote a note: "Don't worry about me. I went to Cairo. I'll be back tomorrow."

I left the house without anyone noticing.

I sat on the plane distracted and silent. It felt like another person was moving me and setting my plans.

Hashim met me at the airport, right at the plane door. There was a big smile on his face. He moved toward me, a little nervous. He was unsure whether to kiss me or just shake my hand. I extended my hand out to him.

"Welcome back," he whispered.

I looked at him feeling a strange tenderness, as if I'd come back to my sad child. I didn't feel the urgency of desire or the compulsion of love, only a calm tenderness like the light of dawn.

I walked next to him through passport control and past the customs lines. Hashim really did have influence. Lots of people said hello to him, lots of people rushed over to ask if he needed anything. I was happy with him, with the way he was charming and courteous with everyone.

I rode next to Hashim in his car. My eyes were glued to his face. He seemed stronger than when I left him. There was a flash in his eyes, a smile on his lips. He seemed like he'd regained everything that he'd lost. He'd regained his personality, his self-confidence. He wasn't confused or shaken or weak. Maybe my return had simply brought everything back to him.

"I couldn't believe the telegram," he said, looking at my face, drinking it in with his eyes. "I was afraid it was a joke."

"Maybe the joke is my return," I said, the image of the yellow suitcase filling my mind.

"It's the sweetest surprise. I was counting the hours separating me from you. But why did you come back? Why didn't you wait for me in Beirut? You know I'm coming soon."

"It's not important. I felt that I wanted to come back to Cairo so I came back."

"I'm always afraid of you giving in to your feelings. But I hope you live your whole life submitting to your feelings as long as they drive you to me."

"This is my feeling today. I don't know how I'll feel tomorrow."

"I trust how you feel today, tomorrow, and the next day."

I smiled. A period of silence passed between us. He was looking at me with one eye, the other on the road.

"Were you sick?"

"How'd you know?"

"Your face."

"I passed out. But I'm better."

"It won't happen again."

"You'll treat me if it does."

"No. I'll keep it from happening to you again."

I smiled silently. I was still thinking about the yellow suitcase.

"Did you take the bag from the Hilton?" I asked, looking out the car window to hide my face from him.

"Yes. The same day you told me about it."

"Where is it now?"

"At the clinic."

"Let's go get it now."

"Why? I'll bring it with my bags when I go to Lebanon."

"No. There are things that belong to the Muhi al-Dins in it which I forgot to give to them. Let's take it from the clinic and drop it at their house."

"As you wish."

"I'm going back to Beirut tomorrow."

"Why don't you wait so we can go together?"

"I can't. My father only let me come for one night."

"Then I'll go with you tomorrow."

"No. It's better if we don't go on the same airplane."

"I don't want to spend another day apart from you."

"It's one day."

He was quiet.

We reached the clinic. Hashim went up. He came back with the doorman behind him carrying the yellow suitcase. He put it in the back seat.

I didn't look at the suitcase, afraid that my eyes would expose me. My heart was beating as if I was the only one who knew there was a dead body in that bag.

We left for the Muhi al-Dins. Once we got there, I called the doorman.

"Take this bag," I told him, pointing to it. "And give it to Rafiq."

"Are you not staying here?" the doorman asked.

"No. Say hello to everyone for me."

The doorman picked up the suitcase without me looking. I was terrified. Hashim drove off.

As soon as we were away from the house, I felt everything in me relax. My tense nerves, my forced smile. I sat back in my seat. I turned to Hashim. I looked at him with a calm smile. I felt that I wanted to kiss him. I couldn't stop myself from kissing him. I brought my face close to him and kissed him quickly on his cheek. I then leaned my head on his shoulder and closed my eyes.

"I'm tired," I whispered. "I want to sleep."

He leaned down and kissed me on my forehead.

He took me to the Hilton and stayed with me until the check-in was completed. He then left me to go up to the room.

I slept. I slept calmly and deeply. There was a happy delicious feeling flowing through me. I'd never felt so calm and relaxed before, as if I'd just thrown a huge weight off my back. The fly slept after it escaped from the spiderweb.

I don't know how long I slept. Maybe an hour or two. I woke up startled by the ringing of the phone. I reached over, my eyes still closed.

"Hello? Who is this?" I asked in a sleepy voice.

"Rafiq," came the breathless reply.

I opened my eyes. I was awake now.

"What do you want?" I snapped.

"What happened?" he asked, his words rushing out.

"Nothing," I said, more sharply. "I don't want any part of this."

"Didn't you go to Lebanon?"

"I went. And I came back."

"Can I see you?" he pleaded.

"No!"

"Why?"

"I don't want to see you! I don't want to see any of you!"

I slammed down the receiver.

I tried to go back to sleep. I put the pillow on my head. I turned over in the bed. I squeezed my eyes shut trying to sleep. But it was no use. I got out of bed, Rafiq's voice still ringing in my ears.

I went into the bathroom, filled the tub, and got into the warm water. I started calming down and feeling better. The story of the yellow suitcase was finished. I was happy it was over, not because I didn't smuggle the money, but because I didn't let them exploit Hashim and his love for me.

What to do with Hashim? I was convinced that my story with Hashim was finished with the end of the yellow suitcase. I paid off my account with him and there was nothing left but for me to go. I knew Hashim was looking at our relationship as something serious. He was thinking about marriage. I didn't want to marry him. He was a big responsibility that I didn't want to bear. His status, way of life, and sense of himself demanded that I give him everything. I couldn't do that. I wanted to maintain my freedom, the freedom of my feelings. Hashim couldn't bear that. He was not that type of man. He was the kind of man who wanted everything. I didn't want him to be weak with me or to exploit his weakness. And I didn't want him to be strong, as he could over-power me. It was better for both of us for us to end it.

All these thoughts swirled around in my mind, and I was calm. I smiled. I smiled at the thought of Hashim, at his sweet personality, his good heart, his love for me. I could see then that I didn't love him. Maybe when I was in Beirut I thought it was love, but it was only a reflection of my remorse about the plan of the yellow suitcase, of my feeling that I was the fly. There was something else tying me to Hashim. Was it friendship? Attraction? I didn't know. It was something big, something sweet. But not love, at least as I imagined love.

I left the bathroom. I looked in the mirror and I smiled. My face had got some of its color back.

I put on my dress and left my room. I passed by the receptionist. I asked him to reserve me a seat on the plane to Beirut the next day. Then I went to the cafeteria as I'd left a note for Hashim that I was waiting for him there.

I met some of the Lebanese kids in the cafeteria and sat with them. I was as happy and free as usual with them until I spotted Hashim coming over to us. I got up before he reached us so I wasn't embarrassed about him in front of my friends.

Hashim met me with a shaken smile, with which he looked at the Lebanese kids and then back at me.

I rode next to him in the car and we headed to Muqattam. Hashim tried to make me talk about the real reason for my sudden return to Cairo. I knew what he wanted to hear from me. He wanted me to tell him that I came back for him, that I loved him. But I didn't tell him that, even just to please him. I didn't want to give him hope.

"Are you still planning to go to Beirut?" I asked him.

"Of course," he said, surprised.

"For me?"

"For you."

"I don't want you to go."

"Why?"

"Because Cairo is the only thing that can bring us together. Beirut will split us apart."

"Why?"

"In Beirut, I'm a different person. And you'll be a different person."

"Love isn't different in different capitals."

"I'm afraid of your love."

"Why?"

"It's bigger than I can bear. Your love is serious. It has traditions. It has a plan. I can't bear traditions or set plans or marriage."

"But you came back to Cairo for me."

"Are you sure?"

A cloud came over his face.

"I won't submit to your feelings," he said sharply. "Your feelings change from moment to moment. These feelings will destroy everyone near you. They'll eventually destroy you too. I won't let you destroy me or destroy yourself."

"You know I am owned by my feelings."

"No," he said more sharply. "You're fleeing, fleeing from everything, fleeing from love, from family, from faith, from your mind, from the future. You think your feelings are behind all that. Fleeing won't help you. You can't flee forever. One day you'll have to control yourself, control what you call feelings, for you to stop fleeing. If you can't, you'll be forced to flee your whole life."

He then stopped the car and turned to me.

"Rihab, you're incredible. You have everything to be happy, to make the people who love you happy, but you haven't found anyone or anything to trace the road for you. Your family was afraid to tie you to anything, anything that tamed your will, your feelings, and your logic. We're all born without taming, but then our family does it, and society too. But you haven't been tamed."

"You'll tame me," I said smiling.

"Let me try," he pleaded.

"You tried for five months. This is how I am."

He was quiet for a bit.

"You're right," he then said. "Maybe because I don't want to tame you for you, but for myself, to tame you for my love. But you don't love me."

"This isn't the love you want. Try to understand, Hashim. When you tried to live in my world or when I tried to live in yours, when you tried to come into my life or when I tried to move up to yours, you were leaving behind your work and friends. I was leaving my freedom and fun to live in your chains with you alone. But we were lost. I felt that you were far from me, and you felt me far from you. We were both happy when we met and each of us was in their own world. I was happy with you when I was a carefree girl. I was happy with you as a serious, important person. We were happy when each of us remained in their own world, each of us was a hero for the other from another world. Believe me."

Hashim was silent for a moment.

"I'm going to Beirut," he said stubbornly.

He then hit the gas, speeding off like a reckless kid.

7

I WENT BACK TO BEIRUT happy. It was a delicious calm happiness. Even Hashim's stubbornness and insistence on joining me in Beirut made me feel happy. It was a happiness deeper than the feeling of conceit, more like a mother when she feels the attachment of her son even though she wants him to get used to standing on his own two feet.

I'd never felt this kind of calm happiness before. My happiness had always had a sharp edge to it. My feelings all had a certain sharpness, happiness, misery, confusion, all of them. I felt a new peak, a peak of happiness, peace of mind, as if I was floating on a cloud. Something had changed in me. I didn't know what. Those months that I lived in Cairo and the crises that I experienced there made me a different person, a person that I didn't know yet, but someone other than the Rihab that I knew.

I spent that evening with Hashim. It was a silent night out. We tried to keep it going until the morning when the plane left as we did before, but we couldn't. We couldn't bear the silence. Hashim was suffering, trying to kill something inside himself. Lines cut through his brow like scars from a sharp knife. I understood his suffering. He was lost in a crisis of stubbornness, from his insistence on me and him living in a single world. He didn't want to acknowledge that each of us was made for our own world. He didn't want to give in to despair. He didn't want to give up on me as the girl he loved and be satisfied with me as just a friend.

I tried a lot to soothe him. I tried to cut the rope of silence that was wrapped around our necks. But when I spoke, I said trifling, insincere things. I gave in to the silence until we couldn't bear it anymore, and we parted at eleven o'clock.

He brought me to the airport the following day, still insisting he would join me in Beirut the next day.

I leaned over to kiss him on his cheek before I got out of his car. He didn't kiss me back. I looked at him, smiling apologetically. I kissed him again.

"Don't you want to kiss me?" I whispered.

"No."

"You're not angry, are you?"

"No."

"Promise me you're not keeping things to yourself. I'm afraid you'll hate me if you do."

"I won't ever hate you. I'm afraid I'll hate myself."

"No. You can't. But we're different in how we see love."

I leaned over and kissed him a third time.

He reached out, no longer able to resist, and pulled me to his chest.

"Goodbye," he whispered, his cheek resting on mine.

I got out of the car.

"Where's your yellow suitcase?" he called out suddenly.

"I left it with the Muhi al-Dins. There was nothing important in it."

He smiled silently.

"I'll be waiting for you tomorrow at the Beirut airport," I said, turning back to him and waving.

He let me go inside the airport alone as we'd agreed.

I arrived in Beirut still feeling that delicious calm happiness. My mother took me and brought me into her room, asking me questions, trying to make me feel like she was an old friend, trying to find out the real reason for my trip to Cairo.

"Nothing," I responded simply. "I had to say goodbye to some friends."

"Do you love him?"

"Who?"

"The guy you went to see." She was looking into my eyes, smiling to reassure me.

"No," I laughed. "I don't love him, but he's a dear friend."

"Are you hiding something serious from me?" she asked, revealing her anxiety.

"No. Believe me. Relax."

She looked at me searchingly.

"You seem like you've grown up, Rihab."

"Maybe."

I paused.

"Tomorrow, a friend from Cairo is coming," I continued as if I'd just remembered something. "I want to invite him over. He took good care of me there."

"Is he the one you went to see?"

"He's a friend of Uncle Nour al-Din," I said, ignoring her question. "My uncle is the one who introduced me to him with a letter that he gave me when I went to Cairo. Do you remember?"

"I remember," she said, looking at me like she didn't believe me.

"I'm going to call Uncle Nour al-Din," I said, getting up from beside her.

I called him and gave him news about Hashim's arrival to Beirut the following day. We decided to go together to meet him at the airport.

I spent the whole day preparing a schedule for Hashim for his time in Lebanon. I even prepared the words that I'd say to him. I prepared for when we'd be alone together. I realized that I was thinking very calmly, as if I really had grown up, as my mother said. I was planning for us to spend as much time as possible with the family to reduce my time alone with him. This would help me to suppress Hashim's feelings and convince him that it's enough to have me as a friend. I was thinking about everything, feeling responsible for him. I really wanted to keep his friendship. His friendship was more important than my friendship with anyone else. It was special, and while it wasn't love, at least not the love that Hashim wanted from me, it was very close to it.

I woke up early the following day. I felt excited, and nervous.

I took our car and went to my uncle's. He was still sleeping so I woke him up. I was able to convince him to have breakfast at the hotel by the airport. The minutes passed slowly. The sound of the airplanes arriving and departing made my heart flutter. All this couldn't be because I was waiting for a friend, even a very dear friend. My heart was trembling from anticipation as if I hadn't seen Hashim for years, even though I was with him yesterday.

The arrival of the Arab Airlines plane from Cairo was announced.

I jumped up, dragging my uncle behind me. We went out onto the landing strip. I raised my head looking for the plane as if I was looking for fate itself.

The plane landed. It pulled up. The door opened. The passengers started descending one after the other. Hashim wasn't the first, or the second, third, fourth, or . . .

Hashim wasn't on the plane.

I ran to the information office and asked if there was another plane. Maybe he was arriving on a different airline. But it was pointless to keep waiting for him at the airport.

I went back home feeling a weight on my chest. I felt my pride wounded, that I'd lost my self-confidence. A big emptiness extended out before me.

As soon as I got home, the servant gave me a telegram from Hashim: "Sorry. I decided not to come."

I smiled sadly. I went to my room. I read the words again. I looked for the day and time it was sent. He sent it yesterday at nine o'clock in the evening. I reread every word, even the government-printed words.

I was sad, but not upset. I felt a muted sadness that is akin to my muted happiness. I had a deep stable feeling that I had lost Hashim forever. My story with him was finished. I started a long back and forth with myself to try to convince myself that this was better, at least better for Hashim. I had tried to convince myself that I wanted to hold onto him, not for his friendship, but because it would please my vanity.

I was thinking calmly. I started thinking about the life I could live in Beirut. Should I go back to the cafés of the intellectuals around the university? Should I go back to living my life moment by moment? It felt like everything I knew in Beirut was frivolous, meaningless. My concerns were frivolous. My friends were frivolous. I felt that I could no longer live my life moment by moment. This existence didn't give me hope for my future. I needed to have hope in something.

The image of Hashim appeared before me without me being able to concentrate on it. I couldn't blame him because he didn't come. I couldn't think about returning to him a third time.

Days passed and I remained in this incredible calm. One morning, I wrote a letter to Hashim.

> All I want is for you to understand. I know it's hard for you to understand me for a simple reason—I don't understand myself. I always told you that I am owned by my feelings, feelings that are not always understandable. Feelings are just spontaneous, and they reflect people's circumstances. Will doesn't control them and neither does the mind. But my feelings for you were something else. They woke up my will and alerted my mind. I felt that I was compelled to you unlike anyone else before. But

when I noticed this compulsion, I rebelled against it. I didn't give you what you wanted and what I wanted to give you. I tried to convince myself that I didn't love you, that all there was between us was a friendship that grew until it got close to love. But this wasn't true. What was between us wasn't friendship. I can see the truth of my feelings now that I'm far from you. When I was in Egypt, I was really convinced that what was between us was friendship. But now, no, I know it was love. Despite that, I had to resist this love. I kept resisting. I was feeling that the wind pushed me despite myself to the edge of the abyss. But I had to resist so that I didn't fall into the abyss. Sorry, you're not an abyss. You're a mountain. You're a strong tree that casts its shade on people to protect them from the Cairo sun. But I had to resist you because I didn't want this love. I still don't know what this future holds, but it's not you. Your love isn't in my future. I have to look for another world to live in, no matter how much confusion, trouble, and anxiety it causes me.

Hashim . . . Do you see another person in these words? I've really changed. I feel like I'm another person, a person with a mind and a will, thanks to you. You don't know how much you've changed me. My compulsion for you has shown me the seriousness of being led by my feelings. I discovered that these feelings might push me to many things that I might end up regretting for the rest of my life. It might push me to hurt people that I don't want to hurt. And I don't want to hurt myself either. All I need is some way to bear my feelings. I'm looking now for principles, values, and logic so I can achieve what I want for myself. Who can believe that Rihab is talking like this? Rihab, who can't stand to be alone with her mind for a single moment, is trying now to give her entire life over to her mind, not her emotions.

My dearest Hashim, thank you for not coming to Beirut. Who knows? Maybe if you'd come, my resistance for you would've collapsed and I would've been forced to admit to myself that I love you and then be swept up by a love that I'm not convinced of.

Thank you for helping me make my decision.

I've been waiting for a letter from you. What was between us can't end in a few words on a telegram . . .

There was more. I thought as I wrote the letter that I was writing to myself more than to Hashim. I was trying to understand myself. Writing helped me with this. From that day, I wrote a lot. I started keeping daily journals. At first, I only wrote down my reflections. Then I started recording a summary of what I was reading. I started reading a lot. I thought all the time about writers, fiction, art, and politics, bits and pieces that I heard from my friends at the cafés. My mouth was filled with them as if I was an intellectual. I discovered in reading a new world, something different from what my café friends had been talking about. Even existentialism, which I'd claimed I believed in, I found to be something else in books, something other than the disheveled hair, pants, flats, and dancing the twist. Existentialism, as I started to understand it, was that the individual had the right to choose his place in society. If I was an existentialist, it was my right to choose my place. Where that place was, I didn't know.

Reading occupied me. I no longer fled from the house all day, as before. I no longer moved around a lot. I thought hard. My mother listened to my calm words. She was delighted. Everyone around me was surprised at my development.

Fifteen days later, I got a response from Hashim. It was the letter that I'd long hoped for. He wrote:

> The secret of my misery isn't your insistence on putting tight limits on our relationship. It's my feeling of weakness. From our first day together, I felt weak. I tried to deny it. I was too conceited to admit that I was weak. I wasn't weak before you, but before myself. After you left, insisting on each of us staying in their own world, I was so miserable that it forced me to face myself, to admit my weakness. Then I decided to resist this weakness, no matter what happened, no matter how much I suffered. I had to rid myself of it. It wasn't easy. I had to close my clinic for a whole month to dedicate myself to this fight. I spent many nights getting drunk, getting drunk to lose consciousness. I spent many nights with women I didn't know. They were just lost efforts, efforts to forget you. Like any ignorant man, I thought I could forget you by doing

everything I could to kill your memory, to kill it with wine and the lips of cheap women. But trying to forget you didn't help me get rid of my weakness since you're not the cause of it. There was another reason. Instead of dedicating myself to forgetting you, I did what you did. I devoted myself to discovering myself. I thought I was weak because I reached forty-five without a place in the world to call my own. No house, no wife. I spent my entire life on the move because I was too conceited to settle down. I believed I could stay standing my entire life, alone, happy with my loneliness. But being forty-five showed me that I needed a place to feel at peace. Forty-five is the age of seriousness. It's the age of the second adolescence. It's when a man opens his eyes and sees a new path stretch out in front of him. He sees the end getting near, an end to everything. He finds himself rebelling against that end, trying to change his life, to flee from the path leading him to the end. He finds that everything he built won't spare him from the end, the end to everything. This is what I felt. I felt that my success as a doctor, my fame, my wealth, my influence, my friends, all that wasn't worth anything. I could dispense with it all. I didn't want it. I was just like an adolescent who turns fifteen and rebels against his parents. He feels that he can dispense with them. He sets out looking for a new life for himself. Adolescence is the age of moving from one life to another, from one state to another. I was at that stage when I met you, I had tried before we met to make it work with another girl, but I failed. I met you with the bitterness of this failure. I was attracted to you from the moment I saw you. I was attached to you. I didn't stop to examine this feeling. It grew and I was pushed forward, pushed forward more than you. By doing this, I lost my balance. I could no longer control my actions. I wanted to reach you quickly, before I got any older. My naive attempts, which you know well, to come down to your age or bring you up to mine. In all this, I was led by my feelings like you. I was pretending to be rational, but the reality was otherwise: I was led by my feelings. The difference between me and you is that you resisted your feelings before I started resisting mine. So, credit to you for making the decision for us to be just friends. If you hadn't, I would've been driven forward in loving you.

I discovered that the secret behind my fear of being forty-five was that I imagined that I'd reached the summit, the summit of success as a doctor, that there weren't any more summits left, only descents and the road to the end. But I haven't reached the summit. There are thousands of years between me and the summit.

I quickly returned to my clinic. I set out working like a lunatic, as if I'd decided to make it through thousands of years in two days.

I should stop writing, Rihab, since the time that I spend writing is taking time away from my patients. They deserve it more than the two of us.

I want you to be reassured. I'm better now. Maybe because I no longer feel love for myself, but for others. I don't feel my feelings, but I feel the feelings of others. Sometimes, I suffer from loneliness. Who doesn't feel lonely sometimes? But it doesn't take long for my work to wipe away my loneliness.

How many times did I read this letter? Ten, twenty times. I don't know. But I read it a lot. I drank from it a feeling of self-confidence, confidence in my decision. I didn't make a mistake when I conquered my love for Hashim. Hashim himself said so.

I didn't respond to Hashim's letter. It was enough that I wrote a response in my diary. I devoted myself to looking for calm on my path. I decided to work.

Do you know where? In Lebanese television. All of Lebanon welcomed me. It welcomed me as a pretty face, the daughter of Hajj 'Abd al-Rahman, the big businessman. Through the TV screen, I represented a new identity for young Lebanese women. I was no longer the girl wearing pants, holding a kohl pen and Kleenex in her hand. Now I carried a purse.

The program that I presented was called *Readings*. Every week, I read a book, summarized it, and discussed it for the viewers. The program was an incredible success. All the newspapers praised it. This success and respect made me feel my responsibility, my responsibility for all of Lebanon, the girls of Lebanon, the guys of Lebanon, men and women. I was happy with this responsibility. It distracted me from myself, filling my time and making me fulfill my potential.

The road opened up before me. Sometimes I imagine myself becoming an ambassador for Lebanon in one of the great capitals. Sometimes I imagine myself as a representative in Parliament. Unending dreams, clean ambition. Everything can be achieved. I now knew the way.

There were many young people around me. One day, I'd love one of them and I'd get married. I now believe in marriage. It's the only solution for organizing life. We can't innovate in life unless we organize it. Those who don't organize their lives lose the ability to innovate.

But this is premature. I haven't found the guy I love yet.

A year passed.

I went to Cairo for a week's holiday. I had to go to Cairo. There wasn't any reason for me to be afraid of my memories there or to flee from them. I hadn't forgotten Hashim. I'd always remember him. His memory doesn't have any pain or regret. His memory was sweet, a perfume that gave me confidence.

I spent four days in Cairo before I called Hashim. I hesitated. I don't know why. Maybe because I was afraid to ruin the sweetness of memory.

"Rihab, where are you?" he called out as soon as he heard my voice.

"At the Hilton."

"I'll come at two," he said quickly, his voice filled with happiness. "Wait for me. I'm busy now."

The conversation ended.

I smiled, still holding the receiver, as if proud of a child studying hard at school.

Hashim didn't come until two thirty. He came up to my room. As soon as he saw me, his eyes widened in surprise. He gripped both of my hands.

"Incredible," he said in his lovely Egyptian accent. "Where's Rihab? You're more beautiful, and older."

"This is Rihab after she got to know you," I said, smiling, filling my eyes with him.

"No," he said with a happy, good-hearted look in his eyes. "After she got to know herself."

He didn't kiss me. He kept holding my hands. His eyes searched every part of my face just as I was still filling my eyes with him. He was a little heavier than I'd left him. His face was stronger. There was no thinness or paleness in it. His hair was whiter, but he seemed younger than his age. His nose too seemed smaller.

We reminisced and laughed.

"Do you know my latest news?" Hashim asked.

"I hope it's good."

"I'm getting married next week."

I felt a moment of silence. Hashim's words settled in my heart. Maybe, no matter how strong I pretended to be, no matter how convinced I was that he wasn't mine, no woman wants to give up her rights to a man, even if that man is firmly in her past.

"You fell in love again," I said, trying to laugh. "And quickly!"

"No," he said, his smile calm and confident. "I'm marrying the woman that my mother engaged me to twenty years ago."

"Did she wait for you all this time?"

"No. She got married and had three kids, but her husband passed away."

"You discovered after twenty years that you love her?"

"I'm convinced she's the right woman for me. I think conviction is the right path to love."

He looked at me pointedly.

"The road from the mind to the heart is easier than from the heart to the mind," he continued. "The mind is more capable of convincing the heart than the heart convincing the mind."

"True," I said, my voice light. "Congratulations."

"I found in this woman a lot of what I was missing. She completes me. I'm ten years older than her, which is good. But when I am with her, I feel like I'm younger than her. Imagine, since we announced our engagement, I've increased my hours at work."

"I think that's the effect of the perfect marriage."

"I'll introduce you to her. We're having dinner at my sister's house."

"I'd love to meet her. But I don't want to bother you. Ask her permission first."

"She knows all about you."

He then jumped up.

"I have to go."

"Aren't you inviting me to lunch?" I asked in surprise.

"After four, when I finish with my patients. Then I'll come back to grab a sandwich with you."

"No," I said, standing to say goodbye. "You now have someone waiting for you."

He looked at me for a long time, about to say something, but he didn't. He headed toward the door.

"I'll come by tomorrow evening at nine thirty," he said.

And he left. A calm smile filled my heart. Hashim had changed. He had changed into a stronger man, into another man, not the one in my memory. Maybe he was always this strong and only a moment of weakness made us intertwined.

He came back the following day, late again, at ten o'clock. He took me to his house in Maadi to have dinner.

I met his fiancée there.

She was an incredible woman.